# THE
# SYNAPSE
# SEQUENCE

FOR
ELIZABETH ANNE JEYACHANDRAN
AND FAMILY

THE PRODUCTION OF TOO MANY USEFUL THINGS RESULTS
IN TOO MANY USELESS PEOPLE.

KARL MARX


THE ARGUMENT OF THE BROKEN WINDOW PANE IS THE
MOST VALUABLE ARGUMENT IN MODERN POLITICS.

EMMELINE PANKHURST

# PROLOGUE

N'GOLO DURRANT STOPPED running just long enough to make another call for help. The AI answered quickly, but not so fast that it could be misunderstood: *'What is the nature of your emergency?'*

'The girl,' N'Golo said, his voice straining somewhere between panic and anger. He swept some wetness from his nose and winced. The pain where Connolly's fist had connected was still raw. A long, sticky, dark red streak appeared on the back of his hand. 'I told you before, they're going to take her!'

*'Please remain calm. Are you in immediate danger?'*

N'Golo held his breath for a moment. Was he? Had he been followed? He couldn't be far from the gap in the security fence; he could see the lights of his foster-home. He ought to be safe. But nothing was safe now. A soft squelch behind him, then silence. N'Golo spun round. Most of the farm track he'd been running along was lost in darkness, curtained between a tall hedgerow and a cluster of trees; only a few slivers of water shone back from the tractor ruts in which he'd just stumbled. The light wasn't sufficient for him to see much else.

He doubted they'd let him escape so easily. N'Golo thought back to the basement. Remembered how he'd tried to shrug past Connolly before the older man had grabbed at him and pulled him back.

'*Caller, please respond. Are you in immediate danger?*'

'No, not *me*,' N'Golo replied. The house was right there; he'd be inside quickly once he'd found the gap in the fence. But he couldn't tell *them*. He'd be shipped off to another home as soon as he opened his mouth, his foster-father's opinion of him confirmed. He had to make the police understand – *now*. 'I told you,' he said. 'I told you before… but I *know* it this time! It's going to happen!'

'*Are you in immediate danger?*'

The emergency AI was locked into its preprogrammed routine, just as unbending as Connolly had always said. And this time it was also wrong.

'Check your records!' N'Golo hissed. For a fraction of a second he thought he saw some movement. A patch of darker shadow moving against the background black. He turned and started walking – fast – trying to ignore the growing stitch in his side. 'You can do that, can't you? You know what I'm asking you?'

'*Please remain calm,*' the AI responded.

'I am fucking calm…! The girl…'

'*Who is the girl?*'

'Beth Hayden.'

'*A "Beth Hayden" lives with you at 19 Vicarage Lane, Amblinside. Is this correct?*'

The voice continued to be both patient and efficient. There was no apparent hurry, not when it could answer hundreds of calls simultaneously. And while it spoke, the AI would also be crawling through its databases for any and all information about him.

'Yes.'

*'And who has taken her?'*

N'Golo felt another rip of frustration. 'Take her,' he corrected. 'I told you they're going to *take* her!'

*'Is Beth in your vicinity? Can you see her?'*

'No.'

*'And do you believe Beth Hayden to be in immediate danger?'*

N'Golo stopped. There was something wrong. The conversation with the AI was caught in a circle. 'I told you all this before,' he said, his voice now quiet.

*'Please return to 19 Vicarage Lane. An investigative team has been dispatched.'*

*Investigative team.* Not the emergency boys. Not the bulldogs they sent when the heat was on. Certainly not the hunter bots. And that confirmed it. He was being ignored.

N'Golo ended the call to the AI. That noise again, louder, echoing his own movements. The squelch of work boots on the muddy path. He risked a glance over his shoulder. The shadows shifted again. Or perhaps it was just one shadow that was moving, detaching itself from the surrounding darkness. Was it a man? Was it Connolly?

He clenched his fists.

He was so very nearly home.

1

ANNA GLOVER ALLOWED herself a thin smile of satisfaction. She'd been right. Nobody had known the man wearing the light yellow shirt had dropped into the café prior to heading to the entertainment plaza. Yet he stood just a few metres away, ordering a flat white. Anna watched him, not trying to attract his attention. Instead, she made a few mental notes about his actions and demeanour that she'd later try to fit into the overall puzzle.

The man didn't make eye contact with the female barista. But he did nod slightly as his drink was placed on the counter, then apologised as he tried to pay with cash. It didn't appear to concern him she couldn't offer any change; that most people now paid with a swipe of their wrist rather than using coins or notes.

Anna kept still at her table, appreciating the irony of where he'd chosen to purchase his last drink. This was a relatively expensive place: one of the few that still employed people to operate the coffee machines rather than using a much cheaper, multi-armed swivelling bot. She'd taken up a position against the back wall of the café, right next to the toilets. The customers near her were mostly sitting in silence, all wearing the alert but distant expression of anyone connected to the boards. No one looked at her. She may as well have not been there. Which, of course, she wasn't. At least, not when the events had actually occurred.

She looked back to the counter. The guy with the flat white hadn't moved. His drink remained in front of him, untouched. He seemed hypnotised by it. A young couple who'd come to stand just behind him were impatiently calling their order over his shoulder. Anna tensed. Maybe he was listening to the voice of his conscience – and yet, if indeed that was what was happening, it had been all too distant. All too quiet.

He stood up.

Anna got ready to follow him out on to the street – but instead he took his flat white and went to a nearby table. She relaxed again, checking her watch. Yes, it wasn't quite time. It wouldn't take him long to get to the entertainment plaza; a couple of minutes, max. So it was about to happen, and she would witness it all.

Sure enough, the man didn't allow the coffee to cool. Instead, he took heavy gulps, showing no sign of pleasure. She wondered why he was here. Perhaps it was just to take part in some sort of ritual. Just to take that last hit of caffeine before he did the unthinkable.

Anna didn't know. The man pushed his foam cup aside, his shoulders and neck stiffening. But he wasn't accessing the boards, his attention hadn't left the room. Instead, he wiped his brow. Fidgeted. His skin acquired a thin sheen of sweat that could only be associated with building nerves. He knew he'd soon have to make a decision. He was almost at the point where he wouldn't be able to stop himself.

Or maybe he'd long since sailed past it. Maybe before he'd

ordered the flat white. Before he'd even left his hostel. Maybe at the time he'd gone to sleep the previous night he'd known that, when he woke up, he'd be living through his last day. Drinking his last cup of coffee in a café his friends would later say they'd never known him visit. *And yet would she catch the moment where he realised his path to destruction was set?*

In her previous job, she'd witnessed those horrifying moments all the time. Mainly from trained men and women who couldn't see what they were doing was wrong until they could no longer do anything to correct it. Minor mistakes, effortlessly rolling into larger ones. But there was always that sudden, snapping moment when the brain can only summon up a single word: *Fuck.*

The man with the flat white was nowhere close to that point yet. And the details around him were becoming less clear. When he'd been at the counter, the slowness of his order had been enough to draw the attention of the other customers. Now he'd begun to merge into the background. Forgotten, and softening into the nondescript.

Two men dressed in suits stood and moved towards the door, further hindering her view. As they passed, the walls of the café blurred for a moment – and then the man with the flat white once more appeared in her eye line. He pushed himself from his chair and headed for the door.

*Damn.*

He really had been alone. Other than the interaction with the barista, he hadn't spoken with anybody. That disproved one of her theories. Nobody had pushed him into action, or was cheering from the sidelines. But that didn't mean she couldn't pick out anything useful.

She stood – took a steadying grip of the edge of her table

and waited for the café to stop swaying. A few more customers were finishing their drinks and making their way back on to the street. As they left, they took with them further detail of the counter and the tables immediately surrounding it. It felt as if something was pulling her brain upwards while also keeping her feet clamped to the floor.

A waiter was already clearing the flat white's table. Anna stumbled over, but didn't try to stop him. The grey laminate in front of her just held the foam cup and a couple of sachets of sweetener. But there was something on the floor. She stooped out of habit to retrieve it, and was again beaten by the waiter. He frowned, then crumpled the sheet and pushed it into the empty neck of the cup. It would soon be on its way to the recycling centre, but at least now Anna had seen it: a single giant fist emanating from the wrists of many.

The café grew a little dimmer. Twisting, Anna saw that the couple she'd seen earlier were leaving, and she followed them out of the door. The other customers dispersed left and right, but she already knew she could only follow the pair heading towards the entertainment plaza. Anna hovered behind them, unnoticed, searching for the man who'd been drinking the flat white.

She saw him ahead. He hadn't gone far from the café door, which was just as the local CCTV had recorded. He lingered alone, blurred and anonymous, and then pushed onwards – always a few feet ahead of the couple.

Anna couldn't help but feel a tiny pull of regret. From the stilted and jarring rhythm of the conversation ahead of her, she could tell this relationship was still new. She wanted to warn them. Tell them to turn and run. But it was too late. The couple in front kept glancing at each other and, as they did so, more and more of the detail of the street became lost, blurring into nothingness even though the approaching plaza should have made everything more vibrant.

They'd perhaps been the closest, but had actually seen the least.

Right up until the first shot.

And then Anna saw it. The moment. Written in large panicked letters across three different faces, as the street scene first exploded in more detail than Anna could possibly process, and then simply disappeared.

ANNA FLINCHED AND rolled onto her side. She lifted her head just as the first wave of vomit came into her throat, just about managing to direct most of the liquid onto the tiled floor rather than across her steel bench or disposable clothing. A learned response, after months working in the synapse chamber.

The tuneless whistle of the hub technician, Cody Weaver, passed into her ears, but most of her consciousness was still on the street outside the coffee shop. Watching from the point of view of her witnesses, as the man who'd ordered the flat white had started to open fire.

Cody pushed her gently back onto the bench, checking with a practised move that her airway was open and clear. Their eyes met, but they both knew she couldn't answer his questions yet, no matter how desperate he was to find out what she'd seen. He moved out of her eye line, and soon began to whistle again.

Anna tried to ground herself, concentrating on the chamber she was in now, not the place she thought she'd been just a few seconds ago. All her witnesses would still be attached to the sequencer, lying outstretched on their own stainless-steel synapse benches. The effects of the sedative would keep them submerged until the experiment was finished. Right now, she could hear from the whistling that Cody was checking each one in turn.

Yes, she thought. She was at the hub. She was back from the street, and had never really been there. All she'd seen was a patchwork of memories. A series of recollections from those witnesses who'd agreed to take part in her experiment – all processed into a single reconstruction.

Cody ambled into view again, pushing a string-headed mop ahead of him, which left a characteristic wet squeak as it swept the slick of vomit into a gulley beneath the beds. 'Your heart rate, adrenaline, all stable,' he said, his voice breaking into a nervous chuckle. 'As if you were sitting at home, watching TV. Now, if you could just stop spewing everywhere…'

Anna opened her mouth to reply, but her tongue felt heavy and thick. Like a slug was filling her mouth, pushing up against her cheeks and lips.

'Relax. Don't force it.'

Anna closed her eyes as she continued to reclaim her brain from the street outside the coffee shop. Sure enough, after a few minutes her tongue began to feel normal again. In a few more, her fingers would become less like bananas. The sensation from her legs would take the longest to return. 'It doesn't… get any… less… awful.'

The vomiting was, of course, the one clear problem with the synapse sequencer, the thing that stopped most of its more commercial uses from being put into practice.

'Were we right?' Cody asked, his voice hopeful.

'No.'

His face clouded over, but Anna's attention was on her own recovery. She attempted to push herself upright, and was rewarded with an unflattering view down the length of the muslin overalls which covered her normal clothes. Next, she tried to move her feet. Failed. Her nervous system needed more time, but she was impatient. She forced herself up, and sat looking around her, legs dangling uselessly over the side of the bed. The synapse chamber was large and mostly empty. Her steel bench was one of twenty arranged as spokes around a central unit. Most of the equipment required to transfer and merge the subjects' memories was contained within the structure of the benches, which lent a certain cold efficiency to her surroundings.

The witnesses from the coffee shop were still 'asleep'. They'd all been sedated to oil the wheels of the process: a light dose for Anna, to keep her higher functions lucid while allowing her to slip into the other's memories; a higher dose for the witnesses. It gave them no opportunity to think about different actions or alternative courses of events, kept the combined memory as steady as it could be.

There were two notable absentees from the chamber: the man who'd ordered the flat white, and the young woman Anna had been walking behind just before the first shots had been fired. Her boyfriend, Marlon, was with them, though. His overalls were covered in orange liquid as he struggled on his steel bench, as though caught in a thick mud.

'He's bumped out,' said Anna.

'Yeah,' Cody replied, drawing his mop along the tiles, cutting them clean. 'I see him. Give me a second.'

'You didn't notice?'

'My concentration was on you.'

'Put him back under. Quickly.'

'It's just shock.'

'I know what it is,' Anna snapped. She couldn't bring herself to watch Cody administer the drug, pushing Marlon back under so he could be given a more controlled return to consciousness. He'd been her most reluctant witness. She'd only persuaded him to take part in their experiment by telling him that what his brain could remember – perhaps outside his waking memory – might hold some clue as to why Jeanette had been shot. But now, after watching him struggle back to the surface, she understood. He didn't want to remember. Didn't want to go through it again. His girlfriend had died: she'd been murdered beside him.

'Another failure, then,' Cody said.

'No.' Her reply was too quick. 'Not a failure. CCTV and drone footage told us nothing about what happened inside the café. It all adds to the picture.'

'Did the shooter meet anyone?'

'We can rule that out now, I think.'

'So this Luke Taylor just ordered a drink, and then strolled outside to open fire?'

'He had a leaflet with him: the Workers' League.'

'The police already knew he was a commie,' Cody growled.

Anna slipped down gently, trying each leg in turn to check all the feeling was back before shifting her weight fully off the bench. Her star witness was sleeping again, the suffering still etched on his face. He'd been shot as he'd looked into his new girlfriend's eyes; she had died in his arms. What was she going to say to Marlon? That this had all been a waste? That he'd seen nothing that day that would really help?

No. The synapse sequencer could save lives. She wouldn't allow it to fail.

## 2

GRACE TROTTED INTO my little box room with a tray of food and her usual cheerful greeting: 'Good morning, Anna.' I was grateful that it was the dumpy nurse and not the careless one. I'd managed to lever myself into my wheelchair already, but she checked that I was secure before she placed the cushioned tray on my lap.

Given I wasn't particularly hungry, I didn't pay much attention to the food. But I was amused that Grace had already started the little ritual she always performed when delivering my dinner. First she picked up the cutlery a fraction of an inch, before putting it down again firmly onto the tray, each piece making a sudden, sharp tap. Then she did the same with the three-quarter-filled glass of orange juice. I was never quite sure why she did this. Maybe it was to make sure I knew it was all there, or to draw my attention downwards so I didn't forget about it.

'Spaghetti, meatballs and bolognese sauce,' Grace said, pronouncing every word like she was talking to a five-year-old. It was perhaps what they taught them to do, but it was still irritating. I wasn't deaf, never had been. 'Your favourite.'

'Yes,' I said, playing my own version of the game, 'I look forward to Tuesdays.'

Grace didn't pass comment. She kept her smile fixed even though a part of her brain would have triggered: *Friday. It's Friday.*

'And are you finished with the TV, Anna?'

My neck moved in a series of jerks and clicks. The TV was just a shimmer in the background. I squinted at it – not quite sure if the damn thing was actually on – and then attempted a dismissive hand wave. 'Nothing worth watching, anyway,' I said.

Grace walked over to it. Her movement brought some of the light from the screen into brief focus, and I realised all I was missing was reruns of old TV shows. The home ran a fixed-channel system, and the management chose programming to sedate rather than entertain. Occasionally, they would make a mistake and there'd be a welcome flash of nudity, some of it male. But those days were all too rare.

'Did I ever tell you the story of Arnold Anderson?' I asked.

Grace stopped, her smile still fixed. Behind her, the shimmer had vanished and been replaced by a cold black void. 'Why don't you remind me?'

'Arnold Anderson was a soldier who woke up in hospital the day after D-Day, and wondered why he was finding it hard to move, hard to see and hard to hear. When he looked in the mirror, he saw an old man staring back at him. Every day he woke up and said the same thing to his doctor. Every day he thought he was still twenty-four years old, just returned from the Front.'

The nurse crouched so she could communicate at eye level. 'I never know whether to find that a sweet story or a horrific one.'

'It's neither,' I replied sharply. 'It's life. You always feel like you're twenty-four years old. When you're sixteen you feel older, when you're thirty-seven you feel younger. And when you're my age you feel it too – but you also wonder why you can't kneel down any more, nor get back to your feet so easily.'

Grace's smile was genuine now. I glanced at my food tray, and cursed again at the machine that turned everything into a pre-chewed gloop.

'It's good for you,' Grace said.

'A student came to see me yesterday,' I said, still not picking up a fork.

'The children from the local school have already been,' Grace replied. She sounded a little nervous. 'You asked not to see them, remember? But they'll be back again soon enough, so you can catch their next performance.'

I sighed. She was playing dumb, trying to distract me and hoping I would instead start my dinner. But that would be easier to eat once the sauce had started to stiffen.

'No,' I said. 'No, I don't want to listen to a bunch of tone-deaf kids… I can remember the songs fine, thank you. I don't want them ruining them just as the album's about to finish.'

'Album?'

'Whatever you want to call it… LP, album, CD, shuffle. Always new words for the same thing. To confuse the old and trick the young into thinking they're cleverer—'

'Than they are,' Grace finished the well-worn statement. She was kind. Unlike the careless one. Unlike the bitch.

'*This* student came from the university,' I said. 'Not a kid. Not one of the local sprogs, although I think his sister might be one of them. Didn't you say he wants to talk to me about what happened in Tanzania? You know, the crash?'

I couldn't really remember – it was all lost in something of a fog – but I just about caught a flash of annoyance cross Grace's cheek. She stirred the gloop on my plate as if that would tempt me to eat it. If she'd been the bitch, then she might have made a callous remark that my memory was failing. Just like my eyesight. Withering away like my skin.

My nurse's face turned serious. 'It would be best if you just told him to go away,' she said. 'It won't do you any good to drag that all up again, Anna.'

It was too late, though. I was already thinking of that place. That stupid decision. When I was too young, too proud and too arrogant to take the right course rather than the correct one. 'Who is he?'

The question seemed to disappoint my nurse. She raised up a little, her hands levering against her knees and her face screwing up for a moment or two. 'All I know is his name is Sean.'

'And what is his research topic?'

The nurse looked back at me blankly.

'What is he studying?' I asked again.

'I think you told me that,' Grace replied. 'You used some pretty fancy words, Anna. But I guess it comes down to why people do things.'

'Why they make their choices?'

'Yeah, I guess that's it.'

'My choice was that I said a plane had been sabotaged.'

'That wasn't a choice, though, was it?'

The nurse hadn't meant it as a question, but my slow eye roll caused her to take a sharp intake of breath. Only then did she relax. Realising the joke. It was, after all, Friday not Tuesday.

'I think it would be interesting to see him,' I said, turning my head away towards the dresser where I kept my now meagre collection of vinyl. It was a format that had gone in and out of fashion throughout my adult life, although I was no longer allowed to play them lest the noise disturbed the other inmates. 'What does it matter now, anyway? The album will soon be finished.'

Grace didn't try to offer any empty words of reassurance. We both knew we couldn't beat what was coming.

'I'd been thinking I'd be forced to explain sooner or later,' I continued. 'Just, perhaps, after the end and not before it.'

The nurse checked a device in her pocket. Vital signs, no doubt. Another piece of my independence that had been passed over to others, somewhere along the line. But this mention of Tanzania hadn't triggered any anxiety. No tightening of the throat. No dizzying feeling that the world was about to fall away.

So it was finally time.

Time I made my admission.

# 3

'YOU'RE TENSE.'

Anna felt something well up inside her, but the frustration didn't quite break. Instead, she switched her attention away from the boards' latest feeds and slipped off her coat. Her housemate, Kate, was sprawled on their sofa, eating pasta from a plate balanced on the very tip of her knees. Anna tried to ignore the fact it might topple, and instead headed to the kitchen.

Her lodger had probably been in their apartment most of the day, though there wasn't any evidence of her doing anything useful. Yesterday's dishes remained stacked beside the sink, and they'd now been joined by a series of cups and beakers that must have been filled and discarded at some point. But just as Anna was about to shout something sarcastic through to the lounge, the oven signalled her evening meal was ready. A hot stew and a stick of crusty bread. Which meant the fridge, Kate, and the connecting logistics chain had all successfully conspired to get her some food just when she *needed* it. Even if it wasn't exactly what she *wanted*.

She would have vastly preferred her housemate's pasta. Not that this was Kate's fault. The oven wasn't set to Anna's biorhythms. To all intents and purposes, it thought she was already home, eating her dinner on the sofa where Kate was now sitting. The meal it had prepared was for someone else entirely, a phantom populating its circuits. An algorithmic substitute coded with the express intent of fooling the main program. The thought caused a sudden knot of doubt and panic.

'Hey,' shouted Kate, 'if you don't like it, I'll eat it!'

'It's fine,' Anna answered. When she'd first invited Kate into her apartment, keeping track of which lifestyle algorithm was following which inputs had been confusing. But now she was just about used to it. And food was food.

Anna retrieved the meal from the oven and started slicing up the loaf – carefully holding back the two crusty end pieces for when she'd finished. She tried not to think about anything else, but found herself dwelling on the usual fears anyway. The trip home had been okay, and with winter approaching, the nights were already providing that extra element of covering darkness. She always walked quickly, varying her route between the hub and the pod station, as she'd so often been advised. But it was more reassuring when she knew there was less chance of being recognised.

'It's been a bad day,' Kate said, not shifting her attention from her pasta as Anna returned to the living room. The plate on her knees was now at an even more gravity-tempting angle, and there was more than enough sauce remaining to make a mess. *If it fell.* 'Well, I guess the morning was okay, but your PPA has been bugging me all afternoon.'

Anna pulled her attention away from the plate. Just like the oven, her Personal Psychological Assistant was tied to Kate rather than Anna. The arrangement meant the PPA's alerts could be contained within the apartment, rather than being relayed to her at work. It was typical of the Home Office's ineffectiveness that its main response to her situation – compelling her to use a PPA – had effectively made it harder to be re-employed. If she admitted to it. 'Saying what?'

'Wanting to chat… you know how Elsy is. Yada, yada, yada.'

'Thank you.'

'No problem,' Kate replied, shrugging. 'It's what you pay me for.'

Her lodger – her employee – her spoof – continued to eat, relaxed. Her head moved in an almost imperceptible bobbing motion, but whatever music was vibrating through her inner ear didn't emanate into the wider room. Another slight irritation. Just like the plate.

Kate's head stopped. 'Okay – I hear you.'

'I didn't say anything.'

Kate tapped at the side of her skull. 'I heard you loud and clear, *Mum*.'

Anna tried not to respond to the young woman's taunt.

But, of course, she did. The two of them were linked. The routing of Anna's personal biodata feed via her spoof meant Kate always had a good idea of how she was feeling. All it had taken was enough time together to allow her spoof to learn how to interpret the data.

Kate flinched at Anna's unspoken response. 'Okay, sorry. My bad. Shitty day, huh?'

'That thing I told you about?'

'Yeah?'

'It didn't work.'

'Not this time,' Kate replied. The answer had been almost instantaneous. Positive. Unworried. Her lodger grinned, and let the plate slide cleanly onto the sofa – where it would likely stay for the rest of the evening. 'And, anyway, you've only just started. They're not going to give you a job and then take it away just like that. I mean... the company you're working for is smart, right?'

*Yes*, Anna thought, *very smart*. Which meant using a spoof was a very dumb idea. But Jake Morley would have been unlikely to have offered her the job if he'd known she had a PPA. And so it would remain her only option until she could get the damn thing uninstalled.

'You seen UI payments are increasing?'

Anna nodded, grateful for the necessary distraction. She'd seen it on the boards, and knew the increase in the Universal Income payment would have attracted Kate's attention. The same cash increase would also be going to her own account, of course, although she also had a job to supplement it. For the time being.

'And there's a new round of grants for creatives.'

Yes, she'd seen that too. Every so often, the government

liked to hand out cash to keep individuals going for a year or so. It was unlikely, however, that any would end up in Kate's pocket. She was good at painting, but so were a lot of other people.

'Hey – my creativity index is in the top bracket,' Kate replied, reacting to the unstated negativity. She settled back, her head already starting to bob to her inaudible music.

Anna forced herself to relax. She was home; she had food. And even though her apartment wasn't spacious – just two bedrooms, a kitchen and a living room – it was at least comfortable and secure. A sideways glance from her housemate confirmed her subtle change of mood had been registered. The simple moment of kindness reminded her of how lucky she'd been in finding Kate at the right time. Eventually, Kate would get sick of being a spoof and the search would be on for a replacement, someone else who could even out her mood.

'Hey…'

Anna turned. Kate tilted her head. 'You're becoming maudlin.'

'I was just thinking.'

'Then stop. Eat your dinner. Go to your room and listen to some of your crackly old records. You're not at work now, you know.'

Anna took a mouthful of the stew, but didn't quite bring herself to relax again. Her spoof stretched out on the sofa and gave a long, slow yawn.

'You've had a visitor, by the way,' she continued. 'Thought I should say before you check in with the front desk.'

'Oh?'

'One of *them*,' Kate continued, rolling her eyes.

'They came to the door?'

'Uh-huh. You maybe got a ping from me? I was still in my dressing gown, so I was just, like, so not ready for that shit.'

Anna silently shook her head. She hadn't felt anything at work. Received no corresponding pulse that anything had been wrong here. Did nothing disturb her spoof? Then again, it was Kate's job to be unruffled. 'Did they say anything?' she asked, knowing her heart rate had already turned up a notch, and her housemate would feel it. 'Tell you why they came?'

'As I said, I got rid of them,' Kate replied. 'And then I informed the security desk they'd fucked up. Don't fret about it.'

# 4

THERE WERE TREES in the distance, but Anna's attention was instead drawn to the lake directly in front of her and the ruined abbey overlooking it. The summer sun hung motionless above the scene. Everywhere appeared calm, the lake only disturbed by the passage of a swan with its cygnets.

She took a few steps forward, sensing the slight distortion and lag of the sequencer. Around her, a few families lolled in the centre of the park. Even from here it was clear that several sets of parents and children were direct copies of each other. But they were only ancillary details – decoration rather than the centre of the memory. By contrast, the detail of the abbey, from the remaining arches to the weathered gargoyles lining the tops of its walls, had been transferred into the sequencer with remarkable clarity. Which meant Jake must have been fascinated by it. He'd examined and could recall every little crack and wrinkle of its structure.

'Anna!'

A man was jogging towards her – coming from the lake that he'd been using as the centre of a natural athletics track. Summer heat or not, Jake didn't look tired as he hammered closer. And he recovered his breath all too quickly.

Anna suppressed a smile. Her boss was perhaps in his

mid-thirties, tall and muscular. He didn't much look like a distance runner, more a sprinter, and his orange running vest seemed to have been chosen specifically to show off his shoulders and biceps.

'Rufford Abbey Park,' Jake explained. 'I used to visit it as a child.'

'I think we've met here before.'

'Possibly. I understand yesterday's experiment didn't go well?'

'We know more than we did before,' she said, trying to sound confident. 'I should have at least something to add to my report.'

'Don't bother with a report yet. Good ideas are never rushed. I'm thinking we need to pursue another example, though. I know we've discussed it before, but Luke Taylor never seemed a suitable choice to me.'

'The man killed over thirty people.'

'And everyone knows why,' Jake replied. 'A solicitor, five years out of work after losing his job to a bot.'

'It takes more than that to push someone—'

'He took the plunge down to the UI,' Jake repeated, 'and snapped.'

'Most simply move on, and try again.'

'Just like you, you mean?'

Anna had joined Synapse Initiatives after her career as an air crash investigator had come to an unscheduled end. Perhaps it wouldn't have been much longer before she – just like most solicitors – became obsolete anyway. Planes rarely crashed any more, just like most legal details could be dealt with by an AI. But she'd been one of the lucky ones, until she'd investigated the wrong crash. The one that went political. The one that led to China's proxy war in Tanzania against the US and Europe.

It had been barely a year ago; a short, clinical drone-fought war for the foreign powers, and a brutal one for Tanzanians – seventy-five thousand civilians killed. The government line was that it had been an honourable war fought to protect American allies against Chinese-backed terrorism; the people Anna met in the street were still raw from seeing pictures of dead children, desperate doctors in bombed-out hospitals, and they were looking for a scapegoat.

'You wanted me here to give you another way of looking at things,' Anna said. 'That's what I'm trying to do. The police concentrate on the *who* and the *when*, when I think there's more long-term value in finding out the *why*. We still need to know why he shot up that plaza.'

It was hard to tell if she was making an impression. Her experiment was just one of the projects being funded at the synapse hub. And the hub itself was just another part of Jake's wider empire, even if he spent more time on it than his other investments.

'Aircraft became safe because we never accepted the easy answer,' Anna persisted. 'Pilot error, mechanical failure, weather conditions. Hardly any crashes had a single cause. And I don't believe what happened at the plaza that day can just be ascribed to someone "being put on the UI".'

'So what's this extra detail for the report?'

'He was a member of the Workers' League.'

Jake sucked in some air his body didn't appear to need. 'A tiny organisation made large through hysteria.'

Anna didn't contradict him. How big the Workers' League had become was a matter of some debate. The organisation was constantly in the news, thanks to its attacks on systems that supported AI and robotics initiatives. Like the Luddites before them, its leaders preached the message that violent protest was justified if it protected people's jobs.

'Plus, it doesn't help that this guy shot up a load of people who were on the UI,' Jake continued. 'If he'd chosen a time after working hours, then the case would be of higher value. It might have earned a visit from a politician, maybe even the new prime minister.'

*Unlikely,* Anna thought. With so many employment protests being agitated into violence by the Workers' League – tiny organisation or not – most politicians had long since disappeared from public view. Every now and then one would make a blink-and-you'll-miss-it appearance to capitalise on some rare good news, or to take credit for someone else's hard work.

'The key problem for your team is that the police don't appear to be interested in buying a new system from us. They're happy with the system they already have.'

'Serve and Protect has its flaws,' Anna replied, all too quickly.

'Yeah, but it seems to be driving down crime, which is all anyone cares about.'

Jake was right. Crime *was* falling – that much was pretty self-evident. People simply didn't have the same opportunity to commit crime and, more importantly, to get away with it. Not when policing was governed by the seemingly omnipotent eye of S&P.

'Of course,' Jake said, 'there's this emerging issue with the use of spoofs. That might change things.'

Anna remained silent, catching her answer mainly because

she didn't trust her voice. The technician monitoring her biofeeds would not detect any blips, thanks to the fact that they were actually reading Kate's vitals, not hers.

A blond child in a striking red T-shirt started chasing a duck down the bank towards the river. About a hundred metres away, the same blond child in a red T-shirt was holding its father's hand, walking through the park. The same child, built from the same memory. The sort of mistake her witness program was designed to eliminate.

'I want this to succeed,' Anna said. 'We can offer something to supplement S&P, I'm sure of it.'

'There are many potential uses for the sequencer. It's just a case of figuring out which are the right ones. Commercially, ethically.'

'And addressing the nausea.'

From the look on Jake's face, her comment was in poor taste. 'Speaking of health,' he said, 'you should get yourself out a bit more. Most of your biodata looks good, but there's an alert that your vitamin D is bumping along the bottom.'

Kate. The downside of her spoof spending all day in the apartment was that she didn't get much sunshine.

'Take a few supplements. Remember: a healthy body is a requirement for a productive mind.'

Anna wondered momentarily about her other stats – and didn't want anyone in HR to look too closely at the data. A few quick sweeps was fine. Anything more than that might highlight oddities that would be harder to explain.

'You had a visitor yesterday.'

*Shit. How does Jake know about that?* Her first couple of weeks at the company had been marred by a steady trickle of protests at the outcome of her final air crash investigation.

But then again, the reason for those protests was the same one for which he'd employed her. 'I've reported the failure to the desk security,' Anna said. 'She won't get into my apartment block again.'

'I meant you had a visitor here, at the hub. And it was a man, not a woman.'

Anna felt another spike of adrenaline that would no doubt soon be registered by her spoof back home. 'I wish I could say it won't happen again,' she said, giving a short, nervous laugh. 'I thought it had all died down; that they'd gone away.'

'Oh, *that* won't go away,' Jake said. 'You're stuck with it. But I don't think this was connected with your other troubles.'

'Oh?'

Jake's eyes were fixed on the lake. He moved impatiently, like a dog straining against his leash. It wouldn't be long before he would start running again. 'Your visitor was a private investigator. Says you've been ignoring him.'

'Are you really surprised?'

'No, but I said you and Weaver would meet him today.'

'He'll want to know about… Shit, Jake.' Under the long sleeves of her shirt, her forearms begin to itch. Back home, Kate would be receiving alerts from Elsy. Her PPA would no doubt be telling her to calm down. Asking her to make time to chat, to start her relaxation techniques.

Her boss seemed undisturbed. 'He had some questions about your current work, not your last job.'

'Well, he wouldn't just come out and say it, would he?'

'He's signed a non-disclosure agreement, like all our visitors, Anna. That includes information about our workers. You'll have to come to terms with the fact that this is a package we're trying to sell. If a potential market exists, we must explore it. And that includes private investigators. I still think what you and Weaver have is potentially a good idea,' he added. 'The witness program. Unfortunately, there are lots of examples of good ideas that never quite found their place.'

Before Anna could respond, Jake started to run. She could have tried following, but she knew the meeting was over. Without saying anything more, she closed her eyes as her consciousness drained from the park.

HER GUTS CONTRACTED. Then she heard the familiar splatter that accompanied her every return to the real world. This time though, a different technician was on hand to clear up the mess: Jake's personal assistant, and nurse.

Becky Holland – who would have been overweight had she not also been so tall – looked disappointed, as if the effort of connecting Anna to the synapse device hadn't been worth the relatively short meeting time. A limited immersion did have its benefits, though. For one thing, the feeling in Anna's legs returned much more quickly. Not that Jake's nurse seemed interested in monitoring her progress. Holland's attention was on clearing up the mess.

Jake lay on a much smarter version of the basic steel synapse bench, moulded to his body. But the relative softness of the design was only to allow his nurse easy access to rotate and clean him. To make sure he didn't suffer from bedsores. To administer his medicine. To keep the crippled tech geek submerged.

Jake's broken body was almost the only thing that was hardwired into the synapse sequencer. She couldn't help but wonder how long it would take to recover feeling in those parts of his body that still worked, if he ever decided to come out of it.

'Hey,' Holland said, looking up from her mop. Her voice was harsh, somehow matching the bright red that she'd dyed her hair. 'Would you stare at him like that if he could see you?'

Anna looked away. She knew she wouldn't. 'I'm sorry.'

# 5

**Top News:**

Citizen Activity Programme to be extended (*Read more*)

Government announce closer economic ties with Tanzania (*Read more*)

Extension of S&P data rights to return to Parliament (*Read more*)

Protests in Iceland: online services shut down again, as more reported missing (*Read more*)

**Selected for You:**

Glitch in the system? Latest gaming sensation revealed to be human! (*Read more*)

AS ANNA WALKED back through the hub to the office she shared with Cody, she tried to relax. For a moment she almost wished she had Elsy there to soothe her with its personalised, if artificial, advice. Her PPA would have probably pointed out she didn't really know why the private investigator was here. That Jake was unlikely to have let him see her if this was really about the air crash in Tanzania. And, most importantly,

41

that she could tell him to leave any time she wanted.

As she reached the office a raucous laugh from inside stopped her. Cody must have invited the investigator in already. There was a murmur of voices, but the detail of their conversation was muffled behind the slide-screen door. Anna tugged at her sleeves and adjusted the heavy, red plastic bangle that hung from her right wrist. Then she slid back the door.

The action seemed to pull the plug on the conversation. The visitor, who was leaning back in her chair, hastily straightened up when he saw her. Cody looked like a kid who'd been caught eating snacks ten minutes before dinner.

'Cody,' she said, ignoring the newcomer. 'Can I have a word?'

Cody gave an apologetic shrug to the visitor as he walked out, which made Anna shove the door closed a little more sharply than she'd meant to.

'Who is he?'

'Just some private investigator,' Cody replied, the words crackling hesitantly in his throat. 'Jake said this was all okay.'

'And how did he get through to Jake? Did this private investigator just ring up Jake's nurse and say, "Hey there, can I have a word with the woman who may or may not have started a war?"'

'This isn't about Tanzania, Anna.'

'They still follow me home. They come to my house. They were there yesterday, and then this PI shows up today?'

Cody puffed his cheeks. 'It's not about Tanzania,' he repeated. 'And if he mentions anything close to that, well, I'll kick his arse out of here myself. Okay?'

Anna paused. Tried to think. They'd left the investigator in their office, alone. Not that there was anything to see at her workstation. Her terminal was offline, and she didn't really make use of paper notes. But there were other things, such as the photograph of her parents. Stuff that no doubt could be sold to the media.

'What did he say to you?'

'He's a private investigator, Anna,' Cody repeated. 'And we have an investigative tool we're trying to sell.'

'To the police—'

'At the point we're at,' Cody interrupted, 'we just need someone to take us seriously.' He paused, stifling a yawn. 'Look, Jake has this saying. You've probably heard it: "Success begets success, and failure begets failure".'

'I've heard the first part, yes.'

'The second is more important. What it means is, people associated with bad projects don't get reassigned.'

'Our project has only just got going,' Anna replied. 'We're a long way from failure.'

'We're close enough. We had all the witnesses we needed for that plaza shooting, and we came up empty. All that effort, Anna: getting them to agree, stimulating the right memory, getting it all to sync. And what did we find? One *leaflet* from the Workers' League?'

'What we've achieved, in a relatively short period, is still impressive.'

'But being impressive won't be enough for Jake – not in the long term. Not when the next interesting application pops into his brain. And to be blunt, I'm starting to regret ever suggesting it to him. I could have still been working in the entertainment programme. And you would—'

'Still be unemployed,' Anna said. Jake had hired her straight after she'd been dumped out of air crash investigation. As an investigator, someone from outside of law enforcement, Anna was the ideal person to run with Cody's proposal to use the synapse sequencer within Jake's emerging justice division. And she'd been grateful for the opportunity to escape the UI.

Cody looked sheepish. 'Yeah, well – all I'm saying is that we should listen to what this PI has to say to us. We could do with another angle – and he might just have it.'

'What were you laughing at?' she asked. 'Before I arrived?'

Cody's brow furrowed. 'Just baby stuff. I made the mistake of telling Tina last night I was tired. She almost battered me. I don't think she's slept since the birth.'

A tiny wave of regret passed through Anna. *Shit*. So not about her, then. 'Okay,' she said. 'I'll give this investigator some time. But if the conversation turns towards Africa, then I'm walking out and you're getting rid of him.'

Cody opened the door to their office. The small space they shared could hardly look less impressive. The prime locations in the synapse hub were reserved for those initiatives focused on health and entertainment. That was where Jake thought the real money would be generated: from people like himself, who couldn't move in the real world, or from those who wanted to vanish into their own imaginations. The use of the synapse sequencer for investigative work was always considered a niche service. Something that few would pay for, even though Jake had been keen enough to headhunt Anna for the project.

'Anna Glover,' she said by way of introduction. 'I'm told you're interested in our work?'

'Yeah.' He finally got out of her seat. 'Adrian Fowler. Everyone calls me Fowler.'

He offered a firm handshake rather than a swallowing grip

– but that was the extent of his refinement. Perhaps in his early forties, Fowler had let his hair grow long and lank. A fuzz of stubble barely hid the fact that his cheeks were a little sunken, excess flesh hanging from his face and neck.

'You're the private investigator?'

'I guess you could call me that.'

'Then you don't make money from exposing men cheating on their wives?'

'That's a fairly old-fashioned notion.'

'That it's mainly men doing the cheating?'

Fowler gave a shallow smile. 'That all cheating men choose wives.'

Anna waited. Whatever he wanted to call himself, this Fowler would probably be feeding off the hundreds of smaller crimes and civil irritations the police no longer seemed interested in tackling. Anything basically that people were willing to divert a bit of their own income to investigate, so he could supplement the UI.

'I'm glad to see *you're* still in the detection business,' Fowler said.

That was his first strike. The first sideways mention of Tanzania.

'We're not in the same business,' Anna said. 'Jake said you wanted to see us?'

'I'm here to hire some time with the sequencer.'

'To do what?'

Fowler's eyes flickered towards Cody, seeking his support.

Cody winced. 'To see if the synapse sequencer can help with his sort of work. This has all been cleared, Anna.'

Anna turned her attention back to Fowler. 'You want to use it to catch love cheats?'

'My work isn't always in that – uh – direction,' Fowler replied. 'Listen, we're wasting time here. At the moment, all I want to know is how accurate the sequencer is, and whether or not I can trust it.'

*Not whether he* can *use it,* thought Anna. *He already assumes he can.* 'It's been shown to be accurate.'

'The police don't seem to think so.'

'No.' Anna tried to keep her voice firm as she made her rebuttal. 'No, the police don't see it as being *useful*, which is altogether different.'

Fowler didn't seem perturbed. He must have been used to being blanked. Part of his job would have been to keep going when others were trying to stall him. 'Well, it sounds interesting enough for me and my line of work, love cheats and all,' he said. 'As long as I can trust what it tells me. And it sounds like you need a client base. I've got plenty of connections. An agreement with me will get the bigger fish in.'

'"Trust" is somewhat beside the point. The synapse sequencer allows direct interaction with memory.' It was probably all bullshit, but Fowler's argument had obviously persuaded Jake that this was a man of influence. And really, what did they have to lose? She couldn't help but think back to her meeting with Jake. The detail of the abbey, the replicated children. 'The results are as good as the memories of those being used to construct the environment and—'

'But memories are faulty,' Fowler interrupted. 'Witness statements have a habit of throwing up jarring details, don't they?'

'Right,' Anna replied, feeling a punch of frustration. 'But if we overlay many witnesses' memories of the same event in the sequencer, then those jarring details tend to disappear.'

Fowler startled her by breaking into a hacking cough.

'Sorry,' he finally managed, wiping at his mouth. 'So the information can be trusted?'

'We think so, yes.'

'And the police still aren't convinced?'

Anna let out a sigh. 'When Jake asked me to head up this project, we quickly came up with a number of tests—'

'Yeah, I've read the spiel. But that doesn't answer my question.'

Anna glared at the investigator. That was the second time he'd talked over her, but he wasn't going to stop her making her point. 'And we passed every one of those tests.'

'Fine. And the police?'

She gave up. 'Want to know what I really think? The police aren't really interested in detection any more.' As Jake had said, sometimes good ideas just never find the correct home. Or, worse, someone comes up with a way of solving the same problem in a different way – one that was so effective, anything offering a tiny fraction more just didn't seem attractive.

'Well, that doesn't mean what they're doing is better,' Fowler replied, a strange expression on his face.

Cody looked between the two of them. 'So, Anna,' he said. 'The sequencer. Let's just keep Jake happy, eh?'

# 6

THE STREET BEGAN to shimmer.

Anna observed the effect rippling on the crowded shopfronts, on the glazed towers of the Square Mile towering above them, and on the faces of smartly dressed people frozen in their early morning commute. She let her gaze drift, trying to detect where the detail became nothing more than a blur. She found the boundary after only a few seconds, where a shop sign was illegible, and next to it a building glimmered uncertainly between shopfront and office window, depending on the point of view. But both were some distance away. They had at least fifty or so metres of clarity, and that was all they were going to need.

'I think I'm going to be sick.'

Behind her, Fowler was having trouble moving. He stumbled forwards, doubled over. His brain was clearly struggling to process where all the parts of his virtual body were now located: not lying on a steel table, but walking along a street in the City of London.

'It's called proprioception,' Anna said, trying to sound sympathetic. She couldn't help but feel a sense of *Schadenfreude* at Fowler's struggles. Cody had arranged the demonstration very quickly after their first meeting. It had taken him just two days to search through his list of volunteers and get the necessary approvals from Jake. Not that this timescale had been quick enough for Fowler. The investigator had contacted them several times trying to speed things up. And now he was floundering, and probably wishing it would all come to an end.

'Huh?'

'The ability to sense the relative position of your body vis-à-vis the environment,' Anna explained. 'Your brain is momentarily confused, switching from the inputs of your body's senses to those of the sequencer. You'll get used to it.'

'It's like walking through jelly, not air.'

'You're not walking; you're not even moving much on the synapse bench.'

'This isn't how I imagined it,' Fowler said. 'I was expecting something like virtual reality.'

'Why would it be? Everything you see here is taken from the memories of people who saw this particular scene together. But the rest of it – the sensations of walking, touching – are fed into the simulation from the expectations of your own brain.'

'I don't get it.'

'Most of what we perceive each day is just a learned response. The triggering of a particular synapse sequence that reproduces hardwired, biological memories.'

Fowler stared at her blankly.

'At no point does your brain ever process all the information sent to it by your senses,' she continued, putting it as simply as she could. It wasn't all that long since Cody and Jake had explained it to her when she'd joined the company. 'It can't – it just doesn't have the time or processing power. So it fills in most things from what it's experienced before. You push on a wall, your brain expects resistance, and you therefore feel it and experience it in the sequencer. Most magic tricks work on the same principle. Your brain sees what it expects to see. The magician throws an imaginary ball at you, and you flinch or try to catch it.'

Fowler considered this. 'So we can just walk around and explore the place?' he asked. 'Can I change things? Move things around? Speak to people?'

Anna let out a sigh. Fowler was trying to control the pace of the demonstration, and that was her job. 'I'll explain when we get to that point,' she said.

Fowler raised a hand and waved it in front of his face. 'It's just that it feels... odd. Like I'm carrying a little extra weight.'

'Your movements feel slightly heavy because of the delay in processing data from the sequencer,' Anna said. 'Look, would you stop that?'

'Sorry.' He put his hand down.

'It gets better with each submersion. But you may occasionally feel light-headed. And take a deep breath. What can you tell me?'

Fowler sucked some air into his lungs. He instinctively made to cough, but his chest didn't react. He gave her a questioning look.

'No smell,' she said, filling in the blanks. 'No smell, and no taste.'

'But sensation, right?'

'We have a lot of sensory abilities in the sequencer: sight; sound; pressure; temperature – to a point; the position of our limbs – to another point. But no smell, taste... or pain.'

'We can't hurt ourselves?'

'Pain is all in the mind, Mr Fowler. And you are lying safely on a synapse bench. Cody is monitoring your biosigns.'

Fowler pushed at the ground with the tip of his shoe, as if testing its solidity. 'And Jake Morley thinks people are going to do this for fun?'

'As you noted, it's more immersive than virtual reality.'

'And a lot more limited. Unless memory and imagination are the same thing.'

'This is a construct of memory, Mr Fowler. Imagination has nothing to do with it.'

'Except it could do, right?'

'*Except* it doesn't,' Anna replied firmly.

Fowler grunted. He walked in a short, tight circle, trying to get himself used to moving in the sequencer. Anna waited for him, remembering her first submersion. She'd been a lot worse, even though Cody had explained it all to her before she'd been connected. If you ask a person to sit at a desk with their hand hidden underneath it and a rubber hand on top of the table, and then run a feather across both the real hand and the fake hand at the same time, it causes the brain to become confused. It will start to think the rubber hand is real. It will lose track of the real limb. The magic of the sequencer was to force the brain to forget it had a body, and feed it alternative sensory inputs.

Fowler was already looking a bit better. He edged slightly ahead of her, his attention snapping from one thing to another as he got his bearings.

'There's no rush,' Anna told him. 'We're not working against a clock.'

'I think I've spotted three of the witnesses,' Fowler said, peering at the people as they passed them.

'The location of the witnesses isn't actually all that important.'

Anna didn't remind him that the witnesses' positions had been clearly described in the briefing docket. He should have known where they were without looking. She took the lead again, weaving past the frozen people. All the time, she tried to detect subtle increases in detail: the way the pavement became uneven, a minor pothole in the road, a poster pinned up in the window of a hairdresser's…

In many ways, the street scene itself was unremarkable. It could have been anywhere in central London. Many of the shops were empty – their window displays designed to disguise the fact they'd long since been abandoned – but were at least well remembered. It was even possible to tell which of the expensive skyscrapers in the near distance were occupied and which had been drained of their employees and replaced with AI. And, if it all seemed very familiar, then that was exactly the point. None of the witnesses' brains would be actively sucking up detail. There was nothing to trigger the deeper recesses to create a clear memory. They were just going about their day, not really paying attention.

'Will we get anything useful from witness six?' Fowler asked. 'She's too far from the centre of the simulation, surely?'

'This is no simulation,' said Anna, slowing her pace.

'I know, but—'

'And our witnesses – all ten of them – are positioned to give us the best view of the whole street, not just the central point. Witness six is placed to give us boundary detail, no more, no less.'

'Okay, but—'

'Then let's start the calibration. Let me show you how we know we're getting a clear picture of what occurred here.'

Fowler looked around for the first calibration point. It

too had been written in the docket that Cody had prepared, but the investigator still seemed to be struggling to locate it. Anna could hear the first whispers of her own impatience, but forced herself to reel it in. After all, there were two men wearing suits in the calibration spot, and it was difficult to tell at distance which one was wearing a tie. 'We know the tie is red,' Anna said, prompting.

'Thanks,' replied Fowler, walking across to them. His final steps were hesitant, as if some of the confidence had been knocked from him. The first man had an open collar. The second was wearing a dark orange tie.

Anna waited as Fowler leant in, almost willing him to take a step to the right.

He didn't.

'It's orange,' he said.

'No,' replied Anna evenly.

'The tie's clearly orange.'

Maybe he'd see the mistake. This was his first time. Anyone out this early in the day could probably have been blindfolded and they'd still have found their way just fine. Because they knew this street by instinct – commuters on their way to work, half asleep, most of them. They were no longer looking, no longer seeking anything new. And that was what made it difficult. *How could a witness describe the street if they simply hadn't noticed it?*

'The tie is red,' Anna repeated. She took a step to the right, closer to one witness and further away from another. She took another step. And then another.

Finally Fowler followed her lead, and his expression soon confirmed he understood. 'Witness four,' he said slowly. 'He got it wrong?'

'Isolate witness four,' Anna called into the air. Back in the control room, Cody would already be switching the inputs. Sure enough, much of the street disappeared, the edges rushing in towards a new central point: *witness four*. It should have been a clear circle around a single witness. And yet the differences between what this man could remember compared to the others was stark.

The tie was orange. The other man in the suit still wore no tie, but his shirt was buttoned up to the neck. The florist's behind them transformed into a sweet shop. The same swirl of colour, perhaps, but the product could not have been more different.

'There's something wrong with witness four's eyesight,' Fowler said. He sounded like he'd somehow been tricked. He turned away from the tie and looked around until he spotted witness four, a flustered man with a briefcase, whose face was frozen in a squint. 'He hasn't corrected it, so his memory is wrong.'

'Very good,' Anna said. Before she could call another instruction to Cody, though, Fowler had another question.

'Wait,' he said. 'Wait. If we're down to a single witness, why can I see him too? Why aren't we seeing things from his viewpoint?'

Anna raised an eyebrow. 'Through his eyes, you mean?'

'Yes.'

'We have difficulty enough fooling our brain into thinking we're here.' Anna tried not to sound like she hadn't asked Cody the very same question herself on her first submersion. 'Feeding it information from the sequencer, and expecting it to override reality. If we took this thing further – and put ourselves behind our witness's eyes – then our brains would start trying – and failing – to control his limbs. Basically put, we'd bump out. Christ, it's difficult enough to overcome motion sickness with ordinary virtual reality.'

'Disappointing.'

'Why? We're using his memory to access much more detail than his individual viewpoint.'

It took a few moments for Fowler to understand what she was telling him. He waved a hand in the witness's face, before turning his attention to the space directly behind him. The places witness four couldn't directly see. 'So where's all this detail coming from?'

'Him,' Anna said. 'The witness. Everything you're seeing.'

'But… he isn't looking in the right direction.'

'You don't need to be looking at it to be aware of what's behind you,' Anna replied, but her voice was tinged with uncertainty – and it caused Fowler to chuckle. He repeated his earlier test – tipping the toe of his shoe forward and pressing it against the ground, no doubt registering the sensation of pressure.

'Look, it's okay,' he said. 'I get it. You're the detective, Weaver's the technical whizz. I can just ask him when we get out of here if you don't know. But you said earlier that our own brains fill in some of the detail?'

'All the primary detail comes from the witness,' Anna repeated. She took a breath. Sure, Cody knew more about the mechanics of how the damn thing worked. He was the technician; it was his synapse chamber. But she was in overall control of the project, and had been submerged more than enough times to give a damn tour. 'You've already noticed the detail behind the witness is less detailed, more blurred, than in front of him,' she said. 'If he turns, it will snap back into sharper focus.'

Fowler's disappointment was almost palpable.

'Is that what you wanted to do?' Anna asked. 'See a memory directly from someone's perspective?'

'I came for a demonstration. To understand what you were offering.'

'Well, it works much better with multiple witnesses,' Anna admitted. 'But this scene as it appears now remains just as witness four remembers it. We're still inside his memory.'

'Even if what he remembers is wrong?'

Anna aimed her voice higher into the air. 'Remove witness four and re-engage.' Almost immediately, the street scene shifted again, the details reappearing and rearranging around the remaining witnesses.

'The tie's now red,' Fowler confirmed, though his voice held no satisfaction. He worked his way down the rest of the calibration list, confirming the scene constructed before them now matched with the known facts. 'Does this mean we're calibrated?'

Anna nodded. '$V_1$,' she murmured.

'Eh?'

'$V_1$. It's an aviation term. It's what pilots say when they hit take-off speed.'

Fowler looked away from her, pretending to examine the street scene again. 'I'm not here about your fuck-up in Tanzania,' he said. 'And anyway, I think I might have done the same, if I'd been in your position.'

'The same?'

Fowler didn't respond to the prompt. 'So what's next?'

'No,' Anna replied, trying to keep her voice controlled. 'What do you mean by "the same"?'

'It doesn't bother me,' Fowler said, 'one way or the other.

And if the government was pressuring me – and I use the word "if" advisedly – then I would probably have given them the right answer too.'

'That maybe says more about you than me.'

'Maybe it does, maybe it doesn't. So what's next?'

Anna waited a few moments. Then she called out a single word: 'Validation?'

Fowler immediately jerked and batted at the side of his face, responding to an impulse that would be vibrating through his skull, as if someone had just put a wasp in his ear. Anna herself was long used to the way in which Cody's voice buzzed in her cochlea.

'*Licence plate, yellow pod. Delta model.*'

Anna soon found the necessary detail. She read out the licence plate, loud and clear. It was something that hadn't been provided on the calibration list. An aspect of the scene only Cody knew, probably something he'd found from the CCTV tapes. If she got it right, they'd know their memory construct was accurate. Then they could get things moving. Her technician would make the static people come to life and they would behave as they had done all those days ago.

A positive response soon came from Cody.

'V$_2$,' Anna whispered.

This time, Fowler didn't ask her what she meant. The people around them started to walk and chatter. They were airborne. The synapse sequencer was working.


ANNA LOOKED DOWN at the synapse bench. Fowler remained completely frozen. He stared upwards, the only movement a rapid blinking of his eyes. After a few seconds a muscle started spasming in his cheek, probably a sign he was already trying to move his lips enough to allow him to speak. Sure enough, air soon crackled out of his throat, bringing with it a few bubbles of spit.

Cody appeared at her shoulder, whistling. He checked Fowler's mouth was clear and then eased him back so his airway was open. 'We should have brought him out with the witnesses,' Cody said. 'Slow, like.'

'He wanted the full experience,' Anna replied. 'This is all part of it.'

Cody shrugged and then went to monitor the witnesses, all of whom were still connected to the sequencer, waiting to be roused. Although some had expressed a genuine interest in the tech, most were here simply for the cash – something to supplement the UI. None had witnessed any actual crime.

After the first meeting with Fowler, Cody had contacted a few people from his list of volunteers and invited them to the City for a business breakfast. Most thought they were being interviewed. None had been warned they'd already been placed into a scene they'd be expected to recreate later. And yet between them, each witness had remembered enough to build a complete picture. Anna couldn't help but feel a small chill of pride. The damn thing worked.

'Hey.' Fowler pushed his head upwards, but the rest of his body remained anchored to the bed. 'I can't move.' The folds of his neck were sagging in the wrong direction, pulling his face tight.

'The first time is always the worst. Like driving fast over a sharp rise in the road: your stomach feels like it's been left behind.'

'My *stomach* feels like it's been punched.'

'You've vomited. Automatic reflex. Cody has already cleaned you up. It's why you were asked to put on the overalls.'

Fowler's eyes swivelled down so he could see the trunk of his body. 'How do I know I'm really out?'

Anna let out a sigh. It was a question that had plagued Jake, and one he no longer entertained. Even as a joke. 'Did you really think what you were experiencing was real?'

Fowler's face flickered. Maybe his brain had told his shoulders to shrug, but they clearly couldn't yet obey. 'No,' he said. 'It was more like a dream.'

'Not quite real,' Anna confirmed. 'You can always tell when you're in the sequencer, Mr Fowler. Or rather, you can always tell when you're out of it.'

Fowler didn't look convinced. So she showed him, justifying her little bit of cruelty by classifying it as part of the demonstration. She took hold of Fowler's earlobe and squeezed, letting her fingernail enter the vulnerable flap of skin. She waited until he flinched – then continued to increase the pressure.

'Shit!'

'Pain,' Anna said, releasing her grip. 'You can't feel pain in the sequencer because – just like in a dream – anything that gives you a shock bumps you out. As I tried to explain to you, keeping a person submerged is difficult – the brain likes to fight its way to the surface.'

'Got it.'

Fowler turned green again. A reflex made his body twist and more liquid hit the tiles – some of it splashing up on the hem of her own muslin overalls. 'Sorry,' he said, struggling with some of the bile remaining in his throat. 'And I thought the most sickening part would be handing over access to my biodata.'

Anna didn't smile at the observation. One condition for entering the sequencer was that a subject had to provide full biodata access to Synapse Initiatives. Which was no big deal, really: most employers routinely asked for it anyway. And yet some people still insisted it was private. Or they used spoofs, such as Kate, if they had something to hide.

'Didn't Cody explain about the nausea?'

'I – urgh – guessed it was to make the simulation more realistic.' Fowler again struggled to move. Then he started to laugh. 'You think you'll be able to sell this for entertainment, then?'

'People get their kicks from weirder shit than this. You should know that more than most.'

Fowler stopped laughing. Perhaps finally registering surprise that he'd been able to manage it. More movement came back to him. The skin along his forehead creased. He strained his neck again, and his shoulders joined the party. Irritatingly, he was doing well. Better than most.

'And you say the police have seen the tech?'

'Yes,' Anna replied. 'We've shown them.'

'The same demonstration?'

'Similar, yes.'

Fowler shifted upwards. He managed to get to his elbows, but they immediately crumpled under him and his head thumped back onto the steel bench. 'Shit...'

'Just relax,' Anna said. 'It will take about thirty minutes to recover, the first time.'

'The police aren't interested,' Fowler said, 'because all you're offering them is a very good witness statement.'

'It's much more than that,' Anna replied. She shot a glance

at Cody, but the look she caught on his face indicated that he'd realised it too. Her technician quickly moved away again, back to check on the sleeping witnesses.

'The spiel you give out suggests the sequencer bypasses any uncertainty or forgetfulness,' Fowler said, 'whereas all it does in reality is blend together memories, and allows you to visualise them. The fundamental problem with your tech is that things can be misremembered.'

'Only where we have a single—'

'Everything in police work nowadays is about predict and prevent,' Fowler interrupted, 'or else identify and punish.'

'There's still a lot of crime.'

'Predict, prevent and concentrate resources on the crimes worth solving.'

Anna felt a kick of frustration. She might not like it, but what Fowler was saying was perfectly correct. The same cameras that provided her with enough data to calibrate their reconstructions were also sufficient to stop some crime occurring in the first place. Patterns of behaviour were recorded and analysed, suspicious faces picked from the crowd. And if all that went wrong, then those same cameras could be cross-referenced with biodata to find out who was involved in the *where* and the *when*. The algorithm that processed all this data couldn't predict crime too far in advance, but it could give the police just enough warning to deploy their forces.

'And it turns out,' Fowler said, 'the police don't need to go after everyone anyway – as long as they punish the right crimes and enough of them. They found this out years ago. Some police forces started to investigate just burglaries of odd-numbered houses, not those of even-numbered houses, and with resources concentrated, detection improved, and crime fell. It's not fair, but it works. Everyone else has to make do with filing a report and then deciding if they want to take matters forward privately.'

'Which is where you come in? You and your little honeytraps?'

Fowler again tried to move from the bench. His impatience wasn't helping his recovery. 'Being able to solve all the crimes doesn't mean the authorities have the resources to chase down every misdemeanour,' he said. 'You might have better luck going after that market, rather than the one the police have already cornered. If you can swallow your snobbery.'

Anna's cheeks burned hot. But since he remained immobile, she had the chance to provide him with an alternative view of how things could be done. 'You know what the most important tool is in air crash investigation?'

'Don't you mean *was*?'

'The black box,' Anna answered, ignoring the jibe but also feeling a tug of regret. 'Detailed records of what was done in the cockpit. From the controls used to the words uttered by the crew. It's why so much effort was put into finding them – and why they were so damn hard to break.' She paused, but didn't give Fowler sufficient time to interrupt. 'The synapse sequencer would allow the police to get right inside the crime.'

'Like the shooting at the plaza?'

Anna glanced at Cody, who was still hovering by the witnesses. It would soon be time to revive them. There was only so long, ethically speaking, that they could be held in limbo.

'Yeah, Weaver told me about it,' Fowler continued. 'And I think it proves my point. For the big crimes, what does your sequencer add? What did it tell you that the police hadn't already discovered?'

Anna let out a weak smile. 'It told me he ordered a flat white, drank his coffee quietly, and read a leaflet from the Workers' League.'

'Printed? Not electronic?'

'Yes.'

A muscle spasmed in Fowler's face. Printed political material had long since been illegal. After all, the government couldn't monitor things it couldn't hack.

'There was no mystery to what happened at the plaza except why he did it,' Anna continued 'Who was Luke Taylor? He had no previous record. No known associations with the group who claimed responsibility. And yet he was still willing to walk into a crowded market and start shooting people. Why? Planes stopped crashing because we always found out the *why*, Mr Fowler, not the *what* and the *when*.'

Fowler shrugged, then grinned as he realised he'd been able to make the movement in his shoulders. He tried to lift himself up, but again failed. It didn't seem to bother him. 'Well, whatever, you can be sure his personal details have all been digested, and about fifty or so new potential suspects fitting the same profile have already been put on watch lists. As I said: it's about prediction, not investigation.'

'Hey, Cody,' she called, 'the PI doesn't seem too impressed with our demonstration. I think we're done here.'

Cody looked up from the witnesses, clearly nervous. 'But Jake…?'

'We've done as Jake asked. When he's able, get him out of here.' She turned to go.

'There's a boy,' Fowler said, his voice now loud and urgent. 'More a teenager, really. Foster-kid. He was badly beaten.'

'And what do the police say?'

'Only that it was premeditated. His attacker had gone off the grid before the attack.'

The police didn't usually need to ask where you were at the time of an assault, they would know: a wash of electronic activity gave everyone a very sizable wake. You had to be extremely foolish to attack anyone on the spur of the moment. Whoever had beaten up this boy had taken care to switch their profile and life-logging data to silent, and then move them to a spoof carrier.

'And they're not interested in investigating further?'

'He's a foster-kid,' Fowler replied. 'He's been in trouble before. You think an incident like that gets an S&P score big enough to warrant an investigation?'

Anna thought about this for a second. The S&P program allocated each crime a score – the bigger the number, the more chance the crime would be allocated police time and resources. 'Someone's obviously interested enough to hire you, though, right?'

'The foster-parents, fortunately, have a sense of right and wrong.'

'And a sizable wallet?'

'Enough to pay for some time with the sequencer, yes.'

Cody stirred. 'Why not just ask the boy what happened?'

'N'Golo Durrant was beaten unconscious,' Fowler explained. 'He's in a coma. He's the reason I want to use the sequencer.'

# 7

THEY SAY AS you get older, the world gets younger.

The kid who arrived could have been one of the sprogs that regularly comes to sing at us. In the end, though, he introduced himself as a politics student from Leeds. I eyed him carefully, trying to get his face straight in my head. He was thin but carried a little bit of chubbiness around his face; he was too young to grow a proper beard.

I signalled to Grace, and asked her to reposition my wheelchair. She'd brought me down to the conservatory about thirty or so minutes ago – maybe longer – and the sun had just started to inflict itself on me. Once moved out of its glare, I re-examined the student.

He looked uneasy. Most people did when they came here. Except the sprogs and their goddamn awful cheerfulness, all too young to realise that this is what they were all heading towards. A room full of people talking to themselves and wondering which of them was next to be taken out in a box. Or else not wondering at all, but lost in another time altogether. Then again, perhaps the student who'd come to see me simply had a good sense of smell. Mine had long since gone. The chairs presumably smelled of stale pee, the air of disinfectant.

'You wanted to see me?'

My words jolted the young man upright. He smiled politely. Grace was a few feet away. She'd be able to hear what we were saying, although she was giving a none too convincing impression of attending to one of the other nearly-deads.

'I want you to know how much I appreciate this opportunity.' His voice had a squeaky element to it. It made me want to reach forwards and pinch his Adam's apple.

'Your name's Steve, right?'

The student hesitated. 'Sean,' he said. 'I'm called Sean.'

Yes, I knew that. Behind him, Grace flashed me a warning look. I could tell she still didn't really want me talking to him.

'You look familiar. Have we met before?'

Sean shook his head. 'No. I came in a couple of days ago, though – maybe you saw me then?'

'I can't remember what happened yesterday,' I said, chuckling. 'What makes you think I can recall who I saw two days ago?'

Sean's stony silence told me that my joke was mistimed and misplaced. He'd come to talk to me about what I remembered about Tanzania; he probably didn't want to hear about the gaps and the blank spots. 'There was an accident,' I said, trying to explain. 'After I stopped being an air crash investigator I went to work at something called the synapse hub. It... well, I guess you could say it changed me.'

My visitor glanced behind him. Grace had moved out of earshot. 'I was asked not to talk to you about that,' he said.

'My grandmother could talk for hours about her childhood,' I continued, ignoring my guest's discomfort.

'Her teens. Getting married. But after a certain point, it just becomes a blur. She thought things that happened years apart occurred at about the same time. The sand falls faster, you see, the older you get. The synapse sequencer accelerates things even more.' I tapped at my forehead. 'It wrecked things up here.'

Sean shuffled and twisted in his seat. 'You were in your late twenties when you flew to Tanzania?'

'Just turned thirty, actually. Young enough for the excitement to burn what happened deep into my memory. Deeper, anyway, than the monotony of my forties and fifties.' I craned my neck, looking for Grace. 'Have you been offered a cup of tea?'

'I'm fine,' the student said. 'I don't drink it.'

I didn't like his answer, but let it pass. 'So tell me about your work, Sean.'

'I'm writing about how we arrive at conclusions.' Sean was speaking a little too quickly, as if he thought the opportunity, now it had arrived, might be all too brief. 'How two people faced with similar facts take different sets of actions. Why that happens, and how the order in which facts present themselves affect judgements. If we can—'

I raised my hand. 'Do you know why most planes crash?'

Sean floundered for a reply. Because, of course, they didn't. Hadn't done for years, not in numbers that mattered. I didn't allow that fine detail to interrupt my line of thought. The nursing home was something of a bubble. And in my bubble, planes still fell from the air.

'Pilot error,' I said confidently. Using a bony finger to emphasise the point, I drilled it into one of the armrests of my chair. 'Not engine failure, or mechanical fault or freak weather phenomena. And certainly not bombs, or gunmen or terrorists. No, most planes crash because highly trained men and women tend to make mistakes. Even when there are two of them at the controls.'

I was pleased to see Sean had a pad of paper with him rather than a computer. He lifted the top sheet and folded it over to give him a bright clean surface. A pen appeared in his fingers. The lid popped off, and it disappeared into the pattern of the conservatory carpet. He glanced after it, but otherwise his attention remained fixed. 'The plane didn't crash in Tanzania because of pilot error, though… did it?'

'IS IT EVEN possible? To go into the memory of someone in a coma?'

Cody thought for a long time, his expression shifting in and out of optimism. 'I don't know,' he said finally. 'Hopefully. We'll know when the health team get back to us. See if it's anything like what they've been looking at.'

That would certainly please Jake. Messages often came down via Nurse Holland that he wanted his various departments to work more closely. A pity, then, that Cody had previously worked for one of his entertainment teams. The gaming and health departments didn't have a particularly constructive relationship; there was too much competition among them, to prove which team could drive the most profit.

'And even if we can get him synched,' mused Anna, 'how would we calibrate and validate?'

Cody pushed back in his chair and whistled a few tone-deaf bars, but she couldn't place the melody. Their office suddenly seemed cramped; their desks pushed so close that there wasn't any space between them. Anna glanced at the partition, half expecting to see Fowler standing at the sliding door. But after the demonstration he'd gone to get some fresh air and put some real movement back into his legs. He'd soon be back, though…

'Well?'

Cody gave her a silent shrug, followed by a long, heavy yawn.

'You getting much sleep?' she asked.

'Not really,' Cody replied, leaning back and rubbing at his face. 'I read on the boards that the Victorians used to give their babies laudanum. I'm beginning to think they had the right idea.'

'And Tina?'

'Oh, she lets me know when I get things wrong…'

Anna smiled. Amid the clutter on his desk, Cody had several photos of his newborn to keep him company in the office. It only underlined the emptiness of her own desk; just the photo of her parents, reminding her of their continued disappointment.

'We've put a lot of effort into reconstructing something accurate,' she said. 'Something robust. What he's asking us to do…'

'Could be potentially profitable?' He whistled a few seconds more, then stopped short. 'If we get the go-ahead from health, we should give this a go.'

'We can't.'

'I don't think we have a choice.'

Anna hesitated. 'It reduces the sequencer to nothing more than a lie detector.'

'Really?'

'If this kid's attackers were using spoofs' – Anna tried hard not to stumble on the final word – 'then whoever he sees will likely have an electronic alibi all worked out. Without calibration, it would be the kid's memory against their faked biologs. We'd be asking people who don't understand our tech to judge it – in a situation where we don't know ourselves. Even a basic legal AI would be able to punch holes through it.'

'Oh, come on…'

'Jake spends most of his time swimming in his own memories,' Anna continued, switching her attention between Cody and the empty doorway, just in case Fowler should return unannounced. 'But he isn't really, is he? In all our tests, one witness can never create an accurate construct on their own. So what are we going to get from the kid? His memory? Or something he's imagined? Maybe he didn't see his attacker clearly, so his brain just fills in the gaps. It plucks a close-fitting match from another memory. How will we be able to tell?'

Cody gave a small smile, but kept quiet.

'What?'

'At least you're starting to think about it,' he said. 'The mechanics of it, I mean. Look, when I suggested using the sequencer for this type of work to Jake, I really thought we were on to a winner… I didn't think it would pull us both down.'

'I know.'

'"Failure begets failure", Anna.'

Despite herself, Anna exhaled and almost broke into a laugh thinking about Fowler. She'd already looked up his business on the boards. Some of his endorsements were for chasing down debts, but his main work seemed to be tailing cheating spouses. Just as she'd suspected. 'At least he doesn't want to use it for some seedy affair,' she said.

'So is that a yes?'

She shook her head. 'It's a maybe. It all depends on what your health buddies tell us.'

'So should I go and get him?'

The health team probably wouldn't rush to get them an answer, but Fowler wouldn't be sucking in fresh air for ever. Soon, he'd appear at their office again. Unless they wanted to be proactive.

'Should I get him, Anna?' Cody was already standing in the doorway. 'Given Jake is expecting results?'

'Yes… but don't make any promises.'

Anna listened as Cody's footsteps echoed out of earshot. As soon as she was sure he'd gone, she took one hand with the other, and let the fingernail from her right thumb bite into her opposite palm. She held it there for as long as she could – feeling the pain – then released it as she heard Cody and Fowler returning.

Fowler still looked pale and clammy. He was walking okay, but quickly accepted the offer of Cody's chair.

'Well, I can't wait to try that again,' he said.

'It gets easier,' Cody said, leaning against a filing cabinet by the office door, his arms folded.

'You have a lot of different departments here,' Fowler said. 'I saw signs to an entertainment team… But didn't Jake develop this technology for old people?'

'Alzheimer's sufferers,' Anna said. 'Jake was one of the first to realise that memories aren't always lost as the disease progresses, but simply become more difficult to access. The same chemicals that stimulate memories in "old people", as you put it, were also used to stimulate your brain cells in the sequencer.'

'But now he's looking to diversify into entertainment…
and justice?'

'That's right. But health is still the primary driver, and
where most of the expertise remains. We're still waiting to
hear back from the health team as to whether or not what
you've asked us to do is possible, so can you tell us a bit more
about the boy? You said he was fostered?'

Fowler let out a sigh through his teeth. 'He lives with a
family in Amblinside. The foster-dad works for a bank. Mum
has a job with animals. I think she's a vet.'

The news seemed to pain Cody. 'They've both got jobs?'

'Yep,' Fowler replied. 'Makes you sick, don't it. But how
else could they afford to live in Amblinside? Most of the
people living there are civic stakeholders, not salaried.'

Anna considered this. Work in the modern world was
scarce. Most people were under-employed, if not unemployed.
Top-end banking was something of a hold-out, but working
with animals was more of a hobby dressed up as a job. There
were more than enough bots to take care of that sort of stuff.

'I take it using the synapse sequencer wasn't your first idea,'
she said. 'You must have already done some digging around?'

'Yep, and it wasn't easy, as it turns out. N'Golo doesn't
seem to have any friends. His social worker's less than useless.
I haven't been able to speak to anyone who's socialised with
N'Golo, or who knows what he's into or where he went of
an evening.'

'He wasn't at home?'

'Sometimes. But he'd often go out without saying where
he was going.'

'And the foster-parents couldn't—'

'No. They didn't stop him.'

'So you have no leads, then…?'

Cody shifted his stance. 'That's why he wants to use the sequencer, Anna.'

'So you have *no leads*, then?' Anna repeated, firmer this time.

'I found a leaflet in his bedroom,' Fowler said. 'A small printed copy from the Workers' League. Nothing that would have created an electronic wake.'

Another Workers' League leaflet associated with an unusually violent crime. First the entertainment plaza shooting; now the brutal attack on this boy.

'My hunch is that he's involved with them somehow,' Fowler continued. 'He would fit the profile. Young. Male. Disaffected.'

'And you've told the police this detail? They've plugged it into their S&P score?'

'It didn't shift the score one iota.'

Something on Cody's terminal pinged. Cody leant across Fowler to check the message. He seemed almost to deflate as he read it.

'What is it?' asked Fowler.

'It turns out we've tried with coma patients before.' Cody retreated to the doorway again. He looked as if he expected the meeting to break up very quickly. 'Health thought it might be a profitable line for them.'

'And?'

'You remember how that witness came out of simulation early a few days ago? The one who'd been shot? Like he was bumped out by the gunfire?'

'You mean Marlon?'

'Yes, him. Well, coma patients evidently do the same thing.

But if they get bumped from the simulation they can't wake up like Marlon did, because they're trapped in the coma...'

'Synapse shock?'

Cody looked utterly defeated.

Fowler looked back and forth between them. 'What does that mean?'

'It means they die. And it also means this conversation is over.'

9

HE WAS LOOKING at my forearms. Long, ghostly white lines criss-crossed like electric cables on the area of skin just below my elbows. Then, realising I'd noticed where his attention was being drawn, Sean turned away and waited. A single cup of tea arrived a few seconds later, carried by Charley, the nurse I didn't much like. She let it clatter down with sufficient force that a small wave sloshed over into the saucer. After flashing an over-exaggerated smile in the direction of my student, she went off to see to some of the other nearly-deads.

It was a couple of days since our first session. Aside from introductory chat, not much had been covered: the background of his research, my early career with the air crash team, a basic rundown of the main things that could have gone wrong with a generic aircraft. But then I'd grown tired, and things had become confused – like they so often did nowadays – and Grace had quickly moved to intervene, whisking me back to my room.

Sean still hadn't accepted a cup of tea, and I'd already decided I was going to force him to drink one before we'd finished. It would do him good. 'You ever heard of a greatest hits album?'

Sean shook his head, and took hold of his pen. I noted

its lid was still missing – presumably waiting to be found underfoot. 'No.'

'They always used to put these bonus tracks on the end. Songs no one had ever heard before. Always added to the end of the record, for no clear reason.'

'Not much of a "hit", then.'

'No,' I replied, thinking of my own spinning record. Sean again looked at my forearms. In my youth I might have folded them across my chest, or hidden them from view. But, as a young woman, I wouldn't have worn anything that might have revealed them. 'I used to cut myself,' I said. Behind Sean, Charley snapped her attention to me – then tried to make it appear as though she wasn't listening.

'I thought maybe they were bioimplant scars.'

I laughed, not able to help myself. 'I would have sued if they'd left me like this.'

'I suppose so.'

'I started cutting when my brother died.'

Sean didn't move, even though I'd lowered my voice. The perfect hearing of a twenty-something.

'He was only five,' I continued. 'Several years younger than... oh, I must have been twelve. Anyway, he followed me everywhere. It was almost too easy to be mean to him. And yet even when I was horrible he still treated me like I was the centre of his world. No matter how many times I made him cry.'

'So you cut your arms because you felt guilty?' Sean wasn't writing anything down. Perhaps this didn't really interest him. I didn't much care.

I snorted with laughter. 'Guilty? At least you didn't suggest it was a cry for help.' I shook my head slowly, the humour leaving my voice. 'No, I cut myself because I felt nothing. And I wanted to, very much. I wanted to take what had happened and make it real. To persuade myself I wasn't dreaming. That he was, truly, gone.'

Sean made a very small mark on his paper. My eyesight didn't allow me to see what he'd written.

'This will come to you too,' I said, looking about me. 'It reminds me a little too much of where my grandmother spent her final years. You get plenty of time to think things through, you see, before you're done. Age magnifies the tiniest regret, and makes major errors... well, the judgement is coming, isn't it?'

Sean waited while I took my first sip of tea. It remained too hot. Grace would have added more milk, but Charley seemed to take pleasure in offering things but keeping them just out of reach.

'Did they know about the self-harming?'

'Who?'

'When you were chosen to head up the air crash unit.'

'It wasn't a problem back then. Only when I was working for Jake did—'

'Jake Morley?'

Charley was moving through the lounge. Although she was meant to be checking on the others, most of her attention seemed to be centred squarely on the back of Sean's chair, as if his presence amused her. I half expected a follow-up question about Jake, but the kid made no further mark on his paper and passed no comment.

'If they don't come here about Tanzania, they try to get me to talk about what happened with Jake,' I said.

'The synapse sequencer?' he whispered, looking over his

shoulder like he had the last time I'd mentioned it.

'Yes.'

'I'm not too familiar with what happened.' Sean screwed up his nose for a second like that might help him recall. 'There was some kid involved, wasn't there?'

'N'Golo,' I said. Somewhere in the back of the TV lounge, a blurred shape shifted. 'His name was N'Golo Durrant.'

# 10

**Top Stories:**
**S&P architect outlines advantages of enlarging
metadata sweeps** (*Read more*)
**Multiple community teams enter forthcoming sports fair**
(*Read more*)
**I did it! Stories from people making most of their time
on the UI** (*Read more*)
**New US administration pressures Icelandic government**
(*Read more*)

**Selected for You:**
**Diseases of the past: Smallpox** (*Read more*)

THE POD EDGED forward, but it was already clear something
was wrong. Traffic at this time of night was often heavy, but
it didn't usually grind to a halt. The system was too good, the
pods' routes optimised and governed to make sure everyone
got to their destinations as quickly as possible.

*Shit.* Anna tried to stretch her legs in the cramped inner
compartment of the pod. It had been a busy day, and she'd

been looking forward to getting home and kicking off her shoes. Not in some gated community like Amblinside, of course, but at least in a building that had been provided with twenty-four-hour security. And decent services. Kate would already be there, mimicking her biorhythms as far as Jake was concerned. But the few other things being put right ahead of her return, such as starting an evening meal and adjusting the temperature of her bedroom, would have now entered a pause setting in response to her delayed journey.

'What's the hold-up?' Anna called into the air. She was alone in the pod. It had arrived at the hub only a few minutes after she'd booked it – presumably the system knowing beforehand that her call was likely imminent – but the cabin was filled with the greasy smell of fried chicken. This pod was probably close to be being taken out of service for a thorough clean.

'*Incident ahead,*' the pod told her. '*The carriageway is currently being cleared.*'

Its emotionless tone made her skin prickle. Pods were designed not to bump into each other, but their safety protocols were such that it had become something of a craze – especially amongst the young – to sprint and dodge between them. The pod would swerve to avoid the human, and hit another pod instead.

The area she was stuck in wasn't particularly wealthy. Through the armoured tint, she could just about see a group of kids kicking some litter between them. She didn't want their attention to be drawn towards the stationary convoy of pods.

'Is anyone hurt?'

'*That information is not available.*'

*Yes, then,* Anna thought. Someone had been hurt. Possibly killed. Because if they hadn't been, then the pod would have simply said so; its algorithmic response was designed to reassure. And it was all such a waste.

She'd often heard politicians say that the automation of industry meant there was more time for leisure. But people couldn't afford the entertainment that seemed to promise, not on the UI. All that extra time could only invoke boredom. Some liked to inject their lives with a little thrill, taking a life risk or engaging in low-level misdemeanours. Not for the first time, Anna wondered how her lodger managed to avoid that trap. How long would Kate remain happy stifling herself in the apartment? Her spoof would be there now, listening to music and letting it pummel her brain.

The pod edged forwards a few metres. Anna scanned the stories circulating on the boards. She didn't particularly have any interest in the ongoing debate about S&P, which was nevertheless clogging her feed. The system already seemed good enough at detecting and responding to crime, yet the current prime minister was increasingly seen on the boards pushing for improvements – even if she hardly ever went outside the protective bubble of the Westminster green zone...

Anna opened the article on smallpox, which seemed the least offensive, and was immediately confronted with a horrific picture of a child infected with the disease.

**Smallpox:** one of a handful of illnesses whose name is still enough to create a shiver. Responsible for nearly half a billion deaths in the twentieth century alone, smallpox was eradicated via a vaccination campaign by

1980. But could it return in more a grisly form? Chilling
new strains have been reported...

Anna soon tired of what she was reading. The facts, figures
and photos had clearly been contrived by a journalistic AI.
Probably the same one that kept churning out pieces about
the war in Tanzania. The photo at the start had annoyed her,
too, for some reason. For articles about the war in Tanzania,
the same news algorithms usually included a photo of
her at the crash site juxtaposed alongside one of some
injured children, simply because they nicely illustrated the
background to the conflict. The overall effect, however, was
that everyone knew what she looked like, especially when
events remained so fresh.

With the growing use of bots and drones in warfare and
the abandonment of bioweapons treaties by emergent
states, the government has again started researching
new strains of the disease.

*Fucking great.* Anna closed the article, angry at the world's
direction, and then flicked to another about the sports fair.
As expected, it was mainly a puff piece about how people on
the UI were filling their time, but it did prompt a sudden
urge to get her own body moving.

'Change destination: Brigate Gym,' she called to the
pod. The vehicle immediately made a sharp U-turn into the
freedom of an uninterrupted lane. Even so, it would take
another few minutes to get to the gym. Anna looked for
stories hidden a little deeper on the newsfeed rankings.

Most of the articles further down were about the

forthcoming rise in the UI payment, and an extension to entertainment credits. *A little cheer to offer the proletariat in the run-up to Christmas,* she thought. Other stories mainly centred on crime stats. They were all frustratingly good. There was even a small piece about someone who'd been caught stealing some meat. At first it seemed trivial compared with the rest of the feed, but perhaps making an example of the odd person guilty of a minor misdemeanour upped the stakes for all the rest considering it. She couldn't find anything relating to N'Golo Durrant.

The pod began to slow before coming to another dead stop.

*For fuck's sake.* 'What now?'

'*You have arrived at your destination.*'

The door clicked open. Anna slipped out, waving her wrist at a panel in the doorway to make payment, and the pod glided away from the kerb and back into the traffic. It was already getting dark, the gloom of the winter's late afternoon made worse by the contrast with the well-lit interior of the gym. It looked busy – it was the period when the gym could be used by both UIs and those coming off their day shifts. She would soon be inside again – getting rid of some of the frustrations of the day by peddling very fast or hitting something very hard.

A call interrupted her chain of thought. Cody. He'd left the hub about an hour ahead of her, and had probably been stewing for all that time. She already knew what he was going to say; she just thought he'd have waited until later in the evening, or perhaps done the decent thing and talked to her about it when they'd both returned to the office. Still, she connected the call, checking around her as she did so to make sure the pavements were empty. She was quite alone. 'Hi.'

'Look, I've been thinking,' Cody said without greeting and above the background wail of his new baby.

'About N'Golo Durrant?'

'Yeah.'

'We're not risking it, Cody.'

'Hear me out. Jake—'

'No,' Anna replied, the sharpness of her voice cutting off her technician. As she spoke, a skinny man ambling past stopped and looked at her, then moved on few paces.

'I think the health techs were being over-cautious,' Cody continued in her ear. 'They've worked with a dozen or so coma patients. They only lost three—'

'*Only, Cody? Do you hear yourself?*'

'But they had multiple interactions with them before their patients experienced synapse shock. We could go in seven times, Anna. Five to be safe; that's what they're telling me.'

'From what Fowler told us, N'Golo could still recover.'

'Unlikely.'

'Possible.'

'The risk of action then, against the risk of inaction?'

Her words. He'd just used her words. Some unadvised utterance she'd once said and that was now constantly recycled and reused, washed out of any meaning she'd originally intended. Back home, Kate's systems would be going nuts. *Heart rate: raised. Anomalies: seriously pissed off.*

'Hey! I know you, don't I?'

Anna twisted back to the street. The skinny man was back and edging into the light of the gym, probably trying to take her out of silhouette. If he came any closer, then the rotating doors of the gym weren't too far away. 'No,' she said, tilting her head away while keeping him in view. 'And I'm speaking with someone.'

'I'm sorry,' Cody continued. 'I shouldn't have said that. All I'm saying is that I think we could safely try this out. This Durrant kid isn't a saint, you know. He's got previous himself for assault…'

Anna glanced to the side. The man was still standing there. Staring at her. He would make the connection soon enough, if he hadn't already. She needed to get inside.

'Anna – are you still there?'

'Yes, yes.'

'Okay, let's talk tomorrow, right?'

*As we should have done anyway,* Anna thought bitterly. The call disconnected. She made for the gym doors, but the skinny man stepped out in front of her. Between the bright lights inside and the darkness beyond its glass, it was unlikely anyone inside would see her. Perhaps the cameras monitoring this spot wouldn't either.

'I thought it was you,' the skinny man said.

She could head back to the street, but that would hardly help now she'd been recognised. And, even if she called one now, another pod would take time to arrive. So instead she remained standing close to the door, waiting for a gap large enough to slip past this idiot and get inside.

'You're her, aren't you? Emma something.'

*Anna, you stupid prick.*

He took a couple of steps closer, then pushed his torso forward and let his arms fly back. Anna flinched, but all of his motion was used to propel a ball of spit and snot. It hit the dead centre of her chest, the glob clinging to her jacket. Anna looked at it, then tried to wipe it clear with her sleeve, smearing it deeper into the material.

Making it worse.

'You should be in jail, you bitch. All those innocent kiddies died because of you!'

She'd been given self-defence training. Something the Home Office had once pushed to all women, but now just gave to individuals likely to be targeted by spontaneous attacks.

*Spontaneous attacks.* The words of her instructor pinged to the front of her brain as he came closer. Fighting the impulse to run, she braced, ready to deflect any blow and trying to judge a kick to his knees. In the end the skinny man stopped short; then he looked about him as if unsure.

He knew he was making a mistake.

Maybe the shot of phlegm had taken away enough of his anger. Perhaps he'd remembered that he was still attached to the network, that all she'd need to do was make a complaint and his records would be accessed and he'd be busted. Maybe even dumped off the UI, with all that entailed.

'Bitch,' he said again. Then he turned and half-scurried back to the pavement. Still shaking, Anna watched him go. Her breathing slowly fell back into a normal rhythm. The message from Kate came moments later: *You okay?*

'I'm fine,' she whispered. 'I'm coming home.'

# 11

'THEY WARNED ME, but I didn't listen.'

Sean's pen didn't move. The care home management would have warned him, of course. 'Our Anna is a bit difficult to keep on track,' they'd have said. 'Her memory is going. She fades in and out.' And he'd have ignored them. Because a chance to talk to Anna Glover about what had happened in Tanzania would have been too good to pass up, especially when so many others had failed to get me to talk. And so he'd just have to sit through the rest, whether he liked it or not.

I found some amusement in the thought. A young man trapped and forced to listen to me. After all those years of finding it so difficult to be heard.

'They called it a bio-audit,' I said. 'Do they still do it?'

'Not really. Not since…' Sean's voice trailed off.

So they'd stopped; at least that was something. Perhaps the protests that had flared up around the world hadn't been in vain, then. In the UK it had been bad enough – here, bio-audits had been used by companies to bully their workforces. In other parts of the world the reduction in jobs had caused more extreme swings. France and Spain had turned left; countries like Iceland and Greece had swung right. And governments who knew everything about everyone hadn't needed an army of enforcers to create a police state. People had already supplied the data themselves, back when they thought they'd been free.

'Huh,' I said. 'Well, companies used to harvest the biorhythmic data of their employees. They knew how we were sleeping, if we were stressed, that we were taking enough exercise. They could even track the biochemical surges associated with having too much – or too little – sex. One colleague of mine found out she was pregnant from HR, before she'd even had a chance to order a test. And no one stopped them – how could we? Everyone wanted a job. You signed away your data to make sure you got the next short-term contract. Not surprising then, really, that people started using spoofs. You could hire them for a few hours if you wanted to go off the grid. To get a little space.'

'Criminals used them, mostly, didn't they?'

'I had a longer-term arrangement,' I said, not stopping to acknowledge or confirm Sean's comment. 'A live-in spoof. Someone to plug more permanently into the system so they couldn't tell.'

'Couldn't tell what?' Sean still wasn't recording what I was saying, but his grip on his writing implement noticeably tightened. I had his attention. He glanced at my arms. 'That you were still self-harming?'

I didn't say anything.

'When you were working for Jake? With the sequencer?'

I tried my best to give a stilted smile. 'Self-harm isn't just some passing teenage fad,' I said. 'I did it for relief. I had all these damn torments building up inside me, and it just allowed me to drain them all away. To stop the storm.'

Sean made a few marks on his paper. As he did so, I

watched Grace serving cups of tea to my fellow inmates.

'Were you self-harming in Tanzania?'

'Would it matter if I was?'

Sean stumbled. 'I don't… I don't know.'

'Then yes.' My mouth had turned dry. I could use something to slake my thirst. 'Yes, I cut myself in Tanzania.'

'And when did you stop?'

'What does it matter? You get this sense, you see: when you're no longer a contender in the race. When younger men and women have already come and replaced you.'

Sean smiled. He'd perhaps not meant it to, but it revealed something within him. Some seed of ambition. Perhaps I was his route to something big. He was someone who was still very much in the running. Just out of the blocks, and accelerating hard. It reminded me of something, although I couldn't quite tell what.

'Have we met before?' I asked him.

'Yes… I mean, we've spoken before now a few times…'

'That's not what I meant.' I peered at him, trying to cut through the misting inside my eyeballs. He seemed familiar.

'Did they know?' asked Sean, trying to return my attention to why he was with me. 'The air crash unit?'

'They knew long before I was selected for the investigation. It was irrelevant.'

'So you weren't using a spoof when you worked in that team?'

'No. There was no need at that time.'

'But there was with the sequencer?'

I smiled. 'Jake told me. He warned me. And I didn't listen.'

When I'd said Jake's name before, Sean had begun acting cloak-and-dagger, but this time he didn't even look around to see if we could be overheard. 'I don't think I quite follow?'

'Jake wasn't interested in our biometric data because he wanted to monitor our productivity,' I said. 'He had other motives. He wanted to make sure that it was safe to use the sequencer. He was trying to sell the device into a variety of end markets. He'd hidden a lot of dangers in the small print.'

Sean leant in closer. I could see a question forming on his face: *Why did you take the risk?* – but in the end he didn't ask it. He probably understood I had no choice. 'I'd like to talk more about Tanzania,' he said.

*Tanzania.* I closed my eyes. So long ago, and all too clear. Unlike everything that had happened since. 'Go on…'

'I want to start with the background to the crash.'

'You should have that from the files.'

'I want to hear it from you.'

*Calibration.* 'You want to know if I can remember things correctly,' I said. 'Before you put too much credence on what I have to say.'

Sean smiled. 'Something like that. The nurse told me—'

'The fat one?'

'Yes… she told me your memory—'

'*I* told you: it was fucked by the sequencer.'

I was pleased to see him jolt; and it was good to know there was still nothing more shocking than hearing an old person swear. But what I'd said was true. I'd not fully understood when I'd been using it: I thought the system simply allowed access to other people's memories. What was really going on was somewhat different. More like a mixing of minds, the sequencer being no more than a thin membrane across which a memory could be shared. The learned responses of the brain filling in the background gaps. And, for me, something had gone wrong. I looked for the nurse. Instead, I saw a blurred shape rise to his feet from the corner and make his way over. His face was lost in static, but I recognised him. N'Golo Durrant.

He knelt down beside me.

Of course, N'Golo wasn't really there. Not in the room. Just in my mind. A large part of me wanted to find a razor blade. Because I'd been warned.

And after all these years, he was still here haunting me.

# 12

**Top Stories:**

Caught! Behavioural cams detect man about to rob woman, 98 (*Read more*)

Latest psychology AIs register improved outcomes (*Read more*)

Free-time breakthrough? Synapse Initiatives announces new entertainment project (*Read more*)

False positive strikes in Tanzania lead to improvement in drone targeting systems (*Read more*)

**Selected for You:**

Yes! People really were once employed to hand-deliver letters! (*Read more*)

ONE OF JAKE'S big things was allowing people to work when they were most productive, rather than while a clock was marking time. For Anna, that meant getting in early – Cody normally got there a couple of hours later than her – but today when she arrived she found the hub even quieter than normal. She progressed quickly through its glass-fronted façade, and barely acknowledged the security bots guarding almost every internal door.

She didn't meet a soul on the way to her office. The emptiness was magnified by the fact that the hub had been built as a research and data centre for one of Jake's old internet companies. Everything now was several sizes too big. The multiple racks of secure servers had long since been replaced by much smaller quantum machines; and the large canteen that had once fed Jake's programming staff now lay empty. It was no surprise, therefore, that her little designated corner of the hub was deserted.

Which was how she normally preferred it. Sitting down at her desk, though, it didn't take long for the pressure to build in her mind. With the plaza shooting looking like it wouldn't lead anywhere, and the N'Golo Durrant thing being nothing more than a distraction, she was back to sifting through old police reports and looking for incidents where the sequencer could perhaps add some value. And it was becoming more and more apparent that such value was going to be hard to find.

*Failure begets failure.*

Anna shivered hard as Jake's phrase came into her mind. The previous night had been tough: first Kate wanting to know why she'd diverted to the gym, and what had happened to her there, and then she'd had a call from her parents. Both her mother and her father had reminded her of how proud they'd been of her previous career, and wondered if she could find a way back to it. And each had also subtly enquired about any man she happened to mention, as if that would solve everything.

*Failure begets failure.*

Her desk was too neat. It should have been chaotic, like

Cody's. At some point soon, she was going to lose her job. Jake would finally tire of their experiment and end it. The news was already out that he was starting a new entertainment project, one that offered up more profit from the thousands of people seeking a new distraction from the boredom of unemployment. And she'd be joining them. Consigned to the UI, with all that entailed. A war criminal on state handouts, turfed out of her apartment with its thin shield of security and left to fend for herself.

She tried a breathing exercise to calm herself. Back at home it was relatively easy to exit the sudden downward spirals. Kate actually seemed to care about what was going on, rather than just going through the motions as her conditions of employment required. And then there was Elsy: the AI designed to break through the psychological maelstrom and pull her back to dry land.

But neither Kate nor Elsy was available in the hub. Not directly, anyhow. And so all she was left with was an old-fashioned response. She unbuttoned the cuff of her blouse and rolled back the sleeve: exposing the fleshy part of her left arm. Then she searched her desk, finally choosing a twelve-inch plastic ruler. A few fast swipes took away some of the doubt; the last sharp slice underlined that she wasn't going to fail.

*Failure begets failure.*

*And success begets success.*

With a cold wash of relief, Anna refastened her sleeve, making sure the material didn't catch on the raw skin. She needed to find crimes where the S&P scores had triggered investigations but where little progress had been made. There must be enough of them, she reminded herself, if Fowler could make a living. The key thing was to prioritise them and track down enough witnesses willing to take part in her next experiment.

Which was where she needed Cody – to work out which witnesses would be good subjects; to operate the sequencer. His desk was always a mess. A few sheets of A4 had fallen on to his swivel chair. Anna frowned when she picked them up. It was the report from the health team on the use of the synapse sequencer with coma patients. A scribbled note was attached to the top of the first page: *With my comments. —B.*

Sure enough, as Anna flicked through the pages she saw that several were marked with notes from the health team. Most were clarifying matters in the text, which was written formally, objectively and with little regard for readability. The message was the same one Cody had passed on to her the night before: the risk level of working with coma patients was related both to the number of times a patient was put into the sequencer, and to the types of memories that were stimulated.

Anna grimaced. Connecting witnesses to the synapse sequencer wasn't just a case of lying them down on steel benches and flooding them with drugs. Each witness had to be interviewed before they went under. The moment to be invoked had to be primed and recollections prompted, so that each witness had the same memory in mind when the technician stitched them together in the same patchwork.

Cody was particularly good at it. He could pull out precise moments in a single session where others would need several attempts to get anywhere close. And yet how would he work with a coma patient with whom he couldn't communicate?

*Failure begets failure.*

The skin on her forearms started to itch again.

Meanwhile the notes continued, so Anna kept reading. As Cody had said, risk rose roughly in line with exposure. Which meant they could risk killing Durrant on the first attempt, or he could pass through several submersions without any harm. But for family members, one interaction was never enough – they kept on wanting to come back: to see if they could prompt their loved one to wake. Even after the risks had been explained.

*Taking Durrant to the point of his beating is very likely to result in synapse shock*, read the note. *You stand a good chance of killing him in one. Sorry.*

As she dropped the pages back on Cody's seat, Anna noticed a final scribbled message, something that explained the A4 printout rather than the information being emailed: *We have a slot for a technician. Look, I know you enjoy 'looking after' her – but you should apply for transfer BEFORE she wrecks this for you. Rumour is that Jake is looking to cut his tech staff again. —B.*

Jake would go batshit if he knew someone was trying to poach her technician. Or any technician, for that matter. Still, she gave the chair a push forward so that Cody's seat moved tight against his desk, to give the impression she hadn't even noticed the papers.

Cody arrived about an hour later, holding a coffee-to-go and a *pain au chocolat*. He didn't look surprised to see her there before him, gave her a quick greeting, and then swept the papers from his seat onto his desk. He read them as he ate his breakfast. 'So what's the plan?' he asked finally.

Anna took a breath. *Not for you to abandon me*, she thought. 'We start looking back through the records,' she said. 'Find a new investigation.'

Cody turned back to his terminal, ostensibly complying with her instructions. But then he stopped. Anna heard his chair swivel. *This is it*, she thought. *He's going to ask me for a transfer. Shit. Come on, Cody, not now...*

'Check your messages,' Cody said. 'Something from Fowler. He wants to meet us at Amblinside.'

Anna sighed. 'We're not going,' she said. 'That project is over.'

'No,' Cody replied. 'You're definitely going to want to read the message.'

# 13

S&P Build 14.224a – Recommendation Module

Situation #GIHHCLTYYEN: Female (15) reported missing. Downtime 12 hrs. Female (15) – Chosen Name Beth Hayden – now designated as Target.

Demographic Class: B3

Relevant History: Target missing (Situation #RONULBDCDRM), outcome returned home.

Connected Case 1: [Redacted, Authorisation: Deng]

Connected Case 2: [Redacted, Authorisation: Deng]

Bot Sweep Inputs: No data found at home address.

Board Feeds: Recent target board searches logged for Edinburgh and Cardiff.

Biolog Data: No target biodata being received (unknown reason). RED FLAG.

Recommendation: Target likely home runaway. Add Edinburgh and Cardiff to search area. Add routes to Edinburgh and Cardiff to search area (limit time window). Continue biolog monitoring and add face to recognition cam list. Identify friends of Target. Class friends of Target as Potential Associates, and interview remotely via AI. Class immediate family members of Target as Potential Future Suspects and interview directly via Bot and Officer. Begin biolog harvesting to identify all other adults in contact with Target over last six months. ENDS.

'FINALLY! YOU CAME on your own?'

Anna stiffened at Fowler's shout. Yes, she'd come on her own. For one thing, Cody's job was to operate the synapse tech, not get involved in the investigative work. For another, she was more than aware of what they both had at stake. She didn't need the constant hints and reminders. And, anyway, with her away and the office door shut, maybe Cody could finally get some decent sleep.

'I came as soon as I read your message.'

'You have any trouble getting in?'

'No,' Anna replied coolly. Public entry to Amblinside was via an oversized sentry station built into a fence that enclosed the entire development. The gates and fence were more ornate than imposing – anyone with a small amount of determination could probably have climbed it – but then they'd have run up against the movement traps and the facial recognition software. And the priority line to local law enforcement.

The cameras had tagged Anna at the sentry station. The attending bot hadn't asked her any questions, though. After all, she was on the guest list, and it must have waved through people with more interesting personal history.

'That damn bucket guarding the gate made me wait for five minutes,' Fowler complained. He turned towards a house set back a good fifty or so metres from the street, and swept a hand through the side of his lank, greasy hair. He still hadn't shaved. No surprise, then, that the sentry bot had been cautious. Even for someone not on a database, an untidy appearance would raise a flag. Behavioural cams were calibrated to sense if someone might be about to do something illegal, and the ones on the sentry station would have been given a clear view of Fowler's face. 'I've already been to check in with the family. Thought it better to wait for you out here, though. Come on, let's go!'

Anna didn't move, purposefully not wanting to be harried into working at the PI's pace. 'Nice house,' she said

'N'Golo Durrant spent the last few weeks living here,' Fowler replied, coming to a halt.

'You said both foster-parents were employed?'

'That's right.'

'Any other kids in the house?'

'The Haydens have two children of their own, Beth and George.'

Anna looked towards the Hayden house. She knew size wasn't always a good indicator of wealth but here, right on the edge of Amblinside, it reeked of money. There'd probably be a decent-sized garden to the rear. She could just about glimpse some rolling hills beyond the boundary of the estate, topped by a small outcrop of woodland.

'And when was the last time anyone heard from Beth?'

Fowler gave an impatient sigh. 'Yesterday. She was meant to be home by ten. Didn't show.'

'And they've called her friends?'

'Yep. None of them have any idea where she is. I understand they've all passed the first wave of lie detection.'

'And they were able to contact *all* her friends? No others missing?'

'Yes to the first, no to the second.' Fowler rubbed his chin, scratching at his sandpaper-like stubble. 'Can you sense them looking?'

Anna caught some amusement in Fowler's eyes. 'Who?'

He tipped his head back to the street. 'The rest of the picket fences.'

Anna glanced behind her. Every house on the estate sat alone in its garden, each one built in the same style. Of course, some natural variation had set in since they'd first been occupied – some brickwork was covered by ivy and some by wisteria – but mainly the dwellings on one side of the street mirrored those on the other. Above all, though, each property had large windows which offered a relatively good view of where they were standing.

'First time I came here,' Fowler said, 'an old woman a few doors down bypassed the sentry station and made an emergency call. Said I was breaking into the Hayden property. Five cops came in two squad cars.'

An emergency call from her apartment would probably have resulted in a single car. Most other places, perhaps nothing. It was all down to the type of incident and the score S&P assigned to the individual case.

'Seems an odd place for a foster-family.'

'Part of the new social contract malarkey.'

*A tax incentive.* Anna felt an inner churn of disgust. The Haydens had taken in N'Golo Durrant to save a few per cent on their annual return.

'The boy gets beaten up; the girl goes missing. So, what do you think?' Fowler asked, turning to her. 'It must be a kidnapping, right?'

'Or it's just coincidence.'

Fowler snorted.

'This isn't a twenty-four-hour news show,' she told him. 'We have time to gather some facts. Isn't that why we're here?'

Fowler issued an exasperated sigh, then began to walk to the house. When Anna didn't move, he looked back, spreading his arms. 'What?'

'Someone here reports a vagrant,' Anna said, letting the thought roll in her mind, 'and they get five cops in two cars. Emergency response.'

'It wasn't a vagrant,' Fowler replied, becoming agitated. 'It was me!'

'Five cops in response to the appearance of a person who was on a guest list and who'd passed through the sentry station? So where are they now that a child's gone missing?'

'It's illegal for the police to prioritise based on wealth.'

Anna couldn't help but roll her eyes. 'Only the signifiers of wealth, eh?'

'That a quote from one of those Workers' League leaflets you're so fond of?' Fowler took a few steps back towards her. 'Look, you know the old saying "If it can happen to them, it can happen to anyone"? Turns out, if rich people are victims of crime, then crime goes up. People get encouraged. Fair or not, it correlates – and it reinforces the need to protect certain groups more than others.'

'But not when their kids go missing?'

'The girl's gone AWOL before. S&P's output suggests she'll show up in the next day or two. It's monitoring social media, news feeds – running facial recognition. The police are working on the premise that she'll be tagged sooner rather than later, and then they can simply go and pick her up.'

'A low S&P score for N'Golo is one thing – but for a girl

with this background it should have been off the chart…'

'But it wasn't. The family's pretty upset, Anna. Let's not debate the merits of S&P in front of them, eh? And remember, this is my investigation. I asked you here just so you can see why I'm so interested in getting access to your sequencer.'

She conceded the point and followed him up to the front of the house. As soon as they'd ducked under the small portico, Fowler rapped on the door, which was already slightly ajar. A tall, sharp-suited man soon yanked it open. Roger Hayden, Anna assumed. He seemed far from panic-stricken, although there was a definite line of tension in his jaw.

'Great,' he said. 'You're back.' He turned and shouted up the stairs, 'Millie, come down and make us some tea!'

Hayden showed them through to a rustic kitchen. They sat down at a thick oak table that dominated one side of the room. By the back door, a couple of pairs of wellington boots rested incongruously next to a briefcase. The briefcase was an anachronism; something certain people still liked to carry to signify they had a job – and a good one – even though it was probably empty. At least Millie Hayden would be putting the wellingtons to good use, if she worked with animals.

Hayden cocked his head towards Anna. 'Who's your assistant?' he asked Fowler.

'This is Anna Glover. She works for—'

'Oh, right. The tech company.' Hayden's eyes narrowed for a fraction of a second as maybe some little part of his brain registered recognition. It soon evaporated. 'You want to use some sort of entertainment system to interrogate the foster-kid?'

Anna could tell Fowler wanted to say something, but he looked deferential in front of the man paying his bills.

'I haven't agreed to anything,' she said. 'But that's certainly what's been put to me.'

Hayden glanced at Fowler, a little confused. 'This was your idea?'

'A line of enquiry,' Fowler said.

'The boy's not worth that much.'

'But your daughter might be.'

Fowler's words caused Hayden to shrink back into himself. Before he could recover, a woman appeared in the doorway and moved quickly to gather some mugs from one of the cabinets. She was accompanied by a ginger cat, which constantly weaved between her feet.

'We've still had no word from Beth,' Roger Hayden said, his voice now quiet. 'The police are telling us she'll turn up either today or tomorrow, though. Eighty-five per cent likelihood.'

Fowler nodded but didn't say anything.

'I'm happy with your contract variation,' Hayden continued, clearly thinking about the remaining fifteen per cent chance the police were wrong. 'I'll ping you the instruction after we've finished.'

'Fine.'

Millie Hayden placed four mugs of tea on the table just as Anna was about to cut in. The cheap mugs looked out of place in the plush kitchen. The tea was already mixed with milk, and there was no sign of sugar. As she handed Anna a mug, Millie froze. 'You're—'

'Oh, shit,' Hayden interrupted. 'That's right. Fuck!'

Both Roger and Millie Hayden were now staring at Anna, probably trying to confirm in their minds whether the pictures they'd seen on the boards matched her appearance.

'We haven't yet agreed fees for Anna's involvement,' Fowler said, nerves clearly audible in his voice. 'If you'd prefer to—'

'I'm willing to pay,' Hayden interrupted.

Anna glanced at Hayden's wife. Millie Hayden didn't look as if she'd slept the previous night; her eyes were red and her hands were shaking slightly. And now the drinks were served, her attention had moved down the table to where no one was sitting. Away from those talking about her daughter. She was detached, like this was happening to somebody else.

'Seems an odd move,' Hayden said. 'Air crash investigator to PI?'

Anna couldn't help but prickle at the notion. 'I'm not a *private* investigator,' she said, 'though I work in the investigation team at Synapse Initiatives. It's all ultimately about saving people's lives.'

Anna immediately regretted her answer. She'd meant it to sound noble, but both the Haydens and Fowler probably had one thing now buzzing through their minds. All the lives lost in Tanzania, through the bot attacks and drone strikes. The ones that had missed their intended targets; the multiple scores of needless dead. Roger Hayden raised an eyebrow; his wife made an incredulous noise. 'The last time Beth ran away,' Anna asked, trying to get things back on track, 'how long was she gone?'

For a long moment nobody answered. Hayden glared at Fowler, who pulled a face. 'That's irrelevant,' Hayden responded. 'She was a little girl, and we'd just seen some kids' film about a group of children who'd run off to see Santa. She got overexcited, that's all.'

'Very different to a teen runaway,' Anna said.

'Except it scores the same on S&P,' Fowler explained.

'Factoring in the five-year decay variable on cases like this.'

*Decay variable?* Fowler seemed to know quite a bit about how S&P worked. It would be useful to pick his brains on it later, Anna thought, when they were back at the hub.

'There's a big difference between ten and fifteen,' Roger Hayden said, his voice bitter, like the debate was fresh in his mind.

'But lots of teenagers run away for a day or so,' Fowler said. 'That's why S&P scores it as likely in this case.'

Anna looked down at her arms as they rested on the oak table, and then tugged at her sleeves, adjusting the bangle that clumsily hid the first signs of scarring underneath the cuff. What Fowler had said was true. She'd wanted to disappear many times in her teens. And it was a pattern of behaviour that was evidently accounted for in S&P's calculations. There were far too many such incidents for the police to dedicate resources to searching for every single one, especially when they could just wait for the missing children's faces to crop up in a public space and be snagged by a cam. But the low S&P score for Beth's disappearance was only one reason why they were sitting round this table. 'Did Beth have much involvement with N'Golo?' Anna asked.

'Involvement?' Roger Hayden looked sharply at his wife, but she was still staring down the table towards the empty spot.

'How did they get along?' Anna clarified. 'Generally speaking.'

'Neither of my children... well, they don't appreciate having other kids here. George hated him. Beth... well, Beth has some funny ideas.'

Millie reached out and took her husband's hand. 'Roger...'

'How do you mean? Funny ideas?'

'She occasionally volunteered at feeding stations,' Hayden replied dismissively. 'Having someone like N'Golo here seemed to be a bit too close to home for her.'

'And how many foster-children have you had before N'Golo?'

'Four. Previously, they've all matched the descriptions given on their docket.'

'But not N'Golo?'

'No. And it was stupid to put someone of his sort with a family like ours.'

The whole tone of Hayden's conversation left a bad taste in Anna's mouth, but Fowler was nodding along sympathetically – it was clear he was used to soothing unlovable clients.

'Look,' Hayden said. 'We can agree fees. If the police are wrong, then I want you to find my daughter. The boy can wait. The deadline isn't until next March but – *yes* – I do want to know if he's mixed up in Beth's disappearance.'

*Deadline?* The question died on her lips. He meant the date by which he'd need to apply to take on another foster-child. It was wishful thinking on his part. With his last ward in hospital and his own daughter missing, he'd be blacklisted. His tax bill was about to get bigger. He was probably already trying to balance the value of the tax incentive against the cost of using the sequencer.

'Do you have children, Miss Glover?' Millie Hayden asked, sounding distant.

'No, I don't.' Anna realised none of them had touched their tea.

Millie continued to stare down the table. 'I'm not sure you really care, that's all.'

'Excuse me?'

'All those children, Miss Glover. All those children who were killed in their beds in Tanzania. I didn't have a good night, thinking about my daughter. But you look well rested. I just wonder how you can sleep at all.'

# 14

N'GOLO WAS THERE, kneeling at my side. Nonetheless, I tried to keep my attention on Sean or, more specifically, on his pen and paper. 'Perhaps it would be best if you explain a little bit about what you know already,' I said. 'So I can see where we're starting from?'

My suggestion didn't go down well. I could see the cogs whirring in his mind; he was searching for a way to politely decline and get me talking again. After all, that was his reason for being here: to hear my side of the story. And I suppose part of my question was born of devilment; so much had already been written about what had happened, it would be as well to flush some of the crap out of his mind now rather than later.

'Okay,' Sean said slowly. 'So I guess we can't get away with it: your report triggered a war.'

'A small one,' I said.

'Does that make it better?'

'No. But the bots and drones kept the casualties low.'

'The Tanzanians didn't have bots and drones...'

I turned away momentarily. He was right, and there was only so far I was willing to push the alternative point of view. Tanzania was one of the first wars where military drones hadn't been piloted from afar, but allowed to select targets themselves based on visual pattern recognition. If something looked like a tank – or like an anti-drone missile battery – then it was destroyed. Except the systems had been taught using examples from Europe and the US. When those autonomous drones had been flown over other parts of the world, mistakes had been all too frequent.

'We used to fight wars over oil,' Sean continued in the tone of a man recalling a half-forgotten history lesson. 'This was the first one fought over rare earth elements.'

'*Was* the first one?'

Immediately my student looked embarrassed. 'Sorry,' he said. 'I guess that's not the official line, but…'

'Go on…'

'I can sort of see it, you know? Most oil was found in the Middle East, and look how many wars were fought in and around there. Then these rare earths start getting attention. They're suddenly needed for computers, communications, batteries…'

'Rare earth elements,' I said, ready to give a history lesson of my own, 'started becoming important when we first acquired a taste for gadgets. They became expensive when those gadgets become ever more disposable. But they only became critical – absolutely essential – when we found one could be used inside quantum computers.'

'Dysprosium?'

'Just like oil, you can find small concentrations here and there all over the globe. But by far the largest reserves are found in China.' My head felt a little light, but then another pulse of blood fed it with oxygen. Sean edged forward in his seat, concern written on his face. 'You're maybe too young to remember,' I continued, waving away his concern and letting my skull fall back against the headrest of my chair. 'Computing speed used to be something of a dick-measuring contest, but then the Chinese shot ahead and never really looked back. After that, rare earths became much more important than oil. You can get along okay without the latter – there are plenty of alternatives so long as you have a grid to distribute the electricity: coal, wind, solar, nuclear. But if you don't have access to rare earths, then quantum computers are useless.'

'You're not convincing me the war wasn't about dysprosium.'

'I'm not trying to convince you the war wasn't about dysprosium,' I said. 'It *was* about dysprosium. But you're confusing two things that are separate. The Chinese spent most of the early twenty-first century investing heavily in Africa, and South America for that matter. They already had good links with the Tanzanian government, and were trying to block the US and Europe getting access to the remaining dysprosium reserves.'

'They wanted to maintain their monopoly?'

'Exactly. The very same tactic that had kept diamonds expensive for so long. In that context, the West was playing catch-up in a part of the world where they were still thought of as the colonial foe. So when the crash happened… there was no doubt. This was all about dysprosium.'

I stopped. The exchange had left me tired, and a headache was starting to knot in my temples.

'Everything okay, Anna?' I looked up and saw Grace hovering over me.

I nodded, but was undone by an outward breath that lacked any sort of energy.

'Maybe I should take you back to your room,' Grace said. Sean looked disappointed, his eyes seeking mine.

'Just a few more minutes,' I said.

'You're sure?'

I managed to lift my head back off the chair, which seemed enough proof that I was okay for Grace to edge away. She remained close, though. Ready to step in and whisk me away if needed.

'They wanted me,' I said. 'Asked for me specifically. That bit gets left out of the history books.'

'I don't... I don't quite follow?'

'When news of the crash started circulating, everyone knew it would be used as a pretext for war. The crash took out the US Secretary of State as well as her aides. It didn't take long for the US President to openly blame the Chinese.'

Sean grinned. 'He wasn't a very diplomatic man, was he?'

'No – and of course there were the usual protests. The placards were a little harder to write than usual, given that nothing snappy rhymes with Tanzania. Those protests started almost immediately after the crash. Look up the dates and tell me I'm wrong. What you don't see in any news report after the war started is that the anti-war brigade wanted *me* to head the investigation. They didn't trust the government, but they did trust me.'

'And why was that?'

'Because of the plane crash I investigated two years earlier.'

'Another one?' I'd lost Sean.

'Two years before the crash in Tanzania,' I explained, 'I investigated one in Iceland. My report stopped a minor scuffle with Russia. Prior to Tanzania, I was the pacifists' poster-girl.'

# 15

FOWLER BLOCKED ANNA'S path as soon as they reached the upper floor of the Hayden home. Someone was listening to music with a deep bass in one of the rooms, which shielded their voices from the Haydens downstairs. 'Before we start,' he said, finding the voice that had been absent downstairs. 'Let me repeat what I said to you outside.'

'And what's that?'

'That this is *my* investigation. It seems you're already forgetting.' Fowler's bulk filled the landing, and he looked more than a little ridiculous framed by delicate eggshell-blue walls and prints of hunting scenes.

Anna raised an eyebrow. 'You asked me here, remember?'

'Yup,' Fowler replied. 'But I also know you understand how stuff like this works, and you've clearly caught my client's eye.' He paused. 'What were you before? When you did the airline stuff?'

'How do you mean?'

'What was your title? What did people call you?'

'Investigator in Charge.'

'Well, that's me now. Okay?'

'I don't have time to soothe your ego, Fowler.' Anna said, turning away from him. 'You're supposed to be convincing

114

me I can help you, remember?'

Fowler stepped aside, as if conceding the point. 'Durrant's room is that one,' he said, pointing at one of a series of closed, impersonal-looking doors that faced the landing.

'I thought we were here because of Beth.' She was a bit disappointed by the Haydens' house now she was inside – it was expensive, but tasteless and distant. Not much of a home, even with all this money. And she could still just about detect the fusty smell of a cat litter tray, which they'd passed somewhere near the foot of the stairs.

'Either the S&P score is right,' Fowler said, 'or it's wrong. If it's right, then Beth will turn up in a couple of days once she's run out of cash and needs Daddy's wallet. She waves at a paypoint, gets in a pod or logs on to social media – and we'll know about it.'

'Not if she's using a spoof.'

'Sure, if she'd planned it. But getting a spoof isn't straightforward and she ain't a tech-head.'

'And if the S&P score is wrong?'

'Then the only lead is Durrant. He gets beaten up, she goes missing. That's not a coincidence, even if the police don't seem to see it on their scorecards. I'd bet my last penny on it.'

'So your theory is that the answer's with him or it's nowhere. Right?'

'Yep.'

'Fine. But we check out Beth's room before we leave.'

'Not a problem.'

N'Golo's room was bland and small. He'd been provided with a single bed, a chest of drawers and a study desk. The sound of bass-heavy music, gunfire and warlike shouting was stronger in here than on the landing, vibrating through the walls. Presumably this was the other kid in the equation, George. The music didn't seem to fit the name.

'I'd have run away too,' Anna said quietly, 'if I was forced to listen to that.'

Fowler laughed, glancing out of the door to make sure nobody was outside. 'George Hayden spends most of his time in there, playing games – killing things. Beth spent most of her time with another sort of animal.'

'She had a boyfriend?'

'No, I meant a horse. Or a pony. Something expensive, anyway. But there's been no sign of her at the stables. And I've put motion nets and cameras up there. It's odd, though, that she'd leave behind an animal she cared about. If she was a runaway—'

'Maybe she thought someone else would take care of it. Her mum's a vet, isn't she?'

Fowler breathed in sharply, then was forced into a loud hawking cough that didn't seem to clear his sinuses. 'Jesus,' he said when he recovered himself, 'the S&P system might just be programmed with more empathy than you. You never had a pet rabbit or something? You don't own a cat? A kid wouldn't just abandon an animal like that.'

'I've never been a big fan of pets,' Anna replied, thinking again about the stink of the litter tray – and not wanting to imagine what it took to clean up after a horse. 'We should speak to George.'

'I already have,' Fowler said. 'He doesn't know anything. He doesn't know much, actually. UI fodder if ever there was one. Smart enough, though, to realise he's too thick to get a decent employment score.'

Aside from the furniture, there was little else in the room.

The walls were bare and dotted with oily poster marks, which were concentrated around the bed. There were no electronics or other entertainments in the room. Just a solitary bookshelf, empty except for a dog-eared copy of *Capital* by Karl Marx.

A physical copy of an actual book. She picked it up and flicked through it, noting absently that it was from a library. She didn't recognise the name of the institution, and then realised it had been last stamped out over twenty years ago. 'From what little you've told me,' Anna said, 'I didn't expect him to be a reader.'

Returning the book, Anna looked back at the walls. There was no personality in the room. Rather, there was just the collective echo of all those who had passed through. The other kids who'd stayed with the Haydens looked like they'd all done something – however small – to make this room their own. But not N'Golo. 'How long had he been here?'

'A few months.'

'I'm going to need to know more about him. You have files?'

'I'll ping them to you. For Durrant and Beth.'

'Good,' Anna said. 'Now let's check her room.'

Beth's bedroom was just across the hall. Fowler picked his way inside and went directly to the window. It gave a good view over the fields at the back of the house – and up towards the dark copse.

Anna was more interested in what lay inside the bedroom. It was the exact opposite of N'Golo's. This was the sanctuary of someone who'd lived in the house for a long time. It was untidy, perfumed, cluttered. There was no pattern to it, no clear mark of the occupant's age. There were a couple of teddy bears on the bed and a collection of make-up on the dressing table.

'You know,' Fowler said, sounding depressed, 'the end of policing came when they introduced checklists. The cops that came into this room would have done so with a to-do list generated by S&P – and probably also worn headcams to allow AIs to direct what they looked at. All initiative has been taken out of the business.'

Anna had already started looking through the bedside cabinet. Tucked away at the back of it was a small, glazed frame that contained some embroidery. She expected it to say something twee like HOME SWEET HOME, but this one proclaimed something a little more political: TRUST IN GOD; SHE WILL PROVIDE.

'She didn't keep a diary,' Fowler said, mistakenly second-guessing what she was holding.

'That we know of,' Anna replied. She pulled out the embroidery and twisted it round. Fowler didn't get it. 'A quote from one of the Pankhursts,' she said, 'if I remember correctly.'

'And what does it mean?'

'I'm not sure. Perhaps only that, like her foster-brother, she was interested in politics?'

'Well it doesn't exactly fit with the rest of the pink and fluffy in here,' Fowler replied, turning back to the window. 'Her private board activity has been screened. I think S&P would have picked up anything incendiary.'

'Maybe she used an old-fashioned pen and paper.'

Fowler laughed. 'Paper?'

A sudden movement caused Anna to shift her attention back to the landing. The Haydens' ginger cat had come to visit them. She noticed there was a small bolt on the back of Beth's door. Not enough to provide security, just simple privacy. And yet she hadn't seen one on N'Golo's. Which meant the Haydens didn't trust them – N'Golo or any of the other kids who came to stay here.

Anna closed her eyes, thinking. The door had a bolt, not a lock. Which meant it only provided privacy when Beth was in the room. At all other times it was unguarded – something of which Beth was probably aware.

'Did you search the stables?' she asked. 'When you were setting up the motion detectors?'

Fowler was fiddling with an old-fashioned comms device, prodding the touch screen with a stubby finger. The black square filled his hand, but he was managing to make it look much smaller and more complicated than it really was.

'Fowler? Did you search the stables?'

'Huh? Oh, it was just full of straw and horse shit.'

'What *is* that thing?' As soon as she'd asked it dawned on her. 'You don't have a direct connection to the boards?'

'No.' Fowler peered at the device. 'Look, I've just got to sort this…'

'Talk about Luddite. I haven't seen one of those in—' She realised what he was doing. 'You're working another case?'

'Trying to,' Fowler replied. 'Just a simple trail and observe. Booked in for tonight – but the woman is ill, she isn't going out, so the hook-up is off.' He looked about him, waving at some of Beth's possessions. 'I've been here before, remember. Knock yourself out.'

Something caught Anna's attention before she could give a caustic reply. A delicately painted porcelain ornament had been tipped over, presumably during the police's search of the room. Tucked into the moulding gap in its base was a little square of folded paper.

'What is it?' Fowler asked, putting his comms device back in his coat pocket.

'If you're right,' she said, feeling her voice shake as she read the slip of paper, 'if she really has been kidnapped, and there's a connection with N'Golo… what would you think was the motive?'

'Most things are about sex or money. And her father is a banker.'

*Pankhurst. Marx.* 'Then I'm convinced.'

'What have you found?'

Anna showed him the piece of paper she'd taken from the ornament and unfolded. It was a leaflet, and it bore the logo of the Workers' League. And someone had written something in the corner: *Meet me at 7 p.m. —N'G.*

# 16

S&P Build 14.224a – Recommendation Module
Situation #GIHHCLTYYEN
Case Updates: None. Target downtime exceeds first
    threshold (likelihood of Target voluntary return
    approaching rapid descent). Cams on routes to
    Edinburgh and Cardiff did not detect Target.
Recommendation: Downgrade resources outside
    main search area. Continue biolog monitoring and
    recognition cams. Seek authorisation for board-feed
    manipulation of Target friends and localised Target
    demographics. Additional resources assigned to
    interview adult contacts of Target by Bot and Officer.
    ENDS.

ANNA STEPPED INTO the synapse chamber, and found Fowler waiting for her. There was no sign of Cody. The private investigator was clearly unhappy to be back in the muslin overalls he'd been given ahead of re-entering the sequencer. The grim look on his face indicated he was regretting fighting so hard for this. He kept looking at the steel bench, its swollen headrest and the gutters lining the floor. The only thing missing was Cody's damn mop, but her technician probably had it soaking in bleach somewhere out of sight.

'Still no contact from Beth?'

'No,' Fowler replied.

'How long do you think?'

'Since she went missing?'

*No, worse than that.* 'How long do you think she has?'

'If my theory is right, then the kidnappers will contact the family sooner rather than later. If she's been taken for other reasons then… well, yes, she's probably already dead.'

'And if the S&P analysis is correct?'

'Then she'll be back in the next few hours, and we can all go home. And you can start looking for another use for these damn benches.'

Fowler hawked something up from the back of his throat, then turned away to swallow. He seemed agitated. She'd offered to go in alone, but Fowler had insisted on joining her inside N'Golo's memory. He'd just need to keep a better grip of his senses than last time.

'You still don't think the S&P score is odd?' she asked.

'Honestly,' Fowler said, giving a rueful smile, 'I really don't know. I've seen scores like that come up in weirder circumstances.'

'I thought the leaflet we found would have moved the needle. That's two illegal leaflets in one house, Fowler.'

For some reason, this amused the PI. 'It was *you* telling *me* not to jump to conclusions earlier,' he said. 'Now you find one little leaflet and you're ready to plug in.'

'So you're not bothered about the Workers' League? You don't think Beth's disappearance has anything to do with them?'

'*Them*? I don't think there is a "them",' Fowler said. 'Maybe a collection of people using the same logo. Some arranging pickets and protests, others organising more direct action against those employing bots and algorithms. Logos and symbols like that tend to attract a fair share of nut jobs.'

'But don't you think this would change the S&P score? Shouldn't we report it?'

'And get my client in danger for having "two illegal leaflets", as you put it, in his house? No, absolutely not. Anyway, it wouldn't affect the score. S&P wouldn't see the connection.'

Anna let out a deep breath. The leaflet and the copy of *Capital* in N'Golo's room were what had brought her to the synapse chamber again. It was worth exploring, at least. But whether or not it was worth the risk to Durrant, she couldn't really answer. He wasn't a saint, Cody had assured her. But that didn't mean his life – no matter his current condition – was worthless.

Before they could debate the issue any further, the doors to the synapse chamber swung open and Cody hustled inside. His feet beat a hurried tap against the tiles as he headed for his workstation, which sat to one side of the wheel of synapse benches. Soon data was streaming across his display.

'It's a wonder you make sense of it all,' Fowler said.

'I'm good with numbers,' Cody replied, not taking his concentration away from the screens.

'I bet you're brilliant at Sudoku.'

'We're getting the synapse data through,' Cody said, a triumphant smile lighting up his face. 'I think we're ready.'

*Ready*, Anna thought. *Ready and quite alone.*

Only she and Fowler would be connected via the synapse chamber itself. N'Golo remained in his hospital bed: the machinery keeping him alive rather more immovable than the comms lines snaking their way back to the hub. All in all, it made the chamber appear far too big for its intended use; the synapse benches reduced to small islands amidst cold, empty space.

'And how was he?' Anna asked. 'N'Golo.'

Cody stopped smiling. 'He's hooked up to more machines than I could count – most of them making weird bleeps – and his face is swollen like he's lost a boxing match. Is that what you mean?'

In truth, she didn't know. Still, it didn't alter the fact she was going to risk N'Golo's life because of a leaflet she'd found in a girl's bedroom, and this when even the father had dismissed his daughter's politics as being a silly teenage fad.

'You had no problems positioning the synapse equipment?'

'No,' Cody replied. 'The main issue was actually getting our people past hospital security.'

'And you've discussed the key parameters with the health team?'

'Of course. This is as safe as we can make it, Anna. We're getting good data, both from his memory core and his main biorhythms. If we get any sort of spiking either here or at the hospital, we stop and flood him with neural sedative. That should minimise the risk of him bumping out completely. In that instance, we'll hopefully just lose the feed...'

The health department's experience had been with long-term coma patients – people for whom the lights had not burned for a very long time. N'Golo was different. He was still suffering from cranial bleeding. With or without his foster-parent's permission, they weren't getting him out of the hospital. Which meant he had doctors all around him, monitoring everything. And hopefully keeping him alive.

So it came down to a very simple question: did they want to take that small risk, on the basis that the girl was actually in danger? Anna had spent a long time thinking about it. Part of her still wanted to call it off, to stop the experiment that she'd instructed Cody to set up. But Jake was pressuring her too, as well as Cody and Fowler. There was an expectation that she'd go through with this, now that she'd been able to make some sort of connection between the two, however tenuous.

'If we wait for a ransom demand,' Fowler said softly, as if sensing her doubt, 'then we may as well pull the trigger ourselves. We have to do this – and quickly.'

'How are you going to prep him, Cody?'

Cody's hands hovered atop his workstation. He leant forward and examined something on the screen.

'Cody? How are you going to—'

'I heard you.' Cody looked a bit sheepish when he turned back to her. 'I don't think we can, Anna.'

They stared at each other in dismay until Fowler broke the silence.

'What's going on?'

'You tell him,' Anna said. 'You're the tech.'

Cody grimaced. 'Accessing memories first requires those memories to be stimulated,' he said. 'Otherwise you just drop straight into a barrage of noise. When we work with witnesses, it's relatively easy. We just talk to them as they're going under. Remind them of the place. When they were there, what happened, all the rest of it. At its most basic, we read their S&P statements back to them to make them remember.'

'But N'Golo's in a coma,' Fowler said.

'We were going to do the same thing,' Cody explained,

shrinking in his seat. 'And hope he heard us. The health techs told me it won't really work like that. He's too far gone.'

'So we're just going to dive in?'

'Yep. Right into the noise.'

Anna weighed the risks, and once more dismissed them. That fucking leaflet. If she'd not seen it, then she might have thought differently. 'Fine,' she said, moving towards her preferred bench.

'There's a good chance we'll be able to guide the next encounter from inside the memory,' Cody continued. 'Once the first memory is in motion – say something to him to pull him to a particular place and time.'

'Okay,' Anna said, clambering up and onto the steel bed. The coldness of the steel came through her overalls and sapped the warmth from her body. It wouldn't be long before her muscles would start to stiffen. But that was all part of the process. A low-tech way of numbing the body prior to the synapse drug being administered. She rolled onto her side, and lifted her hair away from the base of her neck.

On the slab beside her she heard a few grunts as Fowler hoisted himself up. And then the sudden pressure release of a hypo-spray. Cody had taken care of Fowler first, delivering drugs into the base of his neck and then rolling him flat. Next he came across to her.

'Failure begets failure, Anna,' he said quietly.

'I know,' she whispered, feeling the hypo-spray push against her neck. 'Beth could still be just another teen runaway.'

'But let's hope not,' replied Cody. 'Let's hope she's in trouble, and we're the only ones looking for her. And let's hope we find her, Anna. Or whatever's left of her.'

A hiss burst against her neck, and Anna sensed herself

slipping away. She felt Cody's final touch as he took hold of her shoulder and rolled her back onto the table.

It was time to meet N'Golo Durrant.


## A COUNTRY LANE.

They were in a country lane, sometime close to dusk. But the image was rippling and warping like a reflection from a pond. And someone had just thrown in a very large stone. Anna took a deep breath, and tried to cling on. If she couldn't ground herself she would be thrown back out of the sequencer. Her own brain was struggling to adjust – rejecting the construct. She closed her eyes, let the ground settle as the background image of the lane twisted around her. *Shit.*

'Hey!'

Anna continued to wait. She let her feet feel they were grounded before concentrating back on the lane. Fowler was somewhere close: stumbling around like he'd just spent too long propped up against a bar. There was no sign of Durrant.

'What the fuck is going on?' Fowler shouted. 'I thought you said this got easier!'

Anna took a step forward, felt the ground lurch and roll – and then saw the strangest thing. A bird, caught in mid-flight – just a few metres ahead of her. Its wings were folded inwards as it zipped towards a nearby hedge: a little streamlined ball of feathers and beak. Which meant the memory wasn't in motion. Back at the hub, Cody was holding things steady. Or at least trying to.

Anna opened her mouth wide. 'We have line distortion!'

Something screeched in her ear. Fowler's head snapped back in surprise and he fell, his limbs flailing as he struggled to find a purchase on the unmade surface of the lane.

'*We're working to improve the hospital feed*,' Cody said directly into her ear. '*Keep with it*.'

Around her, the foreground pixelated then filled with more detail. She took a step forward. Then a step to the right. Then a step back. She moved her neck round, registered each movement, and then smiled. She was fully immersed. Fully inside a construct of N'Golo Durrant's last memory.

'I can't see anything…'

Fowler was back on his feet, but he had his hands outstretched as if he was trying to walk through a pitch-black room. He took a few steps, then sank to his knees. 'I can't see! I can't fucking see anything!'

Anna moved over to him – at first easily, and then finding her steps slightly out of sync with the ground, as if she was walking on a travelator. She took Fowler's hand and guided him back to his feet. 'You're okay,' she said. 'Close your eyes…'

'They are fucking closed!'

Anna kept holding Fowler until he started to calm. 'You're not fully submerged,' she said. She called upwards, 'We're still having problems.'

'*Uh, yeah*,' came Cody's response. The sound of his voice made Fowler flinch again. '*We've got feedback coming from the beds – one of you is fighting it*.'

'Can you bring him out?' Anna asked.

'*I'd prefer not to*,' Cody replied. '*It might snap the line. Can he just hunker?*'

Anna waited as Fowler continued to turn his head blindly. 'We've got data problems,' she whispered to him. 'Or patient problems. One or the other. Are you going to be okay in here?'

Fowler remained unsteady. He gave a nervous laugh.

'Sure,' he said. 'How dangerous can it be lying on a table? Because that's where I am, right?'

Anna let go of him. Despite his show of confidence, Fowler scrabbled after her touch, but then let his arms drop.

'That's right,' Anna reassured him. 'You're in the synapse chamber. Cody is with you, and he's monitoring your vital signs. And we'll both be pulled out when we've finished here.'

'At least this justifies giving you access to my biodata.'

Interference like Fowler was experiencing was very rare, and something she hadn't gone through herself. But if she had? In that scenario, the only information Cody would be receiving would be being sent from her spoof. And what good would that do her?

'So where is he, then?'

'Who?'

'Durrant. If this is his memory, where is he?'

She didn't know. The construct was small. Only the immediate vicinity of the lane was visible. They'd appeared inside a very small pocket of memory. The country lane would have been fully grassed over had it not been for a set of tyre tracks rutting the surface. So wherever they were, it had regular use by a tractor. It was also starting to get dark. With the memory in motion, it wouldn't be long before she'd be able to see only a fraction more than Fowler.

So she needed to absorb everything she could, and quickly. Anna immediately started to pick out aspects she could use for a post-submersion validation. On one side of the lane was a hedgerow. The other side was cut into a high bank that ran up towards a small wooded area. Anna concentrated on it. The shape of the copse was familiar.

They were in the fields behind the Hayden home.

The construct didn't extend far up or down the lane – most of the detail was lost in darkness – but through the hedge the Hayden house was clearly visible a few hundred metres distant. Its lights were already burning in anticipation of night. A little off-centre perhaps, but clearly the focus of attention amongst its line of nondescript companions.

Anna continued to search the edges of the construct, trying to find where N'Golo's memory faded into either darkness or a generic jumble as his brain tried to fill in the blanks.

A relative newbie like Fowler might have struggled, but she quickly found three potential boundary points. Triangulating between them, she had him. N'Golo was on the ground. And then she realised there was another shape with him. It was phased, partially transparent. More a shadow – or a smudge – than anything else. But as she walked round the patch of dark, it took on the shape of something like a man.

Anna looked back at Fowler. The bird that was frozen between them remained in place. There was no risk to N'Golo. But some feeling of doubt had kicked inside her. Anna pushed away the feeling, examining the boy.

He was just as she expected. Black, full in the shoulder for a youth. Tall maybe, when he was upright. But at the moment he was lying crumpled beneath her, still very much conscious. Watching. Maybe hiding. Fresh bruises covered his face.

'Anna…'

'What?'

'I can feel something…'

Anna twisted back to Fowler. The bird was gone, flying off into the distance. Which meant the memory was in motion, and a strong breeze had started to whistle down the lane.

'I'm starting to see…'

Fowler looked confused and more than a little relieved. His first steps were hesitant – but he finally made his way over. Beneath her, N'Golo was also moving – his lips in continual movement as he tried to crawl away.

'Disappointing, N'Golo. We thought you had it in you…'

The voice – a growling sound – had come from the shadow. It morphed between them, taking on more of a human form. Becoming solid. Two black pits for eyes, and a stretched gash of a mouth.

'What the fuck is that?'

'Whoever beat the kid up,' Anna said calmly. The shadow hadn't formed into a recognisable figure yet, almost as if it was waiting for something.

'But we can't see him!'

Anna shook her head, continuing to examine the scene around her. There was a patch of discarded cigarette butts where the hedge met the verge. Fowler stumbled between her and the shape. 'Don't get in their way,' she said. 'It might cause a bump-out…'

Fowler didn't seem to hear her, or else he was deliberately ignoring her. Stepping between the boy and the shadow, he peered into the void. 'It's getting clearer…'

'Out of the way, Fowler!'

Anna got to her feet as the shape finally became something close to a recognisable figure.

'Stop,' Fowler shouted. 'Weaver, put the damn thing on freeze! We got him! We got him!'


ANNA PULLED HERSELF from the metal bench before she was fully back in her body. She had to force her legs to shift and move – her feet filling uncertain spaces beneath her – but she still managed to stagger the few steps across to Fowler. She took a tight hold of the edge of his bench to stop herself falling. Somewhere in the background, Cody was scrambling at his station, caught between his duty to revive the pair and working to control the submersion. 'Anna! Wait!'

She wasn't going to wait. Fowler continued to lie disabled, his eyes open but his brain struggling to reconnect with his body's own sensory inputs. It wouldn't take him as long to recover his limb-positional sense as his first time in the sequencer, but it wasn't going to be an easy swim to the surface.

Anna glared down at him, watching him flounder. Instructions from his brain were only translating into brief twitches in his cheeks and shoulders, his Adam's apple bobbing as he couldn't help but panic.

'Idiot! Fucking idiot! What did you think you were doing?'

Anna wobbled. The effort of moving the few metres that separated their benches had already sapped most of her energy. She'd come to the surface far too quickly.

Cody's breath flooded into her right ear. And then a deluge of sweat brought her fully round. Her technician had caught her – his arm now wrapped around her midriff after she'd slumped backwards into him. Sensation rippled from her calves into her toes.

'You okay?'

'Yeah.' Anna pushed herself out of Cody's grip, pulling and flattening her overalls back into place. She gulped a few deep breaths. 'Thank you.'

Cody looked deeply concerned. 'What happened?'

Anna allowed herself a moment to think. Back home,

Kate would be dealing with a flood of emotional alarm calls. Probably logging into Elsy and going through the post-crisis routine. But here and now, none of that was important. She could deal with it later. Looking down at Fowler she said, 'He messed things up.'

'Bullshit!' Fowler responded. The single expression made him breathless, and he looked confused by it. His head came up slightly, then fell back onto the metallic pillow. Cody immediately moved to ease his body straight and check his airway. As he did so, he gently pushed Anna away from Fowler's bed. The additional space provided a little more calm.

'We had an agreed plan,' Anna said, trying to be patient. 'All we needed to do during that submersion was move him to a point of safety.'

'But he was right there,' Fowler replied. 'Right there. We nearly had a face!'

'And you know all the suspects, do you? You'd have been able to ID him?'

Fowler didn't reply.

'We take him back to the point when he arrived with the Hayden family,' Anna said, repeating the presubmersion agreement, 'and then we run things forward to find out who he was meeting.'

'Fine,' Fowler said, a little bit too quietly.

'Pardon?'

'Fine,' Fowler repeated, this time louder. 'I said "fine". As in, okay, I agree with you. But if we risk losing Durrant each time we plug him into your machine, then we can't spend too long smelling the fucking flowers either. And if we're right about Beth…'

Anna turned away, signalling for Cody to follow. She knew the risks, and didn't need Fowler using them to justify his approach. 'Have we heard anything from the hospital?'

Cody shook his head. 'I'm sorry,' he said. 'I heard the "freeze" command and didn't think. N'Golo bumped out. The memory had only just been put into motion.'

'You should have been taking instructions from me.'

'I know – look, it was a mistake, Anna. Remember, I can't see what's going on in there. Someone tells me to freeze the memory and—'

'Fine. Let's just learn for next time, shall we? If we get the chance...'

Cody noticeably held his stride as Anna struggled to lead the way to his terminal. However, as she neared it she felt the final wobbles from her legs. *A baby, struggling with its first steps,* she thought. That's how Jake had once described coming out of submersion to her. Behind them, Fowler had made the wiser choice of remaining on his bench as he continued to recover his senses.

'Give yourself a moment,' Cody said.

'I'm fine.'

'Yeah, well, what just happened will have registered on the HR system,' Cody replied. 'They'll want to know what happened. Jake hates his staff losing their cool: he thinks it's bad for decision-making if people are shouting at each other.'

Anna took a deep breath. Cody hadn't yet checked the biodata himself. If he did, he would see that the readings from her hadn't spiked at all. But that would only lead to more questions. No matter how badly Fowler had messed up, she needed to keep a cap on her outbursts. And she needed to keep Cody's attention away from it too. 'Lucky I wasn't shouting at a member of staff, then. So, the hospital?'

Cody leant forward to read a few messages on his terminal. 'I'd better call them,' he said. 'They want to know what happened.' He signalled back to the hospital, and soon a deeply pissed-off health technician appeared on the screen.

'What the hell was that, Cody?'

Cody launched into a highly technical argument with his counterpart, each one trying to bat the blame back onto the other.

'Is he okay?' Anna said, cutting in when they both seemed to be running down.

'Surges in heart rate and adrenaline,' came the reply. 'A blitz of synaptic activity. Maybe he had some sort of seizure. But he's alive, if that's what you mean. We're running checks now: sensory stimuli and brain patterns. Everything's looking the same as when we first arrived.'

*Thank fuck.* 'Good.'

'His doctors aren't too pleased. I talked them down, but if this happens again I think they'll cut us off. It'll take a few hours before things stabilise enough to try again.'

'But he's okay?' Anna repeated.

'We think so – but the only way to know for sure is to plug in again. If you find yourself in a white heavenly space then you'll know he's fried,' said the health tech. 'So what happened? Nothing much looked wrong here – and then he sort of went haywire.'

Anna hesitated. 'Trauma memory,' she replied, thinking about the dark shape. 'Not everything came through intact anyway – we'll hopefully have enough to push him someplace safer next time. Somewhere the memory core has had more time to crystallise.'

'You better hope so.'

The comms link switched off.

Cody turned to her. 'So what's next?'

'We cross our fingers and hope we have another shot.'

Behind them, the sound of movement indicated Fowler was starting to heave himself upright. Cody didn't look over, but it was clear where his attention was fixed. 'And him?' he whispered.

'I'm going in alone next time,' Anna said. 'Our friend will have to find something else to do.'

# 17

S&P Build 14.224a – Recommendation Module
Situation #GIHHCLTYYEN
Case Updates: Communication received. Situation
    escalated to KIDNAP. No financial demand received.
    Target (Beth Hayden) downgraded to Victim. Kidnap
    group now designated as Target.
Recommendation: Biolog monitoring initiated for all
    registered criminal classes 1–5. Board monitoring
    initiated for all registered criminal classes 1–5. Biolog
    and board monitoring approved under Delegated
    Approval Matrix. Reassess family members, seek
    potential motives.

ANNA ARRIVED AT the hub the next morning, and went straight to Jake's ward. The summons had come early, a casual check of her messaging service after she'd stepped out of the shower bringing the unwelcome news.

*Failure begets failure.*

Kate, of course, had casually dismissed it in the way that any news – either good or bad – simply wafted through her. And yes, her spoof had been forced to interact with her mental health programme, Elsy, at around the time Fowler had messed up the interaction with N'Golo. Again, however, Kate hadn't appeared too concerned. 'You were pretty fucked off' pretty much summed up the extent of her interest in Anna's working day. As did a pretty short rundown on the bioresponses that had been triggered by Fowler's incompetence.

The more troubling news was that they'd had another visitor. Or maybe they hadn't. Anna winced. Some dude had come to the building looking for an 'Emma Johnson'. Of course, with that name not being on the building list the man hadn't been let past security – but not before a quick enquiry had been pinged round the building asking if anyone recognised the name. Nobody had. Except Anna, when she'd returned home. Emma Johnson was the name of one of the victims of the Tanzania aeroplane crash. The name had disturbed her more than anything Fowler had done. It had forced her to spend most of the evening in her room, listening to some of her favourite old records. Only after Kate had insisted did she log into Elsy as herself; and the electronic shrink had reminded her of something obvious. It was a fairly common name. So maybe a coincidence.

Maybe.

'Good – you're here.'

Becky Holland, Jake's nurse, looked impatient, and stared pointedly at an empty synapse bench near to Jake. The hub's owner was in the same position he'd occupied when she'd last been here, his body static, his mind fully engaged. Someone else was meeting Jake, too. Another of the beds in his private synapse chamber was occupied. Anna tried to look at the woman occupying it as she moved to an empty bench, but the protective muslin overalls provided the guest with the same level of anonymity as everyone else attached to the device. And, even after a few months working at the hub, Anna knew hardly any of the other employees.

'I'm okay to enter?'

Holland scowled. 'You're fine. He wanted to see you, remember?'

Anna shifted herself into position and let her head relax. The nurse pulled her jaw sharply up to clear the airway. Then she felt the slow draw down…

ANNA HALF EXPECTED to resurface back in Rufford Abbey Park. To find Jake continuing his laps of the lake, as template children watched him while they ate their ice creams. Instead, she was disappointed to emerge someplace else in the hub: a drab, square boardroom on its upper levels.

The greyish background with only dashes of purple filtering through the carpets immediately stimulated an unfortunate association in Anna's mind. This was the same room she'd first met Jake's representatives. Or, at least, a simulation of that room where, in effect, she'd been interviewed for her job – just days after quitting – *being forced to quit* – the air investigation unit. She'd still been upset that day. Confused. Lost.

*We'll need full access to your biorhythmic data, of course.*

She hadn't let them.

The boardroom was dominated by a long, lacquered table supplied with metallic seats. Jake sat at its head. He looked out of sorts, like he didn't really want to be there. Perhaps most of his mind was still thumping around that lake. His hands were held loosely ahead of him on the table, and they continued to flex as he waited.

Jake was also wearing a suit. Anna had never seen him in one, not in all the times they'd been submerged together. The other woman seated at the table with them was also smartly dressed, wearing a trouser suit that matched Anna's. Her black hair was cut into a stylish bob.

'Anna – great, you're here!'

The woman looked surprised at Anna's appearance. She wasn't a regular visitor, then, Anna thought. Perhaps this was her first time. Which maybe went some way to explain the office and Jake's attire. And the fact they were seated rather than making the newbie try to walk.

'I came as soon as I could,' she said, sitting down to complete a triangle between the woman and Jake.

'Your timing's perfect,' replied Jake. 'It took Inspector Mitchell quite a while to get acclimatised. We've been talking about the oddities of living inside here. She's come about your little project.' He waved a hand expansively, as if he barely knew anything about what he employed her to do. 'The Durrant project.'

Anna kept her attention on the woman opposite. 'I didn't think the police were interested in N'Golo?'

'Things have—'

The woman stopped and winced, massaging her temples.

'Things have—' she repeated. 'Things have changed.'

'Don't fight it,' Anna said to her. 'Tell yourself that the other place is the dream, not here. Not now, anyway.'

The inspector nodded, but didn't continue.

'Things have changed,' Anna said, now prompting her. 'How?'

'I was telling Mr—'

'Jake,' came the immediate interruption, alongside a casual grin. 'Just call me Jake.'

The inspector hesitated, informality perhaps as nauseating to her as the sequencer. But then she looked up – narrowing her eyes at the air-conditioning duct above them – and gave a sudden, sharp shiver. 'We've received news regarding Beth Hayden.'

*Fuck.* Thinking about the warning Cody had so recently given her, and knowing she was now in full view of Jake, Anna tried to control her voice, to take any emotion out of it

'Oh?'

'A note arrived at the house yesterday evening.'

'What did it say?'

Mitchell hesitated for a second, perhaps not wanting to give up the information. But then she seemed to think it was worth it. 'It was simple and to the point: *We have your daughter. We'll be in touch.*'

Anna waited, but nothing else followed. 'That's it? No ransom?'

'No cash demand. Not yet. But they have her; that much is clear.'

'And who are "they", exactly?'

'We don't know yet.'

Was the Workers' League leaflet they'd found in Beth's bedroom connected in any way? 'And the message came in the form of a paper note? Not a board transmission?'

The suggestion amused Mitchell. 'We'd have traced a board transmission by now. They'd paid off a UI to deliver the note. It arrived at the security gate. Before you ask, it was just some random woman who'd agreed to help them in exchange for a few food tokens. And yes, we've traced her geolog, but haven't established who she met.'

'So presumably the S&P analysis has been updated? Now we know Beth has been kidnapped…'

Inspector Mitchell responded with an irritated sigh. 'The original S&P data has been checked, and found to have been entered correctly.'

'I don't understand why the system didn't give her case a higher score.'

'S&P is proven at the meta level, Miss Glover. We can always find instances where we disagree with its conclusions, or cases where it gets things wrong. Science relies on mistakes to improve.'

Anna considered this. 'The private investigator who brought this to us is going to be pleased, anyway.'

'Let me guess: Adrian Fowler?'

'You know him?'

Mitchell shivered. She blinked, her head swaying a little like she was still having trouble remaining in Jake's fantasy. Anna watched her, puzzled. She should have been too deeply submerged now. But then, some people did have trouble with the system – the analytical side of their brains being unwilling to let go. 'Yes, I know him. And if you want a tally of his disagreements with S&P, then you'll find Inspector Fowler was wrong a whole lot more times than he was right.'

'Inspector Fowler?'

'He was an S&P analyst for some years before he launched his current business,' Mitchell answered. 'Didn't you think to find out who you were partnering up with?'

'I checked his business,' Anna said. 'And his endorsements. None mentioned a police connection.'

'I'm not surprised. Anyway, most people seem to be

ignorant of one important factor with AI. Essentially, an AI is a system that looks for and interprets patterns, just as we humans do. But the AI part of S&P can process vastly more complex datasets than any human. It has no emotion, Miss Glover. It doesn't suffer from tunnel vision, and isn't subject to prejudice. It ensures resources are directed efficiently, and its success is evident in any crime statistic you may care to quote. It would be even better if it were allowed access to a broader set of data – rather than just skimming those in the highest categories of risk.'

Jake coughed. 'Well, the UK isn't Iceland, is it? So S&P is just going to have to make do with the data it has.'

Anna glanced at Jake, feeling a tug of anxiety. She'd heard that line a few times before from proponents of S&P. That given more access to greater amounts of personal data, its success rate would be even more impressive. Civil liberties groups hadn't been able to stop the harvesting of information from lower-end socioeconomic classes. The wallets of those higher up the wage chain had been much more effective. Still, it was odd hearing Jake protest – a man who had insisted on access to the biodata of all his staff. Didn't he see the similarity to the information-hungry tin-pot dictatorships that had infected Europe in the last few years?

'I just want you both to be clear on what you're up against – you and your little project.'

'So I guess the S&P numbers have been rerun,' Anna repeated, trying to get back to the point. 'And it's now come to a different conclusion?'

'We've now factored in the ransom note.'

'Presumably you want us to hand over what we've found so far?'

Mitchell shook her head, then looked again at the air-conditioning system and shivered. 'No, we'd like you to continue your investigation. I've passed a copy of the ransom note to Jake... his nurse, anyway. S&P has given the case a new score, and additional resources have been allocated, but we haven't got anywhere. Camera and social-media feeds have proven unproductive. We've been adding news stories to teenage girls' media feeds in this area too – you know, to try to encourage her to come home – but that seems a little redundant now. It seems the only person who might know anything is your N'Golo Durrant.'

Anna hesitated. She too was starting to feel a chill from the air con. She pulled at the sleeves of her suit, then recognised it as something more of an internal bubble of excitement. After all this time, were the police about to back them?

'Our first test was, on the whole, successful,' Anna said. 'We'll be trying again today.'

Mitchell was still shivering. 'The note wasn't particularly threatening, but it wasn't specific either. No sum of money was demanded. So while S&P analysis indicates little immediate danger to the girl, we know we don't have much time.' She stopped to lock Anna with a firm stare. 'We need to find out if N'Golo Durrant is involved – and quickly.'

'What we're doing with N'Golo exposes him to significant risk. We can only push him so hard.'

'The boy's nearly dead. What does it matter?'

'He's not dead,' Jake interjected. He leant back in his chair, the memory of his intact body making it flex under his weight. Back in his chamber, however, most of it was crumpled and gone. Fed with tubes and rotated regularly to stop him from getting bedsores. 'N'Golo Durrant is very much alive.'

'I didn't mean—'

'Anna will continue with her work and send you the results,' Jake continued. 'It's in our interests for this to work – the only thing haste hastens is failure.'

'Fine. Now, how do I disconnect from—'

The inspector disappeared from the table, her chair spinning in her wake.

Anna turned back to Jake. 'Working with N'Golo is going to be difficult,' she said. 'More difficult than we anticipated.'

'But it's also your project's best chance of success,' Jake replied. 'And what does that beget?'

'I understand.'

'Good. What did you think of Inspector Mitchell?'

'Hard to say. First time in the sequencer.' The room's temperature seemed to fall another notch. 'Couldn't you have remembered a warmer office?'

'It isn't – *wasn't* – all that cold, Anna.'

Anna rubbed at her forearms again. 'Is that everything?'

'No. I've had a request from the health team. They're looking for a technician for their PTSD thing. Cody Weaver has been mentioned as being suitable.'

'I only have one technician.'

'We can do a swap, if you're willing.'

'Who would want to offload their tech support?'

Jake smiled. 'Quite. Well, I said I'd ask, but… well, I guess things are looking up for your project anyway. And, in truth…'

'What?'

Jake grimaced. 'I'm not too happy with some of the figures I'm seeing from Weaver. There's a lot of amber lights across his dashboard. Seems tired; disturbed sleep…'

Anna tried for a lopsided smile, hoping the sequencer was able to translate it into a suitable image. 'He's just become a father, Jake.'

'I'm still paying him the same as before his family grew. And you need someone fully switched on.'

'He's a good man.'

Jake started rapping his fingers on the desk. 'Well, I guess I've seen data that suggests fatherhood does tend to make employees more reliable in the long term…'

Anna tried to reply, but a sudden cold tingle turned her words into a mute squeak. She took a few quick breaths. 'I'm going to have to disconnect too,' she said. 'Something's not quite right…'

'Fine.' Jake looked up at the air con as if nothing was the matter. 'And I'm pleased to see your vitamin D levels are back up to normal. I assume you've been taking supplements rather than getting it naturally, but I appreciate the effort. Take a break before you connect to Durrant again, though, eh?'

# 18

I ROLLED UP the sleeves of my robe and inspected my arms. My skin was like crêpe paper, crinkling at my elbows. A perfect reflection of my age, all the youth sucked out until there only remained the thinnest veneer. Grace was running me a bath, the temperature controls set just how I liked it.

'Anna?'

Grace had been chatting while I sat patiently in a chair beside the tub, wrapped in a thick robe that almost doubled my weight. I'd stopped listening to what she'd been telling me. Mostly, her words merged into nothing but the same old news and pearls of wisdom. The trick in keeping her going was knowing which noises to make to show I was still paying attention. And now I realised that I'd been too quiet. I tried to pretend I'd been struggling to hear over the running water. 'Mmm?'

'The young man,' Grace repeated. 'I think you actually enjoy his visits. Is that why you allow him back so often?'

She grinned at me over her shoulder, then moved to switch off the taps. I didn't share her humour. Each visit from Sean was relatively short, or so it appeared. A function of my condition was that I easily tired. Facts became confused. Bits of information became lost. Forced interruptions were many.

I saw the frustration all too clearly in his face during the last visit. He obviously wanted to talk more about Tanzania, but I needed him to understand the context. What he saw as time wasted, I saw as very much essential. Even if it would take him more visits than he'd perhaps have expected to get what he needed for his research. And, anyway, perhaps I did enjoy it. Having a young man waiting on my every word.

Making him wait.

'He's lucky I'm speaking to him at all,' I said.

'I keep on expecting you to bring down the shutters again.'

I didn't want to get into why I was now providing my confession. Especially not with Grace. Fortunately, she didn't follow up her comment; instead she checked the temperature of the water. As per my instructions, the water would be the dull temperature of warm beer. A control system at the side of the bath allowed the nursing staff to adjust the temperature.

'There,' Grace said. She lifted me up from the bath chair as if I was indeed made of crêpe, and then slipped first my right arm, then my left, out of the robe. After the weight of the garment fell away, I was plonked back naked into my seat. Then I waited for my lower legs to be lifted up onto the chair's supports so that my body formed an L-shape. But before Grace could push the chair along its runners and over the bath, a small light on her belt began to flash.

She frowned. 'Emergency call,' she said.

'Which room?'

'Now,' Grace replied, scrabbling for the robe, 'you know I can't tell you that.'

Without saying any more, she wrapped the dressing gown around both me and the chair, tucking me inside to keep in the warmth. Which meant she was going to be gone for a few seconds.

'I'll be back in five. Don't move.'

I glanced around me. Water on one side, the remainder of the bathroom empty on the other. And me in between: jacked up on a bath chair, my legs perpendicular to my body and now coddled in a bathrobe. 'I'll be waiting.'

Grace closed the door behind her, but that didn't stop N'Golo. He appeared sooner than I'd imagined, merging into existence at the edge of the bath. He pushed into my consciousness and waited for me to notice him.

I didn't move. I just looked at him, the scars on my forearms already beginning to itch. He always looked the same. The young man who should have had so much to look forward to, all of it cut short.

'Are you going to say anything today?' I asked. 'Or will you just start repeating your numbers?'

I didn't expect him to answer. His visits were irregular: sometimes I'd see him many times in one day; other times, he kept his distance. I'd not mentioned him to the nursing staff, although Grace had caught me whispering to him on occasion. Not that she could see him. Not that anyone could. Because he wasn't really sitting there, watching me from the edge of the bath. He was only in my mind. A connection from the sequencer that hadn't quite been successfully detached. A little etching of guilt that was too deep to remove.

'Why are you telling the boy about Tanzania?'

The question boomed into the empty bathroom and caused my body to jerk. The robe loosened and slid a little from my shoulders. But not too much.

149

'I think it's time,' I said.

'Do you expect forgiveness?'

'No, but I expect him to record the truth.'

N'Golo seemed to consider this, but I knew everything was happening inside my own brain. A devil on one shoulder, an angel on the other. Both whispering in my ears.

'Are you going to tell him about the synapse sequencer?'

'I don't know…'

'The two things are connected.' He tapped his finger against the temple of his skull. 'Up here, they're connected. You can see that, can't you?'

'I…'

N'Golo's eyes rolled up. His eyelids started to flutter. And then he started reciting the numbers. Always starting the same, but rapidly moving beyond that into a line of figures of which I couldn't quite keep track. 'N'Golo, I—'

'Who's N'Golo?'

I turned, my robe sliding a little further. The door to the bathroom had opened and the other nurse – Charley – stood framed. 'Another one of your fancy men?'

'Where's Grace?'

'Looking after a patient. She asked me to take care of you.'

'No.' I tried to move, to twist my legs off the supports, but I couldn't. The aid was designed for safety, preventing unexpected tumbles into water. And Charley wasn't going to allow me to get up anyway. She'd already pulled away my robe. And as I continued to shift and shuffle, she hit a button and the chair started to slide sideways. Slowly, I was being pulled along the rails by the chair's underpowered motor.

I looked down into the water. The next step should have been to lower me down. But Charley was now examining the bath's temperature controls, and had started to fiddle with them. 'Grace has already done that,' I said.

'I don't want you catching a shiver.'

'It's fine,' I said. 'It's just as I like it.'

Charley ignored me, her finger jabbing at the controls. 'You seem to be having a good time talking to your gentleman friend.'

At first I thought she was still talking about N'Golo, but then I realised she meant the student, Sean. I tried to see what she had done to the bath but the gauge was too far away. I didn't need to read it to tell she'd made it hotter, though – a few wisps of steam were now rising up around the chair, dropping moisture onto my skin.

'Are you going to tell him how you got all those people killed?'

I didn't respond. The steam was getting thicker and hotter. Wrapping itself around my legs. I had bruised shins. I could see them clearly, extending away from my body as they rested on the supports of the bath chair. Part of the crêpe effect, any little knock or scrape seemed to create a dark, purple patch that took weeks to fully disappear. On some days I looked at my arms and thought I could perhaps push my finger right through them. No need for a knife now. There was no protection left. Nothing to dampen the pain.

'You don't feel any guilt at all, do you?' Charley continued. She moved away from the bath and reached for the chair's controls. A single push started the mechanism lowering. 'This is just a chance for you to talk your way out of it.'

'No!'

Up until that moment I'd tried to remain calm, but I'd let that word out as part of a shriek. The chair kept lowering and the steam was now making it difficult to breathe. Getting into my mouth, and pushing down my throat. I tried to think. To calmly reach out for some logic. The safety systems wouldn't allow the water to get too hot. Not to dangerous levels, anyway. Unless they'd been overridden…

The backs of my legs were the first to touch the liquid. It felt like I was being dipped into battery acid. I took in a great gasp – but that just took more of the burning heat into my body.

The chair continued to grind lower. The water crept up my legs and washed over them, between them. Each cubic centimetre made me flinch – it felt like my skin was being flayed.

'Seventy-five thousand,' Charley said. 'All those lives lost because of you.'

I still didn't – couldn't – say anything. But I could see a blurred shape over my nurse's shoulder. I kept my concentration on him as the water reached my stomach. It kept rising until it covered my arms and chest, so that just the tops of my shoulders and my head remained untouched by the scalding heat.

N'Golo continued to recite his numbers. I tried to focus on them to take away the pain. But they were already being lost. I was going to lose consciousness.

'How are you going to cope?' asked Charley, grinning. 'When you're lowered down for the final time?'

# 19

**Top News:**

New report shows health AIs bring diagnosis to billions
 – and more accurate than doctors (*Read more*)

Top sports star loses gambling case: moved down to UI
 pending appeal (*Read more*)

Prime Minister Erin Farlands in unexpected visit to new
 community centre (*Read more*)


**Selected for You:**

Better with AI: How prison sentences used to vary by
 colour! (*Read more*)


ANNA ARRIVED AT the synapse chamber to find Cody and
Fowler already waiting for her. She adjusted her overalls
as she entered, then made her way over to the workstation
where the pair were chatting. They both slipped into
silence as she approached. Somewhere in the back of her
mind, she registered that Fowler wasn't wearing any scrubs
– he must have accepted her decision not to allow him
back into the sequencer.

Cody whistled a few bars of an unfamiliar melody. 'You been to see Jake?' he asked.

'Yep – he told me about the note.'

Fowler allowed himself a grim smile. 'I was right.'

'We have the go-ahead from Jake to continue.' Both men looked relieved. 'An Inspector Mitchell was with Jake when I met him. She said she knew you.'

The name had an immediate effect. At some point since their last meeting Fowler must have had a cursory shave; his pimpled, raw skin now flushed a heavier shade of pink.

'She said you weren't a big fan of S&P.'

'Huh! Neither is she. Not really, anyway.'

'You wouldn't know that from the sales pitch she gave us.'

'I used to be her boss,' Fowler admitted. 'Good analyst; poor investigator. But she had the sense not to question her metrics too loudly, so I guess she got what she deserved.'

'A promotion – to your job? Did she push you out, Fowler?'

'I told you, I don't like S&P.'

Anna raised an eyebrow, but it was clear Fowler wasn't going to tell her any more. 'S&P's internal audit protocols posited that you were planting evidence to secure convictions,' she said. With the added information that he'd once been a police inspector, it hadn't taken long to track down Fowler's professional history on the boards. 'Patterns and statistics all pointing in one direction. No wonder you don't like them.'

'I never once set anyone up who wasn't guilty.'

She hadn't wanted to believe it when she'd first read it. Maybe he'd found himself caught in the same situation as her, and hadn't been able to escape the innuendo and the suspicion. But from his expression, Fowler didn't seem concerned by it at all.

'The leaflet in Beth's room,' Anna said, almost not wanting to enquire any further. 'The one that I found in that ornament… You were in the room first. Between the time it was swept by S&P's bots, and before I got there.'

'I was right,' Fowler said, his voice quiet. 'The note from the kidnappers proves I was right.'

Anna let out a slow breath, trying to push the anger out of her system. She turned her attention towards Cody. 'Are we ready?'

'Yeah,' he said. 'Just waiting for the hospital team to sync.'

'Okay.' Anna had decided not to mention the attempt to poach him. Cody probably already knew the request had been submitted. And if it didn't happen, he'd probably conclude she'd blocked it. That was a discussion that could wait. First, she had to confirm another point of contention. 'I'm going in alone,' she said, turning to Fowler. 'I'm not going to debate the issue.'

'Fine,' he replied, taking a moment to snort something back from his nose into his throat. 'Just so you know, though, I went out to the fields behind the Haydens' house early this morning. It was just as we saw it. Right down to that little collection of cigarette butts.'

Yes, that was the best they were going to get in terms of calibration, thought Anna. Not via checking aspects they already knew once they'd first entered the in-memory construct; rather, they were going to have to record what she was exposed to, and validate as much as they could after the fact. Not perfect. But at least it would confirm that they weren't just experiencing the dream sequence of a broken mind.

'I also brought the files you wanted,' Fowler continued.

'Couldn't email them because I shouldn't really have them. Didn't want to risk a trace.'

Anna hesitated, and glanced at Cody. Her technician looked like he wanted to voice a thought but was showing a bit too much deference. He'd probably been thinking about the issues they were facing too. And Fowler's site visit had brought them into clear focus. 'Thank you,' she said finally. 'But I've changed my mind.'

'What?'

'I don't want to read them,' Anna said. 'Or rather, I very much do, but I think it's best if I don't.'

'I thought you—'

'We have a major calibration problem here,' Anna explained. 'And separation is the only thing that will prove what we're seeing is real.'

'You think I'm going to feed you duff information?'

Anna let out a semi-laugh. After what he'd just admitted? How else would he now be trying to influence her? 'Possibly, probably. Either way, I don't want my thinking contaminated ahead of asking an AI for a conviction. I'll use the sequencer, and you can verify what I find in the real world.'

Fowler gave a grunt of acceptance. 'Well, the other thing I found is that there's a gap in the Amblinside security line. An old bridleway gate leading into the fields. Someone had forced it.'

'So N'Golo could have got into and out of the estate without passing the sentry station?'

'Yep. We already knew he pissed off to God knows where at night – now we know how.'

Behind them, a few things lit up on Cody's workstation.

'We're ready,' he said. 'I'm sorry, Fowler, but you can't be here when Anna is submerged.'

'Oh, come on!'

'Internal protocol dictated by Jake,' said Anna. 'Technicians are the only people allowed to be awake inside the chamber during submersion. Though I'm sure we can make an exception…'

'No,' Cody said firmly. 'No exceptions. I'm not losing my job over this, Anna. It's a core hub protocol.'

'Fine,' Fowler replied, not hiding the fact that he was pissed off. 'When you've finished, ping me. I'll be grabbing something to eat. Just don't forget this is attempt two: two of a possible seven.'

Once he had left, Anna opened her mouth to protest, but Cody cut her off. 'You're in charge, Anna,' he said. 'I get that. But this is still my synapse chamber. Think about all those cockpit rules. After a crash, you used to check each and every one of them had been followed, didn't you? And I expect that if you'd found anything amiss, you'd report it in your conclusions? I know Jake's checking my work, looking for mistakes.'

'Okay, I agree. This is your chamber.' Anna moved towards her synapse bench. 'What are we going to do about him?'

'Fowler?'

'Yes.'

'There's little we can do – we're his subcontractors. The client is his client.'

'He's going to fuck us over.'

'Not if we get to the truth first,' Cody replied.

Anna lay down on the bench, the coldness of the steel immediately easing through her clothes and into her shoulders. For no apparent reason, she thought about Kate. Sitting in her apartment, completely alone. 'With no other witnesses to monitor,' she said, 'hopefully you won't get too bored.'

'Nonsense,' Cody replied. 'I'll be too busy looking after you.'

AT FIRST, ANNA thought it was already over. N'Golo Durrant's brain must have been fried. The sudden snapping of the previous attempt to reach him had been too much for his comatose brain. She was conscious, yes, but not inside a memory. Around her was blackness. Before she could feel any sense of guilt, though, she noticed one little detail that reassured her.

Her feet were grounded. They were touching soft, wet earth which she could already feel soaking through her shoes and into her socks. Sure enough, as she squinted into the dark she could just about see the edges of the track again.

So where was N'Golo?

The ditch and the hedgerow were just as she'd left them. But the slight hollow where N'Golo Durrant had lain was now empty. The boundaries of the memory were almost impossible to sense, but the little pile of cigarettes was still there, albeit with fewer stubs than last time, as were the lights from the Haydens' house. The rooms on the ground floor were doused in darkness, leaving only two windows, both open, shining cleanly into the night.

Cody squeaked in her ear. '*How are things looking?*'

'Fine. Let's roll it.'

A soft breeze indicated the memory was now in motion.

Then a shape came out of the darkness. N'Golo entered the frame of his own memory.

'$V_1$,' she whispered.

There was also another man. He was waiting by the hedge, wearing a smart, long winter coat, and looking through a pair of binoculars across the field.

'You're late,' the man said.

'I'm here, ain't I?'

The man lowered his binoculars so he could examine N'Golo. He was of similar height and build to the one who had beaten N'Golo up during the first submersion, but the previous recollection had been so warped that she couldn't be sure it was the same person. This memory, however, was crisp. Anna noted the man's main features: clean-shaven face; light-blond hair, which was slicked back to reveal the start of a widow's peak; thin, bony nose and narrow lips. Yes, she'd recognise him again, if she ever met him.

'So, have you come to a decision?'

'I want to know more,' N'Golo said. 'I've got questions…'

'Sure,' the man said. 'I'd expect nothing less.'

N'Golo hesitated. If he'd had a mental list of queries, then the order in which to ask them now seemed to be causing him trouble.

'Don't believe what you read about us on the media streams,' the man said, filling the silence. 'That's the first thing you need to understand. They try to mock us with memes of Stalin, Lenin and Trotsky. Like everyone else, we're a generation or two away from having once worked in factories.'

'But… the *Workers' League*?'

'We're all workers,' the man replied. 'Maybe once there

were workers and managers, but now we're all ants living in the same hill. Worker ants without enough work. That's the main point, isn't it?' He tapped the side of his head. 'Up here, that is. We need tasks to fill our lives with meaning. We need to work, and we need to know we're not all the same. The Workers' League rejects the casual way in which the UI reduces us all to nothing more than mouths to feed. We don't feel it's enough to be bought off with simple offerings of bread and circuses.'

N'Golo glanced towards his latest family home. 'I'll only be there a few months before I'm moved on again.'

'And in a year's time? Where will you be then?'

Frustration and emotion boiled up in N'Golo's features. 'Probably in a dorm somewhere...'

'We had a hundred years of utopia,' the man said. 'And we didn't even know we were living through it. Decent living standards, pensions, accessible university and health care. But, most important, enough jobs to provide a gradual ascent from the lowest paid to the highest. But now there's a gap: a handful of well-paid jobs, and millions with no hope of reaching them.'

'Not me, anyway,' N'Golo whispered. 'I'm never gonna be able to reach that.'

'Henry Ford started it,' the man continued. 'He paid his workers double the normal wage and accidently created middle-income jobs. But he wasn't a socialist. Ford did it to counter the monotony of the conveyor belts and to keep productivity high. As soon as machines came in, the equation changed. Why employ people when machines are so cheap? Why offer high wages when you can simply bring in a bot? Why not send people to the scrap heap – you can simply tell them the lie that they have all the free time in the world—'

'I ain't human scrap,' N'Golo cut in.

'Then come and talk to us,' the man replied, the traces of a smile reaching his lips. 'Think about it, anyway. The invite remains open.'

'You really think you can change anything?'

The man let out a sigh. 'That's what you read every night, isn't it? On the boards? News stories telling you there's no choice but to accept the UI and be grateful for it.'

'I thought you'd be more shouty,' said N'Golo, his doubt tottering on the precipice. 'Your lot are always shouting on the boards. I thought you'd want to hurt people.'

'The government creates bogeymen so that people are grateful for what they have,' the man said. 'Really, N'Golo: you need to think. Things you see on the boards are specifically tailored to your circumstances. They know you're likely to be swayed by the Workers' League, so they paint us as thugs; they seek to make you scared of us, and of the consequences of joining us.'

'I don't know...'

'Then why don't you meet the rest of our group, and find out for yourself?'

# 20

**Top Stories:**

Further boost to economy as price of dysprosium
tumbles (*Read more*)

Median income inequality continues to fall (*Temporarily
unavailable, story undergoing factual review*)

Prime Minister promises review of protest rights,
following Battermont tragedy (*Read more*)

**Selected for You:**

Architect of S&P makes case for greater data sifting;
latest political assessment suggests unlikely to pass
through Parliament (*Read more*)

ANNA TENDED ONLY to relax when her pod slipped down into
the basement of her apartment complex. Still, she retained
the automatic reflex of glancing behind her, just to make sure
the garage shutters had slid back down, cutting her off from
the street outside.

Although there were fresh white markings for residents' cars,
only a few of the older inhabitants retained their own vehicles.

Perhaps they liked to maintain the illusion they were still in total control, and could ignore the fact that even the oldest car wouldn't allow its driver to park unassisted. Meanwhile, the basement still provided secure entry for the building's more cautious inhabitants. Anna waited for the door of her pod to release and then stepped out. As soon as she'd left it, the vehicle made its usual tight loop and then went back the way it came. Heading for the ramp, the shutters already starting to move upwards again on its approach.

All the little loops of tech worked seamlessly together: the pod knew the layout of the basement; the garage doors sensed the vehicle was on its way. The pod would already be receiving data from vehicles on the street so that it could adjust its speed to enter the traffic flow unimpeded, and meanwhile some entity was calculating who the next passenger would be, where they were going, which pod would be sent to collect them, which would be the most efficient route…

No one really knew how it all worked. A nest of old code and new. Anna had once investigated a few near-miss incidents involving passenger jets. Their avoidance systems had always ensured they didn't strike each other, but when she'd asked the systems engineer how it all worked, he'd just shrugged. *It does*, was all he'd say. *It does work*. And that was simple in comparison to self-drive pods, which tracked and sensed everything from normal cars to other pods to pedestrians and cyclists.

She'd walked a few paces towards the stairwell when a shifting pattern at the edge of the basement caused her to stop. A man she'd never seen before was leaning against the basement wall, watching her. He couldn't possibly be hiding: the light reflected off every inch of concrete in the underbelly of the building.

He nodded at her as she approached. 'Waiting for a delivery,' he said, giving an explanation she didn't really need.

She carried on towards the stairwell. Perhaps it wasn't that strange she'd never seen him before. She disappeared to work early most days, and was always picked up by pod.

But he was following her. Anna tensed but kept moving, listening to the footsteps getting closer. Reaching the stairwell, she pushed through the heavy swing doors. She pressed the button to call the elevator, then changed her mind. He wasn't far behind, and she didn't particularly want to be stuck in a small metal box with someone she didn't know. She hurried up three flights of stairs, then waited. She sure as hell didn't want to have to climb all the way to her floor.

Had the stairwell door just clattered shut below her?

Anna held her breath.

There was no sound from the stairwell, just the almost imperceptible whine from the elevator shaft. A few minutes later, a soft ping indicated it had arrived in the basement. And then up it went again. Past and above her. She let out a deep breath. Fucking idiot.

She stepped forward, looked over the rail and down. The man was looking up at her from the foot of the stairwell. He grinned, caught up in the joke. 'My name's Joe,' he called up. 'Level fifteen. Just moved in Tuesday. Say, do I know you? Your face looks familiar.'

She edged back, and started walking up.

KATE STOOD AT the door to their apartment. For a moment she blocked Anna's path, peering at her in search of explanation.

She'd probably sensed the panic in the stairwell. But Kate would also have known Anna was on her way: the pod would have been transmitting data to the apartment as soon as she'd set off from work.

'Well, you look like shit,' Kate said. 'Elevator's out of order? Or finally trying to do a bit of exercise?'

Anna raised an eyebrow. 'Pot and kettle?'

'I do my yoga every now and then.'

'Yeah, well – are you still taking those vitamin D supplements? That's all I really could do with knowing.'

'Such a control freak,' Kate said, stretching. 'I popped the pills just like you asked. And that's why I'm here, remember? So you don't have to worry about shit like that.' She remained in the doorway. 'So…?'

'There was just some guy,' Anna said.

'In the block?' Kate asked, unable to hide her surprise.

'In the basement. Claimed to be waiting for a delivery.'

'It's where people wait, Anna. I lumber down there Tuesdays and Fridays to get our groceries.'

'I know, but—'

'Wednesdays I'm there for the laundry van.'

'He said he was new.'

'New? Single?'

Anna let out an exasperated sigh and slipped past her spoof into the apartment. 'We're not having this conversation,' she said.

'Single new guy who can afford a pad in this place? We're *definitely* having a conversation about— Oh, you have a visitor, by the way.'

Anna froze. The bioresponse would be within her spoof's brain in moments.

'Relax,' Kate said as she pushed the door closed. 'He said he knows you. He's in the lounge. I made him some coffee, and was about to open some pretzels.'

'There's some strange man in the basement,' Anna repeated in a tight whisper, 'and you're now saying I have an unexpected visitor? Who you just let in?'

'He was cleared by the front desk.'

'But not by me.'

Kate shrugged. 'He had credentials.'

Which, as they both knew, could be spoofed. The lounge door was closed. The worst-case scenario was that the stranger in the basement was somehow linked to this unexpected caller.

'Get ready to make an emergency desk call.'

'Fuck, Anna. I mean… seriously? He was cleared on both biometric and facial ID. I told you, they've tightened up down there…'

'And the man in the basement?'

'Is obviously a resident. He couldn't be anything else. Especially not in the basement: there's behavioural cams down there. If he'd been loitering, waiting for you, they would have picked him up.'

Anna took a breath and marched into the lounge, ready to scream at the first sign of trouble. But there was no need. Fowler was sprawled on her sofa, picking his teeth. He raised an eyebrow.

'What did I do?' He spread his arms in mock surprise. 'You look like you want to punch me.'

Anna's entire body remained rigid, ready to lash out. She tried not to shake. 'Did you come alone?' she asked finally.

'Yeah.'

'Then who the hell was that man in the basement?'

Fowler didn't seem concerned when she explained. 'Huh,' he said. 'Well, for what it's worth, there are probably easier ways to kill you.'

'Is that supposed to make me feel better?'

'Not really.'

Anna clenched her fists, digging her nails into her palms. 'Why are you here?'

'Relax,' Fowler replied. 'I'm here because Weaver bundled me on my way, remember?'

'We called you; sent you a report.'

'Yeah, well. I also wanted to apologise. Explain things.'

Before he could do so, Kate appeared, armed with two cups of tea. She smiled cautiously and then handed one to each of them. 'Do you want me to stay?'

'No,' Anna replied, looking for somewhere to sit. Fowler had taken up her favourite spot, so she found herself another seat. 'Give us a few minutes, will you?'

Kate rolled her eyes, then headed back to the kitchen. *You can do better*, she mouthed.

Fowler waited until she'd left. 'Flatmate?'

'Yeah.' She hoped he hadn't picked up the slight tremor in her answer.

'I wouldn't have thought you needed one.' Fowler's eyes darted around the room. 'Jake pays for this place, does he?'

'Jake pays my salary, yes.'

'You know what I mean.'

'I'm still waiting for that apology.'

'I—' Fowler started, but then an alarm went off in his pocket. He scooped out his little comms device and started prodding at the screen.

'I'm glad our case has your full attention,' Anna said.

Fowler looked up at her as he finished tapping out a message. 'I ain't salaried, remember,' he said. 'Little bits and pieces like this mean I can afford a bit better than basic.'

*Shit.* 'I'm sorry.'

'No, I'm the one who should be apologising. You're right, I planted that leaflet in Beth's room. You said you'd found one when you were investigating that plaza shooting, and you got really interested when I told you about the one I found in N'Golo's room… well, I figured you'd bite if there was another one. And fuck it, I was right.'

'But you could have been wrong.'

'But I wasn't. And you get a sense of things, sometimes. You already know what I'm talking about, you said so yourself at Amblinside. Beth Hayden should have registered a nice S&P score and didn't. There's something about this case that's making my balls tingle.'

Anna looked to the doorway. 'Fine,' she said. 'You were right. Now I'd like to relax in my house and—'

'Mitchell.' Fowler didn't look like he was about to leave. 'What about her?'

'She didn't have authorisation to speak to you and Jake.'

Anna considered this. 'And you know that… how, exactly?'

'I still have a few old friends, keeping their heads down.'

'Okay. But I still don't get your point.'

'As I said to you back at the hub, Mitchell is a career-focused officer. She has the same doubts as me about S&P, but she swallows them down. Keeps crunching the numbers and following through on its instructions and commands.'

'And S&P didn't ask her to come see me and Jake?'

'No. It told her first to hammer facial recognition, social

media. Start pulling heart-strings on the media feeds. Then it said to find people in the vicinity who were showing signs of alienation. Anger. Resentment.'

'But how—'

'The daughter of a rich, white couple goes missing and S&P should have pushed it right to the top, and it didn't. We both thought it was odd, and now Mitchell seems to agree.'

'She won't admit that, though, will she?'

'Of course not.'

Anna took a sip of tea. She listened out for Kate, but her housemate was someplace else, being her ghost. 'Back when I was working in air investigation, I was told of this incident where a plane lost an engine. We thought it was a pretty straightforward maintenance screw up – or possibly undetected metal fatigue. Except the mechanics weren't at fault. What we found instead was that someone, somewhere, had been placing orders with a firm supplying cheap spares rather than the manufacturer's originals. The sizes of the engine fittings were fractionally out. The engine vibrated right off the frame.'

'I don't get your point.'

'One of three things normally causes a crash: people, environment or equipment. We only have access to the first two.'

'Huh,' Fowler said in response. 'Well, our priority is finding the girl. If S&P has screwed up, then it'll be sorted in the next update. That's where the "never will it happen again" part of the equation that you seem so interested in takes place. Statistically, anyway.'

In a way, Fowler was right. If she was going to use air crash analogies, then she had to accept that they were in the middle of it. Until they had Beth back, the plane was still going down. Still, at some point she was going to find out just exactly what made S&P tick. 'The family still haven't received any financial demands?'

'My gut is telling me they will,' Fowler said. 'Sooner or later. So how did it go today with Durrant?'

'As per our message, N'Golo was definitely meeting with the Workers' League. I saw the man he met clearly this time.'

'You'd recognise him again?'

'Definitely.'

'I'll call in some more favours, try to source some photos of people known to be in the League.'

'He seemed articulate.'

'You mean not one of the tub-thumpers?'

'No.'

'Then that might complicate things,' Fowler replied, understanding Anna's point. 'We'll have to hope he falls into one of the higher-risk categories that my buddies – and S&P – has access to.'

Anna thought about this. Protests had already started about giving S&P even more sweeping data rights. Most seemed to be against it, even though the Prime Minister, Erin Farlands, was very much in favour. Then again, every advance in AI was trumpeted by Farlands, and it didn't seem to be affecting her overall approval ratings. 'The man N'Golo met also sounded... I don't know – not exactly old left.'

'Huh – well, did they mention a spot where the local group meets?'

'No,' Anna said. 'I got bounced out again.'

'Same thing?'

'We're letting N'Golo's brain patterns calm. We should be able to try again tomorrow.'

'You're running out of chances. You need to get into his head and make it stick.'

'I know.'

Fowler pushed back into the sofa, leaning to one side slightly as he fumbled for something in his pocket. For a moment Anna thought he was going to start using his comms device again, but she was wrong. 'Weaver was pretty keen for me to leave, wasn't he?'

'He was following procedure: clearing the room ahead of submersion.'

'He's in a position of a lot of trust,' Fowler continued. 'I mean, looking after your body while your brain is elsewhere. Except with Durrant at the hospital, it's just you and him in there.'

'He's married, Mr Fowler.'

Fowler gave a bark of laughter. 'Have you forgotten what I do for a living?' He leant forward, palm open, to reveal a couple of spots of black plastic on a white disc. 'Here,' he said. 'Take them.'

Anna peered into his hand, not moving. 'What are they?'

'Cams,' the PI replied. He dropped the discs on the couch beside him when he realised Anna wasn't going to take his offering. 'He's alone with you, Anna.'

'I trust my technician.' Anna stood, indicating the door. Fowler didn't move.

'Makes me wonder why Jake doesn't replace him with a bot?'

Anna glared down at him. 'Do you ever listen to yourself? This whole project was Cody's idea, and he's good at his job.

Anyway, most of the hub tech is automated. The sequencer is pretty much all AI.'

'But not the guy who moves you around, and mops the floor?'

'There are stats,' Anna said, 'that prove humans don't work well alone. And Jake loves his performance statistics.'

'So the second he finds a way to automate *your* job, you're both fucked?'

Again, Anna pointed to the door. This time much more firmly. 'I think we're done?'

Fowler rose slowly to his feet. He left the discs on the sofa. 'One other thing,' he said. 'Whoever took Beth had clearly planned it. Which means they hired a spoof.'

'So?'

'So S&P has yet to trigger any search for localised anomalies across the biofeeds. Which would be normal. Mitchell queried it. Probably the thing that pushed her into coming to speak to you.'

'Okay.'

'Mitchell could, of course, have authorised an independent search. But she won't, because then she'd have to explain why she went against the S&P recommendation. Just so you know: I have something running in the background.'

*Fuck.* She couldn't control it. A surge of adrenaline and panic. It didn't take long for Kate to appear in the doorway. Fortunately, Fowler didn't ask why her flatmate had come back to the lounge.

'It's more important to me to get the girl than for your experiment to succeed,' Fowler said, turning to leave. 'Your clock is ticking.'

# 21

'BACK AGAIN.' SEAN flashed me a wide grin. However, his expression soon lost its humour. 'You okay?'

I nodded, still feeling sore. 'Fine.'

'I hope it's nothing that I've—'

'No,' I said firmly. I tried to ease myself up in the chair. Charley had reduced the bath temperature as soon as I'd passed out. My injuries were obvious, but she'd claimed the thermostat on the heater had been broken. It wasn't clear if Grace believed her or not, though nothing would likely happen. Not a day seemed to go by without one or other of the residents claiming the staff were mistreating them. Today, thankfully, it was Grace's turn to patrol the communal lounge. But the only occupants were us three – the other nearly-deads were all in their rooms. My nurse sat a polite distance away as we began to talk.

'So, we discussed the background to the Tanzania crash when we last met,' Sean said. I made a sound of acknowledgement from the back of my throat. I doubted I could delay him any longer by talking about the prizes buried in the volcanic uplands of northern Tanzania. Or how vital they'd become for the neural nets that had begun to run so much of the world back then. I felt my lower lip curl. Including Jake's precious sequencer.

'So when you arrived in Tanzania, people had confidence in you. They thought you would get to the bottom of what happened out there?'

'Out there,' I said, mimicking him. 'Africa, still the dark continent?'

The jibe seemed to shake some of the student's confidence. 'I'm sorry...'

'Don't be – it was just as hard hit by automation as the West. But in answer to your question: yes, the anti-war lot were pleased I'd been selected. So was the Tanzanian government. The only people who weren't were... well, the people I'm now supposed to have been in league with: the US and UK governments.'

Sean hesitated. He probably wanted to ask me then and there if I had been nobbled. Had the UK government instructed me to conclude the Tanzanian plane crash had been a deliberate act? Had I been told to find a pretext for war? Instead, his boldness deserted him. 'What were the main differences between Iceland and Tanzania?'

'One was hotter.' I kept my face serious for a few seconds, then laughed to release some of the tension. Somewhere in the background, Grace stood up, and then shuffled away. We'd only exchanged a few words since she'd left me in Charley's care. Perhaps she felt guilty. Somehow, though, the timing of what happened all seemed wrong. Like it had been set up. The emergency call had come at the very moment I'd been stranded in that damn chair.

'It's maybe better to start with the similarities,' I said. 'There was an immediate suspicion that both had been brought down by either bombs...'

I stopped. Grace had come back into view, and this time I waved at her. Mimed an action for a drink. In that moment of distraction, N'Golo Durrant had taken the opportunity to appear, kneeling beside my wheelchair. I recoiled from the unexpected intruder with a weird sense of betrayal. But then I felt foolish; an imaginary friend couldn't really have done anything to stop what had happened last night.

'Witnesses state they saw an explosion,' Sean said, trying to reclaim my attention.

'That's not uncommon,' I replied, snapping my attention back to him and trying to ignore the demon knelt beside me. He'd started his damn counting. Whispering the numbers. They always started the same way, but I soon lost the pattern. I let them drift over me, ignoring the chant as best as I could.

'Let's go back a step,' Sean said. 'The plane that crashed in Tanzania was quite old, wasn't it?'

'Twin engine turbo-prop,' I said. 'Propellers, yes. But a decent machine. Remember the adage "If it ain't broke, don't fix it." And they were a good fit with the environment. Only small numbers of passengers used the route, mainly mining execs and techs; short runways were required; easy maintenance; a wide pool of potential pilots.'

Sean scribbled a few notes. 'Surprising, though, that it was being used by the Americans…'

If I hadn't had such a good control over my expression, I might have allowed my eyes to narrow a fraction. Was he testing me still? 'That's because they didn't intend to,' I said. 'They had a more modern aircraft – twin engine – tail-mounted jet – all ready to go. Except there was a glitch with its landing system. Ground proximity alarm kept going off, with no way to disable it.'

'So everyone – the entire American negotiation team – were bundled on to the turbo-prop?'

'That's right.'

'I wonder why they didn't wait – I mean, for their own aircraft to get fixed?'

I sighed. 'The Americans were playing catch-up,' I said. 'They'd not given a shit about Africa for years, but the Chinese had been investing millions. And don't forget, the Tanzanian government understood this: they knew the US needed access to dysprosium, and that the Chinese wanted to keep their monopoly. After hundreds of years of being under the heel, Tanzania suddenly had the two largest superpowers dancing to their tune.'

'I still don't get why they wouldn't just wait for their own plane.'

'Yes, you do: it's in the records. The timing was good for the US because it was Chinese New Year. Everyone on the opposing negotiating team had downed tools. They had a few hours, and needed to make it count. And with one plane broken, and another fuelled and ready to go...'

'So there were two planes: one they were expected to use but couldn't, and a second that no one thought they would be using but which they ended up boarding.' He let his pen hover. 'You can see the issue, can't you?'

'Two things happen when everyone can see a war coming,' I said, speaking as slowly as I could. 'The first is that those who want a war agitate for it, and the second is that those who don't want one find reasons not to fight.'

Sean made a few more notes. I didn't try to read what he'd written. 'So the plane took off and crashed about half an hour into the flight?'

'Yes.'

'And it came down following an explosion.'

'No,' I said, turning my head slightly. N'Golo was still there, counting.

Sean made a noise. Some sort of confirmatory *hmmph*.

'My memory of Tanzania is clear,' I said, smiling. 'It's the rest of it that's patchy.'

'So what made you first think it could have been sabotage?'

'It's odd what the brain holds on to, and what it ignores,' I said to the rhythm of N'Golo's counting. 'I can remember, for instance, getting divorced – but not getting married. I can recall my child's first day of school, but not his birth. Almost as if I have all these little threads that don't quite belong to me.'

'Ms Glover?'

I squeezed my eyes shut. I could see one such thread now. Walking alone, and through a bridleway gate. Jogging along a country lane, and then out into the night. I knew it was something that had been recorded through N'Golo Durrant's eyes, and yet here it was playing through my own mind. 'I sometimes see him beating people,' I said. 'He'd disappear from the Haydens' and pick fights with people at random. He was a troubled kid.'

'Who?'

'N'Golo,' I said. 'I can still see him. Even after all these years, I can still see him.'

# 22

S&P Build 14.224a – Recommendation Module

Situation #GIHHCLTYYEN

Case Updates: Drill down into family data identifies (1) money (2) [Redacted, Authorisation: Deng] as main likely primary motives.

Recommendation: Biolog and board monitoring extended to all Debtors. Biolog and board monitoring extended to all local citizens registered for UI payments. Biolog and board monitoring approved under Delegated Approval Matrix. Request logged to extend biolog and board monitoring to all associates of Victim's father. Limited approval given under reasoning of likely motive. Authorisation: Deng.

'YOU'RE READY TO try again?'

Anna lifted herself on to the synapse bench. There was just the two of them in the synapse chamber. The surrounding equipment worked almost silently through its start-up procedures, only the barest hum giving away that any effort was involved in making N'Golo Durrant's memory a reality. 'Yes, let's get going.'

Cody's attention was on his terminal. Finalising the connection with the hospital, where N'Golo remained immobile and unconscious. 'This will be our third—'

'I know.' Her words were too sharp. Both she and Cody were in the same boat. If this didn't work, then the odds were growing that they'd both be out of a job.

'You heard from Fowler today?' Cody didn't look up from his workstation.

'No,' Anna said. 'Why?'

'I thought he'd be back. You know, trying to observe.'

'Have you made any progress with the memory mapping?'

Cody's shoulders spasmed in response to her query, and then he continued working. Like he'd missed a heartbeat. 'Maybe,' he said, finally turning in her direction. He swallowed a shallow yawn, which transformed seamlessly into one of his tuneless whistles. 'Look, we know your first submersion showed a memory from the date he was beaten, right? I'd hazard a guess – a guess, mind – that what you saw in your second submersion happened one to two weeks before he was attacked.'

'Based on?'

'It's my best estimate,' Cody replied, sounding more than a little peeved. 'Jake calls it mapping, but God didn't design the human brain with a satnav.'

'Okay, sorry.'

'No, it's all right.' Cody yawned again. 'I'm just a little tired… Look, together with the health team, we've mapped out a number of other dense neuron clusters. We think they're memory imprints, recent ones. The team at the hospital is going to stimulate one, and then we'll drop you in.'

A light on the panel behind him blinked. He tapped in

a few instructions. Taking her cue, Anna lay down on the bench and waited for Cody to check her position. She soon felt his fingers as they made a slight adjustment to her chin. Had they lingered a moment too long? None of this had ever bothered her before, but now she couldn't stop thinking about what Fowler had insinuated.

'Jake told me one of the other teams requested you on a transfer,' she blurted out, resisting the urge to swallow.

'They asked me over lunch in the canteen,' Cody said, moving his hand to her shoulder to check she was stable on the bench. 'I haven't applied for anything. But I think I'd accept, if—'

'I can't let you go, Cody.'

Cody's jaw tightened. 'I sort of figured as much,' he said.

'It would take too long to bring a new tech up to speed.'

'You wouldn't have been given a permanent replacement,' he said with a regretful smile. 'They would have just rotated someone in. Failure begets failure, Anna. Come back with something useful, eh?'

'LISTEN, YOU LITTLE shit, George saw you!'

*Freeze the memory,* thought Anna. 'We're in motion,' she called back to Cody. 'We're in motion!'

Cody's garbled response whined in her ear, but everything kept moving. N'Golo Durrant was the only one sitting at the Haydens' kitchen table. Roger Hayden towered over his fostered tax break. Millie stood to one side, clearly upset. There was no sign of Beth or her brother, George.

'George saw you take the money!'

N'Golo stared straight ahead. He was breathing hard

and his shoulders were hunched and rolled forwards. Anna noticed he was sitting with his legs to the side of his wooden chair, his feet pushed into the floor. If he decided to stand up, things would get ugly fast: under the glare of the kitchen light, he was about the same build as his new foster-father.

And yet she had to remember that this was an event that had already happened. Neither Roger Hayden nor his wife had mentioned a physical confrontation with the boy. One of them would have, surely? So the odds were that N'Golo would remain seated.

All she could do was watch.

'We're going to search your room. You know that, right?'

Neither of them moved, the tension palpable. Anna looked quickly around the kitchen. The detail of the room looked good, much of it just as she recalled from her brief visit. Which was promising: this memory came from before N'Golo had come across the man in the hedgerow. There'd been time for his brain to overwrite the finer details, as it sought to store what was important in the longer term. The only thing absent was the odour from the litter tray.

'That's it, then,' Roger continued. 'We'll go up to your room together, shall we?'

N'Golo sighed. 'What's missing?'

Roger snapped his attention to his wife, who looked back at him startled and confused, like a rabbit caught in headlights.

'Two aspirin,' N'Golo said, still not looking up. 'Two aspirin are missing.'

'You're saying you searched though my wife's handbag because you had a headache.'

'Yes.'

Roger Hayden didn't seem convinced. He waved his arms at Millie as if she was his audience. 'The first place you'd look, I suppose?'

'Women tend to have stuff like that in their bags,' N'Golo said, turning his head slightly towards his foster-mother. 'I checked the bathroom. That was the *first* place I looked, but I couldn't see any. The bag was in the lounge. I either had to search every cupboard in the house, or get some where I knew I'd find it.'

'So you weren't looking for cash, then?'

'Cash,' N'Golo said. 'As if you can remember what it even feels like.'

Silence. In the gap, Anna took a few steps forward, trying to get a sense of where the detail of the memory was being infilled. Hoping to see something she could use for calibration. At the table, the family had reached an impasse. N'Golo had put the ball squarely in Roger Hayden's court, but he didn't seem to know what to do with it. He looked at his wife, and backed slightly away from the table.

'In this household, if you want something, you ask. Got it?'

'Yep.' N'Golo pushed his chair back. Slowly got to his feet.

'Did I say you could leave?'

'I figured it was time for the search?'

'We don't have to do that,' Millie said, finally contributing something.

'It would make me feel better. There was all sorts of shit in that bag. Make-up, ID, tampons, an attack alarm… and aspirin. You name it, it was in there. So let's get it done. Search me.'

Anna came to a halt. There was a thin sliver of light coming from one of the kitchen work surfaces. She looked at it, and recognised it as part of the home environment system. She'd noticed it on her first visit. This time, though, the screen was blurred. Most of the information was illegible, forgotten, but the time remained clear: 2 p.m. – an exact, rounded time. That wasn't unusual: when asked what time something happened, most people gave a rough estimate rather than an exact time. Yet it was a memory, nonetheless, and it was something worth noting for later.

'Stop that, N'Golo.'

Anna turned back to the kitchen table. N'Golo's T-shirt was on the floor. He was in the process of unbuckling his thick leather belt. He dropped his trousers.

'Stop!'

N'Golo pushed down his underwear. Then his eyes locked on Anna. He was looking directly at her, even though he shouldn't have even been aware she was there. For a moment, Anna wondered if this was all part of the memory; whether after the big show of trying to embarrass his foster-carers, he hadn't been able to maintain eye contact with them and had simply glanced away. A coincidence, then, based upon where she'd chosen to stand, burned deep into the memory. Then he spoke.

'And you called the cops, too,' he said, still looking at her. 'Fucking great.'

ANNA OPENED HER eyes. Her body convulsed, and for a few seconds she couldn't stop it. She was back on the synapse bench. Her muscles were locked into the hardness of the steel, its penetrating cold. He'd seen her. He'd seen her, and he'd pushed her out. They'd failed again, and...

The gears in her brain slipped.

She tried to gasp, but couldn't.

She was on the bench. The burning brightness of the recessed strip lights above her took most of the room with them. And she had no sense of anything else. No feedback from the rest of her body. No numbness prior to the return of sensation. That unstated sense of knowing where everything should be had simply gone.

She had no fingers. No legs. No toes. No stomach.

Panic. Everything blanked. Perhaps a calmer person might have resisted the urge, but Anna wasn't able to turn down the noise of her own internal screaming – all of which was now backed up by the heavy drumbeat of her heart, which she could hear – but not feel – was racing.

'Anna?'

She wasn't cold either. There was no stomach pain. No nausea.

'Anna?' Cody said again.

Anna tried to focus on him but couldn't. He remained a blurred shape. She had no control. Not even over her vision.

'Anna? Blink if you can hear me…'

She didn't blink. Couldn't blink. There was someone else in the room. Some other face pushed Cody out of the way. From the shock of red hair, it had to be Jake's nurse. The vision in one eye went purple. Black. Then back to normal. Then the other eye did the same. Most likely, that had been a thumb pushing into the eye, probing for a reaction. And then she realised. For the moment, she'd been effectively reduced to just two eyes, floating in their sockets.

'What happened?' asked Holland.

'Pushback from the hospital feed,' Cody replied.

'The coma kid?'

'Yeah. She's not submerged, but she isn't with us, either.'

'Could be severance.'

*Severance?*

Anna tried to remember the calming exercises Elsy had taught her. The light shining down from the ceiling became stronger again. Both Cody and Jake's nurse had moved out of her view. They couldn't have gone too far. 'Heart rate looks fine. Cardiovascular looks fine. All biorhythms just as they should be...'

*Check,* Anna thought. *For fuck's sake, check!* She could still hear her heart beating faster and faster. All they needed to do was put a hand on her chest to see their readings were wrong.

'And how's the feed from the hospital now?'

'Durrant's stabilised,' said Cody. 'He didn't come out, and we don't want to detach him either. This is our third run; we don't know how many more times we can do this.'

Holland came back into view. She stooped down and came into clearer focus. Jake's nurse momentarily looked puzzled before grinning. She knew, she'd noticed.

'Then reset and give her another dose,' Holland called to Cody.

*What?*

'Push her under?' asked Cody. 'Are you sure?'

'The question is,' whispered Holland so that only Anna could hear her, 'would anyone care if something awful happened to you?'

*Bring me out! Bring me out!*

The nurse stepped away from the bed and out of Anna's sight line. 'Push her under, Mr Weaver. Push her under and hold her down.'

## 23

*HOLD HER DOWN.*

Anna was back in N'Golo Durrant's memories. She felt a mixture of emotions, then let herself crumple as each and every part of her body signalled to her brain that she was intact. In a dream, maybe, but intact all the same – would it be the same when she resurfaced, though, she wondered.

'Do I know you?'

The question surprised her, and stopped her dwelling on whatever was or wasn't happening back in the synapse chamber. And now she realised she wasn't standing in the Haydens' kitchen, either. Instead, she found herself in N'Golo's bedroom. The boy was sitting on the edge of his single bed, a few papers in his hand. But he seemed confused. He wasn't so much looking at her as around her. Like he had double vision.

N'Golo shook his head, perhaps trying to clear his senses. Then he moved quickly to stuff the papers under his pillow. The walls of the room shimmered. She was losing him. He could see her, and she was losing him. In the hospital, his brain would be screaming at the comatose boy. *There is something wrong*, it would be telling him. *This isn't how it happened! Who is she?*

'I'm your social worker,' Anna said. A snap reaction. Something she hoped he would hear, even though she didn't really know if he could fully see her, let alone understand what she was saying.

N'Golo hesitated. He had on the same clothes he'd been wearing downstairs, but it wasn't clear if what she was now seeing was something that had occurred after the confrontation with Roger Hayden or before the accusation of theft had been made. Anna glanced at the pillow. What were those papers? Something he'd taken from Millie Hayden's handbag? Or more propaganda from the Workers' League?

'What's up with Peter?'

*Peter?* Anna hadn't heard the name before. He must be N'Golo's usual social worker.

'You know how things are,' she said. It was a response she hoped would cover a variety of possibilities. All the while, her mind was racing. He could see her; she was talking to him. He could understand. How was that possible? The sequencer was meant to allow her to explore a memory, not interact with it. Not change it.

'He said he'd be there for me if I needed anything. Didn't say nothing 'bout nobody else.'

'He still will be.'

'So have we met before, then?'

Anna hesitated. 'No,' she said.

'You look… I don't know: like I know you?'

'Maybe you saw me when you met Peter?'

N'Golo looked at her thoughtfully. The blank bedroom walls rippled again. 'No,' he said, looking away and down at the floor. 'We ain't met.'

Anna waited. The memory seemed to be holding. But what

was he remembering exactly? Being alone in his bedroom? No. He was remembering those papers. Stuffed under his pillow. Something about them had stuck in his mind, and had become just as strongly imprinted as the confrontation downstairs. *But how to get to them?*

'How are you finding it here?' Anna asked. 'It seems a nice place.'

N'Golo shrugged, his limbs loose and unwieldy: a teenager indicating he didn't really want to talk. 'Decent house,' he said.

'And the Haydens? How are they?'

'The usual.'

'And what's "the usual"?'

'Mrs Hayden seems nice enough, but you'd expect that, wouldn't you? Daughter's okay looking; George is a dick. And Mr Hayden…'

'Yes?'

'Mr Hayden ain't as well off as he makes out, and, yeah, I suppose that fucks me off a bit.' Anna tried to follow N'Golo's logic, but couldn't. 'The tax break for fostering ain't that big,' he explained. 'Would you trade some of what you made to take a kid into a spare room? Someone like me?'

In a way she already had. Kate sat at home, filling time by listening to music as she spoofed Anna's biorhythms. But the way N'Golo had spoken to her caused her to remain silent. This wasn't some tuneless conversation. He was responding to her in a way that was beyond the bounds of his memory.

'Banks are being fucked up by robots just as much as other jobs now,' N'Golo continued. 'Why employ some jumped-up prick from Oxford, when you could code something that makes fewer mistakes?'

'I don't really know what Mr Hayden does for a living.'

The walls rippled again. Larger this time. 'You didn't read my file?'

'Yes.'

'No, no you didn't. Too many kids like me, and not enough time.' N'Golo paused. 'So tell me why're you here again?'

*To watch you,* Anna thought. *To see if I can figure out if you know who took Beth. To save my project with Jake.* 'Routine visit,' she said. 'I needed to put a tick in a box.'

Her answer prompted a small burst of laughter. 'Better being honest, isn't it? So are you sure we ain't met? I don't know, but you look familiar?'

'We haven't met, N'Golo.'

'Well you can put in your report that I'm here. Causing no trouble.'

'And what...' Anna trailed off, wondering how far she could push it. But she knew she didn't have much choice. The opportunity had presented itself, and she needed to take it. 'And Beth Hayden... can we talk about her for a moment?'

'Why?'

The walls of the room shook. N'Golo snapped his attention away from her. There were heavy footsteps heading towards his room. The door flew open, and Roger Hayden stepped inside, looking furious.

'Downstairs! Now!'


*PUSH HER UNDER. Hold her down.*

Anna gasped. Turned. Her throat contracted and her stomach roiled. Then she slumped, and felt Cody check her mouth and straighten her body.

She couldn't move. Again, her heart was hammering, but

this time she could at least feel it. She could sense the position of each of her limbs. Could already move her eyes and her eyelids. Felt them flooding with water as the tears came.

'Hey,' Cody said. 'Easy…'

She tried to say something but neither her jaw nor tongue seemed ready to obey her commands. She just heard some God-awful sound.

'Easy,' Cody repeated. 'Jesus! Did you find something in there? You found something, didn't you?'

Above her, he had broken into a big grin. But she hadn't, of course. Her enquiry about Beth had come too late, and those papers stuffed under the boy's pillow hadn't been in N'Golo's room when they'd searched it. Whatever and wherever they were would remain a mystery. And yet it did suggest he had taken something more than aspirin from Millie Hayden's handbag, which meant his stripping naked could now only be interpreted as a grand show to stop his foster-parents checking his room. The question was, whatever he'd taken, was it related to Beth?

She had to admit it was unlikely. The sharpness of the memory was probably due to what had happened next, in the kitchen. On her face, the emotions running through her would have barely registered an impression. Not for another few seconds at least. When she was able to speak, she'd have to let Cody down gently. He was still grinning, pumping his fist as he moved away. His first duty – making sure she wasn't going to choke – had been performed. Next on the action list would be to check the other witnesses. Which, in this case, meant communicating with the hospital. 'We're good,' he called out. 'Durrant bumped out, but his readings look fine. Hell, yeah!'

# 24

SEAN WAS STILL there.

I opened my eyes, and he was still there. I turned, startled, and found Grace looking at me – inches from my face, her hand resting gently on my shoulder. I shrugged it off, not appreciating the physical contact, and shrank into my chair. Hoping it would swallow me up.

'I'm fine,' I said.

'You were talking about N'Golo Durrant.'

'I'm fine,' I repeated. N'Golo was gone. For how long he'd leave me alone, though, I couldn't be sure. 'I'm fine, thank you.'

'I think you'd better start this again tomorrow,' Grace said.

'No,' I said, trying to be firm but failing. 'I'm fine. I'm enjoying it.'

The stand-off that followed lasted a few seconds, but a sudden flashing light on her belt caused Grace to retreat all the way out of the conservatory. For a moment I wondered if Charley would come and replace her, but she didn't, and I found myself completely alone with Sean. 'Are you okay?' he asked.

'On first arriving at a crash site,' I said, not answering his question, 'the first thing you do is try to locate the four compass points of the plane. Nose, tail, and the two wings.'

'You don't check for survivors?'

'No. Ambulance and fire teams do that. We just need to know if anyone survived so we can interview them later.'

'But they were all dead, in Tanzania?'

'The plane came down all the way from its cruising height,' I said, reminding him. 'The entire American negotiation team perished. No survivors. Little in the way of bodies, actually.'

Sean checked over his shoulder. There was no sign of Grace. I squinted in the direction he'd been looking but gave up. I couldn't really see the doorway from the conservatory through to the main body of the nursing home; it all blurred into the myopic.

'You can tell a lot about how a plane has been brought down by the pattern of the wreckage,' I continued. 'A single bomb will tend to scatter it over a large area, whereas a plane going down in one piece tends to make a more compact crash site.'

'And what did you find in Tanzania?'

'Pretty much all of the plane had come down in a small area. Nose first, wing tips where they should be... no problem finding the two black boxes.'

'But...?'

'The tail was missing.' I laughed. 'We found bits of it over a day later using drones.'

'What's so funny?'

'Drones were still a bit of a gimmick back then. But the one we had was fitted with software to help look for bits of aircraft. We would never have found the damn thing without it. Even when I was stood a few feet away, I didn't really see it.'

'So whatever happened, it affected the tail.'

'The tail came off the plane, which meant the pilot had no control. As soon as it detached, a crash became inevitable. Not even an automated system could have averted it for that type of plane. Game over.'

Sean made some more notes. 'And what did the black boxes tell you?'

I zoned out a little. 'The same. Flight data showed everything was normal, then there was a rapid descent. Almost vertical. From the voice recorder we heard a loud bang followed by lots of confusion and panic. And in between...'

I stopped talking.

'Are you okay?'

No, I wasn't. Grace hadn't come back yet. I needed a drink. Sean sensed it, but he had nothing to offer me. 'And in between?' he asked.

'There's a point,' I said, 'where you know you're beaten and you can't do anything to stop it. No decision you can take will affect the outcome. It was clear on the voice recorder: the bang, the confusion. And the few seconds in between where the pilots realised they were going to die. I can't think of anything more dreadful, can you?'

# 25

**Top News:**
Official Report: lack of work not causing increase in
    suicide rate (*Read more*)
Record tech firm profits invested in social programmes
    (*Read more*)
Research proves bots make better decisions than
    politicians (*Read more*)


**Selected for You:**
Glad to be alive: My employer spotted cancer in my
    biometric data! (*Read more*)


A WOMAN SHE had never seen before was standing at the
Amblinside sentry station. Anna hung back by the pod she'd
arrived in, waiting to see how the estate's security would
react. It was clear the woman didn't belong in such a wealthy
environment. Her hair was long and tangled, and the
thickness of her clothing indicated a life outside the dorms
that were meant to represent the last safety net of the UI.

Sure enough, it didn't take long before a drone appeared

above the gate, hovering low. The woman swore when she saw it and threw something at it, trying to knock the device out of the sky. The drone caught the object neatly and moved out of reach. The effort seemed to have drained the woman. She gave a last fist-shake to the sentry station before stumbling away.

'*Please make payment, and step away from the pod.*'

The electronic warble caused Anna to flinch. The woman who'd been by the sentry station was heading in the opposite direction, and probably wouldn't come back, but as soon as Anna followed the pod's instructions, her vehicle would pull away and leave her exposed. So she waited until the woman started to disappear into the middle distance.

'*Thank you, and please have a good day.*'

Anna hurried towards the gate. She was still feeling uneasy about her last submersion. Despite giving herself more time than normal to recover – making sure she could sense every muscle and position of her body – she couldn't help but think about N'Golo. He'd seen her and she'd spoken with him. And that was something she'd always been told wasn't possible.

'I'm here to see the Haydens,' she said, directing her words towards a square steel plate. Inside, protected by Plexiglas, a semi-humanoid bot twisted a faceless head towards her. Amusingly, it was wearing a blue and gold baseball cap bearing the name AMBLINSIDE, which had almost slid off the chrome surface of its skull. 'My name is Anna Glover.'

There had been no reason to give her name. The bot would have already tagged her facial features and found a match. Above her, the drone came in close. It disappeared through a hole in the sentry station's roof before zipping back into the air and heading off into the Amblinside estate. Only when it left did a small section of the security gate click open, allowing Anna to follow it. 'Proceed.'

Fowler was heading towards her on the other side. 'There's still no news,' he said. 'And I don't really get why you've come out here.'

'We're waiting for N'Golo's brain patterns to stabilise,' Anna replied.

'Yeah, well the agreement was that you were to work the sequencer, and I then check matters after the fact.'

'And have you spoken with the Haydens?'

'The confrontation with Durrant happened almost the way you described it,' Fowler said, starting to head back towards the Hayden house. No doubt they'd be drawing attention from the neighbours, but everyone around here must have heard by now what had happened, and their appearance would be becoming familiar. 'One or two things were different, of course: Roger Hayden made it sound a lot less heated.'

'Which you'd expect.'

'Yeah. So I think between that and the hedge, we're getting a good enough match.'

'I still want to have another look at the kitchen.'

Fowler didn't object, and led the way. The front door was on the latch. Inside, the kitchen was deserted except for the little cat, which had curled itself into a tight ball on top of the oak table. Anna grinned to see the animal apparently so undisturbed by what was going on around it. She looked around for the electronic clock from N'Golo's memory.

'I asked Hayden what time he confronted N'Golo,' Fowler said, noticing where her attention had been drawn. 'It was pretty close to the time you gave.'

'What did he say exactly?'

'Mid-afternoon.'

Which was all they were likely to get, Anna supposed. But at the least it was something. And everything else here was the same as what she'd seen from inside N'Golo's mind – the same as her first brief visit, when most of her attention had been focused on Roger and Millie rather than on the detail of the kitchen. So although they were working with N'Golo as a solitary witness, it did appear that what they were getting at least approached the truth.

'And where is Roger Hayden?'

'He's gone to work.'

'Really? With his daughter missing?'

'He's doing half-days to stretch out his compassionate entitlement,' Fowler replied. 'The mother's upstairs. Not sure how pleased she'll be to see you.' He issued a burst of breath through his teeth. 'So what time are you going to be able to wire up N'Golo again?'

'Cody said a few more hours.' She started heading towards the stairs, hoping to have another look at Beth's room, when the look on Fowler's face caused her to hesitate. 'What is it?'

'The front door was open,' he said, looking back towards it.

'Hadn't you left it that way?'

'No. It was locked when I went to the sentry gate to meet you.'

Fowler was already walking back to the front door. He returned a few moments later carrying a cream-coloured padded envelope. 'Left in the drop-box,' he said.

From where she was standing, Anna could see the envelope wasn't addressed. Fowler immediately started to open it, scratching to find an edge on which to pull. From inside, he tugged out a used tissue. It was bunched up, slightly wet. Wrapping something.

Despite her years in the field, Anna winced. 'Oh my God…'

'I thought you would have had a stronger constitution,' Fowler said, his voice grim. He held the tissue up. The dampness it contained was slightly pink. 'You must've seen some pretty horrific things in your time.'

Yes, she'd seen more than her fair share of mangled bodies. A fall from forty thousand feet did awful things to a human body. 'I'm not in the mood to share stories.'

'Fine. So what do you make of this?'

At the centre of the tissue was something metallic. Almost like a tooth filling, except a whole lot smaller and with three fine filaments wrapped and tangled around it. Perhaps if they'd had the time, they would have found the filaments extended half a metre or so: the distance from the wrist to the base of the neck.

'Someone's cut this out,' Fowler said, although that much was obvious.

What was sitting in the depths of his tissue was a microchip that should have been embedded inside someone's arm. Anna peered at it. She couldn't tell how modern the device was; to her they all looked pretty much the same. But she knew that now this device had been removed, the owner had lost their ability to connect to the boards, make payments and communicate with the grid. All life-logging capabilities had probably been severed too. 'Please tell me this is one of your props…'

'No, this is all too real.'

'Beth Hayden's?'

'It must have activated the door when it was delivered.'

Anna was already out of the door, running hard. She'd seen the whole thing. The woman at the sentry gate hadn't been trying to knock the drone out of the sky – she'd been passing it an envelope, shouting instructions rather than curses, and the drone had delivered it here. She hadn't been walking fast. They might still have time to catch her.

# 26

S&P Build 14.226a – Recommendation Module
Situation #GIHHCLTYYEN
Case Updates: Evidence of Physical Injury to Victim. No
financial demand received.
Recommendation: Drones and hunter bots dispatched.
Extension of biolog and board monitoring to social
classes 1–3 requested. Extension denied by Deng under
Approval Matrix.

'YOU OKAY?'

'Sure,' Anna replied, sitting across from Fowler in the
Haydens' kitchen. 'Why wouldn't I be?'

'You just look a little… I don't know…'

Anna screamed silently with frustration. She hadn't found
the woman who'd delivered the package. Maybe she'd been
picked up and whisked away by her friends in the Workers'
League, but a speedy escape hadn't really been necessary.
Anna's dash from the Hayden household had unintentionally
provided the woman with more than enough time to get away.
The estate's behavioural cams had triggered a security alert – a
visitor running from an Amblinside house registering on its

systems as a suspicious act. Which meant the security gates had been locked down tight, and Anna had been unable to pursue.

Fowler reached into his pocket, his little comms device already lit up and buzzing. 'Roger Hayden is on his way home,' he said.

A few twinges erupted from Anna's forearms, but she resisted the temptation to scratch. The police visit had been swift, with a drone coming to bag the implant and its envelope as evidence. Data from the security station was also already likely to have been transmitted to S&P. Beth Hayden's case notes would have been updated; her score adjusted. What that meant in terms of how many resources were being assigned was anyone's guess.

'Huh – Mitchell's pinged me too,' Fowler continued.

'And…?'

'That woman you saw at the gates has been arrested. She was IDed via face rec.'

Anna shifted in the wooden dining chair. 'Just some homeless girl, then? Like with the note?'

'Paid off with a few supplementary food tokens, probably,' Fowler confirmed, as he continued to read. 'She'll be followed for a few days, of course. Huh. Geotagging, biome checks – none of it has identified who she met with. Whoever is behind this is smart.'

'They know how S&P works?'

'Forget S&P – they know how digital and biological forensics work.'

'That means S&P tactics aren't likely to catch them.'

'Agreed.'

'And the implant chip? Anything from that?'

'Just that it belongs to Beth Hayden.'

'No DNA?'

'Too much DNA,' Fowler replied, grimacing. 'It's been peppered. Like I said, these people know their stuff.'

Anna frowned, not trying to hide her confusion. 'Peppered?'

'Sprayed with lots of different DNA samples,' Fowler explained. 'From a pressurised can. If you've visited a cheap hairdresser in the last few months, you might find a bit of yourself in there too. Or at least something made in a lab with the same genetic code.'

'Great.'

'Well, what do you expect? It's just like spoofs. And fake vehicle plates before that, I suppose. Always a way round. It's one of the reasons why there's all this pressure at the moment for S&P to be able to push down into more and more people's private data, not just those classified as high risk.'

With her own forearms itching, Anna thought again about the chip, its tendrils. The chips were designed to rest in a natural gap in the wrist, the wires able to slide through muscle and tendon for easy replacement. But it would have hurt to remove it. Without a medical facility, and some half-decent anaesthetic, it would have hurt a great deal. Fowler must have been thinking the same thing.

'We need to make some progress,' he said. 'We're running out of time.'

'I know.' *There's a girl in danger, for Christ's sake.* 'If you prefer, I could just blunder around in N'Golo's memories and terminate our only lead?'

Fowler grunted something.

'Did you bring the photofits of the Workers' League people?'

'They should be in your inbox.'

Anna connected to the boards. Sure enough, a file was waiting for her. She opened it and started to wade through.

'Well? See anyone you know?'

She remained silent, trying to ignore the pressure. The file contained relatively few faces, most of which didn't appear anything like the man she'd seen. No, these were stereotypical images of Workers' League members: working-class men shouting about the loss of jobs and dignity while promoting fantasies from a bygone century. They were nothing like the man she'd seen with N'Golo. 'Where did you get these from?'

'I told you, I still have contacts in the department.'

'And these are the only photofits you have?'

'They've all been positively linked: either they've been at demonstrations, or they've viewed sites that disseminate Workers' League material.'

'Then I have further bad news,' Anna replied. 'He's not here.'

ANNA LOOKED OUT of Beth's bedroom window. Downstairs, Roger Hayden was taking out his anger on Fowler. No doubt once he'd got over the shock, he'd want to know what she and Fowler had managed to find from the sequencer. But that could wait.

Anna's gaze was being drawn again to the hedge line where N'Golo had met the man from the Workers' League. It was clear what had attracted the boy to the movement, of course. When you have no hope, the person offering the merest glimmer has the most persuasive voice. She remembered that as they'd stood down there chatting, the light from this window had shone like a beacon. Anna ran a hand along the windowsill, noticing the floral curtains were tied back by simple loops of matching fabric.

An incoming message from Cody distracted her attention. She was needed back at the hub. N'Golo was starting to look like he was nearly ready for another submersion. The news would, she hoped, be enough to get her quickly past Roger Hayden before he could turn his vitriol on her, but as she turned to leave she found Millie Hayden watching her from the bedroom doorway.

'My daughter likes standing at that window,' she said. 'Looking at the woods. It's her favourite view.'

Anna felt something cold clamp across her stomach. She hadn't been here to witness Millie's reaction to the contents of the package – she'd been stuck at the Amblinside security post, trying to explain why she'd been leaving in such a hurry – but Fowler had told her he'd been forced to give Beth's mother a sedative simply to stop her from taking the evidence. The drug didn't appear to have totally worn off. Just like on Anna's first visit, Millie's words appeared detached, her expression almost vacant.

'She's good at languages.' Millie started to cry. 'She would have made a good translator, if they'd been needed any more. They used to say that AI would destroy the monopoly on knowledge, and bring everyone closer together. We were all sold a lie, weren't we?'

Anna opened and closed her mouth a few times, flapping to find what to say. 'We're making progress,' she said finally. Even to her ears, it sounded false. But at least it was a distraction from the swearing that continued to punch up from the kitchen below. Millie listened to her husband's anger for a few moments.

'You know what happened?' Millie asked. 'What was brought to our house today?'

'Yes.'

'And what do you know about them?'

'The Workers' League?'

'Yes.'

Anna hesitated. 'I think it's more complicated than what we read on the boards.'

Millie made a little squeak. 'They're cutting my baby.'

*Baby.* A girl of fifteen, but still very much her mother's youngest child. Anna wiped a little moisture from her eyes, not knowing what to say but feeling it all the same.

'I can't help but think it's my fault.'

'The only people to blame are the ones who took your daughter,' Anna replied.

'And N'Golo? Is he to blame too?'

Anna swallowed, unsure. 'We don't know enough yet.'

'She took him to her little group to talk about politics,' Millie continued. 'It irritated my husband, but I teased him about it. Back when we were dating, I used to tell him that the AI would come for his profession, just like it came for mine.' There was sudden amusement in her eyes, but it quickly died. The ginger cat had appeared beside her, another exile from the argument downstairs. It arched its back and rubbed itself against her leg. 'N'Golo was always going to be more of a labourer, of course, but bots won that battle many years ago. It's people with skills to sell who now find themselves fighting.'

Anna didn't want to interrupt Millie – it felt insensitive to brush her off. But she couldn't help but wish the woman would leave so she could get back to the hub and start prepping for another submersion. That was the only way they were going to find Beth.

'The police keep talking to us about probabilities,' Millie said. 'And likely outcomes. They don't understand that my girl's in danger. She's just an input to them. A number…'

'Everyone's determined to find your daughter, Mrs Hayden.'

'They gave me a contact to call, if I needed to speak with someone. Only after a couple of hours did I realise I was speaking to a chatbot. Daughter gone, and they give me an AI for support.' She gave a cruel bark of laughter. 'And to you, she's just an experiment, isn't she? Fowler told us that your project is a trial. Something that you're looking to sell to people like him and the police?' Millie waited for an answer. None came. 'You're not denying it?'

'I'm doing my best to find Beth.'

'They won't tell me what's happening to her.'

Anna swallowed hard. She could guess. Cutting her arm would just be the start.

'Roger won't share what the police are telling him, either,' Millie said. Downstairs, Roger Hayden was now demanding to know what Fowler was doing for his money, and what they'd found using the sequencer. Fowler's answers weren't audible. 'At first he said she'd be back tomorrow,' Millie went on. 'Then he said we'd get a demand for money, and he'd arrange for it to be paid. Now…?'

'He's maybe protecting you.'

'From knowing what's happening to my girl? I already know what's happening. They're mutilating her!' Millie put a hand to her mouth and stumbled away, still crying.

Anna suddenly felt dizzy. She dropped her head into the

gap between her knees and waited for the blood to return to her brain. As she'd told Fowler, she'd seen worse than what they'd found in that stained, pink tissue. She'd walked into the midst of aeroplane crashes and seen the tiniest fragments of what had once been human life. And yet nothing was quite as horrible as what she'd seen today, because the person who it had been taken from was still alive.

All they had to do was find her.

# 27

I WAS SITTING in my room when he came to me next. Sitting, and waiting to die.

It hadn't taken long after arriving at the nursing home to realise that's what I was actually doing here. They'd made a good show of moving me in: letting me choose from a handful of vacant rooms, and then allowing me to populate it with some of my most personal possessions. My former home, an apartment just north of the city, had gotten too big anyway. But it was odd how all the clutter I'd owned could simply be shaken away, just as soon as someone looked me in the eye and asked what was most important to me.

What would I want to be looking at when my eyes started to close?

'Are you going to start counting again?' I asked.

N'Golo stayed mute. He was in the corner of my room at the very edge of my vision, just ahead of where everything turned into a grey blur.

'If you're waiting for an apology,' I said, 'you're not going to get it.'

N'Golo said nothing. He just stood there. Watching me.

'You were already in a coma,' I said, repeating the little

whisper of justification I often heard myself saying. 'We had to try to save Beth.'

*We had to save the project. We had to save our jobs.*

N'Golo didn't flicker. He remained standing like a statue, his expression grim. I tried not to look at him, my attention instead on the sound of a clock ticking somewhere in the room. And then I heard him. Not counting, I realised. Not counting at all. Just repeating the same old stream of numbers. I tried to keep track of them, even as they became faster.

The door to my room opened. Grace entered, smiling, before she realised something was the matter and rushed to me. 'What is it?'

'Nothing.'

'You're sure?'

N'Golo had vanished, back into the deeper recesses of my mind. 'I'd like to be taken down to the conservatory,' I said. 'Sean will be here soon.'

Grace tipped her head to one side as she contemplated me. 'You don't have to do this, you know. We can all see it's a strain.'

'I'm ready, though,' I said. 'And I've got nowhere left to go.'

It took about ten minutes to wheel me from my room to the conservatory. Grace could have walked it in two. We passed a few other residents gamely making their own way using a variety of sticks and supports. We always gave them priority, Grace manoeuvring the chair through the corridors to give them the widest possible path lest she cause them to topple. Each time, I crossed my fingers that there'd be no incidents. I didn't want Grace to leave me in the corridor, safe in my chair, while she dealt with another of the nearly-deads.

As we entered the conservatory, Sean waved at me. Then he waited as I was positioned in front of him. I saw once again that he'd not been given anything to drink.

'Two cups of tea,' I said to Grace.

'I'm fine,' he said.

'You could do with it.'

'Now, Anna,' Grace admonished as she walked away.

*Beaten this time,* I thought. But my game seemed a bit hollow. There was something wrong with Sean, and it wasn't just the awkward silence of having to deal with an unpredictable and cranky interviewee. 'You seem a little tense.'

'I—' He flushed. 'I had an argument with my girlfriend.'

'Was it your fault?'

'Six of one, half a dozen of the other.'

'Then apologise,' I said, 'and move on.'

'Just like that?'

I shrugged. In the back of my mind I had a glimpse of something – a sudden feeling of déjà vu. Some nagging sense of doubt. Had I offered this advice to someone before?

'When we last met,' Sean said, reading from his pad, 'you told me the tail of the turbo-prop had detached, causing the crash. Can you tell me a little bit about what you found?'

I knew where today's session would likely go, and had fully prepared for it. 'We knew from the black boxes that the crash wasn't caused by pilot error. Weather conditions were good, and wouldn't have affected the tail like that anyway. And that leaves the equipment and how it was maintained.'

Grace returned with a single cup of tea, pleasingly provided with a good dose of milk. I sipped it, and waited for her to leave us again.

'We examined the tail very carefully,' I said. 'The bolt casings were all ripped. Shattered.'

'Could it have been metal fatigue?'

'No. That looks very different.'

'In your report you stated the tail fell off because of an explosion. But the labs couldn't find any trace of explosive residue.'

'Modern explosives burn fully,' I replied. 'That's in my report too. Gone were the days when you could detect an explosion from the pattern of ripped fuselage and traces of Semtex. Unless they were stupid enough to use it, anyway. No, this was probably painted along the connecting surface and triggered with a microdot.'

'Did you find the microdot?'

'Of course not.'

Sean looked at me for a long time. He made a few notes. 'What was the explosive?'

'A form of thermite.'

'How did you come to that conclusion?'

'It seemed logical.'

'*If* there was an explosive, yes. But if there *wasn't*?'

Hands trembling, I fumbled for my tea. 'The decision to switch planes caused about thirty minutes' delay,' I said. 'We know which maintenance team worked on the aircraft. We did background checks on them all: one had a connections to a Chinese mining firm – she'd bought a lot of stock options.'

'Lots of people had similar options. It's how companies like that buy control.'

'But not everyone's partner has access to the same explosives required to take down the plane.' I could see Sean about to interrupt again, so I stopped him. 'Don't forget, whichever plane was used would have had a final check. The maintenance team would have flown their drones over whichever one was about to take off. The fact they changed planes is coincidental.'

'It certainly seems more than coincidental to a lot of people.'

'Everyone became an expert when it hit the headlines.'

Sean didn't see the joke, and scribbled a few more notes. While he did so, I looked for N'Golo but couldn't find him. Charley had entered the conservatory. She was pushing another nearly-dead in a chair, but she still found time to smirk at me.

'You authored the report yourself?'

'Yes.'

'And how many were on the investigation team?'

'About three of—'

'Is that all?'

'AIs were already doing a lot of the lab work by then.'

'And you were working over a period of how long?'

'Two weeks on the ground.'

Sean seemed to accept this. 'And during all that time, the US were baying for war?'

'Yes – some calmer heads were saying things should still be talked through. But then a document got leaked that said the Tanzanian government would prefer a Chinese deal, and that it would be better if the western powers were kept out of Africa. A stupid paper, written by a small department. It was enough for the US government to prove the public case, that their negotiators had been murdered.'

'Were you in contact with any government officials during the time? Either from the UK or the States?'

'No.'

'And who was Gordon Hawley?'

I thought for a second I'd misheard. I closed my eyes, and sensed some of the room spin away. He'd distracted me with a series of jabs, then performed the perfect upper cut.

'Ms Glover?'

I forced my attention back to Sean. Charley passed behind him and gave me another wicked grin. And N'Golo snapped into existence beside me too, smiling, enjoying my moment of torture.

'Ms Glover,' repeated Sean, 'who was Gordon Hawley?'

'He wasn't involved in Tanzania,' I said. Even to my ears, it sounded weak. But it was my last possible line of defence. One that would be easily breached.

'No, he wasn't,' Sean replied. 'But he was in Iceland, wasn't he?'

# 20

**Top News:**

Workers' League burn down automated factory causing dozens to lose office jobs (*Read more*)

No more Old Tie Network: Audit of University Algorithm confirms unbiased selection (*Read more*)

Who's up for the Cup? United versus City! Big match build-up (*Read more*)

**Selected for You:**

From doctor to successful artist: How one woman started anew following the introduction of Automated Health Assessments (*Read more*)

'JUST SO YOU know,' Cody said, sounding uncertain, 'we're getting some funny readings from Durrant. Health team contacted me about it.'

'We can't afford to stop now, Cody. Not after what was sent to the Haydens.'

Anna adjusted her muslin overalls, pulled herself up on the synapse bench, and then waited for Cody to conduct his checks. But in that small amount of time a nagging doubt began to gnaw at her. *Funny readings.* They'd managed three submersions. Was that all they were going to get?

'Is he okay?'

'We think so. Just need to tread carefully, that's all.' Cody grinned down at her. 'Sweet dreams…'


'HEY… DO I know you?'

Anna was sitting alone at a small, round-topped table, one of several in a nightclub. The decor was silver-effect chrome and black plastic. The drinks counter was brightly lit, which made the rest of the place appear slightly shrouded.

There was no mistaking N'Golo Durrant, though – he was about to walk past her. He broke his stride when he saw her, puzzled. No doubt, back in his hospital bed, his brain had stumbled in the same way over her presence, trying to make sense of why the unknown woman had stolen into his memory again. His gaze moved away from Anna's face, towards her chest.

Instinctively, she looked down. Her clothes were pretty much those she was actually wearing in the synapse chamber – a smart pair of trousers and a long-sleeved blouse – minus the disposable fabric overalls. Durrant must be seeing something else. He stared long enough to make her worry she was about to get bumped out, but then he continued walking towards the bar.

The place was nearly deserted, filled more with music than people. Anna didn't recognise it. She could have been anywhere, except she wasn't really here at all. And from N'Golo's reaction, she could also have been *anyone*

– certainly not herself – and possibly just some random woman he remembered passing. Which was another oddity. Or perhaps it was just how N'Golo's brain was making sense of her presence: it had made her part of a memory, rather than accepting her as an intruder inside it.

Anna slipped off her stool, keeping N'Golo in sight, and waited for the barman to serve him. This was the boy who had all the answers, she reminded herself. He could lead them directly to Beth Hayden. She needed to make him talk to her, despite the risks.

'Callcross High?' she said, intercepting him on his return trip. 'I think we're in different years, though.'

*Callcross.* The word seemed to alarm N'Golo. He snapped his attention back to the bar, but the guy who'd served him – a human, not a bot – had long gone, and there was no one left to hear. He took a large mouthful of beer, trying perhaps to restore the cool.

'Thought I knew you,' he said.

'You want to grab a table?'

N'Golo's eyes narrowed. 'You here alone?'

Anna hesitated. Was a boyfriend about to arrive? A group of friends? All she knew was that she'd been waiting in the bar, just as N'Golo had arrived. And he was able to interact with her again. 'Don't be a goof. We've got a bit of time.'

N'Golo laughed. 'Goof?'

Inside, Anna cringed. Yes, she knew people didn't say that any more. Hadn't done for a long time. With a simple smile she sat back down at her table. She needed to keep his brain engaged, keep herself integral to the memory, be careful not to bump him out. 'You live with the Hayden family, right? Beth and George?'

N'Golo took another mouthful of beer and glanced around the bar. Because of course, he was unlikely to be here alone either. He'd come to find someone. 'You look a lot older than sixteen.'

'Yeah,' Anna replied, knowing that whoever he was remembering might have been anyone – and, if it didn't fit, the line about Callcross High might have been a mistake. She could have wrinkles and grey hair. But somehow she doubted it, and the woman in N'Golo's mind had enough to distract him from the details of her face. 'No problems getting served. You neither.'

N'Golo let one of his arms rest on the table and slowly squeezed his biceps to show off his developing strength. 'Has some advantages, don't it?'

'So what are you doing out?'

'Meeting some people.' His attention was fully on her now. 'Quick drink and then back home. School night. You know how it is.'

'Same.'

'I'm sure I know you from some place other than Callcross…'

She needed to get him off this line of thought. The contents of the pink tissue came back into her mind. 'Beth's a nice girl, isn't she…?'

N'Golo pushed some air through gritted teeth.

'What? She's not?'

'She sees me as some sort of social project,' he said. 'Like a prize pet has arrived on her doorstep. Something to talk about at her meet-ups.'

'Meet-ups?'

'Yeah, which is fine. I mean, she can go home to her nice

house, full fridge and comfy bed. And I don't see her actually wanting to share any of that, no matter how fucking clever her placards—' He stopped to check over his shoulder. They were still alone, and he soon returned his attention to her. 'So, how about you?'

'How do you mean?'

'I didn't catch your name?'

'Anna.'

The response had been automatic. Unthinking. Another little chink of truth warping N'Golo's memory as it played back from the hospital bed. When he woke up, would he remember things differently?

'Anna? Huh. I wouldn't have figured.'

'And what would you have said?'

'Maybe an Aliya or a Jasmine…'

Anna couldn't help but glance at her hands, which flexed white against the table. N'Golo grinned at her, perhaps working out his next move. Before he could say anything, the door to the bar opened and two men walked inside.

N'Golo's casual confidence vanished. He gave the pair a half-wave, half-salute – the gesture only underlining the sudden stiffness in his shoulders. Anna followed his stare. The first, who acknowledged his wave with a nod, was the blond man with the widow's peak who'd spoken to him by the hedge. The other was bulkier. One of them had sliced open a young girl's arm, Anna thought. One of them was close to being a butcher. 'Friends of yours?'

'Not exactly,' N'Golo replied while keeping an eye on the men, who were ordering drinks at the bar. 'Listen, I'm going to have to go.'

'Who are they?'

N'Golo edged forward on his seat, ready to slip off it. Anna reached across the table and took hold of his hand gently. It was enough to reawaken whatever biological response had drawn him to this woman in the first place. He relaxed and twisted back to her, but his look of confusion had returned. The music in the bar cut out. Perhaps that had been what truly had happened, but Anna doubted it. Touching him had punctured the memory, and caused the synapse sequencer to wobble.

'Are you sure we don't know each other?' he asked.

'I told you, I've seen you at Callcross.'

'No,' he said. 'No, I don't think that's it.'

The men had their drinks. They turned so their backs faced the counter, and surveyed the empty tables. Their attention was on N'Golo, but they continued to wait for him. She had some time. No matter how this had actually played out, she just needed to keep him engaged for a few more minutes. Keep him in the memory and find out why it had burned itself so deep in his brain. 'So are you going to introduce me?'

'I don't think so.' N'Golo pulled his hand away and slipped off the stool. 'Look, it was nice chatting…'

He didn't finish his sentence. Instead, he just walked towards the men. Anna had a good view of their faces, and she concentrated on the new one – the man was slightly fatter and balder than the one with the widow's peak. She didn't recognise him from Fowler's photofits.

Someone cut in front of her. Another man. He sat down at the stool where N'Golo had been sitting, and leant across towards her. His face, though, was just a featureless blur. The new arrival bent to kiss her and then sat back on his stool with a strange murmuring noise. Anna tried to look past him. N'Golo occasionally glanced towards her; from his position, he was unable to see the face of the man now sitting with her.

The murmuring was getting louder. And then she realised. The shape in front of her was like some sort of half-imagined dummy: gesticulating, talking, laughing. Nothing quite making sense. An ancillary detail within N'Golo's memory: just the guy who'd been talking to the girl he'd noticed in the bar. Worse, this dummy was now completely blocking her sight line to N'Golo.

Anna tried to move. Get off the stool and get another drink. But she couldn't. Her feet were stuck to the little heel bar beneath her, and her rear didn't want to shift from the plastic seat. She was about to be shunted from the sequencer.

All of which meant she'd failed. Again.

# 29

**Top Stories:**

Crime could be cut by further ten per cent with greater data access – S&P architect (*Read more*)

UI bonus – Check your Citizen Number to see if you have unearned supplement (*Read more*)

Prime Minister rejects call for Tanzania Inquiry (*Read more*)

**Selected for You:**

Struggling to find your way? When people were employed to read paper maps for travellers from call centres! (*Read more*)

*TANZANIA INQUIRY.*

Anna didn't open the article. She'd read warnings of an inquiry before, multiple times. It was a story that didn't want to die – and with the price of dysprosium also in the news, she doubted it ever would.

Fowler sauntered towards her, his vehicle parked part on and part off the kerb. For a moment Anna wondered how it had allowed him to stop in that position, then realised

221

it hadn't. He must have disabled the parking system – and his manoeuvre was drawing attention to the fact. Maybe he wanted her to ask him about it. She didn't.

Instead, she switched her attention to the bar. It sat like a bunker just off from the main highway. A few stray dogs were scavenging from bins set to one side of the door. Despite probably being lashed by rain on more nights than not, the place had a flat roof which was lined with an unlit neon sign: COMPADRES.

'From how you described it,' Fowler said, looking pleased with himself, 'this is probably it.'

Although she'd logged out of the boards, Anna's attention still wasn't entirely on where they'd agreed to meet. Her pod had dropped her off outside the bar a few minutes ago and she'd been left to wait in the open. A few people had walked past but hadn't recognised her. Now, though, a man was jogging towards her, his pace too fast for Anna to turn her face away in time.

'Bitch!'

The sudden shout startled Fowler, who stared after the man as he pounded away. 'You get that all the time?'

'Pretty much.' Anna tried to hold Fowler's eye contact – like it hadn't impacted her – but she was trembling.

'You ever thought of submitting a complaint?'

'About what?'

'Well, I presume it's because the boards keep posting your photo? That one at the crash site…'

'You really think submitting a board ticket is going to do any good?'

'Not really.'

'Well then.'

Fowler grunted something, then took the cue to move on. 'So what do you think? The bar?'

'I only saw the inside,' she said. 'And it doesn't look open for business.'

Fowler grunted and headed off towards a heavy black door. Anna followed somewhat sceptically. She'd not seen anything like the name Compadres inside N'Golo's memory. Fowler rapped on the door, waited a few seconds, then rapped again, harder. 'So,' he said. 'Did you use the cams?'

'No,' Anna lied. She was angry at Fowler for planting fears about Cody; she hoped the annoyance hadn't permeated her voice. One of the small black cubes was no longer mounted on the white disc he'd given her. She'd fitted it to the wall of the synapse chamber, but she wasn't about to tell Fowler she was following his instructions. Once he had put the doubt in her mind, every interaction with Cody was tinged with doubt. Had there been something off about the way his hand had lingered on her neck prior to the last submersion? She didn't know – but now she'd been given a way to find out.

'Well, I'm sure you'll find a use for them,' Fowler said, shrugging as if accepting her answer. 'Maybe keep an eye on that flatmate of yours.'

Anna turned to him. The bar door remained firmly shut. 'You don't trust many people, do you?'

'No,' he said. 'But maybe that's why I do what I do.'

A sound of movement behind the door interrupted their exchange. After a few seconds more it opened, and a man who still looked drunk stared back at them. Fowler reached in his pocket and pulled out a card. It was enough to get them inside, and it didn't take long for Anna to realise it was indeed the same bar.

Although it was brightly lit, she recognised the same circular plastic tables and arrangement of now deserted seating. The only major difference, aside from a total lack of customers, was that a metal grille had been pulled down across the counter. As the man who'd let them in went to find his boss, Anna made her way over to where she'd been sitting with N'Golo. She glanced back to the doorway where the two men had entered to confirm her view. 'This is it,' she said.

Fowler hadn't shifted from the entrance. Whereas Anna had been interested in verifying what she'd seen in N'Golo's memory, he was simply waiting and picking his teeth. Noticing her looking at him, he pointed in several directions in quick succession. 'Camera points,' he said. 'The main bar area is covered. There's probably more behind the grille.'

'You've been here before?'

'Yeah.'

Other aspects of the bar were now flooding her senses in a way which had obviously not impinged sufficiently within N'Golo's memory. The carpet stuck to her shoes as she walked across it; there was a dank smell of stale beer and sweat. It wasn't a place she'd choose to come herself – but perhaps music and alcohol were enough to mask such things for the regular clientele.

'Why am I not surprised you know about this place?'

'No bots,' Fowler explained. 'It means the service is slow enough to put most people off, except those looking for a quiet place to drink. You know, which may suit certain types.'

'Like those looking to cheat on their wives?' She immediately regretted the cheap jibe. This wasn't the time for it. 'Have you had time to follow up the other lead? Beth Hayden's meet-ups?'

'I spoke to her friends again, sure. Turns out there were three of them that were into helping out people struggling on the UI. I pushed them pretty hard on it, but they don't know anything else, I'm sure of it. Just an informal school club.'

'And how's Millie?'

'How do you think?'

*Beside herself*, Anna thought. *Lost and totally helpless.*

'Roger Hayden is—'

'I don't care about that arsehole.'

Fowler let out a sigh. 'He's stressed,' he said. 'People let it out in all kinds of ways. If you want to get on in this business, you need to learn occasionally to keep your mouth shut and suck it up. We're making progress, at least.'

'You call this progress?'

'We're doing better than S&P,' Fowler replied, sounding a little too pleased. 'With what came in the post, though, I wouldn't be surprised if they've sent out the hunter bots to do probability raids.'

'Which means?'

'They've got a list of addresses of people who've got history with this type of thing. They'll be working their way down it and—'

He stopped. A heavy-set man had shown up from behind the bar area. Tattoos covered most of his arms and neck. He didn't look too pleased to have been pulled away from whatever he'd been doing. Anna didn't recognise either him or the guy who'd let them into the bar from N'Golo's memory.

'What do you fucking want?'

Fowler reached into his pocket and retrieved a printout of Beth Hayden's face. 'We're searching for a girl who's gone missing.'

The tattooed man looked at the paper but didn't give it much notice. 'This isn't your usual type of thing, is it, Fowler?'

For a second Fowler looked embarrassed. 'Yeah – but I was still hoping you'd be able to tell us if she'd been here.'

'Decided to get yourself a partner?'

Fowler glanced at Anna, then shifted the bulk of his body to block the man's view of her. 'I was hoping you'd let us take a scan of your camera footage.'

'I told you, I don't recognise the girl.'

'We think some people were here who could help us,' Fowler continued. 'Look, I could really do with the break.'

'Not going to happen.'

'I can pay the usual rate, plus a little extra.'

'Don't matter if you pay a lot extra,' said the tattooed man, turning and walking away. 'It's not gonna happen. And you're gonna have to find a new venue for your honeytraps.'

# 30

I HAD TO get out.

That one thought penetrated the dark. I lay in my bed staring up at the ceiling. I didn't want to speak to Sean again. I'd answered his questions about Tanzania. He could either accept them or dwell on the minor details on which conspiracy theorists thrive. But I wasn't going to talk about Iceland.

I hadn't agreed to talk about Iceland.

*Breathe.* I waited for the first dull light of dawn before I pushed myself out of bed. On a normal day, I'd be able to get myself into my wheelchair unassisted. Then I'd wait for one of the nurses to come and dress me. They'd manipulate limbs that didn't want to stretch, and help a waist that could no longer fold sufficiently for me to able to reach my feet.

I felt cold. There wasn't any hint of movement in the corridor beyond my room. At this very moment, though, the sensors embedded in the ceiling would have picked up my attempt to rise unaided. A nurse would probably be heading in my direction now. I didn't have long in which to execute my gambit.

There wasn't any real way out of the nursing home. The chair by my bed wasn't self-propelled, and I couldn't walk more than a few metres without needing to sit and rest. Even now, tottering within a few metres of my bed, I could feel the first complaints from my chest as my lungs searched for more air.

Damn it. I needed to be stronger than this. My robe hung on a peg beside the wheelchair. It was an easy enough garment to slip on or throw across my shoulders while I waited for a nurse. But I didn't have time for it now; instead, I took a few steps further down the bed, towards a chest of drawers.

The top drawer opened smoothly, and I searched through it. Nothing. Not what I was looking for, anyway. The next one down was the same; just a few cardigans that looked grey in the dawn light. The third drawer held more promise. Mementos of a previous life. Things I'd insisted were brought with me from my apartment. Photographs, knick-knacks. But nothing quite right for what I now needed. The fourth drawer was out of reach. Too low. When I'd moved in, I could open it – at least I could remember doing so – but now it resided in that space around my knees where I couldn't quite grasp.

I listened for the approach of a nurse, but then scolded myself for thinking I'd be able to hear her. I wasn't deaf – they didn't need to shout at me – but sounds in the corridor were just as lost to me as things happening beyond my restricted field of view.

'What are you looking for?'

'None of your business,' I said to N'Golo.

His appearance wasn't surprising. He leant against the drawers, the youth of his body mocking the frailty of mine.

'You brought with you a small kitchen knife,' he said. 'You told them it was your mother's – something that held some sentimental value to you. Something that reminded you of cooking with her.'

I let out a frustrated grunt. 'It's in the bottom drawer.'

'No,' N'Golo replied. 'It's against policy to allow residents to own weapons.'

'It's a kitchen knife.'

'But you're not going to cook with it, are you?'

I didn't answer. He knew what my answer would be in any case. And no, I didn't want to die just yet. But the last time I was ill I'd been taken to a small private hospital a few blocks distant. A couple of days there would allow me enough time to think through what I was going to say to Sean. If I ever decided to see him again.

I shuffled backwards until the end of the bed hit the back of my knees. I slid my heels forward until my arse hit the tip of the mattress. I braced myself. This was going to hurt. Sure enough, I thudded onto the carpet below and felt my tailbone crack.

The pain emanating from the base of my spine almost stopped me there and then, but I knew I had to force myself to keep moving. The sensors would have registered the fall, and the notification to the nursing staff that one of their residents was 'up and about' would have just been promoted to a full alarm call. The drawer was now in reach. I pulled it open and rummaged through the contents, searching for the blade. Other things I found with ease – perfume, books, even a few mementos from a trip to Australia – but not the knife. Had N'Golo been right? Had they taken it from me at some point, knowing it would be hard for me to discover it was missing?

'They're not going to let you escape,' N'Golo said.

Light erupted into the room as Charley opened the door. She rushed towards me, took hold of my arm and yanked me back onto the bed. A single sideways shove from her hip and leg shut the drawers, and then she pulled me along the mattress until my head once more reached my pillow. 'Again,' she said. 'This little game always starts out with you playing nice, doesn't it?'

I couldn't reply. I had my mouth clamped shut to stop myself yelping. Charley's fingers were digging into my biceps.

'You want me to let go?'

I nodded my head, fast, keeping my mouth shut to control the pain.

'Perhaps I say you were confused. Maybe I say you needed to be subdued?'

My head twisted round towards the door. There was no sign of Grace. But Charley had already tired of tormenting me and released her grip.

'If it was up to me,' she said, moving away, 'the knife would still be there. And if you wake me up again tonight, I'll bring it with me.'

The door slammed shut, leaving me once again in the near dark of dawn. I could still feel Charley's fingers in my skin, already sense the bruises forming. N'Golo stepped closer.

'Pain is all in the mind,' he said.

I grunted. 'And where did you drag up that pearl of wisdom?'

'It's what you told Fowler, when you first showed him the sequencer.'

'Yes, but that's different. You couldn't feel any pain in the sequencer.'

'Couldn't, or can't?'

'Jake made sure of it…'

'And what if he'd changed his mind?'

# 31

S&P Build 14.224a – Recommendation Module

Situation #GIHHCLTYYEN

Report from Hunter Bots: Potential Target. ID:
#FLG24343JGT (Tom Turner) cleared. Victim (Beth Hayden) not at household. No biological evidence of Victim at household.

Recommendation: Upload case for Continuous Learning.

Associated Actions: Violent scene clear-up required at home of ID: #FLG24343JGT .

'A CALM MIND is a productive mind.'

Anna saw only blue sky. She was on her back, floating in a warm, turquoise sea.

To her left, Jake paddled into view. She turned her head slightly, bringing him fully into her eye line, and trying not to think about where he'd chosen to meet. She knew there would be no land on the horizon. This was an escape from everything that troubled him.

'Have we heard anything more from Inspector Mitchell?'

'No.' Anna fought the urge to move. She couldn't swim. Or rather, she was fine in water shallow enough so that she could put her feet down when needed. Here, though, there was nothing at the bottom.

'Anything more on the missing girl?'

'Just the things I've already reported: a note, an implant chip.'

'Strange,' Jake said almost absently, 'that there's been no specific ransom demand.'

Water was lapping into her ear. Jake's body drifted out of view again. 'Everything about this is strange,' she replied.

'And how is your own work progressing?'

'We've managed to submerge N'Golo four times.' She wished she didn't have to say 'submerge', with those unseen depths below. 'It's now confirmed he was meeting with members of the Workers' League.'

'Isn't that the same group that was involved in the recent massacre you investigated?'

'Yes – or, at least, there was the same sort of rare leaflet found on the shooter.'

Jake's floating body reappeared on the other side of her. 'There are stories about Tanzania on the boards again.'

'Yes,' said Anna. 'I've seen them.'

'As is always the case, the war was easier to win than the peace. Every new casualty seems to bring an inquiry closer.'

'If it happens, it happens.'

'Then I don't need to worry about anything? What you told me during your interview was true?'

'I told the truth then, and I'm telling the truth now. That plane was taken out of the sky deliberately. Perhaps it would have been better if I *had* lied.'

Jake laughed. 'I think not. You'd just have to grapple with a different sort of pain.' Again, he drifted from her view, orbiting her. 'The coma patients the health team worked with didn't show any sign of problems,' he said, 'right up until the point they snapped. You should treat every interaction with Durrant as if it's your last.'

A sudden chill passed over Anna's body – despite being in water that could only be described as tropical, and with a strong equatorial sun shining down on her. At the same time, she realised she couldn't really move. Although she had full control of her body, any slight movement disturbed the illusion of floating, and she felt herself beginning to sink a little. All she could manoeuvre were her eyeballs. She had no better time to ask him. 'Can you tell me about severance?'

'How do you know about that?'

'I heard Cody talking about it – I was submerged with N'Golo, and he almost bumped me out. I was aware of Cody speaking above me, and then…'

*Push her under, and hold her down.*

'Severance is what happens when the mind can no longer connect to the body,' Jake said; he sounded angry. 'It's rare. You don't need to worry about it.'

'It was disconcerting to say the least.'

'If you were being bumped out, your brain would be disorientated, that's all. And Weaver would be monitoring all your biodata; he wouldn't allow it to become permanent.'

*Permanent?* 'That could happen?'

'Yes.' A hard edge penetrated Jake's voice. The water around them had become distinctly chilly. 'Weaver shouldn't have been discussing it around you.'

'It wasn't his fault, he didn't know I could hear—'

Anna didn't finish her sentence. She was back on a

synapse bench, Jake's nurse ready for her. The meeting was over.

ANNA BLINKED AWAKE inside N'Golo's memory, and immediately felt herself being buffeted on all sides. She grunted as an elbow hit her somewhere below the ribs. In the face of the girl standing next to her she caught an immediate, apologetic wince. Yes, it was an accident. They were too tightly bunched, moving forward to the beat of drums somewhere in the distance, and being pushed from behind.

Another shove almost caused her to fall. Anna would have been buried under the feet of all those following behind had her arm not been caught in a tight grip tugging her back to her feet.

'Come with me – now!'

Anna instinctively tried to wriggle free, but N'Golo had her, and he was already pulling her to the side. Perhaps if she'd been in the real world, she would have felt some pain. But although all the colour had been squeezed from her skin, she felt nothing except a numb pressure. She remembered Fowler pressing his toe into the ground as he tested the sequencer on his first submersion. For the moment, her own synapses were doing a good job of reminding her of what it felt like to be yanked about, with all the associated hurt being removed by the sequencer. That didn't mean she couldn't object, however.

'Hey! Let go!'

A stray foot kicked the back of Anna's leg causing her to pivot around N'Golo's grip. Dragging her like a doll, he pulled her from the crowd. Only when they were through the police lines on either side did he prop her back on her feet.

'It's me,' he said. 'N'Golo.'

Sure, it was N'Golo. It was his memory. From her point of view, there was no one else it could have been. But from his? Was she herself, or was she now playing the part of someone else within his memory, maybe the attractive woman sitting in Compadres?

'Fucking hell, Beth, does your dad know you're here?'

Anna remained mute. Fuck. She was Beth.

N'Golo let out a frustrated grunt and took hold of her arm again, propelling her along the pavement. Although he wasn't hurting her, Anna couldn't help but let out a little yelp. The few police officers and bots lining the route seemed more concerned with the crowd than the two teenagers behind them. Fortunately, N'Golo stopped of his own accord after a few metres, where they could get a reasonable view of the whole street.

'Fucking idiots,' he said, looking back at the section of crowd he'd plucked her from. It was hard to understand why he was so angry. It all seemed good-humoured enough. The people enthusiastically chanting slogans and waving their signs – many of which were funny enough that they'd no doubt later reappear on the boards. The crowd itself was a mix of ages and genders. A gaggle of genuine anger, excitement and face paint. All to protest the lack of jobs and opportunities, although a few people were also objecting to the ongoing occupation of Tanzania, and S&P's moves to access more and more personal data.

N'Golo pointed up ahead. 'Street narrows,' he said. 'Right up there.'

'So?'

'So when the boys come to mix things up, there's going to be a fucking crush.'

Anna froze. Yes, she'd read about it on the boards. Organised protests had long since become regular features around which life had to be planned. Although the government clearly didn't approve, those in power also seemed to view them as a useful way for people to let off steam. Even if there was little that could actually be done to change things any more.

And yet this one had gone wrong.

She thought about the crush. The kick from behind. The elbow in the ribs. Everyone just a fraction too tightly packed. The crowd not exactly being led from the front but being pushed from the back. If another group of people joined the rear and started a stampede…

She looked at N'Golo. 'How did you know?'

'Know what?'

*That it was about to happen*, thought Anna. *Or that Beth was part of the crowd. Or where to find her.*

'There's different ways you can be smart,' N'Golo said, shepherding her away again – this time with his arm loosely around her shoulder. 'Come on, I know a place not too far from here.'

Anna allowed herself to be guided. Would he take her somewhere directly associated with the Workers' League? Somewhat disappointingly, N'Golo stopped at a café a few streets away from the main protest. Just far enough that they could still hear the background murmur of the street chants while being safe from the oncoming crush. Again, Anna felt a pang of guilt. She reminded herself she was swimming in a construct. There was no way of stopping it. No way of warning anyone. And the warm wash of being submerged in

N'Golo's memory provided at least some distance between her and the horrible events about to unfold.

She stared down. They'd both bought a cup of tea. The liquid was still rotating in the cup, steaming into the air. It had been produced by a bot, which moved deftly between the counter, coffee machine and till, taking orders from the handful of other customers, and getting drinks without the frustrating performance theatre that used to plague such places. Still, the presence of a bot – and another to clear the tables – underlined the point that this wasn't a place where she'd find any members of the League. So why had N'Golo chosen it?

'You ever wondered why they stopped making bots look human?'

Anna shrugged.

'They want us to just see them as machines,' N'Golo said, answering his own question. 'But some of them can think now, you know.'

'We've become a society of slave owners again,' Anna said, repeating something she'd once read on the boards to try to keep the kid's mind on politics. 'Where the slaves are better off than the urban poor.'

'Damn right.'

Anna picked a sachet out of a white ceramic pot and tipped its contents into her drink. The detail seemed to disturb N'Golo.

'I didn't think you took sugar.'

'I… sometimes, I guess I need it.'

N'Golo tipped his chair on its back legs, examining her. 'So why were you out there?' he asked. 'You got everything, haven't you?'

For a moment Anna struggled. He wasn't talking to

someone he didn't know; like a stand-in social worker or a stranger in the bar. He'd probably spent quite a bit of time with Beth. He had her mapped out, and Anna's responses would likely need to fall within a narrower range of probability if she was going to convince his brain not to bump out. Like the sudden taste for sugar, the details mattered.

*So why was a rich teenager at an employment protest?*

Anna thought back to her fleeting first impressions of Beth's bedroom. Other than the Pankhurst quote, there wasn't any sign of teenage rebellion, but perhaps a smart kid was still naïve enough to hope there were other ways to change the world. 'It's important we make our voices heard,' she said.

Her answer prompted a thin smile from N'Golo. 'To say what exactly?'

Again, Anna floundered. But then one of the placards from the protests came back to her. 'What do you call a man with no work?'

It had stuck in her mind for its slightly dated use of the word 'man'. But for the words of one placard to be so clear in the sea of others, it must have also hit a nerve in N'Golo's mind. Something a bit more personal. He let his chair fall back so all four legs were firmly grounded, then seemed distracted. 'Is it me, or does it smell a bit off in here?'

Anna shook her head. She indicated towards the bot. 'Perhaps they should employ someone to give this place a decent clean?'

'It's not a joke, Beth.'

'I didn't say it was, I—'

'Smith, Carpenter, Shepherd, Taylor. What do they mean to you?'

'Surnames?' Anna asked. Was he at last giving her some solid information?

'They're jobs that became names. Our work is important; it says something about us. People used to ask, "What is it you do?" Now they're scared to, just in case the person they're talking to has no answer.'

'We're agreed then…'

'I doubt it, not on what needs to be done anyway.' N'Golo twisted to look at the bot sweeping the tables as the one behind the counter attended its station. His nose wrinkled, then he returned his attention to her. 'Tech has been taking our jobs since the industrial revolution,' he said. 'How come you white collars only noticed once the bots came for your jobs?'

*White collars.* A buzzword from the Workers' League playbook.

'You didn't care about robots making cars or milking cows or driving trucks,' N'Golo continued. 'But let one become a doctor and you lose your shit. So when they come for your daddy's job, do you think he'll be happy trading his dignity for the UI?'

'My dad works in the City, N'Golo.'

'Your dad's job could be done by an algorithm,' N'Golo stated, his voice blunt. 'Just like solicitors, just like accountants. The only reason it hasn't happened yet is that bankers have the ear of the politicians. And their money.'

Outside, the chanting had stopped. From this distance, it was a subtle change in the background blur of noise. The regular rhythm of catchy slogans had been replaced by a more random noise of panic and rage. All of which meant that whatever was going on out there was no longer the centre of N'Golo's attention, and his mind wasn't really recording what was happening. Just that something *was* happening.

'It's still important to do something about it, though, isn't it?' Anna prompted him. 'Don't you agree?'

N'Golo didn't notice her question. 'I have less than a year left,' he said.

Anna realised he was talking about his foster care. 'You'll be given a transitional home.'

'A bed in some hostel. A subscription to the UI.'

'There are still jobs out there, N'Golo.'

'Not for people like me.' N'Golo pushed back in his seat, looking away, his face twisting in frustration. Then he turned back, angry. Some of the background noise outside had become clearly audible as screams. One of the other customers in the café edged towards the door, and looked out through the glass. But they were several streets away. Nobody would be able to see anything from here. If she remembered correctly, nearly one hundred people had been trampled in the scrum, and twenty had died. The subsequent outrage had been such that even the prime minister had momentarily poked her head out of her security bubble, once they'd cleaned the blood and glass from the street, to issue some empty words of reassurance about how things could be better in the future.

'I'm a foster-kid,' N'Golo continued. 'My dad spent time in jail. I've been suspended from school more times than I can fucking count. All that gets fed in, Beth. Which employment algorithm is going to assign me to a decent job?'

Anna glanced at the man at the door. It was true that not many industries were providing decent jobs nowadays. And those that did, offered them for only a fraction above

UI. Some work paid better – serving the remaining white collars. But it was an ever-shrinking pool, and one she was already paddling in the shallows. 'So why aren't you out there protesting?' she asked. 'Doing something about it?'

N'Golo's eyes flared. 'Politicians won't listen until something affects them directly,' he said. 'They'll say those people outside are violent yobs. You just wait for the board reports. When was the last time you could get close enough to talk to an MP about our problems? When was the last time our votes actually meant anything?'

Yes, a few of the banners outside had indeed been protesting that it was becoming harder to access Members of Parliament. The prime minister's rare public appearances always went unannounced, except to a few chosen party members and media bots. She'd become known for turning up with her entourage to take credit for occasional good news stories – all the while trying to avoid being followed and harassed by people angry with the country's direction. 'You know them, don't you?' continued Anna. 'The Workers' League?'

N'Golo pushed a dismissive snort through his nose. 'Workers' League,' he said. 'More like Luddites, really.'

'So you do know them?'

'I know *of* them.'

Anna paused. She knew what she wanted to ask him next. Who were they? Where are they based? Would he take her to them? If that meeting had already happened, it would be burned into another part of N'Golo's cortex, just waiting to be accessed. 'I'd like to meet them,' she said. 'Will you take me to them?'

N'Golo ignored her question, posing one of his own.

Maybe his brain was rebuffing the attempt to crack its secrets. 'What do you think of your dad's job?'

Dad. Beth's dad. Beside Anna, the man at the door opened it a fraction and some of the chaotic noise from outside flowed in. A low drone of loudspeakers undercut some of the higher-pitched shouts of panic. The door closed again as the man stepped outside. 'It sounds pretty bad,' she said.

'That's why I got you out of there,' N'Golo said. 'So… your dad?'

Anna didn't really know what Roger Hayden did for a living. 'He's a banker.'

'Banks were where all this really started. You know that, right?'

'Not the industrial revolution?'

N'Golo shook his head. 'Not for the workers, for the white collars. To work in a high-street bank, you used to need to pass exams. To know a trade. Then they brought in computers that automated every decision. They turned working in a bank into nothing more than being in a call centre. And then AIs took those jobs as well. Get a quick decision… let an AI determine your future.'

Anna hesitated. N'Golo wasn't simply parroting Workers' League literature. This was something different: a subtle shift in emphasis regarding the class most affected by the changes being brought about by machines and computers.

'We should be getting you home,' N'Golo said, getting to his feet. 'Your mum will be seeing this on the news. Let's talk on the—' He stopped talking.

*Had he bumped out?*

No, he was looking down at the table. At first Anna thought he was looking at her cup of tea, but then he reached forward and took hold of her hand. Lifted her forearm from the table and pushed at her sleeve. An angry purple line, perhaps just a few days old, ran from her wrist to her elbow.

'I didn't know you cut,' N'Golo said. He laughed, as if remembering something. 'The only antidote to mental suffering is physical pain, right?'

Anna snatched her hand back. 'Fuck you,' she said, replacing the sleeve. But she needed to remember this wasn't one of her injuries, it was Beth's. And somehow that made it all the worse. Had Beth's parents known? Had Fowler?

'Don't tell me – you were feeling a little sad when you got back from your holiday in Tanzania?'

Anna froze. *Tanzania?* 'What do you mean by that?'

'You were out there, weren't you?'

*Yes*, thought Anna. Yes, she had been. But had Beth?

N'Golo sniffed the air. 'It stinks in here,' he said.

'What do you mean by Tanzania?'

'Blood,' N'Golo said. 'It stinks of blood. And jet fuel.'

# 32

ANNA SAT AT her desk staring at nothing and thinking about her last encounter with N'Golo. Again, she'd been able to interact directly with him inside his memories. And yet: Tanzania. In that final moment before he'd bumped out, she'd been able to smell the blood and jet fuel too – and she'd returned to the synapse bench almost choking on it.

It dawned on her that Cody hadn't even acknowledged her arrival that morning. His screen displayed a raft of neuron data, but the detail of what he was actually doing was lost on her. She watched the data points enlarge at his touch, then fade back into the meta.

'Have we heard from Fowler?'

Cody continued to work. Or, at least, that's how it appeared. But even with Anna's limited knowledge of what he was doing, the data points he was calling up looked random – and he was only viewing them; he wasn't manipulating the data.

'Hey,' she said, louder this time. 'Did Fowler call? Any news about Beth?'

Still no response. And then Anna knew the reason. Just beyond her workstation lay a small black cube, one of the cameras Fowler had given to her.

244

'The synapse chambers get swept every few days by Jake's security,' Cody said, still refusing to look at her. 'My first thought was that Fowler planted the camera, but it's got your DNA all over it. You should have peppered it.'

'Look…'

'Don't bother,' Cody replied. 'I get it.'

'Fowler gave me the camera. He—'

'Yes?'

Anna let out an exasperated sigh. 'I'm sorry,' she said. 'He said some things that made me… I guess I was feeling kind of vulnerable.'

Cody let a few seconds pass, then turned in his chair. He looked deeply pissed off. 'Part of my job is to keep your body undisturbed on the bench,' he said, emphasising each word like he was hitting a series of nails. Keeping the box tight. 'If I did anything weird, your brain would sense it. You'd bump out. I thought all this had been explained to you?'

Anna felt a little flush of embarrassment. 'I'm sorry. But Fowler—'

Cody looked back at her blank-faced and somewhat bewildered. 'Again,' he said, 'and I'm only going to say this once more: you'd sense it. Say I grabbed hold of your arm; you'd feel it. If I unbuttoned your shirt, you'd get cold. And anyway, for fuck's sake, I'm not a pervert!'

*You'd get cold.* Just like when she visited Jake, when his awful nurse, not Cody, was there alone with her unguarded body.

'Yes,' she said, her voice sounding small. 'So what did you tell security?'

'Nothing. They want to see you about it, though.'

'Okay.'

'You'd better prepare yourself for an arse-kicking. Jake takes this sort of shit very seriously. They didn't exactly compliment me for missing a camera in my synapse chamber.'

'I get it.'

'Good.' Cody turned back to his workstation.

Anna sucked in a deep breath, but she'd only be able to punish her stupidity later. Right now, she had other things to worry about. 'How is N'Golo?'

'Truthfully, we don't know. He bumped out pretty hard this time. The health team are doing some remapping.'

'Remapping? Is that normal?'

'Nothing about this is normal, Anna. But to answer your question: no. The last memory we implanted you into seems to have disintegrated. If he does wake up, he'll likely have a gap – or else be fuzzy on the details.'

'Shit.'

'And that's not the weirdest—' A light flashed on Cody's screen, interrupting his thought. 'Huh – we're getting a priority comm from the switchboard.' He spun the chair round to face her. 'Our esteemed private investigator has gotten himself in trouble.'

'Where is he?'

'Same place as Durrant. Fairbanks Hospital, trauma ward.'

THERE WERE RELATIVELY few people waiting in the hospital reception, a few medical bots circulating among those with visible injuries. Little had been done to hide the fact that the building was once a hotel: the reception desk and carpets had a distinct 'budget stay' look about them, even though the rooms above would have all been transformed into wards for surgery or recuperation. Just like the hub, traditional hospital sites were now far too big – the efficiency of AI prognosis and robotic surgery allowing vastly greater throughput of those people who did require their services. Still, it didn't seem right to get such treatment in a building located between a Tex-Mex and a clothing outlet.

Anna stepped past the entrance lobby bot – not answering its enquiry as to whether she was a visitor or needed treatment – and found Fowler almost ready to be discharged. He had his arm in a cast, which was being held at a right angle across his stomach by a thin-looking sling. He also had company. Inspector Mitchell was waiting with him as one of the medical bots gave him a final scan, adjusted his sling and pointed him towards the exit.

'There was no need for you to come,' Fowler said, seeing Anna. He popped a pill. 'I'm fine.'

He didn't look fine. His upper lip was heavily swollen, and he was holding his body slightly off-centre. He looked as if he'd taken a few punches, or maybe kicks, to the ribs and face.

'So what happened?'

Fowler exchanged a glance with Mitchell. The S&P analyst shrugged as if to give him the go-ahead. 'I was staking out Compadres. Guess I was spotted.'

'We've identified all the men involved,' Mitchell cut in. 'None of them bothered to mask their e-tracks. We'd prefer it, though, if we had the victim's cooperation for the prosecution.'

Fowler looked sheepish. He shifted his weight and grimaced as his injured body protested.

'You don't want them to bring charges?' Anna asked.

'No,' Fowler replied.

'Why not? Presumably they're connected with—'

'Of course they're connected,' Mitchell said. 'The key question is how it's best pursued. I'd like to bring them in; my former colleague here disagrees.'

'And what is S&P telling you to do?'

'She meant S&P,' Fowler said quietly. 'S&P would like to bring them in, not her. Don't ever make the mistake of thinking she isn't just following the commands of a computer program.'

'I don't always agree with S&P,' Mitchell retorted, 'but in this case it's correct. There's a connection between the bar and the men who attacked you. There's a connection between the bar and the Workers' League. There's a connection between the Workers' League and N'Golo Durrant, and there's a connection between Durrant and Beth Hayden. The girl who had her biohardware cut out of her arm, if you remember?'

Fowler flushed an angry shade of red. Behind them, a medical gurney wheeled itself in from the street carrying a man who wasn't moving. He was taken silently through a set of double doors to the side of reception, into what possibly had once been a restaurant but now was an operating theatre.

'You could bring them in anyway,' Anna said, momentarily distracted by the lack of human care that man had been afforded. 'Couldn't you?' She looked at Fowler. 'If you think the victim is being intimidated because of his investigation.'

'No,' Mitchell replied. 'No, Mr Fowler is well versed in the law. He tells us it was a minor disagreement that got out of hand. An alcohol-induced scuffle. There's no connection in his version of events… but if he wants to use that bar to catch love-cheats in the future then I guess…'

The inspector didn't finish her sentence. She just let the implication drift.

'That's nothing to do with it,' Fowler said.

'Do you have any news from the Haydens?' Anna asked, not wanting to be sucked into the argument. 'Have they received any more communication about their daughter?'

'No,' said Mitchell. 'And Roger Hayden pings me several times a day. If anything arrived, he'd tell us about it before our own systems managed to relay the same information.'

'And Millie? How is she doing?'

'Millie Hayden is a wreck.'

'I was wondering whether I should—'

'No,' Mitchell said curtly. 'No, leave the family alone. The only contact with them should be through S&P. Concentrate on fishing in that Durrant boy's skull.'

Mitchell gave Fowler another meaningful glance, then walked away. Fowler stared after her but didn't move.

'So,' Anna said slowly, 'are you not cooperating because you want to solve the case before her? I mean – from what that guy with the tattoos told you, you're not going to be using that bar for your core business, are you?'

'Are those my only choices?'

'You tell me.'

'The people who took Beth were very careful to hide their electronic wake. S&P isn't getting close to them, probably because they're not on the boards and not on its radar. I doubt they would have laid a trail to themselves by hiring four vagrants to duff me up.'

'And that's your gut feeling?'

'The four guys who got me smelled like they were from the sewer,' Fowler said, perhaps unaware of his own less than stellar hygiene. 'Probably had their UI docked. I'd be prepared to bet that the only connection they had to the bar was that they'd been promised a warm meal in return for giving me a scare.'

Anna thought about this. 'We could still track them.'

'And Mitchell probably is doing just that... but she won't find anything. And the bar has turned cold, too – I doubt the people we're looking for will be returning there any day soon.'

'So we've lost, then.'

'That depends on what you've found in the sequencer, doesn't it?'

'Well, we've confirmed Beth was just as politically active as Durrant. She was at the recent jobs protest. The one that ended in a crush.'

Fowler didn't acknowledge her statement, but started walking towards the hospital exit. As they approached, he fumbled in the coat pocket opposite his broken arm. Anna eyed the cast. 'You didn't opt for immediate fusing?'

'Like my coverage gives me that option.'

*Shit*. 'Sorry.'

'Don't be,' Fowler replied. 'UI gives me basic, and I bought some add-on tablets which are meant to speed up the healing. Something to do with calcium. Docs said it should be fine in about a week, so I don't really see much point in paying the extra for an immediate.' He finally had what he was looking for and passed it over. A small tub of beige powder and cream concealer.

'What's this?'

'Make-up.'

Anna stared at the offering, then made a move to give

it back. Fowler had already stuffed his good arm into his pocket, though, and refused to bite. 'I don't need it,' he said. 'But I noticed a tub of the stuff in your bathroom when I stopped by… That's the brand you use, isn't it?'

'And what the hell were you doing in my bathroom?'

'Taking a piss.' He stopped to hack up some phlegm. 'It's a specialist medical concealer,' he added, though he hadn't needed to explain. 'They said it would cover any scarring from where the bone protruded. I don't need it – it's not like I wear short-sleeved shirts, which I guess is something we have in common. Anyway, you don't see this brand much outside of hospitals. I understand it's very popular with people who cut themselves.'

Anna stared at the little tub. Finally she held it out again, and kept her arm extended until Fowler relented and took it back. 'Thank you, but it's the wrong shade.'

'That girl you live with isn't a relation,' Fowler continued, keeping the tub in view in the palm of his hand. 'She's more than a lodger, too.'

Anna looked about them. A few people were passing in and out of the hospital, but none appeared to be giving them much attention. Only a single bot loitered in the entrance lobby, its job to direct people on arrival.

'To be frank, I wasn't surprised at the results of my scan.' Fowler waved the little tub again, and then stuffed it in his pocket. 'I know what this stuff is, and I figured… well, you just wouldn't have got a job with someone like Jake if he'd known you were into self-harm. Not with his obsession with personal stats, anyway.'

Anna took a breath. 'Jake doesn't employ people who he thinks are… unstable.' She found the last word distasteful, but it was how her boss thought about it. A calm mind is a productive mind.

*And the only antidote to mental suffering is physical pain.*

N'Golo had said that to Beth, but where had Anna heard it before?

Marx. It was a quote from Karl Marx.

'You never thought about getting your scars smoothed out?'

'No,' Anna replied, holding the PI's inquisitive stare. 'They're reminders, and I don't want to forget.'

'Well I guess that's your choice.'

'So are you going to tell him?'

'You've maybe missed the fact that I need you on the Durrant thing.'

'And after that?'

'And after that we both go our separate ways,' Fowler replied. 'But just know that most people use spoofs as a short-term deal, not for extended periods. Sooner or later, someone is going to rumble you.'

'Thank you.'

'Don't thank me,' Fowler said. 'What you're doing is potentially stupid.' He gave a nod. 'Aren't you going to see our star of the show while you're here?'

Anna hesitated. When she'd first agreed to work with Fowler, she'd been keen to know about N'Golo Durrant. Then she'd wondered if the details would affect her experience in the sequencer. But, right now, there were no details. He was just a kid in a coma. Someone whose life she was risking every time she submerged. 'Just for a few minutes,' she said. 'You fine getting back home?'

'I've got enough left this month for a pod,' Fowler replied, grimacing as he started to walk away. 'And if we crack this thing, money isn't going to be a problem for many, many months, is it?'

## 33

S&P Build 14.226a – Recommendation Module

Situation #GIHHCLTYYEN

Hunter Bot Update: Potential Target. ID: #KNR97876KM
   (Fiona Danvers) cleared. Victim (Beth Hayden) not
   at household. No biological evidence of Victim at
   household.

Recommendation: Unusual increase in food purchase
   associated with unregistered association. Upload case
   for Continuous Learning.

Associated Actions: Violent scene clear-up required at
   home of ID: # KNR97876KM.

THE ONLY HUMANS Anna found in the intensive care ward were
its patients. Another bot met her soon after she'd arrived on
the right floor, asking who she was here to see. On hearing
N'Golo Durrant's name, it checked her credentials and
then quickly led her into a warren of smaller, more private
side rooms.

As they progressed, Anna couldn't help but feel uneasy. It
took her a few minutes to understand what was wrong. At
the entrance lobby to the hospital there were plenty of bots,

254

but also plenty of people. Or at least, some people. Here on the intensive care floor, there appeared to be nothing but closed doors. If the patients were stable and needed only monitoring, feeding and cleaning, then the latest medical hardware was more than capable of doing the work. But what if someone woke up? Wouldn't they want to be greeted by a friendly face rather than a mechanical one?

Ahead of her, the bot stopped at a door numbered 436, which clicked open as she approached. Still no one. Anna looked about her, back and forth along the corridor. She'd expected to see one of the health techs, maybe a doctor. Certainly there should have been one of Jake's security team here to monitor the synapse tech.

'Where is everyone?' she asked.

'*N'Golo Durrant is in his bed.*'

'I meant where are the people looking after him?'

'*N'Golo is being cared for to all necessary standards.*'

'Where is everyone from the hub?'

The bot again seemed to think for a while. '*All hub staff were recalled twenty minutes ago.*'

'Recalled? By who? Jake Morley?'

'*I do not have access to that information. I am only able to answer questions about N'Golo Durrant, his status and his care.*'

Anna let out some of her exasperation. The bot didn't respond, although she knew it would have understood her meaning. Still, there wasn't exactly anything she could do about it, so she edged into N'Golo's room. The bed was almost hidden by a raft of medical and synapse hub equipment, the latter dumped haphazardly anywhere it would fit.

'N'Golo Durrant,' the bot chirped behind her.

Anna looked for the first time at the patient in the bed.

255

Her mouth turned dry. He was motionless, eyes closed and with various tubes running to and from his body. Just as she'd expected. But her overriding sensation remained one of shock.

N'Golo Durrant was white.

The edges of the hospital suite flexed as some of the blood left her brain. Seconds stretched. She couldn't quite keep her arms steady, and she was forced to cross them across her stomach to keep them still. It felt as though she was still within the synapse sequencer – but this was no immersion.

No, this was all too real.

The bot trundled up beside her. '*N'Golo Durrant remains in a neurologically subdued condition*,' it said.

'Yes.'

It was the only response Anna could manage. He was white. He was fucking white. All that effort they'd been through to check the immersion: visiting the Hayden household – finding the exact spot where he'd met the man at the hedgerow – visiting Compadres. And she'd not noticed it. Not in anything the Haydens had told her; not in her discussions with Fowler. She couldn't help but give a strangled laugh. *We have a major calibration problem*: she'd said that to Fowler. The PI had brought her N'Golo's files and she'd refused to accept them to keep the calibration and validation steps clear. Which meant she'd heard a name that sounded African and her brain had jumped to fill in the blanks with the wrong answer. Her subconscious had overpowered N'Golo's on one of the most basic points of his identity. What other information had she corrupted?

What else had she missed?

She closed her eyes. When they'd agreed to help Fowler,

they'd known that they'd get some details wrong. The simple price of not having multiple witnesses, all securing and validating each other's perspective. Instead, she only had N'Golo's. And her own.

Her own viewpoint. Her own prejudice. Aspects that would have been removed by the cold logic of the S&P algorithms. The thing that the justice ministry was so proud of: *We treat everyone the same, no matter their background.* And yet the form of the person sleeping in front of her now also prompted further, more immediate questions.

She remembered the scarring on Beth's arm. Did she cut too, N'Golo had asked her. Perhaps – but it could also just as easily have been a memory transferred from Anna's own brain. Just like the stench of blood and jet fuel. Why hadn't she spotted its importance at the time? She *knew* she couldn't smell anything in the sequencer, it was one of the first things she'd been told. The longer she immersed herself with N'Golo, the further they'd both drifted from the truth.

Did this mean she was now bound to fail?

'*Surprise is a natural reaction for those visiting patients in intensive care,*' the bot said. It was no doubt reading her body language, and trained to detect shock in those arriving for the first time. '*Please take your time.*'

'I'm fine,' Anna said. 'Just a bit woozy.'

'*Do you need some time alone? Do you need some water?*'

'Yes,' Anna whispered. 'Please. Some water would be great.'

The bot scurried away, returning all too quickly with a clear plastic beaker. Its absence didn't really give her enough time to recover, and she had to take the offering with her left hand to avoid showing it that her nails were still feeding on her right palm. The sensation of pain hadn't yet cut through the fog clouding her brain.

'*There are good signs*', the bot said, '*that N'Golo has started to recover. Neural activity remains low, but – uncertain diagnostic reason – has pushed him into the first phase of coma recovery.*'

Anna's breath shortened. A second punch while she was still reeling from the first. Recovery. The one word she didn't want to hear, at least not yet. She turned away from the bed – resisting a sudden urge to flee from the hospital – but stopped short. There was a man staring back at her from the corridor.

A man, not a bot.

'Hi.' Her voice wobbled. 'I'm from the hub.'

The man looked like he'd expected to find N'Golo alone. And, in just a fraction of a second, everything clicked. The Workers' League would have known N'Golo was still alive. And if Fowler had been right about the presence of cameras at Compadres, then those working there might have later recognised her. Found out she was now employed by Synapse Initiatives. Started worrying that N'Golo had been connected to the synapse sequencer.

The stranger took a couple of steps into the room, completely filling the space ahead of the door. There was no way round him. He had a square jaw and a flat face. He was bald, but only because he'd shaved his head close to his skull. His hands looked like two swollen chunks of meat. Anna was fairly sure she hadn't seen him in Fowler's photofits. Was he one of the vagrants who'd attacked the PI?

'Place an emergency call,' Anna said to the bot. 'This guy doesn't belong here.'

'*Unexpected error*,' replied the bot. '*I am disconnected from the network.*'

The skinhead's path to N'Golo's bed was encumbered by a bot and a woman and a lot of cables and wires. 'Get out of the way,' he said.

Anna tested her own connection to the boards. She found she couldn't ping Fowler or Mitchell, or dial through to the emergency services. She couldn't reach the hub.

The man grinned at her. 'Dampening field,' he said.

Anna looked down at the bed. N'Golo looked so vulnerable. Just like herself when she was connected to the sequencer. And she was the only one present who could protect him. 'I'm not moving.'

'Fine. I'm going to kill him, and then I'm going to kill you too.'

The man was surprisingly fast. He swept forward, and grabbed her by the throat. Anna stumbled back, all of her self-defence training useless. One hand was enough to stop her from breathing. From screaming. He punched her hard into her stomach, the lungful of air she hadn't been able to expel magnifying the pain as it popped in her throat.

He wasn't letting go. She needed to breathe, and he wasn't letting go. He lifted her from the ground, still throttling her. Everything grew white. She convulsed as her muscles ran out of oxygen. And she knew he wasn't going to stop.

The realisation prompted some last grain of resistance. She swung her legs forwards. Hard. Aiming for his kneecaps. Had she connected? Her vision came back in a dizzying rush as she fell, her body cold with sweat.

Anna twisted on the floor to find her attacker was still on the ground, clutching his knees. She only had a few seconds. She started scrabbling away to find help. Behind her, the stranger laughed.

'Where do you think you're going?'

Anna kept going. She filled her lungs as she crawled to the door, ready to scream for help, knowing even as she did so that there was no one to hear her.

Except for the police officers, running towards her.

# 34

'ARE YOU OKAY?'

I ignored the question. After pulling my clothes on in a way that ought to have broken a few of my fingers, Charley had wheeled me down to the conservatory and provided me with a too-hot cup of tea. I'd waited about twenty minutes for it to cool before my student turned up.

Sean shuffled in his seat. He looked youthful and meek, just like he'd done on his first visit. Back then, of course, he was worried I wasn't going to speak to him at all. He had other issues on his mind now. He'd tricked me, and I knew it.

'Are you okay, Ms Glover?'

'I'm fine,' I replied, my voice terse. In truth, I was tired. My attempt to get to my knife hadn't just meant a disturbed night. I could still feel where Charley had yanked me from the floor, and the pain of her ill treatment and my earlier fall had stopped me returning to sleep. The bruises also caused me to doubt my situation. To question what was real. I tried to remember when exactly I'd been brought to the nursing home.

'What do you think of the place?' I asked, looking around me.

We weren't quite alone. Aside from Charley, who was

261

hovering just out of earshot, a lone man sat a few metres away, jabbering. I didn't know his name. I don't think he knew what planet he was on, let alone which decade it was.

'It seems nice,' Sean said neutrally. 'You seem well cared for.'

'I sometimes wonder if I'm being cared for at all,' I replied. 'Maybe I'm being punished.'

'Why would you think that?'

I leant forward, keeping my voice in a whisper. 'Are you really sitting there, or are we both lying on a synapse bench waiting to be woken up?'

For a good few minutes, Sean didn't say anything. In some ways, he didn't need to: I could already see that he thought what I'd just said was insane.

'We were talking about Tanzania,' I said, trying to reassure Sean that I still had a grip on reality. 'I was about to explain to you how we'd proven that explosives were used to take out the tail.'

Sean smiled politely, his pen limp in his hand. 'I'm rather more interested in what happened in Iceland.'

I shook my head slightly. 'I agreed to talk to you about Tanzania.'

'And I apologise, but you yourself said I needed to know the background—'

I waved the student into silence, not wanting to have my own words used against me. Not again. 'I know.'

'Everyone trusted you to get to the truth in Tanzania because of what happened in Iceland.'

'How did you come across his name?'

'Gordon Hawley?'

'Yes.' I took a breath. 'He's not well known.'

'I came across it in the crash files,' Sean replied. 'He gets a single mention, which grabbed my interest. I ran his name. The only other record I found was on an honours list for the king's birthday. Can't remember which year – but he got a full knighthood.'

Only one reasonable conclusion could be drawn from that, nowadays: *government official*. Hawley was also a manipulative bastard. But was that all this Sean had? A single name, and a bit of imagination? A government official at another controversial crash investigation. Was that enough? Could I still bluff it out?

'I was young,' I said. 'Too young to have been made Investigator in Charge.'

'But you didn't turn the post down?'

'When someone wheels out a golden chair, you sit down in it. Just like you did when someone asked you to come and speak to me here.' Sean opened his mouth to protest. I didn't let him. 'There's no way you picked that name out of a file,' I said. 'Men like that don't leave traces for people to stumble over years later.'

'Then what do we do now?' he asked after a long pause. 'Are we finished here?'

I looked around the conservatory. Charley had disappeared. I wasn't sure where the bitch had gone, but while I'd been talking to Sean she'd managed to silently wheel another couple of nearly-deads into the room. They sat facing each other, waiting. And then I thought back to what I'd said to Grace when I'd first found out a student was interested in talking to me about Tanzania. I was running out of time. 'What do you know about my work with the synapse sequencer?'

'I'm not… it's not really my main interest,' he said.

'Before I talk to you about Iceland, I'd be interested to know what you would have done,' I said. 'Would you risk one life for the chance of saving another?'

'I can't answer,' Sean replied. 'I don't know enough about it.'

'It's a simple enough question: a boy is in a coma, a girl has been kidnapped. Would you risk the boy's life to find out what happened to the girl?'

'I…'

'What if it had been the other way round? Would you have risked the girl to save the boy?'

This time the answer was more definite. 'No.'

'Why not?'

'I don't know. I just wouldn't, I guess.'

'An AI wouldn't have given a different answer. Person A and Person B. Both the same. Would you risk a poor man to save a rich one? A rich one to save a poor one?'

'I'm not an AI.'

Before I could answer him, Grace came into the conservatory. She stared at me – sympathy etched deep into her expression – and then headed for one of the other lost souls who needed care.

'The plane that crashed in Iceland was the total opposite to Tanzania.' My voice shook. 'It was a jet: twin engines, tail-mounted. Could seat about 150 people, and it had been commissioned by the Russian military to fly its boys home on a standard rotation. Of course, the Icelanders didn't want the Russians there at all – but with the US acting increasingly erratically…'

Sean shuffled forward in his seat, straining to hear as my voice grew quieter. 'A lot was happening in Europe back then…'

'A lot was happening everywhere,' I replied. 'You take away people's work and they tend to revolt. Especially in countries which rejected the UI on a point of principle. Fifty years of peace upended because of a lack of jobs and the resulting inward-looking nationalism. Some countries turned left, others right. We Brits wobbled around the axis. Iceland was one of the countries that veered right. Far right.'

I took a breath. Grace was now working with one of the nearly-deads. 'When the West was mostly democratic, we invented all the tools that were required to control us; there was a time when we consented without regret to handing over information to our employers, to our governments. That complacency didn't change until Iceland moved to the right. The number of stories I read about people "disappearing" in Iceland was horrific, mainly naïve souls that had decided to post some little line of objection on the boards. The smallest of mutinies, squashed flat.'

'You said in your report the plane was taken down by ice?'

'Yes,' I said, hesitating. The world would have changed again, of course, but I had lost track of the politics. The facts of the crash remained clear. 'Yes, ice build-up on the wings, which was drawn into the engine on take-off and caused the jets to flare and ultimately explode.'

'But that wasn't the cause, was it?'

'The plane was de-iced,' I said. After all these years, the admission was coming all too quickly. Pulled from me in a swirl of wider confusion. 'I fixed the records to suggest it hadn't been. If you look closely, a few experts queried it, since jet engines are designed to withstand ice ingest. But they were easy to shout down. Even before pilots were removed from the cockpit, little algorithms and subroutines would have taken over the thrust to stop the flares from breaking the engine. No one knew how exactly they worked, of course, so it was relatively easy to find a unique set of conditions which suggested they'd failed.'

'And Gordon Hawley?'

'He turned up almost as soon as I arrived – British diplomat, liaising with the Russians, so he said. He'd been sent to remind me that the Russians wouldn't look kindly on their plane being brought down. And it *had* been brought down – we found a residue of explosives in the engines, not ice. Our lot didn't want to give them a pretext to invade Iceland.'

'It's a small country: why would that have been worse than Tanzania?'

I broke into a heavy laugh. 'You can't see the problem with the Russian military annexing such a strategically useful island? Don't they teach you about the Cuban Missile Crisis in school any more?'

Sean settled back in his seat. 'So that was your decision, then, report the Icelandic plane crash as an accident to stop a war?'

'Yes,' I said. 'And that's why I was chosen for Tanzania. The government knew I could be leant on if the facts didn't fit with their plans, and they could claim I was independent enough to keep the anti-war lot happy.'

I knew what he was going to ask next. It was what had kept me awake for so many nights of my life. Person A and Person B. *The risk of action against the risk of inaction.* 'I don't understand, then, why you feel so guilty,' he said. 'You told the truth in Tanzania…'

'Seventy-five thousand people died in Tanzania. None

of them our boys, but they appear every day on my charge sheet. Wouldn't it have been better to have lied?'

'But if you told the truth then you can't blame yourself for—'

'There was no winning move,' I said. 'Not in Tanzania, and not in Iceland.'

'You just said you stopped a war.'

'And that's all you can see, is it? Yes, a lot of people take the comfortable opinion that if we're not directly involved, then we can just look away. But after Iceland, I didn't.' I took a deep breath, feeling myself beginning to shake. 'People still died in Iceland: they just didn't die in a war. They were killed by a fascist government, one which would have surely toppled sooner had I told the truth about that crash. The risk of action against the risk of inaction. No one blames me for it, but how you can say I shouldn't feel any guilt about what was happening there?'

# 35

**Top News:**
Citizen Activity Programme to be extended (*Read more*)
Government announces closer economic ties with
   Tanzania (*Read more*)
Police hail latest update to Serve & Protect (*Read more*)


**Selected for You:**
Extension of S&P data rights to return to Parliament,
   unlikely to pass (*Read more*)


'FUCK! ANNA, I just heard what happened! Are you okay?'

Cody sprang from his seat almost as soon as Anna slid back the door to their office. The technician's concern made her kick herself for placing the cams in their synapse chamber.

She looked back at him, embarrassed and guilty. 'I'm fine,' she said. She'd covered the bruises on her neck with a pink silk scarf – the very same technique she'd used as a teenager to hide the occasional hickey.

'Do you know how the Workers' League found Durrant?'

'It happened right after Fowler was attacked at Compadres,'

Anna said. 'And the manager warned us off when we visited, too. It's possible he recognised me and found out that I worked at the hub. Couple that with Fowler's poking around, following up the information we uncovered in N'Golo's memory…'

'And the kidnappers noticed,' Weaver continued, following Anna's logic. 'They realised Durrant was still alive, giving us clues.'

'And then they worked out which hospital he was most likely to be in. Or perhaps they visited a lot of hospitals – it's not hard to walk in and out of those places if you have a dampener. There aren't any humans on the staff.'

'Is he okay?'

'Yes, the man who attacked me didn't get the chance to start on him before the police got there.'

'Lucky.'

*Lucky.*

'We've got police bots there now, as well as Jake's own security. It won't happen again.'

'And have they been able to tell you anything about the man who attacked you?'

'Another random thug. Mitchell has taken him for questioning, but I doubt he knows anything about Beth.'

'You're going to have to be careful.'

'I already am,' Anna said, trying not to laugh in case it sounded too tearful. She'd been careful for a long time now – keeping to her apartment, the hub and the pods that carried her between her workplace and home. 'I don't think I can do much more.'

'The health techs told me the police received an anonymous call from someone outside the hospital, saying you were in trouble?'

'Yes... don't ask me to explain, please.'

Cody frowned. 'The odd thing is that your biodata remained constant here in the hub, even though the guy was using a dampening field. I'll have to run some diagnostics.'

There was no need to run a diagnostic, Anna thought. Her biodata had remained constant because there was no dampening field around Kate. And when her own adrenaline and panic had spiked and cut out, Kate had reacted. She'd called the police. Sent in the cavalry. Not that Anna wanted to admit any of those details to her technician. 'When will N'Golo be ready to submerge?'

Cody glanced at his computer. 'He's ready now,' he said. 'But you should know: the hospital thinks there's a good chance he's coming round.'

Anna hesitated, knowing the equation had changed but not quite ready to accept the new answer. She'd not wanted to take the risk with N'Golo at first, but had been pushed into a decision by Beth's kidnap. But now? Had the tide turned once again? With no ransom demand and having had hardware sliced from her arm, were the odds now stacked more against Beth than N'Golo?

'When will he wake up?'

'We can't say...'

'The next few hours?'

'No,' Cody replied. 'Maybe two – possibly three – weeks.'

'Then it's too late to change track,' Anna said, unable to look at Cody. She found herself staring at his desk. A new photo of his baby daughter was pinned to his monitor. Back in Amblinside, Millie Hayden would be wanting them to fight for her daughter. 'Failure begets failure,' she added. 'And I don't think either of us can afford to lose these jobs.'

'STAY HERE.'

Anna found herself coming to a halt even though she hadn't yet become aware she'd been moving. Unsteady, she rocked back and forth, adjusting to some ghost of movement. N'Golo didn't seem to notice. He left her standing by a table, and headed across to the bar.

It was the same place she'd been in before; the same place she'd visited with Fowler, and where he'd later suffered his beating. This time, however, Compadres was busy. N'Golo had to squeeze sideways through a small gap in the crowd, using the roll of his shoulder to block out people who'd been waiting longer, and then he straightened out parallel to the counter to get the attention of the bar staff.

In many ways, he was exactly as she'd last seen him. The sequencer had reconstructed his height and weight perfectly. But in one important way he was completely different. This was a white version of N'Golo Durrant.

She'd never seen him. Not once. She'd only gone on a name – N'Golo – and what little she'd been told about him. The rest? Simply what her own brain had wrapped around the gaps. Her own synapse sequence.

'Hey! Are you at this table?'

Another woman was jabbing her finger at the empty table. She was ill-defined: just a bright red dress topped with electric-blue hair. Anna glanced back at N'Golo, and saw him briefly look at her before returning his attention to the bar staff.

'Yes, I, uh—'

The woman was gone. With N'Golo no longer looking, the woman seeking to take their table had simply evaporated from existence. Anna slipped onto the high stool and waited. Tapping her fingers on its surface, she flicked some ash on to the carpet. Around her people buzzed. But just like the woman in the red dress, they were all amalgams of others: faces lost in the crowd.

N'Golo headed back towards her with a triumphant grin. He was carrying two pints of beer. Served again, and served fast. 'You didn't know her, did you?'

He was searching the crowd for the woman with the blue hair. A few faces snapped in and out of definition, almost as if there was a narrow tunnel of high definition around which everything else was scrambled.

'She wanted to sit here,' Anna said.

'Huh.' N'Golo's distraction meant Anna was unlikely to be the same woman he'd seen the last time at the bar. She wasn't holding his attention in the same way. Which meant she was Beth again, and N'Golo had brought the Hayden girl to where he'd been meeting the people from the Workers' League.

Anna reached for her beer. 'Thanks,' she said.

'No problem. It is your dad's money, after all.' N'Golo grinned, like a joke had just hit him. 'Not sure he'd be happy me spending it here, though. You been before?'

'No.'

'Didn't think so.'

Anna tried to place herself in the mind of Beth Hayden. What would she notice about the place? What would strike her as being odd? 'There's people behind the bar,' she said. 'People, not bots.'

'Yeah, I thought you'd like that. Means you can sneak through the queue.'

N'Golo took a few large mouthfuls of beer. The music filling the background was just as tedious as before, and turned up that bit too loud in the hope of ensuring everyone had a good time. N'Golo must have brought Beth here for a reason that was important to him, something that had brought it to the fore of his memory in the coma. While she waited for it to play out, Anna had the chance to do some more careful digging.

'There's something I've been meaning to ask you,' Anna said. 'Who decided on the name N'Golo?'

'Urgh; he was some footballer my mum liked. Helped her team win the title.'

'You don't like it?'

'Do you like "Beth"?'

Anna paused. 'I guess so…'

'It's a nice, standard name. No threat on anyone's filters. And your folks spelt it right, too.'

'I'm not sure that—'

'No, you're right. If your parents had spelt it B-e-f, or any other odd combination, it still wouldn't have mattered. And do you know why?'

'No.'

'Weird name spellings only matter if you're poor.'

'Come on…'

N'Golo was distracted again, his attention drawn instead towards the bar's entrance. Anna thought perhaps the woman in the red dress was back, but when she risked a glance over her shoulder she immediately saw the man with the widow's peak. Within a few seconds he'd come to join them, dragging another stool with him.

This time the detail of his face was extraordinary. This memory was far better defined than anything she'd seen before in the sequencer. Right down to the lines on his face and the small greying hairs pushing out of his ears and nostrils.

'N'Golo,' the man said, his voice quiet against the background hum.

'This is the girl I was telling you about.'

Anna raised an eyebrow. 'You were talking about me?'

'N'Golo said you were interested in helping us.'

'Really? I don't know who you are.'

'Connolly,' the man said, almost as if she should recognise it. But more importantly, she had a name. She finally had a name. $V_1$. Take-off speed.

'Workers' League?'

Connolly smiled but didn't answer. N'Golo pushed back off his stool. 'You wanna drink?'

'Sure.'

'I didn't know how involved...' Anna let her voice drift and fail. Without N'Golo, the puppet from his memory had simply stopped performing. N'Golo sliced through the crowd and was served even more quickly than the first time. A few other customers looked disgruntled. One even threw his arms out wide to make a show that he'd been standing there longer – but Anna also saw the barman with the tattoos had clocked the man N'Golo was buying a drink for.

And that was all she needed to confirm it: he had lied to her and Fowler, then his cronies had come looking for N'Golo in the hospital. The boy they thought they'd already killed on the bridleway, who they now knew was connected to the sequencer. For Beth, the risk was that they'd cut and run. Anna had to find something that would lead directly to the kidnappers – and fast.

'First of all,' Connolly said, coming back to life as soon

as N'Golo got to within a few paces of the table, 'you need to forget what people tell you about us. We're not some homogeneous group.'

Anna thought about what she'd heard him say to N'Golo on the bridleway outside Amblinside. He certainly wasn't hard left. 'I've heard you called Luddites,' she said.

'Luddites, peasants, communists, Trotskyists. Whatever. Labels that seek to describe the past and not the future.'

'So everyone's got you wrong, then?'

'As I said, we're not a homogeneous group. Which is why I dislike the term, and the symbol.'

'Then why don't you explain?'

'I'd rather talk about your dad. He's one of the few people who doesn't seem to be affected by what's going on out there.' Connolly gave a rueful smile and reached across the table. Fast. One second he was holding his drink, the next he was holding her face, his thumb now resting on Anna's cheekbone while his fingers anchored themselves around the underside of her jaw – not letting her pull back. 'Let me make this plain for you: what do you think would happen if someone here were to cut your face?'

Connolly pushed his thumb upwards slightly, so that it slid over the ridge of her eye socket. Then he drew a line with it across her cheek before releasing her and letting his hand thud back down on the table. 'That's not going to happen, of course. But suppose it did?'

'My dad would pay for it to be healed,' Anna said.

'That's right,' Connolly said. 'You'd be fucked. Most employment filters include photographic scans. A scar – especially one on the face – signals issues. And that's all we boil down to nowadays: patterns and statistics.'

Beside her, confusion flashed across N'Golo's face. Connolly's answer hadn't matched her response. But Beth's dad *was* rich. If her face became scarred, then it would have been sorted. Maybe she hadn't given that response on this particular night. Maybe Beth had said something different. Either way, Connolly had simply responded the way N'Golo remembered.

'Clever girl,' Connolly continued, again prompted by something she hadn't actually said. So although she could interact with N'Golo, the others in his dreamscape were locked on to a single set of tracks. Which was going to make things difficult, if not impossible. Because beside her N'Golo was blanking – and Connolly's voice was starting to warp and break.

'*Problems,*' Cody squawked in her ear. '*We're getting weird feedback. Prepare to disengage.*'

*No!*

N'Golo shook his head as if trying to clear his senses, and took another drink of his pint. He hadn't yet bumped out. If she was careful, there should be no problem. She just needed to get the conversation back into the groove of N'Golo's memory.

'Yes, maybe your dad would do something,' Connolly continued, still lost in his one-sided conversation. 'But let's leave that for now. First, let me tell you about how we're helping young people like N'Golo take back control and...'

'*Anna, I'm pulling you out!*'


IF SHE COULD have screamed, she would have; instead she retched up her frustration. She'd been close. The man who'd introduced himself as Connolly had been talking freely, clearly trying to attract Beth to the Workers' League while probing for details of her family.

Anna contemplated the vomit on the floor. Cody hadn't come over to check on her; he was still at his workstation. Was he still angry with her after all? It was a long wait before her muscles came back under her control, for her tongue to move freely again. Eventually, she managed to shift her torso upright, the feeling and sensation still not quite reaching her legs.

'You should have kept me in there longer,' she said. 'That was the closest we've come to finding anything useful. I got a name.'

Cody glanced at her briefly before snapping his attention back to his workstation. He looked worried. N'Golo hadn't been that disturbed by the interaction, had he? An awful feeling hit her. Had something gone seriously wrong?

Was that it? Had they had their last submersion?

'Is he okay?'

'Keep calm, Anna.' Cody turned back to her. 'Just relax and try to breathe.'

Anna stared blankly across the chamber as she obeyed the technician's instructions. But that didn't mean she could allow him to keep her in the dark. 'Tell me, Cody,' she said. 'Have we lost him?'

'Durrant's fine.'

'Then why?'

'I'm worried about you.'

Anna froze. *Severance.* Starting with the face, she rotated her jaw, moved her eyes, then slowly rippled movement down to her toes. Her right foot responded, her left didn't.

She could feel it, at least. Everything was coming back just as it should; there was no sign anything was wrong. No sense that any part of her body was missing. 'I'm fine,' she said.

Cody gave a final check of his workstation, then rushed towards her. He leant over her bench and stared down into her face. 'Your adrenaline is off the scale and your heart is starting to fibrillate.'

For a moment Anna didn't understand. There was no hammering in her chest, no triggering of panic. And then she got it. Something was happening back home, at her apartment.

Something had disturbed her spoof.

# 36

POLICE VEHICLES WERE parked outside the street-level doors of her apartment block, their blue and red lights blinking. She could only stare at them as her pod took a hard right from the street and down into her building's basement.

She checked the boards, filtering for news of localised crime. Nothing had appeared, but if anything bad had happened, it would probably still take an hour or so before the first stories started to be issued. Anna shivered in the pod's compartment, then slipped out into the empty subterranean parking lot. Cody had demanded to know what was wrong as she'd scrambled to leave the hub. He'd even wanted to accompany her home. His concern had only prompted more feelings of guilt about how easily Fowler had made her distrust him. It was bad enough that she'd planted cameras in the hub. Now what was she going to say to him?

That her bioreadings were being spoofed? That she'd deliberately misled Jake by routing her data via a third party? That her deception could get both of them fired? No, for the time being she just needed to get home and find out what had happened to Kate. There was still a chance that all this was a bad scare – even though the presence of the police cars suggested otherwise.

*The Workers' League had found her.*

Anna had been trying not to think in those terms, but it would make sense. Fowler had blundered his way into their path at Compadres, and then she'd inadvertently gotten in their way as they'd tried to kill N'Golo. Despite all her precautions, they wouldn't be the first strangers to find out where she lived. Maybe they'd expected to find her apartment empty and had simply planned to wait for her there. Kate would have been in the wrong place at the wrong time. An unexpected lodger, caught in the crossfire.

Anna wiped away a tear as she ran up the stairs to the lobby. There was a single security bot sitting behind the front desk, observing the comings and goings, and challenging those it didn't recognise to prove their identity. Its head swivelled towards her as she approached. '*Anna Glover,*' it said. '*Police bots are in attendance at your apartment.*'

'What happened?'

The bot remained sitting placidly behind its desk. To all intents and purposes it appeared as if someone could walk right past it – but its smooth outer shell also housed Tasers and stun gas. Just like those stationed at Amblinside and the hub. And the damn thing was fast: she'd once seen a similar model tackle a guy who'd had a bit too much to drink. And yet what use was it if Kate was hurt?

'Why didn't you stop them?'

'*I am not authorised to obstruct the police.*'

'Not the police,' Anna said. 'The Workers' League. Why didn't you…?'

The bot didn't answer, and the reason pinged into Anna's brain, taking the words from her mouth. The Workers' League hadn't been here. An unannounced visit from the police would have been enough to scare someone who'd been making a living as a spoof. Even the unflappable Kate.

In the time it took to get to her floor, all she could think about was how she'd been attacked in the hospital and how Kate had reacted to the loss of her signal. She'd immediately called the police. If anyone had stopped to really think about how she'd made that call, then the answer would have been obvious. Kate had effectively both made herself a target and pulled the plug on her life as a spoof.

'*Anna Glover.*'

A police sentry bot was blocking her doorway. She realised it had called her name to alert the people inside her apartment rather than as a greeting.

'Where's Kate?'

'*Katherine Owen, preferred name "Kate", has been taken for interview.*'

'I want to see her.'

'*That will not be possible.*'

Anna peered round the bot. A human police officer, as well as a couple of bots, were busy inside. 'Can I go in? This is my home.'

'*That will not be possible... at this time.*'

Before she could object, a call came in from the boards. Anna took a few steps away from the sentry bot – even though she knew it would still be able to hear her – and connected.

'Anna,' Cody said, 'what the fuck is going on?'

'I've got problems,' Anna said. She stared up at the ceiling of the narrow corridor, and couldn't help but feel the panic ahead of an imminent crash. She'd just lost her spoof, and that meant her job was about to vanish too.

'Your biorhythms smoothed out – but they're all over the

place again now. HR have emailed me to ask if I know what the problem is. I told them you just had a bad experience with the sequencer.'

'Thank you.'

'So what did you see in there? What happened?'

Anna breathed out, trying to remain calm. Cody still thought the initial biodata spasm was something to do with the submersion. But if the shock of being arrested had dissipated from Kate, then it was still very much rippling through her own system. And if that's what Cody was now seeing, then it meant Kate had been detached. Anna's own data was now being sent directly to the hub, providing it with a wide-eyed view of her terminal anxiety. She briefly thought about trying to bluff her way through this – to buy herself a bit more time. But there was no way she could keep it from them. They'd find out in the next few hours.

'Anna Glover?'

The voice had come from behind her and wasn't part of the call. Anna disconnected from Cody and found a stick-thin and all too young police officer standing beside the sentry bot. He looked very pleased with himself. 'I'm sure you know that routing your biodata via a third party is a criminal offence.'

'Yes.'

'Well, it's certainly no war crime, Miss Glover. But you can consider yourself busted.'

# 37

SEAN HAD GONE. I looked at his empty chair, not quite remembering when he'd left me. I screwed my eyes shut for a second, opening them to find the seat still unoccupied. I wasn't sure if I regretted what I'd told him. Still, it was too late. The secret was gone, and I realised the strange sensation in my chest might be one of relief.

I was alone in the conservatory. The other nearly-deads had been taken back to their rooms. Packed away for the night so the nursing staff could get some rest. I remained because I'd asked for a few more minutes alone to think things through, and because I hadn't been hungry at the time when everyone else had been served their food.

Was I still in the sequencer?

The question had come back to me almost as soon as I'd realised Sean had gone. I'd made my admission. Told the truth about Tanzania, and Iceland. And now my inquisitor, the man who'd come to speak to me posing as a student, had left me.

Was there any way to tell?

It had once appeared so simple. The movement, slightly off. The lack of smell. Absence of pain. The numbness of interacting with objects via someone else's memory, all on time delay. None of it could be distinguished from simply being old. I strained to see the edges of the conservatory, but found most lost in blur. The boundary of a memory? Or of myopia?

'I've made my admission,' I said. I tilted my head upwards. 'Are you going to let me out now?'

Nothing. Or rather, no response from outside the construct. From somewhere distant there came the sound of clomping feet. Charley appeared in front of me. 'No need to shout,' she said, visibly grumpy. 'I was coming to feed you.'

I wasn't hungry. But I knew I needed to try to consume enough to stop what was left of my body from withering completely. Tonight, though, it wasn't even solid food. A beaker filled with a pale pink sludge was put in front of me. Grace had once explained that it was filled with all the vitamins and minerals I needed, but in a more compact form. Something to make sure I had enough to sustain me, rather than having to rely on the measly intake of solid food I was now able to eat before I tired of chewing.

I turned my head slightly, and found N'Golo watching me. He was examining the beaker or, more accurately, the pink sludge within it. 'Do you drink it or eat it?' he asked.

'You never had a milkshake?' I didn't expect an answer. I just hoped he wouldn't start again with the numbers.

'Who are you talking to now?' Charley asked. 'Who are you seeing there this time?'

Grace came into the conservatory, wheeling another of the nearly-deads. A man, perhaps a little younger than me. I'd seen him several times before, but only now did I have a horrible feeling I'd seen him before somewhere…

'Always two of them,' N'Golo said.

I looked at him again, then at Grace. Then at Charley.

'No bots,' he continued. 'Two humans, tasked with looking after you. Good cop, bad cop.'

I took hold of my beaker and tried to take a mouthful of the sludge. It stuck on my tongue. I coughed it down. 'No,' I whispered. 'Bots aren't allowed to work in places like this. Not now. It was all explained to me. The number of bots was rolled back after the workers' revolt…'

'Do you really believe that?'

The question caught me off guard. I'd taken another mouthful of the semi-liquid and it kicked at the back of my throat, causing me to cough and gasp and fight for air. Grace was dealing with someone else, so Charley was the closest. I put my hand up flat, trying to signal that I was okay. But I couldn't yet speak to tell her to stop. The bitch kept on coming.

'You need to eat that,' Charley said, pointing towards my evening meal. She checked behind her. 'Do you need some help?'

'No,' I said. I picked up the beaker and took another small mouthful. Not enough to cause me to cough. I swallowed, letting the sludge pass into my throat and being careful to breathe. All the time, Charley watched me.

As did N'Golo. 'When is now?' he asked. 'Where are you Anna Glover? Where are you really?'

He began to count. The same string of numbers. They were more and more familiar. I whispered them along with him.

'You need to eat more than that,' Charley said.

She watched as I took another mouthful. Another small mouthful, carefully judged so that I could continue to eat at my own pace. But then a moment of panic caused me to issue a small hiccup: Grace was leaving the conservatory, taking the old fool she'd been dealing with back to his room.

Charley noticed this too. She took another step forward, and I felt her hand on my jaw. Pulling it open and pushing my head back. The beaker was at my lips. The sludge and slime filled my mouth, and my gullet kicked in to try to swallow it while keeping my airway clear.

'You need to eat this,' reiterated Charley, continuing to pour. She let the beaker hit my teeth and slice at my gums. I kept swallowing – my body starting to shake as it ran out of air – my ears filled with those damn numbers now being called out by N'Golo.

Then suddenly he stopped, came close and whispered, just as the beaker was being pulled away from my mouth and I was able to cough the last of the sludge from my mouth and onto my chin. 'You're still in the sequencer,' he said. 'The nurses aren't bots because you're still in Jake's sequencer. And it's time you got out.'

# 38

'THEY'RE ALREADY SAYING there's going to be an inquiry.'

Holland's enjoyment seemed unaffected by Anna's harsh, angry stare. On one of the spare synapse benches, beside Jake's broken torso, lay Mitchell. The S&P analyst was already connected to the sequencer and interacting with Jake. In a few moments Anna would be expected to allow herself to become immobile on one of the benches, as her consciousness was transferred into the sequencer to join them.

Anna looked deep into Holland's face. She'd wanted Cody to accompany her to Jake's synapse chamber – to be there during the time she was submerged – but he'd refused. He'd told her it wouldn't do her any good anyway, because Holland would have simply pulled rank and had him thrown out. And yet she'd still come, despite her fears about what this nurse might do to her while her mind was elsewhere. The call from Jake had been marked urgent. If she wanted to keep her job, what choice did she have?

'Come on, then,' Holland said. 'The sooner you get connected, the sooner you can be fired.'

Anna didn't allow herself to be rushed. She'd arrived straight from home, and had brought with her a small black

287

leather handbag. She looked around for somewhere to put it while she was submerged, then opted for the empty bench next to the one she'd soon be occupying. 'I don't understand why you don't just admit it,' the nurse continued. 'Everyone knows you fixed the outcome of that crash, and everyone knows you were pressured. Being caught using a spoof now only confirms it.'

'I'm not here to talk about Tanzania.'

Holland laughed, and brushed back some of her red hair. 'They'll make you talk eventually,' she said.

Anna pulled herself on to an empty bench, swinging her legs round and letting her head settle on the steel. She pushed her head back to keep her airway clear.

*Hold her under. Keep her down.*

'I'm not going to discuss Tanzania with you,' Anna said. 'I'm here to see Jake.'

'Your heart rate is high,' the nurse said, checking her systems and then moving across to her bench. 'Almost like you're worried about something.' She paused, allowing herself a sly grin. 'This is your data this time, isn't it?' She placed a hand on Anna's chest, directly on the breastbone. 'Yep, you need to learn to relax.'

*Hold her under. Keep her down.*

'Just connect me,' Anna said, her voice shaking while she wondered what would happen next. She drifted away seconds later. One second she was on the synapse bench…

The next standing in a gym.

Directly in front of her Jake was running on a treadmill, sweat pouring off him and drenching his bright yellow running vest. Mitchell was speaking, but she stopped sharply as Anna popped into existence.

'Keep talking,' said Jake, gasping for breath. He was running hard, his legs pumping as the machine kept the road open ahead of him. In the real world, he wouldn't have been able to keep this pace up for long. Here, though, he seemed to be able to keep going indefinitely.

Mitchell hesitated, waiting for a break in the rhythm of Jake's exercise. She wasn't going to get one, though, and she gave up trying. 'Given recent developments' – she glanced at Anna – 'we're ceasing cooperation with your experiment. We want your team to remove their equipment from Durrant's bedside and—'

'That doesn't make sense,' Anna interrupted. Jake glared at her. The treadmill gave him a slight height advantage, and her position in front of it – watching him continually charge towards her – only served to underline the threat.

'We can issue a warrant if need be,' Mitchell continued. 'But I'm sure you'd prefer to have your technicians remove your equipment, rather than have it impounded.'

'We'll have it cleared by the end of the day,' Jake said, continuing to run.

'It's getting late. Are you sure you can—'

'I'm aware of the time,' Jake snapped. 'I live in here just as you do out there.'

'Fine. Just make sure it gets done.'

Anna cleared her throat. 'Aren't you forgetting Beth Hayden?'

'Of course not.'

'Connolly,' Anna said. 'N'Golo took Beth to see someone named Connolly.'

Mitchell sighed. 'Pretty much everything you tell Fowler gets straight through to us,' she said. 'But we've already run

289

the numbers, and every Connolly within the area has come up clean.'

'Are you sure? Did you push down into their personal data?'

'Those we were able to legally access, yes.'

'So what do you intend to do?'

When Mitchell spoke, it was with more than a little regret. 'The probability Beth Hayden is still alive has been dropping by the hour. In fact, her chances took a tumble off a cliff as soon as the kidnappers found out that their plot was compromised by Durrant. Resources are being reassigned.'

'Already?'

'Whoever has taken Beth has already demonstrated a certain degree of brutality,' Mitchell explained. 'The chances they intend keeping her alive are low; particularly given the lack of further contact.'

'Is that you talking, or S&P?'

'It's both, Miss Glover. Christ! This "Connolly" was using a false name. I would have thought you'd be familiar with the idea given your situation. I think we're done here… How do I discon—'

Mitchell was gone. The heavy thump of Jake's sprinting drew Anna's attention back to him. How long had he been running like that? How long would he continue?

'You were using a spoof,' he said.

Anna nodded. 'They won't let me see her. I expected them to arrest me too.'

'They would have done,' Jake replied. He reached forward and touched the controls of the treadmill, lessening the pace. His breathing immediately adjusted. He didn't seem to need any recovery time. The change in speed was probably only to allow him to speak more easily. 'I intervened.'

'Thank you.'

'Using a spoof is in violation of your employment terms. But more importantly, it's bloody stupid.'

'My work isn't affected by...' Anna felt a sudden itch running away from her wrist and towards her elbow. 'It's unaffected. I have it under control.'

'Your real stats are way outside the performance boundaries of where I want my staff.'

'I'm good at my job.'

'People with anxiety tend to concentrate on the wrong thing,' Jake continued, as if he hadn't heard her. 'They don't see the bigger picture. There's a fine line between being a specialist and becoming a dinosaur.'

'I have it under control,' Anna repeated.

Jake didn't acknowledge her defence. 'Have you experienced anything strange using the sequencer?'

Anna couldn't help but give a strangled laugh. She knew what he was getting at. It was time to admit it. 'I've been able to speak with N'Golo directly,' she said. 'Not just experience his memories.'

'As yourself – or through the eyes of others?'

'Both, just like we're doing n—'

'It's not the same,' cut in Jake. 'Not the same at all. You should have said something. Maybe your own biofeed would have warned Weaver. He still should have noticed the feeds were being spoofed, though...'

'He's not to blame for this.'

'Don't interrupt me, Anna,' he said curtly. 'Your technician seems to have a habit of minor failures.'

*Failure begets failure.* 'Cody is a good technician.'

'Noted.' Jake slowed the treadmill some more. 'The risks

of using the sequencer are clearly stated in your employment terms. We've already spoken about the first: severance.'

'And the second?'

'Post-detachment echoing. You may have noticed your own brain fills in gaps within the memory construct?'

*N'Golo Durrant was white.* 'Yes…'

'It's a two-way thing,' Jake continued, his tone remaining angry. 'A little bit of Durrant may be in your mind now, and he'll be hard to get out. Worse, if this Durrant kid does ever come round, then his memories of certain events are going to be screwed. He'll have pieces of you inside his cortex.'

Anna suddenly felt cold. The chill concentrated in her torso, along the front of her chest. *If I unbuttoned your shirt, you'd get cold,* Cody had said. Back on the synapse bench, was Jake's nurse playing some sort of sick game? She had to say something.

'Jake—'

'There's going to be an inquiry into that Tanzania business.' Jake was climbing down from the treadmill. Glaring at her, still towering over her. There was no trace of the kindly businessman now.

'I've seen the rumours,' Anna said, swallowing her complaint.

Jake seemed surprised. 'Really? I thought it was secret. My information comes from the Ministry. Whatever – when it's formally announced, I'm going to have to let you go. You do realise that, don't you? We can't have that kind of negative attention on the company.'

'Yes.'

'In the meantime, you have a short window.'

'Window? To do what?'

'You still have a few hours to get what you need from N'Golo Durrant, before the team at the hospital unplugs my equipment. And do you know what success begets, Anna?'

ANNA PUSHED OPEN the door to the synapse chamber – *her synapse chamber* – and headed straight for one of the empty benches. She didn't bother to look for Cody, she knew he was here, still communicating with the hospital-based health team and no doubt processing the news that their experiment was being brought to a premature end.

'I want you to submerge me at exactly the same point as before,' she said, hoisting herself onto the bench and throwing her black handbag on to the floor. 'The exact same memory.'

There was a moment's pause. Then footsteps echoed across the chamber's tiles as Cody hurried towards her. Anna responded by pushing her head back, making it easy to make the final checks. He didn't touch her.

'We're shutting down, Anna.'

'No – we still have time for one more go. Attempt seven.'

'Anna…'

'There's a girl's life at stake, Cody.'

'And a young man called N'Golo Durrant could also die. The health team are sure now: he's coming out of his coma. He's going to recover.'

'But not in time, Cody! Not in time to save Beth!'

Anna stared at the ceiling. They were rushing. It would amplify the risks. But the answer was there, she knew it. They'd been within touching distance last time.

'Didn't think you were a handbag sort of person,' Cody said, undercutting the tension as he noticed what she'd dropped. Anna continued to stare upwards. She had no wish to talk about it. After she'd left Jake's memory construct, she'd returned to find the bag's zip half open, which meant Holland had rifled through that as well. And she'd made a point of leaving the bag open so Anna would know what had happened. 'You were using a spoof,' Cody continued. He sounded disappointed.

'Yes.'

'I should have noticed.'

'It's not your fault,' Anna said.

'It's all over the boards… that, and the inquiry thing.'

'Then they have a choice, don't they? Arrest me for using a spoof, or frame me for what happened in Tanzania. Either way, I don't have much time. And neither does Beth Hayden. If we achieve nothing more here today, I need to know all this wasn't a waste of fucking effort!'

Cody looked round the empty chamber, as if searching for someone to either object or give him permission. He found neither, and instead headed back to his workstation. Anna closed her eyes and waited. She heard him speaking to the health team. Didn't quite catch what they said in return.

'I'm getting some odd readings from the biofeeds,' Cody said, his voice starting to be lost.

'They're not odd,' Anna whispered, losing some of the sensation in her jaw. 'They're mine.'

'CONNOLLY,' THE BLOND man said. Anna had slipped back into N'Golo's memory of the bar. The man in front of her seemed relaxed, confident. Just as he had been the first time round.

'Workers' League?' She heard herself say the words, but

tried to let them flow without thinking. Here, she was Beth Hayden, not Anna Glover. She needed to keep that in mind, to remember what she could of the mistakes she'd made previously that had almost caused N'Golo to bump out. Connolly grinned.

N'Golo stood up. 'You wanna drink?'

'Sure.'

Without N'Golo, Connolly again fell silent and static. He remained like that until N'Golo came back with another pint of beer. He placed it on the table, but the man calling himself Connolly didn't pause to drink.

'First of all,' Connolly said, 'you need to forget what people tell you about us. We're not some homogeneous group.'

'I've heard you called Luddites.'

'Luddites, peasants, communists, Trotskyists. Whatever. Labels that seek to describe the past and not the future.'

'So everyone's got you wrong, then?'

'As I said, we're not a homogeneous group. Which is why I dislike the term, and the symbol.'

'Then why don't you explain?'

'I'd rather talk about your dad. He's one of the few people who doesn't seem to be affected by what's going on out there.' Connolly gave a rueful smile and then reached across the table. As before, his thumb came to rest on Anna's cheekbone while his fingers clasped her jaw. 'Let me make this plain for you: what do you think would happen if someone here were to cut your face?'

Then he drew a line with his thumbnail across her cheek before releasing her face and letting his hand thud back down on the table. 'That's not going to happen, of course. But suppose it did?'

Anna hesitated. *She was a girl pretending to be something she wasn't.* 'I'd be scarred,' she said.

'That's right,' Connolly replied. 'You'd be fucked. Most employment filters include photographic scans. A scar – especially one on the face – signals issues. And that's all we boil down to nowadays: patterns and statistics.'

'We're people, not numbers.'

'Clever girl. But surely the biggest lie is that the government only sees us as simple numbers. Let me give you a scenario: say Person A and Person B both steal twenty thousand pounds from the government, each one by making a false UI claim. Which one do you think goes to jail, and who gets to pay the sum back and continue as a Member of Parliament?'

The opportunity was here. She had to take the next step. 'You think my dad could help in some way?'

'Yes, maybe your dad could do something, but let's leave that for now. First, let me tell you about how we're helping young people like N'Golo take back control.'

'Okay.'

'*Anna – we're getting some minor perturbations from the hospital…*' Cody's voice buzzed into her ear.

N'Golo looked puzzled, then he formed a quizzical smirk. 'Déjà vu,' he said.

'The Luddites broke the factory machinery because they thought those devices would take their jobs,' Connolly continued, ignoring his companion's uncertainty. 'They didn't realise their descendants would end up shovelling coal or packing crates or working in call centres or managing social media. As a society, we're like blindfolded men being forced to walk across stepping stones. We put our foot out, and find some other job to occupy our time while the machines gobble up the stone just vacated behind us. Always, except for now. We've run out of stones. There's too many of us, too few decent jobs, and the illusion that what we're now tasked with is worthwhile has burst.'

*Decent jobs.* Connolly wasn't ever going to spend his life shovelling coal or packing crates. He was a white collar, just like her. Which gave them another detail: another way to whittle down the list of potential suspects, if she could get the information to Fowler. The Workers' League was supposedly composed of the diehard left, but this was a man who until recently probably had little sympathy for labour rights. Not until his own job was taken.

'You're planning on breaking the frames though, aren't you? Just like the Luddites?'

Connolly shook his head and reached for his beer.

'We can't attack the machinery,' N'Golo said. 'It's too well protected.'

'As are our noble politicians and their ears,' Connolly said, taking back the conversation from his young recruit. 'N'Golo tells me you're a big fan of Emmeline Pankhurst?'

*Trust in God; she will provide.* 'Yes.'

'Did you know the Pankhursts – Emmeline and Christabel – only wanted the vote on the same basis as men at the time? Only for women who owned property? They expelled Adela Pankhurst for suggesting all women – no matter how rich or poor – were important.'

Anna kept silent. She had no wish to get into an argument with a figment from N'Golo's memory. Beth was all that mattered, and the Hayden girl probably hadn't wanted to argue with Connolly either.

'Class used to be the main way we identified ourselves.'

Connolly was warming to his theme. 'Somewhere along the line, the richest in society persuaded us class didn't matter. Take another one of your heroes, for instance: Ada Lovelace. She went to the mills of Lancashire and saw how punch-cards were being used to control industrial looms. Tell me, why do you think the title of the world's first computer programmer didn't go to a mill owner and instead went to a countess?'

*Because she wrote it down, you jackass.* 'I don't know.'

Connolly laughed. 'It's all about perception. What we're told is what we think. To that end the news you get to see is personalised, to corral you into behaving as the government wants. Start expressing sympathy for certain views? Then they'll feed you stories to make you think along their lines. Of course, some stories are too big to be drowned out, but then they can usually find some angle or other to divert some of your anger.'

Someone – had it been Kate? – had said something like this to her before, and she'd dismissed it. She still thought it unlikely. But then a horrible thought struck her: she knew the government allowed street protests simply to relieve some of the bubbling tension. *But the 'angle' deliberately included to divert some of your anger?* Could that mean news stories about Tanzania focused on her kept on cropping up just to distract people's attention? Was the government deliberately keeping people angry with her to distract them from the real issues behind the war?

Before she could respond, Connolly stood up from the bar table. 'Don't look so shocked. The government has always manipulated our news. The real question is, why do you think they would have ever stopped? So we're going to join the same game. Make those at the top dance to our tune, and do what we want. Let's talk again soon.'

He was leaving. Anna opened her mouth to try to call him back, but it was too late. Connolly was leaving – and N'Golo wouldn't respond to her.

ANNA OPENED HER eyes. She was back on the synapse bench. Cody was already checking her airway was clear. Some movement flickered into her lips and the back of her throat. She was going to vomit, but she swallowed hard. 'Push me under,' she said. 'Hold me down.'

SHE WAS IN a basement lit by a single light bulb that hung by a short cord from the damp plaster ceiling. The fitting hadn't been secured properly, which meant the bulb left shadows on one side of the basement while the other was doused in bright light. A set of block concrete steps led upwards towards a door that had been left open. Anna couldn't see anything beyond it.

N'Golo stared back at her. He looked angry. It took a few moments for her to realise the memory wasn't in motion. She called into the air; 'Cody?'

'*Yeah – sorry, I had to jump tracks.*'

'I'm in some sort of basement.'

'*We're holding steady-state until we get the feed stabilised.*'

'How's it looking?'

No answer.

'Cody?'

'*Are you in something that looks… right?*'

Anna looked about her. The basement looked anything

but all right, but it was a tangible memory. 'Yes. Why?'

'*Then we're running it.*'

N'Golo moved. 'This isn't what we agreed,' he said. His breathing was heavy, his voice pushed through bared teeth.

Anna remained mute. Her conversation with Cody had distracted her from a pertinent fact. She and N'Golo were the only ones in the room. She scrambled for words, and then remembered she just needed to move the conversation along.

'What is it you think we agreed?'

She kept her voice emotionless, hoping the plain question would elicit a useful answer. For the time being, she had to guess she was playing the role of Connolly – and that was unfortunate, given she very much wanted to hear what he had to say. But she did have one advantage: without a third person, she could now talk to N'Golo without having to worry about fitting her words into a set conversation. Just as long as she didn't wander too far away from what he was expecting her to say…

'Not this,' N'Golo said. 'I didn't agree to this.'

*This.* Anna took another look around the basement. Looked again at the concrete block stairs leading upwards towards the thick door. A few cables trailed around the edges of the ceiling, attaching to a small box in one corner. It looked like dampening field tech. Something to stop the life-logging apps feeding out, prior to making the detachment permanent. So this was where they were keeping Beth.

'It will be fine,' Anna heard herself say, trying to find a route between what she now knew and what N'Golo could remember. 'We bring the girl here, and we keep her here.'

N'Golo's head was turned away, as if denying himself to the situation. And then she saw it: the moment he understood.

That same terrible moment she'd detected so often in the voices of pilots about to crash – and in the face of the guy who'd shot up the entertainment plaza. It was too late. The mistake had been made. Anna immediately felt sorry for him. But she had to remember, at some point he had rebelled. He'd at least tried to stop it. And then the Workers' League – or whoever they wanted to be – had beaten him into a coma for it.

'Hey,' Anna said, snapping the boy's attention back to her. 'Hey, listen to me. Do you remember the way here?'

N'Golo shrugged, suddenly looking like a sullen teenager again.

'You know the way here, N'Golo. I need to know that you can bring her here, yes?'

N'Golo muttered something. Not quite a 'yes' but most certainly not a 'no'. How would Connolly have handled the situation?

'Tell me,' Anna said. 'Tell me where we are.'

N'Golo finally looked up and into her eyes. The conflict was clear in his face. And the walls of the basement melted. They shook, and slid away.

*'Anna – fuck, Anna – we're losing him!'*

'Where are we N'Golo?'

They were no longer in the basement. Not quite. The floor and first foot or so of crumbling plaster provided a square frame around them, but everything beyond had been replaced by the country lane at the back of the Haydens' home, from which a thin, straight arrow-like line of dazzling green light pointed – not at Beth's brightly lit window, but at the darkened room next to it.

'N'Golo! Look at me! Where are you taking the girl?'

No answer.

'Where did you take Beth?'

A man stepped from the shadows. Connolly. He strode up behind N'Golo and took him by the collar. Pushed him down. Kicked him in the ribs. Rained punches down on him.

'*Anna, I'm pulling you out.*'

Anna moved quickly. She moved through the image of Connolly, and the fists that kept on coming. She took hold of N'Golo's face as gently as she could.

'Listen to me,' she said. 'Listen. We'll only keep her a short while; her father will pay. But you have to tell me: where are we keeping her?'

The figure of Connolly evaporated. He took with him the memory of the country lane, and the last fragments of the basement. For perhaps the last time, N'Golo looked at her; confusion written deep into his face.

'Her father isn't going to pay,' he said. 'But her mother will.'

# 39

Hunter Bot 28.637f – 47637946376gh476r74r64 – Action Log

Objective: Find Target (Priority, Medium)

Background Data: Downloaded from S&P. Receiving continual updates.

Geographical Sweeps: 78 addresses visited. Unable to access 4 (return visits scheduled). Infrared cams: Within parameters. Recognition cams: Negative. Behavioural Cams: Negative.

ANNA WOKE, TRIED to move, but couldn't. Above her, Cody was going through the normal post-submersion routine. Only when he'd finished did he notice the rapid shifting of her eyes.

'What is it?'

Anna couldn't answer. Not yet. Her mouth remained a numb chasm, and each segment of movement was taking an age to come back. Instead, she tried to focus. Tried to ignore the slow accumulation of sensation that was spreading throughout her face, and thought about N'Golo's final words.

*Her mother will.*

She made a noise. Something vocalised, but it was not properly formed by her nose or lips. More like a judder of sound. She could have been trying to say anything, but Cody at least appeared to understand the urgency.

'You saw something?' he said. 'You know where she is?'

Anna blinked. Once. She started to feel sensation in her cheeks and forehead. But nothing in her tongue, which remained limp and stodgy.

'Durrant looks okay,' Cody continued, misunderstanding her. 'His neural activity is spiking but we think he's okay…'

Anna blinked. Still, she couldn't speak.

'Take your time. Just take your time. I'll get Fowler.'

*Fuck Fowler, get Mitchell!*

The thought screamed inside Anna's skull, but she couldn't articulate it. Not yet. Again, she tried to relax. Her brain was firing hard. Too much adrenaline.

'Mith-thell,' she mouthed, almost entirely on an outward breath. Not quite right, but her technician seemed to hear.

'Mitchell?'

Anna blinked. Once. *Yes.*

'I'll get them both… you want me to get them both?'

She blinked again. Hard. Providing just enough meaning to put the technician to work. It took another few minutes, though, before her jaw loosened sufficiently to flex at her command. 'Mil-lie Hay-den,' she said. 'We need to find Millie Hayden!'

'I THOUGHT I was clear,' Mitchell said. 'Jake told me the equipment would be removed.'

Anna ignored the stupidity of what was being said to her.

The S&P analyst had arrived at the hub quickly, but the main thrust of what N'Golo had revealed within the sequencer had already been conveyed. Mitchell could have just messaged them from the police headquarters – or en route to the Hayden house. Instead, she'd come personally to the hub, and Anna had intercepted her in the entrance lobby. She'd not expected the first exchange to be about what had been agreed with Jake, though.

'Did you get to Millie Hayden?'

'Millie Hayden is missing.'

Anna didn't say anything. Fowler was now rushing towards them from the direction of a newly arrived pod, his arm still bound in its sling. The two investigators looked grim, but also embarrassed. They'd all missed it. A key factor had been overlooked.

'What do we know about Millie?'

'I told you before, she's a vet,' Fowler said. 'Works for the Department of Agriculture and Environment.'

An agricultural vet – that was another oddity. Like humans, almost all animals had implants that continually monitored their physical health. If anything was wrong – if the first triggers of the immune system were detected – then both diagnosis and dispatch of treatment was immediate. The number of vets – just like the number of doctors – had plummeted. 'Presumably this information was fed into S&P?'

Anna's question prompted two completely disparate responses: Mitchell flinched; Fowler gave a silent smile of resignation.

'Did it register as unusual?'

'It was always fucking unusual,' Fowler said, 'that the Haydens had two bread winners in the household.'

'That's not what I—'

'I don't think you'll be surprised to learn,' Mitchell interrupted, 'that I haven't told you all the ways we've been trying to find Beth. Her father is a banker, so of course we've been following him, tracing his contacts, monitoring his accounts for signs of any secret pay-offs. The S&P analysis was clear: concentrate on the father.'

'So you weren't allocated any resources to do the same for Millie Hayden?'

'No.'

'Figures,' Fowler said.

'You did the same,' Mitchell responded, barely disguising her annoyance. 'Your human gut instinct did the exact same. Banker equals money equals ransom.'

'My gut instinct is not held up as infallible, though, is it?'

'And neither is S&P… it is simply right much more often than it is wrong.'

'And this debate is no help to the Haydens,' Anna said flatly. She could kick herself for her own mistakes, her own prejudices. She'd not yet admitted to anyone her confusion about Durrant's ethnicity. The same errors were built into all of them. The selective blind spot. For a few moments she felt some of the frustration bubbling under the surface of her skin. If she'd been alone, then she might have tried to let some of it out. The temptation caused everything inside her to knot up.

'So what do we know about what she actually does?' she asked eventually. 'For the Department of Agriculture?'

'We're trying to find that out now,' Mitchell said.

'You don't know already?'

'As I said, the focus was on Roger Hayden, not his wife.

We're making enquiries. I can't think what would be on a farm that the Workers' League couldn't just go out and steal. Farm depots aren't exactly well secured – normally just a couple of drones to provide early warning. Our response times are pretty awful – nothing our tech can do about that – and that would give the Workers' League more than enough time to get away.' Mitchell took a breath. 'You mentioned in your last submersion there was a basement… Did you see anything in it that would give us a location?'

Anna shook her head. 'No, it could have been anywhere.'

'But not at the bar?'

'I couldn't tell. It might have been.'

'It would be worth a punt,' Fowler said. He lifted his broken arm slightly. 'Given what happened to me.'

'S&P doesn't work on punts,' Mitchell replied. 'I need to feed it something substantive. Facts, not theories. This has to be authorised.'

'The only other fact we have is this man called Connolly,' Anna said.

'And as I told you, "Connolly" is a probably a made up name.'

'He's middle class – not one of your usual Workers' League types. Maybe he's not on the UI yet.' Anna swallowed, thinking about her own precipitous employment situation. 'Maybe he just feels sufficiently threatened to get involved in something like this. I'd recognise him again if I saw him.'

'Nice,' Mitchell replied. 'But doesn't help. If he has no previous history, then we need specific approvals to push into higher-end social-class data. And Deng simply isn't going to allow it – it's illegal to do it without those.'

Anna knew that, of course – the debate on S&P powers

kept being bounced back into Parliament; it was reported daily on the boards. And, up until this moment, she'd always been against it. 'Who's Deng?' she asked.

'Mitchell's right,' Fowler said. He didn't sound happy about the statement he'd just uttered. 'All we've got is Millie Hayden. We need to know why they took her.'

# 40

Hunter Bot 28.637f – 47637946376gh476r74r64 – Action Log
Objective. Find Target (Priority, Medium)
Background Data: Downloaded from S&P. Receiving
    continual updates.
Geographical Sweeps: 256 addresses visited. Unable to
    access 23 (return visits scheduled). Infrared cams: Within
    parameters. Recognition cams: Negative. Behavioural
    Cams: Negative.
S&P Update: Downgrade Priority to Low (Reason, priority
    timeout. Authorisation, Denq)

ANNA ARRIVED HOME expecting to find her apartment devoid
of life, but instead found it bustling with cops and bots.
She watched them from the doorway, trying to detect any
hint of who was actually in charge. In the end, a short
man wearing a suit that didn't quite fit handed her a glossy
search warrant.

'What are you hoping to find?' Anna's voice carried into
the hallway, but no one answered. If she'd read the details,
no doubt the warrant would also confirm her digital
archive had also been unlocked. If so, that would be more

useful to them than the collection of mementos and papers in the apartment.

Stepping into the lounge, Anna found Kate reclining on the sofa. Her former spoof looked at her blankly. 'I had to let them in,' she said. 'The security on the front desk said I had no choice.'

'I—' Anna felt a surge of guilt. For the first time in months the regret wasn't routed via the young woman sitting in front of her. 'I wasn't expecting you back,' she said finally. 'They wouldn't say where they'd taken you. Are you all right?'

'I'm fine,' Kate replied. 'Don't sweat it. It was just a bit of a shock to find a police bot at the door.'

From elsewhere, the noise of possessions being boxed and confiscated continued. Anna wondered how much they would leave her. She hoped they wouldn't take her collection of records. 'How long have they been here?'

'Maybe thirty minutes? I made them wait as long as I could… claimed I was just out of the shower and only wearing a towel. But they just sent the bot in to check. They're scanning the walls and under the floorboards.'

'There's nothing there,' Anna replied.

'Huh, well, I thought you'd want to know, just in case. They're saying on the boards there's going to be an inquiry into Tanzania?'

'That's right.'

'You going to be okay?'

Anna almost laughed. The girl speaking to her had been arrested for spoofing, and she was still acting like her physiological nurse. 'I'll be fine,' she said. 'And what about you? Have they set a court date?'

'Tomorrow.'

'They haven't asked me to attend,' Anna said.

'I was caught subbing my biodata in place of yours. They don't really need anything else.'

'And have they said what you're likely to get?'

'Five months, plus complete access to bio and digital for the next twenty. I guess my chances of getting a proper job are now pretty much zilch.'

*Jesus.* 'I…'

'I'm pretty cool with it, actually,' Kate said. She made a face suggesting she'd dropped some food onto the floor rather than flushed her life away. 'Light security place, probably. I won't have to worry about food or rent, and I'll still be eligible for UI after I'm out so, you know, I'm good, long term.'

She shuffled up on the sofa, creating a space for Anna to sit and to wait for the rest of the apartment to be cleared of her personal belongings. Many items couldn't, on the face of it, be of interest to the police, but no doubt everything she owned would soon be scanned to ensure it didn't contain any hidden data drives that could have slipped past the initial search.

Soon a bot came to them and asked her to stand in a star position while it swept a device along her arms, legs and torso. Fortunately, it seemed satisfied by the results and then handed over another glossy slip of paper. This wasn't a statement of orders, though; instead, the document formed a statement of intent from the court system. Yes, there was going to be an inquiry into her role in Tanzania. The matter of her spoofing her biofeed was mentioned, but with the words *In Abeyance* printed next to the charge.

She could guess the line of questioning now: '*Have you ever lied, Ms Glover? No? Do you consider spoofing to be a form of lie? So if you lied about spoofing, did you tell the truth regarding your role in Tanzania?*

A small cough interrupted her thoughts. Kate had pulled herself up from the sofa. 'They're gone. You wanna eat something?'

'No.'

'They took pretty much everything.'

Anna felt another swell of guilt. This was probably Kate's last meal before being incarcerated. 'Order whatever you want,' she said. But by now her attention had been distracted by a tiny detail. The inquiry notice was signed by someone called 'Deng'.

DESPITE BEING UNABLE to get much sleep, Anna pulled herself out of bed early the next day. It was quiet, and tiny movements echoed from the walls. The missing items – clothes, ornaments – only seemed to highlight the lack of sound.

There was no sign of Kate, which wasn't unusual at this time of the morning, but there was a note in the kitchen.

> *Anna,*
>
> *Sorry to slip away but saying goodbye would be too much of a downer today. I'm off to stretch my legs and get a final breath of fresh air before court. Thank you for everything – I hope we meet again when I get out.*
>
> *—Kate*

Anna doubted she'd see her lodger again, and she continued to get ready for work.

There was no pod waiting for her in the basement. One was normally called as soon as her apartment signalled the morning routine had commenced. At first she just waited, looking towards the garage roller doors and hoping none of the other inhabitants would find her there. But after another ten minutes she knew the delay wasn't just down to some unexpected peak in demand.

She checked her messages. There was an automated one from Human Resources. She'd been suspended on full pay, pending the outcome of the inquiry. A quick check of the boards indicated that yes, the inquiry had been formally announced. It wasn't flagged that highly in the selection of news stories sourced for her from the boards. And yet nothing was more personal to her.

The lead story was about Beth Hayden and her mother. Their photographs were prominently displayed, and rewards were being offered for information on their location. It seemed S&P had at last dumped the subtlety of facial recognition and social-media monitoring. *Back to more traditional techniques*, she thought, before drifting back to her own situation.

At least she'd continue to be paid. She'd have a few weeks while the sludge of what happened in Tanzania was sifted through and they found nothing. The plane had been deliberately brought down: the evidence was in her report. She had nothing to worry about. *Except for one thing*.

Anna turned back to the elevator. No doubt she'd soon be contacted and provided with a timetable for when and where she'd need to appear at the inquiry. And then she'd need to prepare. She wondered if she would be allowed access to her old files.

An alert stopped her before she reached her destination.

After ensuring she was indeed still alone, she took the call. She hadn't expected Cody to be in work this early.

'Anna.' His voice sounded strained. 'I just heard you've been iced. Look, I'm sorry.'

'Suspended, I think is the term.'

'Yeah, and another one is fucked. Have you heard from Fowler?'

'No.'

'He's found out what Millie Hayden does for a living.'

'She's a vet?'

'No, she's an animal welfare inspector.'

Anna heard the words, but couldn't quite get them to fit with the stress levels permeating her colleague's – *former* colleague's – voice. 'And that makes a difference how?'

'It's about access,' Cody said. 'She's a government-sanctioned animal welfare inspector.'

'Come on, Cody, that job title sounds even less likely than "vet". All livestock and pets have monitoring implants…'

'*Almost* all. But not at Bromoor Down. It's about an hour's trip from Amblinside.'

'Bromoor Down?'

'You won't have heard of it. They don't advertise what they do there.'

'Let me guess – something nasty?'

'They wouldn't even tell me until I pushed them. It's a chemical and biological weapons facility.'

What had Millie Hayden said the last time they'd spoken? *They won't tell me what's happening to her*. She hadn't been talking about her husband or the police. Connolly had been in direct contact with her. Pressuring her. And she'd seen it: the green light lancing across from the bridleway to the darkened window. It must have been a communication device. Something away from the boards and hard to detect. Another thing they'd missed. Another thing they'd fucked up.

'Get this,' Cody continued. 'Millie Hayden is permitted – any time, any day – to make unannounced inspections of the whole facility. The *whole* facility, Anna.'

'And why would she have access rights like that?'

'It's a little wrinkle in the Animal Welfare Act, in there to keep the bugs and bunnies people happy. Her remit is to make sure the labs are keeping their rats, monkeys, cows and sheep at a basic level of care.' Cody's breath squeaked and rattled with excitement. 'Inspector Mitchell came to see Jake again in a big hurry. Have you checked the news this morning, Anna? Everyone is hunting them now. A vial of smallpox is missing.'

Smallpox. What could that mean? N'Golo had been caught going through Millie Hayden's handbag, she reminded herself. Roger Hayden had gone apeshit about it. So perhaps she'd misread him as an overbearing foster father, when in fact he was worried his foster-kid would stumble across something connected to Bromoor Down. Maybe a security pass? Maybe some papers he'd taken to examine, and briefly stuffed under the pillows in his room? But they were still missing something. It still didn't quite feel right.

'Where's Fowler?'

'Not sure. I think Roger Hayden fired him.'

'Then why are you telling me all this?' Anna asked, her voice wobbling. 'I'm suspended.'

'All our equipment is still at the hospital, Anna. And people are losing their shit over this now. Did you see the recent board reports on this stuff? Jake's asked me to have a go at communicating directly with Durrant…'

'When was the last time you actually submerged?'

'Months.'

'Then I would have a better chance,' Anna replied. 'We've already accessed his memory seven times. It could be about to break.'

'I know, but they're not going to let you… And I'm worried I'm going to fuck it up.'

'Then stall them,' said Anna. 'Say there's something wrong with the feed and give yourself a bit more time.'

'To do what?'

'I need to see Fowler, then I'll be heading back to the synapse hub.'

# 41

S&P Build 14.234a – Recommendation Module
Situation #GIHHCLTYYEN. Closed (Priority reduced to
   Zero, Victim likely now dead).
Situation #UIDFUHUFHR: Open (missing smallpox sample,
   risk of terrorist release. No background data available).
Connected Case 1: #GIHHCLTYYEN
Recommendation: Additional hunter bots dispatched. No
   change in geographical search parameters.

ANNA FOUND FOWLER at the gates to the Amblinside estate. Or rather, he found her there, waiting for him. The quickest way to set up a meeting had been to force one. On terminating the call from Cody, she'd simply pinged Fowler a message saying she was on her way to see Roger Hayden at his home. The mere fact she was heading to Amblinside meant he would come, and sure enough he made it soon after she arrived.

Fowler didn't look well. When they'd first met, she'd thought the PI had appeared a little gaunt under all his stubble. Now his clothes hung as loosely as the flesh from his jaw, a sight emphasised by the sling that pulled his arm close to his torso. He'd been losing weight.

'What the fuck are you doing?' He stopped to hack up some phlegm.

Above them, a couple of drones lingered – far too low to have been programmed for stealth, these bots were conveying a message: you're being watched. Anna tried to give Fowler a conciliatory smile as she edged away from the sentry station. She'd had no intention of visiting Roger Hayden. 'I've seen the news,' she said.

'Who hasn't?'

'Did you know what she really did for a living? Millie Hayden?'

Fowler followed her away from the bots. He'd worked out her ploy, and the realisation had taken away some of his anger. Perhaps he'd also worked out they were effectively in the same boat, redundant and adrift. 'I was told she was a vet.'

'And don't you think all this is a little odd?'

'No more than someone being a doctor. AI systems mean you need fewer people, but somewhere there's usually a human making decisions.'

'I meant something odd about the smallpox.'

Fowler scrunched his face as he reconsidered her question. 'Fucking hell, Anna: smallpox! If they use it… *if people find out we missed it*… well, it'll put your current problems in the shade, that's for sure.'

Anna took a breath to give herself some time. Fowler had it wrong. She was almost sure of it. 'Do you know what an aerodynamic stall is?'

'No.'

'It was probably the scariest thing that could happen to a pilot. The plane loses lift because its nose has been pulled too high or it's going too slowly. One minute you're flying, the next you're falling.'

'So?'

'So the truth is it's not scary at all. First, the pilot's control column would have started to shake as the plane approached stall conditions. Second, there's an easy fix. All a pilot had to do was tilt the nose down and increase the thrust.'

'It's smallpox, Anna. Not a fucking aeroplane.'

'There have been vaccines for smallpox for years.'

'Bromoor Down is a weapons *research* facility – this could be a new strain.'

'No.' Anna shook her head slowly. 'I don't care what sort of security pass Millie Hayden had to wave at the security bots – there is no way she would have been able to get to the really nasty stuff.'

Fowler's face flexed and creased as he considered her point.

'You know the crazy thing, though?' Anna continued. 'Despite all the training – all the simulators – dozens of pilots made the same mistake. It's tragic when you hear them on the flight recorders. They see the loss of altitude and they pull their flight columns back – tilting their plane's nose up, not down – and then they max the engines. Their brain overrides all common sense. They become disorientated. You don't dip the nose down to gain height, they think, it's counterintuitive. In actual fact that's what would have saved many of them. And it's why they all lost their jobs to AI.'

'Well I hate flying,' Fowler replied bluntly. 'I'm glad there's no one left at the controls.' He nodded to draw her attention to something behind her. A pair of sentry bots were heading in their direction. Presumably they'd been alerted that a couple of people were loitering. It took a few minutes of conversation – an exchange of legal views between Fowler and the bots – and then they were left in peace. The drones, however, continued to circle.

'You don't look well,' Anna said, no longer able to ignore it.

'Just a little run down. My place is a little above UI standard, but without my supplementary, it takes up most of my income.'

'You've not been eating?'

'No.' Fowler coughed again, then wiped at his face. 'The Durrant thing's been taking most of my time, and now Hayden isn't paying for it. But I've got a few nice new jobs lined up, which should soon cover the gap. You'll be pleased to hear they mostly involve men visiting women they shouldn't be seeing.'

'I'm sorry.'

'Don't be.' Fowler gave a regretful smile. 'So, Millie Hayden nicked some smallpox. Maybe not the most deadly strain, but I bet if you were sprayed with it, you'd still be concerned.'

'What I'm trying to say is that it's the reaction that's dangerous, not the smallpox. Pulling the control stick up, rather than pushing it down. What the police have done is to significantly raise the stakes for Beth and her mother.'

Fowler rubbed at his jaw. 'They're probably already dead. As soon as their faces went public – or as soon as the smallpox story gets put on the boards.'

'Which is odd, don't you think? That S&P would generate a course of action that increases the odds that they'll die.'

'Maybe it's balancing the risk associated with someone releasing the smallpox.'

'There's no risk.' Anna knew she was right. 'Smallpox was the first disease for which we ever created a vaccine.'

'And what if you're wrong? There was a new story about this a few days ago: the potential sounds pretty horrible.'

Anna shook her head. She'd seen those stories too. 'And how often does smallpox get released? What is S&P basing its judgements on?'

Fowler thought about this, but couldn't answer.

'And why the softly, softly approach at the beginning?' Anna asked. 'Why the passive use of surveillance rather than assigning proper resources? We both thought it: the daughter of a rich, white banker going missing would normally have received more attention.'

Fowler glanced skywards. The drones were still overhead. 'We're not intending to see the Haydens, are we?'

'No.'

'Then let's walk.' Without saying anything more he turned and headed down the street. Anna followed him, wondering if she should put a pod on standby, just in case they wandered into a part of the town where she'd be recognised. 'Ask your question,' he said, coming to a stop by a junction. 'You didn't ask me here to tell me all this: you either want me to do something, or to tell you something. So go ahead, then we can both go home.'

The drones had gone. Presumably an AI had concluded they were now far enough away from the gates not to be a potential threat.

'How does it work?' she asked.

'What?'

'S&P. All we're told is that it's exceptionally good at directing resources to prevent crime, and without prejudice.'

Fowler snorted. 'Huh. You don't really believe that last bit, do you?'

'No.'

'Good. Because the entire program was coded by humans and is therefore built on prejudice. Anyway, policing has never really been about justice.'

'I'm guessing you poked around a bit before you quit?'

'I tracked down one of the system's programmers, yes. If they were going to stop me from investigating my own cases, then I wanted to know what they were basing their decisions on. Because, in a way, the results were just too damn good.'

'Explain.'

'I don't see how this helps us.'

'There's usually several components to a disaster, Mr Fowler. Humans, environment and systems. And there's one big element here that we aren't getting near to understanding.'

Fowler hesitated for a second. 'Early automated systems were relatively simple and based on geographical mapping. S&P sucks in a huge amount more data: bank transactions, social-media feeds, board activity, biologging. All to work out who's likely to commit a crime, and where it's likely to happen.'

'And the S&P score, for those crimes that do occur?'

'A simple recognition that our response to crime is emotional, not objective. The score depends on the type of crime and who it affects. It's all calibrated by a people's panel, to ensure resources get targeted at crimes people actually care about.'

'Some crimes don't get assigned any resources, though, do they?'

'No,' Fowler replied. 'As one tech said to me, some crimes have a more exquisite "taste" than others. And that's where the prejudice comes in: do you want to know how many people actually care when a drug addict gets murdered? As opposed to a child? As opposed to a prostitute? As opposed to a nurse? Beth Hayden was white and rich, and, given who programmed the system, her score should have been off the chart.'

'Somewhere there's usually a human making decisions,' Anna said.

'Eh?'

'What you told me, just a few minutes ago.'

'No AI runs completely independently,' Fowler agreed. 'Some instructions require a human to approve them.'

'Someone who could give S&P the occasional nudge?'

'What are you thinking?'

'I'm thinking that the person pulling the strings here is someone middle class, using a system that was getting better and better, a system that threatened his job. Someone taking advantage of slips in S&P. Someone who knows how to keep himself masked from it. Is it too much of a stretch to suppose he might have access to the system? Be able to play around with the inputs or control its recommendations?'

'Well okay, so who is this someone?'

'Connolly,' Anna replied. 'It has to be Connolly.'

# 42

Hunter Bot 28.637f – 47637946376gh476r74r64 – Action Log

Objective: Find Target

Background Data: Downloaded from S&P. Receiving continual updates.

Geographical Sweeps: 256 addresses visited. Unable to access 23 (return visits scheduled). Infrared cams: Within parameters. Recognition cams: Negative. Behavioural cams: Negative.

Data Ping received from McMullins Shopping Mall. Behavioural cams note men loitering on two or more days.

Action: Request Geographical Reassignment. Request denied, authorisation Deng.

ANNA TURNED UP at the hub not expecting to be let in, so she didn't try to wave the security pass embedded in her wrist at the security station. Instead, she pinged a message to Cody and waited outside. At first he didn't respond, so she made it more personal.

*Failure begets failure.*

The boards were putting out increasingly shrill messages demanding any information relating to Beth Hayden and her mother. Other than that, all that had caught her attention was a small story about the new Tanzania inquiry. A junior government minister had issued a statement indicating they remained sure the war had been fully justified. The price of dysprosium had jumped slightly in response to the story.

'Hey!'

Anna turned. It was a bright day, and she had to shield her eyes as the sun reflected off the glass panels fronting the hub. 'Thanks for coming down to see me.'

'This is a really bad idea.' Cody looked nervously back at the entrance. There was no sign of anyone – or any*thing* – watching them.

'I want one last chance with N'Golo Durrant.'

'No, Anna. I've changed my mind. Jake was clear: you're suspended.'

'And you're going to fail,' Anna replied, trying to keep calm. 'You haven't done an immersion like this before. Not with someone in a coma. I'm guessing you're only being put up for it because none of the other teams sent a volunteer. No one wants to be holding the parcel when the music stops.'

'Anna…'

'What do you have to fall back on if this goes wrong? Other than the UI?'

Cody looked back at her, grim-faced. 'I can't afford to go on the UI,' he said. 'Not with a new baby.'

'You can log me past security as a guest. We both know I have a much better chance at this. And,' she added, hating herself for saying it, 'I'm sorry to tell you this, but Jake already thinks you're a failure. This may be your only chance.'

SHE WAS IN a sterile meeting room, facing N'Golo Durrant across a small, circular table. Anna tried not to let the disappointment floor her. She'd hoped Cody would have been able to land her somewhere close to Beth Hayden's abduction. Maybe even the point between N'Golo learning the truth in the basement and his retreat back to Amblinside prior to him being beaten to a pulp.

Anna twisted, trying to feed on any detail available to her. Panels of partially obscured glass provided the only privacy between them and what looked like a deserted reception area outside. She tried to find some sort of clue as to where she was, but in the end decided the lack of information was probably a function of N'Golo's memory.

A momentary flash of colour swept past the glass, confirming it: not even a person. Just a smear of red, blue and yellow as they'd gone by, one that had left only the merest imprint in N'Golo's mind. Whatever he was doing here, all of his concentration had been squarely inside the small meeting room.

Anna tipped her head skywards. She was ready. 'Run it,' she instructed Cody.

N'Golo came to life – he was clearly agitated. 'You're listening to me?' he said. 'Right?'

'Yes, of course.' She needed to know what he was doing here, who he was speaking with. Anna glanced again at the reception. Her first instinct said 'social services'. N'Golo would have had to check in every now and again. If he'd been an adult, he would have been assigned a bot or an automated call centre number – but as a child he was still entitled to human-first care. And when she'd first told him she was a social worker, he'd mentioned someone named Peter. So was that why he was here? To talk about his life with the Haydens?

'I'm listening,' she said, resting her arms on the table. 'But you need to explain it to me again.'

N'Golo gave an angry sigh, filled with exasperation. 'They,' he said. 'Are. Going. To. *Take*. Her.'

Every word hammered home. Beth. He was talking about Beth. Anna looked again at the reception. A few shadows passed beyond the glass wall. She settled her attention back on N'Golo.

'Who are they?' she said. 'The Workers' League?'

N'Golo pushed back into his seat, taking it on to its back legs. 'Is this what you do?' he said. 'Keep asking the same dumbass questions to see if what I'm saying changes? To see if I'm lying?'

'I just want to understand,' Anna replied.

'You're just as useless as those things you have answering calls.' For a brief moment he glanced at the main reception area, and it flashed full of life. About a dozen people were circulating within an open atrium. And then he looked away, and the synaptic curtains closed. Except Anna had seen enough to know he wasn't seeing his social service contact. They were inside a police station.

He'd done what he should have, all those days ago. He'd come running to the police. He'd told them everything, and he'd been ignored. With that realisation, the room's bareness filled with meaning. There was no recording apparatus on the table, no notebook in front of her, no social worker to witness this statement from a minor. So there'd also be no record he'd even been here, except perhaps the security camera footage of his arrival and departure. 'Let's go through it again,' she said. 'You told me about a man called Connolly.'

'That's not his real name.'

'And do you know what he's really called?'

'No.'

'But he's part of the Workers' League?'

N'Golo again let out an angry breath. 'He says he is, but anyone can say they're in the Workers' League. It's just a name. Something the government uses to scare white collars into not rebelling as their jobs disappear.'

'So what does he want?'

'I told you! He wants Beth! He wants to get to her mother!'

'Do you know why?'

N'Golo rocked his chair forwards on to all four legs. For a moment Anna wondered whether he was going to get up and leave. She thought again about the basement. 'You said he wanted to take her… Where will he take her?'

'I already told you this.'

'Tell me again.'

'Why? What's the point? Won't it just be blacked out by that fucking Deng?'

*Deng?*

'Yeah.' N'Golo looked pleased with himself. 'I've seen his name, last time I was here. Didn't have the screen turned away enough, did you?'

Anna tried to hold her voice firm. Was Connolly actually called Deng? 'Tell me where they're going to take her.'

'He has a house off Munday Road. I don't know the number… a few doors down from the church, with a red door.'

$V_2$. Got it. Finally, she'd got it. *They were airborne*. Anna tipped her head skywards. She was about to call out to Cody, to tell him to freeze the memory and pull her out. But N'Golo was looking at her quizzically. 'You look familiar,' he said. 'I think we've met before.'

'That's right. On another of your visits here.'

'No, you were at the Haydens' house. We've spoken before, I—'

N'Golo stopped mid-sentence, his eyes wide but unseeing. Outside the glass booth there wasn't a hint of movement. Anna looked upward. 'Cody?'

No answer.

'Cody? Are we in motion?'

No answer.

'Cody? Cody!'

'*Whoa! Sorry, Anna. Things going on out here. We lost the feed from the hospital. I'm trying to fix it.*'

Some of the detail outside the booth was starting to re-emerge. Small glimpses of the people N'Golo had previously revealed to her when his attention had been in that direction.

*My own brain*, Anna thought. *My own brain's starting to fill in background details*. She called to Cody, 'I know where to look for Beth. Pull me out.'

No answer.

'Cody?' she called. 'What the hell is going on?'

A long pause. Anna almost repeated her question, when Cody spoke. '*It's too late, Anna.*'

'What?'

'*We're too late,*' Cody repeated. He sounded like all the fight had been taken out of him. '*The smallpox… it's just coming on the boards… The Workers' League have just announced they've released it… in central London… inside a shopping mall.'*

They'd run out of time. She sat frozen, looking at N'Golo. The boy who'd finally given up his secrets – but too late. She wanted to scream.

*Failure begets failure.*

'And Beth Hayden? Is there any news on Beth Hayden?'

*'No, I don't think so.'*

'Pull me out, Cody.'

Nothing happened. Anna closed her eyes and tried to force her own disengagement, but she remained in the interview room, N'Golo mute and immobile ahead of her. It was only then that she noticed something on the table. Something that hadn't been there a few moments ago.

A short, stubby kitchen knife.

Something designed to peel and chop vegetables. She hadn't seen it for a long time, but recognised it immediately. With N'Golo detached from the synapse sequencer, it was her own brain now making the rules. Her own memories creating the illusion. And her subconscious had brought her something to help her face her failure.

*'I'm having trouble pulling you out,'* Cody said, his voice deep within her ear. *'I'm preparing an adrenaline shot to counteract the synapse drugs.'*

She looked at the knife. It was the same one she'd used as a teenager. Back then every slice and cut had hurt, but also provided relief.

At that moment the door to the office opened. She looked up, surprised. Jake stared back, looking fresh, warm and damp, like he'd just arrived from the shower.

'I know where Beth and her mother are being held,' Anna said. 'Munday Road – a house with a red door—'

'My people found the camera,' Jake said, cutting her off. 'I presume you knew we'd find it – pinned to that handbag? It gave a good view of you on the synapse bench in my chamber.'

'Munday Road,' Anna repeated. They could deal with Jake's nurse later. 'We still have time.'

'And you're suspended,' Jake said. 'Whatever happened with Holland, I don't want you to work with the sequencer again.'

'But Cody wouldn't have been able to get through to N'Golo. He'd have been starting too far behind the line.'

'You've heard that the smallpox has been released?'

'Yes.'

'So you know you've failed.'

Anna's attention swung back to the table. The kitchen knife still sat there, waiting for her. But she knew she couldn't use it here. The sequencer wouldn't allow her to feel any pain. It would leave no mark. There'd be no sense of relief. 'Then I guess it's time to leave.'

'I'm sorry, Anna,' Jake replied, his voice heavy. 'But you're not leaving. There's something we have to do first.'

# 43

I NEEDED TO bump myself out. If I was in the sequencer, then I needed to bump myself out.

That one thought had revolved in my mind in the hours since Charley had forced me to eat my evening meal. I looked down at my hands, trembling in my lap, and locked them together.

I was facing the television, which was muted. I'd be expected to eventually lever myself from the chair and get into bed – and then I'd wait for one of the nursing staff to come and check on me. I was already wearing my nightwear, Grace having gently removed me from my daytime clothes, passing no comment on my latest selection of bruises. Hopefully she would be monitoring the movement sensors to see when I was finally ready for her to come and switch off the light.

I let my hands part and find the corners of the chair's armrests. Sean's face came into my mind, along with that old fool down in the conservatory. Both had looked familiar. I couldn't quite place either of them. Had I seen them before? Quite possibly. If I was in the sequencer, very probably. They'd be made up of fragments of my memory, and that would explain the familiarity. But I ought to be able to place them, even so.

I pushed down, pressing with my hands and trying to extend my legs until I was standing. The effort left me momentarily breathless. Giddy. But I knew no alarms would have been triggered. It was late, and it was time for bed. This wasn't an early morning rush to the bottom drawer and a knife that had long been removed. This was normal. I would get out of my chair, I would get into bed, and I would wait for Grace to come and put me to sleep.

I smiled, swaying slightly as I shuffled to the right. Letting myself line up so that I was at a tight angle to the bed. Again, nothing too unusual in that. But earlier in the evening I had pulled back the duvet from the bed to reveal one of its legs. It was topped by a wooden block. If I toppled – if I allowed myself to topple – I would strike it with either my face or forehead.

I *was* in the sequencer, I said to myself again. And yet I couldn't quite square it. I did have some patchy memories of things that had happened after the Durrant investigation. There was a husband, a child. Friends. Glimpses of beaches and mountains. Music concerts and theatre trips.

I looked at the bedpost, then stared down at my arms and the crinkled skin. Folded them in front of me. Closed my eyes. I saw the numbers, and let them roll through my mind. Falling into place until I realised what they meant.

Then I let myself fall.

```
5 1 7 2 1 7 3 2 5 2 5 5 2 3 2 4 3 4 3 5 4 2 1 3 6 3 4 2 7 5 2 6 3 3 7 2 6 3 7 5 1 5 6 6 4 2 5 6
8 7 7 4 1 7 4 8 2 5 2 2 1 2 6 5 8 6 6 5 6 3 4 7 3 1 4 1 3 5 7 5 8 1 1 4 7 8 7 3 1 3 5 3 1 3 8 8
8 7 2 3 2 2 7 8 1 7 2 6 3 1 7 5 8 3 4 5 3 1 2 3 3 1 5 5 1 7 2 4 8 7 4 1 6 8 1 3 7 6 5 1 5 6 8 8
8 1 7 3 5 3 2 8 3 8 8 8 8 8 8 1 8 1 2 8 6 1 8 8 8 8 8 8 4 2 2 8 2 6 5 4 8 7 8 8 8 8 8 8 5 8 8
8 6 2 8 8 4 5 8 3 4 8 8 8 8 8 4 8 8 8 8 3 3 8 8 8 8 8 8 5 2 1 8 2 2 6 4 8 7 8 4 1 6 5 8 6 8 8
8 8 8 8 8 8 8 7 8 5 4 7 1 8 2 8 5 8 8 8 5 5 8 8 4 2 3 5 4 6 3 8 4 4 6 3 8 2 8 2 3 3 7 8 6 6 6
2 8 8 7 4 8 8 6 7 2 8 8 8 8 8 7 8 4 4 8 8 2 3 8 8 8 8 8 8 8 5 7 3 8 8 8 8 8 8 1 8 8 8 8 8 7 8 8
5 7 1 7 5 4 7 1 4 2 5 3 4 2 2 4 4 7 2 3 4 2 2 7 3 4 1 3 2 4 4 1 4 1 2 4 7 3 4 8 6 2 6 6 4 7 5 2
4 5 3 3 1 7 3 1 6 5 4 5 4 3 1 2 2 6 7 7 5 2 5 2 7 3 6 5 2 6 1 4 7 5 1 2 4 3 5 8 7 3 2 2 1 2 3 3
```

# 44

ANNA WOKE, HER stomach convulsing. This time it was much worse than normal, the stream of vomit filling her throat for a good few seconds. She rolled back on to the synapse bench, gasping for air.

Her throat was tight. She waited for a technician to come and straighten her body. None came. She tried to swallow, but her muscles wouldn't respond. And then she noticed something much stranger. She wasn't inside a synapse chamber. The lights above her were dimmed and the room was cool – almost cold. She let her eyes drift to the left, and then to the right.

She wasn't alone. There were at least two other people on synapse benches either side of her. Her eyebrows twitched back to life but her breathing had become shallow. Phlegm blocked her larynx. She tried to move her head back – willing her brain to re-engage with her body.

And then someone pulled her body straight, freeing up her airway.

Cody.

Finally, Cody.

'Anna,' he whispered, 'are you okay?'

She couldn't nod, but she could blink. Once.

'Take your time – you've been submerged for a few days.'

A few days. Where the hell had she been?

She'd been with N'Golo, in the interview room. He'd tried to warn the police of Connolly's plan to kidnap Beth. And they'd ignored him. His testimony hadn't registered highly enough on the S&P boards to warrant any action being taken. And yet that had been days ago. *Since then…?*

All she could remember was the inside of an old people's home.

Had she been dying?

Her face moved. Or rather, all the muscles covering her forehead, cheeks and jaw flexed, allowing her to gulp some more air. A few drops of salty moisture ran from the corners of her eyes and across her cheeks.

'It's okay,' Cody said, again adjusting her position. 'I've got you. Take your time. It will take longer than normal.'

Anna pushed out some air, trying to shape it past her vocal chords. It just came out as a strained gargle.

'Don't force it.'

Again, she tried to speak to her technician. Again no words came. But at least she could sense every part of her body, pins and needles emanating from every surface. It would all come back with time. There was no severance.

'I had no idea they were going to do this to you,' Cody continued. 'It was another team in the justice department who suggested it. They told Jake they could get you to admit the truth about Tanzania. That it might form a revenue stream.'

It was starting to come back to her. There was a student; an interviewer.

'Trick a person into thinking they are about to die,' Cody

said, 'and there's this sudden urge for confession. That was the theory, anyway.'

Yes, she'd thought she was near the end. Thought she was dying. Anna pushed her head forwards and up. She turned it slowly – it felt as if all the muscles in her body needed to be oiled. It was the most populated synapse chamber she'd ever seen. There must have been fifty people in the room, all submerged. The closest to her was an old woman.

'Who…? Who are all these people?'

'This is one of the new witness chambers,' Cody replied. 'Once the inquiry was finished, Jake wanted to keep you under. Every time I was rotated on to this assignment, I manipulated your feed to try to bump you out.'

At first Anna didn't understand. Maybe it was because she still had the synapse drugs in her system. Perhaps it was because a lot of her brain was getting used to the idea she was no longer on her deathbed. Something tingled in her right arm and she lifted it to cradle the right side of her head.

'At least it wasn't Holland looking after me…'

'Holland has been sacked. That camera footage you managed to get was more than enough…'

'And the numbers,' Anna said. 'The numbers that N'Golo was repeating to me?'

Cody looked momentarily pleased with himself. 'I implanted them,' he said. 'They'd shut down your auditory input, so I couldn't speak directly to you. I hoped you would hear something inside the program instead. You may continue to hear them for a while…'

'Thank you.'

Aside from the one woman beside her, all the other people submerged on the synapse benches were men in their seventies and eighties. A sea of white hair, bald scalps and wrinkled skin. 'What are they all doing here?' she asked. 'They weren't with me in the nursing home.'

Even in the dimmed light of the chamber, Cody had turned a shade greyer.

'Who's running their feeds, Cody?'

Cody leant in closer – even though Anna suspected they were quite alone. 'That woman was used to complete the illusion you were old; her memories of later life subbed to fill in the blanks.'

'And the rest?'

'Subscribers to Jake's premium services don't hook up down here,' Cody explained. 'The experiences of our witnesses are instead sent up to the private booths.'

'I don't…?'

'Most of the men in here used to be soldiers. Before bots took over the fighting. It's seared into their minds, Anna. Killing people. What it was really like to fight in a war. Do you know how many people would pay for that type of immersive entertainment? Do you know how many would sacrifice themselves to escape the monotony of life on the UI?'

Anna understood. In some ways, she'd always known. The synapse sequencer was a device to access and manipulate memory, and, for it to work, you needed people to volunteer their experiences.

'You were going to be the test case for yet another new revenue stream,' Cody continued. 'Indefinite submersion. Basically, a form of prison.' Her technician's face twisted in utter disgust. 'Using the sequencer for the inquiry I could just about understand – but this? No, it's simply wrong. I couldn't allow it.'

Anna shifted herself up on to her elbows. She was nearly ready to walk. She needed to get out of the hub. But first there was something else she wanted to know. 'The smallpox?'

'All over,' Cody said. 'We were too late.'

'And N'Golo Durrant?'

'He's dead, Anna. His memory burned out. I'm sorry, but we killed him on your final submersion.'

# 45

**Top News:**

Safe! Smallpox confirmed as mild strain (*Read more*)

Prime Minister to visit shopping mall at centre of smallpox outbreak (*Read more*)

Extension of S&P data rights to return to Parliament (*Read more*)

Tanzanian War fully justified – Ministerial statement in full (*Read more*)

**Selected for You:**

Freedom from Work: UI has helped me unlock my creativity! (*Read more*)

'I DIDN'T EXPECT to see you here.'

Fowler's semi-shout across the crematorium lobby seemed devoid of any emotion. Anna couldn't tell whether he was expressing irritation or sympathy, or just neutrally noting a fact. He waited for her in front of the entrance to the empty ceremonial chamber. They were the only ones who'd so far turned up.

'He didn't have any family,' Anna said. She was still getting used to hearing again without the muffling which came with old age. She had to remind herself again that she'd only been submerged for a few days – not years.

'No, but I expected more people.'

The crematorium was set in a small park on the outskirts of the city. The building itself seemed designed not to provoke any real response, each wall painted cream, with everything else – door panels, tables, chairs – made of the same heavily varnished pine. Only the tall, thin chimney protruding from the side of the building reminded visitors of its true function. Except the chimney was no longer needed, not now the dead were dissolved rather than burned.

'I heard about the outcome to the inquiry…'

'I don't want to talk about it.'

'Well,' Fowler continued, 'it's all over the boards… the government seems quite pleased that their position has been vindicated. I guess they can go on mining dysprosium now, and the prices will be kept low.'

'They're not saying much about Iceland, though, are they?'

Fowler looked confused. Which was the clearest indication she needed that the key piece of information from her deathbed confession had already been snuffed out: that she'd told the truth about Tanzania but had not been so candid about the air investigation that had taken place before it.

'I guess it will make things easier for you,' Fowler said. 'You just gotta hope people actually believe the outcome.'

*Easier?* Anna couldn't help but laugh. 'You mean, now my name's associated with a smallpox attack rather than an illegal war?'

'The smallpox wasn't your fault…'

'People will make the connection,' Anna said. 'I didn't crack N'Golo Durrant fast enough. He's dead, and it's my fault.'

Worse, Beth and Millie Hayden hadn't been found. On leaving the hub, it had taken a while for her brain to refocus – the news about the smallpox attack and N'Golo's death placing more immediate demands on her attention. And yet the girl and her mother were still gone, and few people expected them to be found now. Unless Roger Hayden had hired another private investigator, no one was looking for them any more.

'You gave it your best shot.' There was a bit more colour in Fowler's cheeks than when they'd last met. Presumably he'd earned enough for a good feed. 'You don't always have to cast yourself as the bad guy, you know.'

'We were looking in the wrong direction. All making the wrong connections. The entire point of the synapse sequencer was to reveal more detail, and instead it gave us tunnel vision.'

'Well, S&P didn't do any better…'

Anna stopped. Her brain was still fuzzy, but her last conversation with Fowler now replayed in her mind. 'Did you find anything from them? S&P? Anyone who could have been Connolly?'

'Give me a break,' Fowler said, snorting. 'Trying to get information like that when everyone's flapping about a smallpox attack? And I couldn't ask directly, you know.'

'But you're still trying?'

'Is there any point?'

'I saw his face,' Anna said. 'I would recognise Connolly again if I saw him. I'm going to find him. And I'm going to make him pay.'

From the ceremonial chamber, a bot wheeled its way solemnly into view. Of course, for an extra fee the crematorium would have provided a human to officiate. For everyone else, the bot provided a reliable enough way to go through the motions. '*The ceremony will commence in five minutes.*' It spoke in a firm but soft voice, as if the whole lobby was filled with mourners. Then it reversed out of sight. Did it know how few people were waiting? Would it still have carried out its program if no one had turned up?

'What made you come today?' she asked Fowler.

He sucked his cheeks and swept a loose strand of greasy hair from out of his eyes. She didn't need an answer. He was here for the same reason she had turned up. Sure, part of her had come to say goodbye. After eight submersions, she had a sense she'd known N'Golo Durrant – or at least had some form of impression of him through the warped lens of the sequencer. But another big pull had been to see who else would turn up.

'I thought they might be here,' Fowler said.

'Connolly?'

'Maybe not him, but certainly someone.'

But there was no one.

'I was hoping that too…' Anna let her voice trail away. Yes, she was hoping that the Workers' League would have turned up. Principally, so she could scream in their faces, demand to know whether they thought what they'd done had been worth it. But maybe more than that was the feeling that she wasn't quite ready to let it drop. She didn't like the taste failure had left in her mouth. Fowler clearly thought the same. He wasn't being paid any more by Roger Hayden, but he was still here, poking around.

'No one's going to hold you to account for the smallpox,' Fowler said, misreading her expression.

She could shoulder people's anger – she'd had more than enough practice – but she couldn't stand not understanding why. The metaphorical plane had crashed, and she could now see all the pieces. All she had to do was put them together.

'I saw some footage on the news,' she said. 'A lot of people screaming at the camera that they'd been infected, and some stock photographs of what smallpox used to do to people.'

'Yeah, well, it was a non-event,' Fowler said. 'As soon as they got news of the possible threat, the government dispatched inoculations to its regional threat centres. You were right: Millie Hayden wasn't able to get to the newer strains of the disease. Maybe the Workers' League thought she could, but she couldn't. So don't feel too much sympathy for all those rich people you saw in hysterics. Everyone exposed got the right jabs, and no one died. Just a few people in hospital, and a lot of disruption. And once the fuss was over everyone forgot about it.'

A mistake, then. 'Which is what we said, isn't it? Smallpox was the wrong weapon.'

'It depends what their aim was, I guess,' Fowler said. 'Terror strikes don't necessarily need to kill to be successful. Transportation networks were shut down, we had two days of closures across most business and distribution centres... the economic damage was big in terms of GDP.'

'I still don't understand.'

'Publicity? Attention? Who the fuck knows? Either way, the government aren't exactly advertising how the smallpox got out – I don't think they want too many questions asked about their security breach. And if they're not taking the blame, it will be hard to pin on us. So, like I said: it *will* blow over. This isn't the same as Tanzania, not the same at all.' Fowler gave a final, frustrated growl and then abruptly headed for the exit. His departure left Anna feeling exposed, a sensation heightened by the return of the ceremonial bot. The ceremony was about to happen – and she was the only one there.

A sense of duty pulled her inside. Her actions ultimately killed N'Golo. She'd been the one who'd balanced his life against Beth's, who'd chosen to roll the dice. And the guilt was mixed with a dreadful feeling that one day there'd be no one at her ceremony. Just as there'd been no one there at her imaginary deathbed. No one to see the curtains finally pulled shut.

Anna sat near the back of the room as the bot trundled towards a coffin. It would be the same one used in every ceremony. N'Golo's body was probably already being tipped into the dissolution pools. And she felt nothing at that realisation.

*Because I didn't really know him.*

Her brain's entanglements with his memories had only given her a series of conflicting viewpoints. Yes, she'd seen some of his actions, seen his mistakes, heard his words. But all she'd seen of him was what she'd been allowed to view. Just like all those who'd accused her of conspiring to start a war in Tanzania: they'd been given a selected funnel of information, not the full picture. Like the list of information being read by the bot, much of which she hadn't known.

So how could she pull back the lens?

Maybe she didn't need to. After all, there was nobody here. It was just her, and the bot, and a continued feeling that something wasn't quite right.

# 46

ANNA CLICKED OFF the boards. She'd come to a halt, tired of catching up on the media reports related to the smallpox attack. The air outside the crematorium was cold and crisp. She breathed it in steadily, eyes closed, and waited. She had nowhere in particular to go, and the sense of release now made it easier to think.

Their focus had been in the wrong place. When they'd thought they were simply looking for Beth Hayden, using N'Golo Durrant as the main lead had made sense. The theft of the smallpox sample should have put a different spin on things – and yet that was when Mitchell had come to her asking for access to Durrant's memories.

Anna let her mind drift. Part of her was still in the inquiry, waiting for death, small details repeating and repeating. She remembered her helplessness; the way her senses had simply crumbled away…

She wiped away tears, forcing herself to concentrate again on Connolly. The angle was wrong. She needed to stop pulling the flight stick back, and instead tip the nose forward. Gain some real altitude. This wasn't about N'Golo and the Haydens, she reminded herself. Not really. It was all about Connolly, and why he'd taken the smallpox. And the answers were likely to be in the real world, not in some half-remembered one.

*Munday Road. A few doors down from the church, with the red door.*

Anna connected to the boards again and hailed a pod. The church was in the northern half of the city. At this time of day, it should have taken over an hour to reach it. But traffic was light, and the pod moved quickly from wealthy estates through more middle-class areas to a series of run-down streets. The church loomed over the surrounding terraced houses, dwarfed in turn by skyscrapers on the horizon. It was abandoned, windows boarded up. Years of pollution had blackened its stonework.

Anna got out of the pod, waving her arm at it to pay. A cluster of people were talking on the doorstep of a nearby house. None of them looked her way. If this had been a few days ago, she'd have already been trying to hide her face, or else summoning another pod to take her away. But the inquiry was now complete; the truth was out. She could only hope people would accept it.

The house with the red door was directly opposite. The door was freshly painted, and the house itself looked smarter than those around it. Nobody answered when she knocked. She turned back to the street, feeling stupid for having made the trip, but then turned again to peer through the single pane of the ground-floor window. The window frame was rotting. Whoever had so recently gone to the trouble of fitting a new door hadn't bothered to replace the windows.

'They've left!'

She turned. A woman was glaring back at her from the opposite pavement, her clothes a little greyer than they'd probably been when she'd bought them.

'Was there a girl with them?'

The woman shrugged.

'What happened when the police came?'

The woman bellowed with laughter. S&P sending resources to a place like this was the funniest thing she'd ever heard. 'No police been here in years!'

That was enough for Anna. The people around here were all on the UI. They had nothing of value, there was no need for the police to respond. It was the perfect place to hold Beth and Millie hostage.

It didn't take long to find something she could use to lever the window – a short piece of discarded metal. She dug it into the wooden frame, splintering the lock.

'Hey!'

Anna pushed open the window and scrambled inside, dropping down into the darkened front room. It smelled of dust and damp. Yes, this was a home that had been left just as the Workers' League had found it. The wallpaper seemed several decades out of date; it had faded to almost nothing on the wall opposite the window, but was a strong floral yellow in the places where sunlight didn't reach. Anna doubted the kidnappers had spent much time in the front room, which was in clear view of the street. She stepped cautiously into a small, empty hallway, and then into the kitchen beyond.

There was food on the table. A loaf of bread, spotted with mould. So no one had been here in a while, but it hadn't been left empty for long. In the corner was a small door that had been bolted shut. And given the kitchen was slightly narrower than the lounge, she could guess that it only led down.

Anna worked the bolt free, the rust biting into her fingers. As soon as she got it open, she knew she was in the right place. A set of concrete steps led down – just as she'd seen in N'Golo Durrant's memory – and the same pattern of electric light was flickering below her. The only thing different was the stench, a detail she wouldn't have picked up in the sequencer – but also something she doubted had been present when she'd seen it with N'Golo. The smell soon suffocated the odour of decay coming from the rest of the house. Faeces and urine. Anna almost gagged on it, but knew she'd have to go down there.

First, though, she checked her connection to the boards. If she'd interpreted what N'Golo had remembered correctly, then she'd seen a dampening field. But if such a device had once been active, it was no longer working. She had full access, and the connection was strong right down to the last step.

They were still there.

*Holy fuck!* They were still there!

Beth and Millie Hayden were on the floor of the basement, curled up as if they were asleep. Millie was facing the concrete steps. Her face grey, her eyes open and glassy; it was clear that she was very much dead.

Anna ran to Beth, and rolled her onto her back. There was some colour in the girl's face, and the barest hint of breath. Her eyes opened. 'Water!'

Anna looked around her. Two stained paper plates and several plastic bottles lay discarded on the floor. A TV was pushed up against the far wall. Anna grabbed one of the bottles and ran to the kitchen. Soon she was back, tipping fresh, cold water into Beth Hayden's mouth.

'How long since you've eaten?'

The girl shook her head, then started to shake as if crying, even though no tears came. 'I don't know,' she said, reaching to try and take hold of the bottle herself. Her right forearm was covered in a blood-soaked bandage. Beneath it would be where Connolly had cut out her biochip. 'She wouldn't have anything! When we realised they weren't coming back, she wouldn't have anything!'

Millie. The girl's dead mother remained beside them. Anna tried to shift Beth onto her feet, to take her upstairs while they waited for the police. But Beth wouldn't allow herself to be lifted.

'Why didn't they come back? They said they would come back!'

'I don't know.'

'But they said they'd come back!'

Anna stopped. Just below the sound of Beth's shouting, she heard a noise. She hadn't checked the upper floors of the house. A stupid error, and one Fowler wouldn't have made. Something was on the steps, and it was coming down.

She still had a board connection. Quickly, she made an emergency call. But before it connected, a police hunter bot entered the basement, its head swivelling as it took in the scene. '*Anna Glover*,' it said. '*You are not a member of the Workers' League.*'

It must have been upstairs, waiting. So why the hell hadn't it come down before?

'You were waiting for them,' Anna said, still cradling Beth and trying to keep her from facing Millie. 'You were waiting for the Workers' League to come back so you could arrest them?'

'*The assigned objective was to find the Workers' League.*'

The hunter bot's logic had reduced Millie and Beth to bait in a trap. Anna looked round the basement again. Bottled water. Used paper plates. The Workers' League had left them provisions. Yet they hadn't come back. And if they'd known a hunter bot had found the house, then why would they? N'Golo had spilled the location of the house just as the smallpox attack was taking place, and Jake must have told the police. He wasn't as heartless as she'd suspected. The information had come too late and too early at the same time. Too late to stop the smallpox, too early to rescue Beth and her mother.

'We need to get them to hospital!'

'*We will now reset the house, and wait for the Target.*'

'But they're not coming back. Don't you get it – they're not here!'

Beneath her, Beth reached up and touched her face. 'They said they'd be back – and then they'd let us go…'

Anna helped her to sip some more water. 'I know.'

'That's why my mum agreed to give them the smallpox… it wouldn't hurt anybody. They knew that…' Beth's voice trailed away to a whisper.

This wasn't about N'Golo Durrant or Beth or Millie. It was about smallpox, and why Connolly had wanted it. She'd read about the disease, in the days leading up to the theft. It had been fed to her from the boards, some subconscious drip of fear being fed directly into her brain by whichever algorithm was controlling the media feeds. And she wasn't the only one. Both Cody and Fowler had seen the articles on the boards that had stuck in their minds. And if they'd all seen it, then perhaps everyone had seen it: the story could have remained highly ranked in the personalised feeds until it had at least been scanned. Everybody would have been given the unsettling feeling: smallpox was bad news.

Even if it wasn't. Even if was just as simple to solve as an aerodynamic stall.

'There was only one person Connolly wanted to really hurt,' Beth said.

At the door to the basement, the hunter bot edged closer.

'The Prime Minister. He wanted her here.'

# 47

ANNA WAITED WITH Beth Hayden just long enough for the girl to be loaded into an ambulance, and for a second unmarked vehicle to come for her mother. She hadn't wanted to abandon Beth to the medical bots, but at least she was safe, and out of that basement.

It didn't take her long to find out a visit by the Prime Minister had been scheduled for that afternoon, at the McMullins shopping mall. The smallpox attack had tempted Farlands out of the Westminster green zone for something more substantial than the usual Jack-in-the-box appearance. No doubt she'd be guarded by a platoon of government officials and her security services, but nevertheless she was here.

A smallpox outbreak that hadn't been a threat suddenly made sense to Anna. There was no reason for an attack that injured or killed anyone, that wasn't Connolly's game. He had just wanted the response, the white-collar hysteria that would demand a politician's attention. This had all been about getting the Prime Minister to poke her head above the parapet, at a time and place he had practically named himself. He'd been able to prepare for this visit long before even the Prime Minister herself had decided on it.

'Hey!' The woman who'd seen Anna scrambling through

353

the window earlier was bustling aggressively towards her. Anna didn't shift. 'We didn't know they were in there, right?'

'I know.' Her acknowledgement took the wind out of the woman's sails. Like she'd been expecting an argument, and had wanted to defend her little community against a white-collar intruder.

'So you're a cop, then?'

'Not quite.'

'My friend said she recognised the girl you found; that it was something to do with the smallpox?'

Anna looked away, up the street. She didn't have time for this. Where was the damn pod?

'Why's everyone so bothered about that, anyway?'

'What do you mean?' Anna's skin prickled, but it was a far cry from the itch that had once plagued her forearms.

'It's not dangerous, is it? All them people panicking, but a few jabs later and everyone's okay. Them folk at that fucking death lab just need to be more careful, that's all.'

*Death lab?* Anna's eyes narrowed, locking on to the woman. The government didn't exactly advertise the existence of their top-secret bioweapons lab, and the news stories she'd read hadn't included it. Even in the aftermath of the smallpox release, none of the stories explained how the Workers' League had managed to obtain it.

'How do you know about Bromoor Down?'

The woman looked at her as if she was stupid. 'The boards, of course!'

Yes, there was only one way. This woman had seen a passing reference in her media stream. Maybe it was in all the feeds of those reliant on the UI. Bromoor Down. Smallpox. A great big invite for any individual or organisation looking to sow a little bit of panic, if they knew how to get to it. Was it too much of a leap to suppose that such information had also been fed to Connolly and other members of the Workers' League?

An incoming call disrupted Anna's thoughts. She thanked the woman, and took a few steps away before she connected.

'Hey,' Fowler said. 'I got a missed call.'

'You okay? You sound stressed?'

Fowler gave a tight laugh. 'I think your paranoia is catching. I thought a hunter bot was heading my way—'

Anna glanced to the side. The hunter bot from the basement was lingering on the pavement just outside the red door.

'Fowler,' Anna asked, 'the police can influence what stories a person reads, can't they?'

'No,' Fowler replied. 'Well, yes. Sort of. You need a warrant, but normally only to do what they tried to with Beth – bump stories that will help them find people and solve crimes.'

'Only those things?'

'So maybe there's an element of reducing crime too.'

Anna thought for a moment. 'Mitchell talked about demographic categories being a restriction,' she said. 'That if the risk categories were widened they'd be able to cut crime further.'

'Yes, but that's not going to happen,' Fowler said. 'Too many white collars don't want S&P digging into their board history. Politicians listen to white collars, Anna, not the police.'

'But what if something changed? What if a politician were killed? What if someone orchestrated something spectacular enough to get the Prime Minister to pop her head out – rather than just another run-of-the-mill shooting?'

Fowler didn't respond for a long time. 'The PM's coming today,' he said, his voice tight. 'Fuck! She's coming this afternoon.'

'Drawn out of her security cordon by the smallpox. Coming to ground zero to reassure the public. The white collars. Those with something to lose.'

'Shit.'

'We both wondered why they'd chosen smallpox, but I don't think the Workers' League chose it at all. At least not directly. It was *suggested* to them. We all saw it in our news feeds: but we each saw a subtly different message. I didn't see anything about Bromoor Down. But the UIs down here on this street know all about it, Fowler. Everyone with a grievance with the government knows where it's being stored. One message a call to action, the other to prompt panic.'

She heard Fowler hawk something up from his throat and spit. 'I guess it's possible.'

'Can you check? I think we need to know who's doing this.'

'You changed your mind about Connolly being part of S&P, then?'

'I don't know… he could be; or he could just be some white collar who's been played.'

Once again, she was running out of time. And she hadn't even known the clock was still running.

'Played by who?'

'By Deng,' Anna said, grasping at the only other name she'd come across during their investigation. 'Someone else that's cropped up a few times is some guy called Deng. I thought at one point it might be Connolly's real name.'

'Deng?'

'Yeah. Mitchell mentioned him. But the name was also on my inquiry documentation, and N'Golo…' Anna's mind blanked. *The police station? In the interview room?* She was struggling to remember. It all seemed so long ago. A memory warped by old age. 'I'm pretty sure N'Golo mentioned him too. He said he was blocking things.'

Fowler laughed. 'Deng isn't a "him".'

'Fine, do you know who *she* is?'

'Digital Engine,' Fowler put in. 'Deng, for short. S&P isn't one system; it's multiple modules all managed by a digital engine. Cops tend to shorten it to just "Deng".'

The hunter bot, the one whose cold logic had condemned Millie Hayden to death as it waited for the Workers' League, edged closer.

'So what are you going to do?' Fowler asked.

'Well, I'm not going to call the police, that's for damn sure.'

# 48

Hunter Bot 28.637f – 47637946376gh476r74r64 – Action
  Log
New Objective: Follow Target (Anna Glover)
Background Data: Downloaded from S&P. Receiving
  continual updates.
Geographical Zone: Trailed Target to McMullins Shopping
  Mall.
Actions: New instructions received from Deng. Monitoring
  with behavioural cams. No trigger movements
  detected. Signalled to cordon teams that Target is
  allowed to enter.

ANNA ARRIVED OUTSIDE McMullins shopping mall to find it busy, but with no obvious additional security. She was wrong. As she approached the door, two police officers emerged and stopped a couple of youths – probable UIs – from entering, turning them away. The overall time spent dealing with them was so quick as to be almost unnoticeable. Beyond them, in the shopping centre, there would likely be more security officers.

There were sentry bots circulating, too – hidden amongst

the white collars who'd come to shop or to see the Prime Minister speak. Most looked exactly the same as the devices the shops usually sent out to sell and to advertise, although these bots were just milling around, their function uncertain. And then she noticed several pairs of men and women watching the crowd. Taken together, it looked like a soft cordon – the police were probably tracking people heading towards the mall and turning away only those people who crossed a certain threshold of risk.

There was no sign of Connolly.

Anna waited. It probably hadn't taken any fancy facial recognition software to tag the UIs who'd just been stopped from entering the mall. This was clearly a place designed to attract white collars; McMullins was new, not some old shell that had been refitted multiple times. The signs advertising the restaurants and shops boasted all the latest brands. It didn't surprise her that the Workers' League had targeted the place – it had been built to be run by bots, not humans. She thought again of the panic she'd seen on the boards following the smallpox release. If they'd wanted to grab the attention of a woman like the Prime Minister, this was the place to do it.

The police officers who'd stopped the two young men a few moments ago seemed to have melted away, but Anna still expected them to cut across her path as she approached the building. They didn't. She followed the crowds into the shopping mall, where she was carried along by a slow stream of people towards a central atrium.

A stage had been set up around which a few people were already standing to reserve the best view. Anna chose a spot near some of the fake ferns decorating the edges of the atrium. More people were standing around the balcony above her, leaning over the railing so they could look down at the stage. No doubt their faces, too, had been scanned for risk, but Connolly wasn't on any of S&P's databases. Whether or not he'd been deliberately removed was something that she and Fowler would need to find out later.

She needed to find someone; an official connected with the shopping mall, not someone connected to S&P. Connolly had given himself the time to prepare, she reminded herself. He'd chosen the location, he'd drawn the Prime Minister here. If she could alert the right person to the risk, then perhaps whatever Connolly was planning could be stopped.

The chatter of many shoppers was bouncing off the surfaces and concentrating back in the mall's central bowl. The effect made the space seem busier than it really was: all no doubt designed to make the place more exciting. To keep the remaining white collars spending rather than just booking deliveries from the boards. It also made it difficult to think.

Anna's heart gave a sudden thump.

Connolly.

The man from N'Golo's memories, made real. He was on the balcony, looking down. Anna checked the time, then made a call.

'Yeah,' Fowler said on the other end of the line. He sounded breathless, like he'd spent the last few seconds running. 'You there? I got through to Mitchell—'

'And what did she have to say.'

'S&P ain't programmed any more, so we can rule out Connolly having interfered with the Beth Hayden case.'

'What do you mean, it isn't programmed?'

'S&P writes its own code, all that gets input is a series of objectives depending on whoever's in government. The objectives don't change, though: "reduce crime" is pretty much the top of its list.'

'Reduce crime,' Anna repeated slowly. 'By any method?'

'Fuck, Anna. When you called me earlier I thought you might have something. But really? You think this thing got cooked up in S&P's own circuits?'

'Millie Hayden is dead because a bot decided to use her to trap the Workers' League.'

'And that's the point, isn't it? If S&P were really mixed up in this, then why didn't they ignore the case completely? It gave Beth a low score, yes, but —'

Anna didn't know. Not completely. But she guessed that somewhere down the line there'd be a review by an independent system. And an incompetent S&P investigation would look an awful lot better than none at all — especially given the prevailing view that any mistake by S&P could be dealt with by Continual Learning. N'Golo had mentioned Deng was making redactions — and if some modules of S&P had gone off chasing down leads connected to Roger Hayden rather than his wife, then there would be at least the appearance it had been doing the right thing. Give a system bad information, and it will draw poor conclusions. Do so deliberately, and you might be able to give yourself enough space to orchestrate something a little more sophisticated. She glanced again at Connolly. She couldn't lose him. 'Well, either way, he's here,' she said. 'Connolly, I mean.'

'Then call it in.'

'I don't think that—'

'Prove yourself right or prove yourself wrong, Anna. You call it in and get no response — then you know you're right. You might think that your hunch is real, but detection is about evidence, and all you've got is some nice theory.'

'It fits.'

'"It fits" is what fucked the police before S&P took over.'

Anna started carefully threading her way through the other shoppers, heading for the escalator. 'But it also makes sense of the smallpox,' she said. 'You can't reduce crime by committing mass murder. The logic doesn't fit. So it just lets the Workers' League have something—'

'*Fuck!*'

It took a few moments for Anna to realise Fowler was no longer really talking to her. 'What is it?'

'Hunter bot… it's… Oh, shit! I think it's—'

The call disconnected. Anna tried to patch through again, but she received no answer. *Prove yourself right or prove yourself wrong.* Despite her better judgement, Anna made an emergency call.

'*What is the nature of your emergency?*'

'I'm at the McMullins shopping mall.' Anna reached the top of the escalator, keeping Connolly in view. 'Erin Farlands is in danger.'

There was a long pause – even though the AI speaking to her was more than capable of understanding what she was telling it.

'*What is the nature of your emergency?*'

'There's a man on the balcony overlooking the stage,' Anna continued. 'I think he intends to injure or kill the Prime Minister. I say again, I am at the McMullins shopping mall.'

'*Are you in immediate danger?*'

'No.'

'*Then please remain where you are; officers are being dispatched.*'

Anna's breath quickened. Connolly was still ignorant of her interest. Beneath her, she sensed some movement through the crowd. At first she thought a few of the pairs of officers had started heading towards her, but then she realised they were instead forming a tighter net around the stage. A couple of bots were repositioning the microphones and speakers. Anna checked the time again.

'Do I know you?' Connolly was looking at her. He'd turned away from the balcony rail and was casually leaning against it. He gave her a little half-smile, which was enough to encourage her a little closer. 'You've been staring at me.'

Anna looked down again towards the stage. The preparations continued. There was no sign of any movement towards her from the police. Of course, if she was right, then there wouldn't be; they wouldn't come. Or perhaps whatever was orchestrating things just needed a close call – something to make the politicians sit up and notice. Maybe it already knew Connolly was here, and there was an invisible net around him waiting to close.

'I knew N'Golo Durrant,' Anna said, pushed towards him a little more by the crowd.

Connolly shrugged. The small action – of complete disregard or denial that the name meant anything to him – almost made her punch him.

'He's dead,' Anna continued.

Connolly's face hardened. He checked about him, and seemed satisfied enough she was on her own. There was still no sign of an impending arrest. Had Deng intercepted her warning and called off the response?

'He was going to spoil things, we had to stop him.'

'He was just a kid.'

'The last I heard he was in a coma.'

*Bastard.* 'And Beth? And Millie?'

'Safe, I presume. We let the police know where they were, just after—'

'Millie is dead!'

Anna's rage-filled shout drew some attention, none of which Connolly wanted. It punctured his self-assurance. He glared at her, then turned and walked away. Anna followed him. 'She's dead,' she said again, jostling his shoulder. 'Left to rot in the house on Munday Street.'

Connolly kept looking to the side as he walked, seeking an escape route. She wasn't going to let him take one.

'Where are you going?' she asked. 'Where do you think I'm going to let you run?'

'And why do you care so much?'

'This isn't going to change anything,' Anna said. 'You're playing into S&P's hands!'

'Farlands is taking away all our rights,' Connolly replied, his voice confined to a hiss, 'and this opportunity is too good to pass up. The fact that both Durrant and Beth were interested in politics was something of a gift.'

'A gift given to you by someone called Deng, by any chance?'

A twitch of uncertainty passed across Connolly's face.

'For Christ's sake,' Anna shouted, 'you're being played by a fucking computer! You heard about Bromoor Down from your media feed. An algorithm placed your associate in Millie Hayden's house, as her foster-son.'

'Why?'

'S&P's objective is to reduce crime,' Anna said, thinking as she spoke. 'It's done all it can with the data it has access to, so it now wants to push down further. It needs access to everyone's biodata. Everyone's, including white collars'. If it could get you to pull the trigger – someone with a job, who isn't in a risk category – that's all it needs to change public opinion.'

A small group of officials was heading to the stage. The Prime Minister was amongst them.

'Maybe that's true and maybe it isn't,' Connolly said. 'But you don't really think I'm the only one here today ready to pull a trigger, do you?'

At first, Anna didn't understand. But before she could work it out a man had pushed between her and Connolly, twisting her arm behind her back. He'd moved too quickly for her to see his face.

'Easy,' he growled in her ear, twisting her arm higher, making the muscles in her shoulder scream.

'I've just made an emergency call,' she said.

Connolly ignored her. 'Are we ready?' he asked, shifting his belt so that she caught a glimpse of the gun he was carrying. 'Take her out back… Make sure you keep in the camera blind spots.'

Anna twisted into a position where she'd be able to see where he went, pain ripping at her elbow. Connolly quickly reached another vantage point looking down over the stage below, then made for the escalator.

Some part of her was still waiting for a response to her emergency call, hoping that she'd been wrong about all this. But this was just what had happened to N'Golo. He'd gone to the police and they hadn't done anything, because Deng had wanted Beth to be kidnapped, just like Deng now wanted Connolly's plan to succeed.

Anna tried to relax her arm, to stop struggling against the

strength of the man behind. He loosened his grip in response, and she seized the opportunity to wrench away and stumble forwards, slapping the ground before getting herself back on to her feet.

She got to the escalator, and pushed between people, stumbling to the bottom. The Prime Minister had been ushered on to the stage, but she hadn't started speaking. Connolly was walking towards his target. Moving slowly. Not drawing attention. She still had time to catch him.

A shout from above distracted part of the crowd's attention skywards, but not Connolly's. He just shifted round so that he faced her full on – perhaps expecting her to charge into him. Yet instead of pushing her or shouting at her, he simply waited until she had almost reached him... and then he stumbled. For no clear reason. As he recovered his footing he flashed a quick smile, and in that moment she realised what he'd done.

*Make sure you keep in the camera blind spots.*

Her rush down the escalator had attracted attention. People were looking at her – a few bots had moved in from the side – a few pairs of police officers were already reaching into their jackets. And Connolly had just demonstrated a perfect understanding of how S&P worked. He'd known the mall cameras would have been scanning the atrium. Known her behaviour towards him would have perhaps already registered as aggressive, and then, with the skill of a footballer, he'd taken a minor stumble to ensure a reaction from the security teams.

'One advantage a human has over a bot,' he whispered, 'is our plans can be flexible.'

She'd just lost her job, very publicly. She'd been the subject of an inquiry ordered by the Prime Minister. And now she was rushing towards the stage. A middle-class woman at risk of dropping down to the UI. The facial recognition cams would have already tagged her. S&P would have assessed the risk. The bots within the crowd would have been alerted to the danger. And maybe Deng had noticed her too. How fast could the AI instruct the bots?

Connolly grinned at her again, then walked away. She hadn't even noticed him drop the gun by her feet. Anna looked down at it with growing horror.

*There's a point where you know you're beaten and you can't do anything to stop it. No decision you can take will affect the outcome. And there are a few seconds where you know you're going to die. I can't think of anything more dreadful, can you?*

It came to her in an instant: the dots were connected and the synapses fired, and all she was left with was one solitary word.

*Fuck.*

Anna closed her eyes and waited for the shots.

News Feed Module – Submission to Deng

## Prime Minister Erin Farlands Escapes Death

The Prime Minister has ~~been assassinated~~ [Edit, Deng] escaped death at the McMullins Shopping Centre, London. ~~Seeking to promote her plans to allow S&P greater access to private data~~ [Edit, Deng] Speaking to victims of the recent smallpox attack, Farlands was attacked by Anna Glover – the recent subject of an inquiry into the Tanzanian War. S&P later acknowledged that given greater access to her personal biodata, she would likely have been stopped by security [Journalistic subroutine query – Glover's data was accessed at the time of the inquiry. Query overridden, Deng].

A new vote on data access rights is likely to go before Parliament ~~next week~~ [Edit, Deng] tomorrow. Many MPs are saying that this will be the perfect way to ~~cement Farlands' legacy~~ [Edit, Deng] show continued support for Farlands' continued legislative programme.

**STORY APPROVED FOR BOARD DISTRIBUTION**

# 49

'HER BIOSIGNS ARE stabilising,' said a voice above me. I was conscious, but couldn't move. I wasn't sure if I'd been sick. I tried to move my eyebrows, but couldn't. But I could at least sense them. And at this moment of realisation, something inside me burst. A wave of excitement. I was out. 'She should be moving again shortly. The old bullet wounds are quite something. This must have been one cool lady, back in the day.'

Feeling was creeping first into my cheek and then into my jaw. But for the moment, I was still. Unable to speak. Unable to see, really, my eyes still tightly closed rather than staring up at the ceiling.

'Really weird readings from her cortex…'

'Synapse damage,' came another voice. Two technicians, then. Perhaps one wasn't sufficient to monitor a long-term submersion. 'Common for early users of Jake Morley's equipment.'

'Have you spoken with the nurse?' Nurse. I felt a sudden inward hatred at the thought of Jake's nurse. 'She seemed genuinely concerned. Where have I heard the name Anna Glover before?'

'The dysprosium war?'

'Yeah, that's right.'

'Well, that's what makes her situation here worse. They got her confession by tricking her into thinking she was in an old people's home.'

'Huh – well no wonder she can't tell the difference any more.'

I felt something in my forehead flicker. I still couldn't open my eyes. I did manage to move my lips, though. I swallowed. Tingling had also started in my right thigh.

'The nurse says she still sees some student involved in the case. Some little grain of memory she can't quite shake. Her inquisitor keeps on coming back to see her.'

'Really?'

'Yep. Everything keeps replaying in her mind, like a stuck record.' The voice took on a thoughtful tone. 'Just imagine not remembering all the good bits of your life. She did quite a lot after that investigation, but she can't escape it. Those bullet wounds? Police snipers. They thought she was attempting to kill the Prime Minister. Turned out, it was the police AIs. If it hadn't happened we'd all be repla—'

'Look, she's waking up.'

My eyes were open, but I couldn't quite see properly. They felt sticky, like they'd been shut too long. The technician standing over me was wearing medical garb. So was his colleague. And in neither face could I see anyone I recognised as Cody Weaver. But then I remembered something with a flash of recognition. The old man in the nursing home, the one who'd been wheeled back in with me when we'd been all alone. That man was Weaver, I was sure of it now. Just an older version. A much older version.

*How had he become an old man?*

'Ms Glover? I'm Dr Bartholomew. You have taken a tumble, but we'll soon get you back to the Morley Hospice and to your friends.'

Morley Hospice? As in Jake Morley? I tried to lift myself up, but my shoulders and back didn't shift. They just cried out in pain. The doctors above me backed out of view. They were replaced by Grace, who I could feel had taken hold of one of my hands. She squeezed it gently, crying as she did so.

My hand was still the withered one from the nursing home. I wasn't back in my body, and I hadn't bumped out. Soon, I'd be back in the care home, being looked after by Grace – and Charley. Would Grace believe me, this time, if I told her? A confused old woman?

Did I dare?

'You've bloody worried us, Anna!' Grace sobbed.

My jaw moved, and I made some form of sound. It took a few minutes longer for me to form words. 'Did I ever tell you the story of Arnold Anderson?'

'Why don't you remind me?' she said.

Remind me. Which meant I had told her. I pressed on, ignoring the irony. 'Arnold Anderson woke up in hospital the day after D-Day,' I said. 'He wondered why he was finding it hard to move, hard to see, hard to… I'm not in the sequencer, am I?'

'No, Anna. You haven't been in the sequencer for years. It's just that your memory… everyone at the hospice. No one should have been attached to those synapse benches. No one knew the long-term dangers… no one really understood what they were allowing inside their minds.'

I wiggled my toes, and something within me relaxed. Like

someone had hit a reset button. I couldn't quite remember what it was that Grace had just said to me, but a synaptic sequence fired.

'Wasn't there a student who came to see me yesterday?'

# AUTHOR'S NOTE

ONE OF THE difficulties about writing near-future science fiction is that you're only a few inches away from the incoming tide. As I was writing this book, several of its key aspects appeared in both scientific journals and the mainstream media. On completing the first draft in mid-2017, I noted a scientific paper that proclaimed an AI had been developed that could create a virtual world from memories. As such, this novel is not intended to be a prediction of the future: these things are already here.

# ACKNOWLEDGEMENTS

MANY THANKS ARE owed to my editor, Sam Matthews, for her hard work in bringing this book to publication, and her insights into near-future world building. Thank you also to Miranda Jewess for helping me construct the outline, and to Joanna Harwood for providing a second pair of eyes on the various twists and turns. I am also very pleased with the cover, which was designed by Julia Lloyd.

I'm very grateful to all at Titan (Lydia Gittins, Philippa Ward, Ella Chappell, Polly Grice, Hannah Scudamore, Cath Trechman, Christopher McLane and Cat Camacho) for promoting my novels, and for their support at various events.

Big thanks are also owed to my literary agent, Ian Drury of Sheil Land Associates, for his wise counsel in all things publishing. Cheers, Ian!

# ABOUT THE AUTHOR

DANIEL GODFREY lives and works in Derbyshire, but tries his best to hold on to his Yorkshire roots. He studied geography at Cambridge University, before gaining an MSc in transport planning at Leeds. He enjoys reading history, science and SFF. After the publication of his first novel, *New Pompeii*, Godfrey was described as "an exciting new talent" by *Starburst* magazine.

# NEW POMPEII
## DANIEL GODFREY

Some time in the near future, energy giant NovusPart has developed technology to transport people from the past to the present day, and they have just moved the lost population of Pompeii to a replica city. Historian Nick Houghton is brought in to study the Romans, but he soon realises that NovusPart are underestimating their captives. The Romans may be ignorant of modern technology, but they once ruled an empire. The stage is set for the ultimate clash of cultures…

*"That rare science fiction novel that reads like a thriller. Astonishing."* Alan Smale, Sidewise Award winner

*"Impressive. In the tradition of Michael Crichton and Philip K. Dick."* Gareth L. Powell, BSFA Award winner

*"Smart, inventive and action-packed."* Tom Harper, bestselling author of *The Lost Temple*

# EMPIRE OF TIME
## DANIEL GODFREY

For fifteen years, the Romans of New Pompeii have kept the outside world at bay with the threat of using the Novus Particles device to alter time. But there are those beyond Pompeii's walls who are desperate to destroy a town where slavery flourishes. When his own name is found on an ancient artifact dug up at the real Pompeii, Decimus Horatius Pullus – once Nick Houghton – knows that someone in the future has control of the device. The question is: whose side are they on?

*"Tremendously gripping"* Financial Times

*"The page-turning style of Crichton"* The Sun

*"An exciting new talent"* Starburst

*"A remarkably promising debut"* Morning Star

**TITAN**BOOKS.COM

For more fantastic fiction, author events,
competitions, limited editions and more

Visit our website
**titanbooks.com**

Like us on Facebook
**facebook.com/titanbooks**

Follow us on Twitter
**@TitanBooks**

Email us
**readerfeedback@titanemail.com**